Jan Lloyd

War Torn

BOOK 2

The French Girl

Disclaimer

This is a work of fiction. All characters, places, and incidents in this book, even those based on real people, real places, or real events, are the product of the author's imagination or are used fictitiously.

I would like to dedicate this book to my two beautiful granddaughters, Tabitha Alice, and Demelza Faith, in the hope that they will never experience war, and that they will grow up in a free, happy, and safe world.

I thank my two editors, developmental editor Lucija Dupljak for her many brilliant suggestions, and Gennifer Ulmen for her keen eye.

I also thank my lovely friend Lorraine for her enthusiastic support of my writing, and my children Meghan and Owen who have been called upon to read many chapters many times.

I thank my husband Ant, for freeing up the computer at the drop of a hat and offering advice. I give my thoughts to my dear brother Brian, a fantastic historian, who passed away in 2019. It feels like it was only yesterday that we spoke.

About the author

Jan Lloyd is a retired teacher of mathematics and science who lives in beautiful Mid Wales with her husband, Cavalier King Charles Spaniel, and very old cat.

When Jan isn't writing she enjoys walking in the forest and the many beautiful valleys near her home. She also enjoys gardening, and anything to do with animals who have four legs, as well as reading a good historical novel.

Jan wrote the bones of the first two War Torn books over thirty years ago, and after being told by a publishing house that there was little interest in WW2, she put the manuscripts in her wardrobe where they remained until her daughter asked to read them. The War-Torn novels were resurrected and Book 1 was published in March 2023.

If you would like up to date information on the War-Torn series or have any questions about the books, why not sign up on Jan's email list by visiting her website www.janlloyd.uk where you will be invited to download free chapters and information regarding the War-Torn series. Follow Jan on twitter, twitter.com/oghanlloyd.

Chapter 1

Frances tentatively knocked on the door of the office in the Jourdhaus and waited until Frieder's voice ordered her to enter. The last time she had seen him, he had slapped her hard several times across the face to stop her hysterical laughter. She wondered if his sending for her now had something to do with that journey from the Fuhrer Haus in Munich back to the camp at Prittlbach. Was she to suffer some sort of further punishment for her behaviour? She knew she had made him angry, she meant to, but she had also upset some of the men from the orchestra, for which she was sorry. She felt the thumping of her heart in her head, and the nervous trickle of sweat running down her back as she pushed open the door.

"Ah Meyer," he said, using just her surname, the same way he talked to the men in the orchestra. "So, it seems you are leaving us tomorrow."

Frances's stomach churned. It was worse than she had thought; they were sending her away from Dachau. Where to this time, for God's sake, not back to Auschwitz, surely?

"Well?" he asked. She stood, stupidly staring at him, unable to speak. "You're to be released," he repeated. "Aren't you the lucky one?"

So that was it. Otto, her onetime friend, had delivered after all. He had been filled with remorse after raping her following the concert for Adolf Hitler and had sworn to get her out of Dachau. But leaving Dachau had its price; they would deliver her into his custody, and there she would have to undergo further abuse from him. Compared to the fear, abuse, and degradation of the last fifteen months, though, she knew she would survive. She would survive just so that she could take her revenge on him. She would do so when the time was right. The girls in the bordello had told her she must. She also had to fulfil the promise she had made to her friend Miriam, to get revenge against all things German.

Frieder was still speaking to her. She shook her head, struggling to concentrate on his words. Her mind was still full of that last sickening encounter with Otto and how she would make him atone.

"You're to be given new clothing when you leave here, and then you will go back to the brothel for one last night. In the morning you will be picked up and brought back here to the Jourdhaus, and then they will release you into the custody of that idiot man who seems to be obsessed with you. The thoughtless fool has ruined the programs for all the concerts I have planned around you." Frieder shook his head with disdain. "When you return here tomorrow, bring your instrument with you and hand it to the officer of the day."

Frances still hadn't spoken, but what should she say? Should she thank him? she wondered.

There was a sharp rap on the door and Frieder shouted, "Come."

The door opened, admitting a female guard. "I've come for the woman," she said.

"Wait outside," Frieder ordered. "She'll be out directly." As the door closed behind the guard, he crossed the room and stood before her. "You haven't said a word," he said, trying to meet her eyes, which she had kept on the floor throughout. "This is goodbye."

"Yes, I suppose it is. Can I go now?" she asked, lifting her head, and meeting his icy stare.

He nodded, and she moved to the door. Just as her hand took the handle, he called out, "Good luck, Frances Meyer. You have a rare talent. Keep it safe and keep yourself safe too."

She turned, briefly giving the ghost of a smile. "Thank you, Herr Frieder," she said and stepped out into the corridor, closing the door behind her.

* * *

It never occurred to her she might not want to leave the confines of Dachau, but now, as she heard the approaching footsteps, it seemed to her a momentary haven. She detested Otto, and she would steel herself and take revenge, first on him, and if she survived, then on anything German, as the opportunities arose.

It would be a cleansing, a great purging if she could make them suffer for what they'd done to her, to her friends, to the thousands. The crimes she'd witnessed, the crimes she had done nothing to prevent. Her common sense told her there was nothing she could have done, that survival was the order of the day, her guilt told her she could at least have tried.

She looked around her at the sparsely furnished room, trying to find a comfortable place to stand, wondering how she would feel when she came face to face with Otto again. Would she cope and be able to carry through with her plan, to bide her time and go along with him? Hate filled as she was, it should be easy. As the door handle turned, she crossed to the barred window, taking deep breaths to calm herself. She heard the door open and the click as it closed again. With head held high, she turned to face him.

Kristian Mueller stood taller than she remembered. Or was it just the uniform that made him appear that way? Cap in hand, dressed in blues and clean shaven, as she had never seen him before. The last time she had seen him had been in the prison at Brest. He and his U-boat crew had picked her up from a lifeboat in the middle of the Atlantic Ocean and, after a rocky start, she had fallen in love with him. On returning to Brest from patrol, the SS had arrested her for things they thought she knew.

She reeled upon seeing him. A mass of emotions crashed through her head, only a few of them pleasant. She fought to contain herself, and recovering from the shock of him being there, she noted that his hair was a couple of shades lighter. It was free from grease, sweat and salt, thick and wavy. His face without the beard was more delicately put together than she remembered. The jaw and chin pronounced, but not at all heavy. And she thought how good he looked.

He threw his arms wide in anticipation of an embrace but as their eyes met, they slowly dropped to his side and they both stood staring at one another. The room became an unbridgeable chasm.

Mueller was perplexed. In his mind, she had run into his embrace, the old feelings immediately rekindled, but the scrawny grey skinned woman with short hair, wearing ill- fitting clothes, who was staring back at him from across the room, was a stranger.

Her voice when she found it came as a whisper. "Kristian?"

"Christ Froggy, what's happened to you?" he asked. Her body stiffened, and she stood for a while, unable to speak. She had been expecting Otto, but here was Mueller, looking so upright and clean, so damned handsome, that her heart lurched in her chest. She fought for control before answering.

"I don't believe you don't know," she replied, holding his gaze with the fire in her eyes. She wanted him to leave. She wanted to believe he was like the rest of them and that he had tricked her into falling in love with him. "Go, Kristian, go now. Just bloody well go, you're too late. It's too late for us. You shouldn't be here."

He shook his head and pushed the thick hair back from his forehead in confusion.

"But I am here," he said, crossing the room to her.

She backed away from him, eyes wide, shouting, "No! No! No" until she had backed up against the wall, and the denial became a scream. Mueller waited a few moments; his better sense was telling him to go. It was telling him that this woman wasn't the girl he'd been searching for, but then he saw the fear in her eyes, and it reminded him of the last time he had seen her some fifteen months previously, when the SS had taken her. Taking her in his arms, he held her tight as she fought against his embrace and continued shouting. "No, Kristian. Go, go now."

"Hush, sweetheart, shush now," he murmured over and over until he felt her body relax into his own and she quietened. They stood for a while until she shifted in his embrace, and he loosened his hold on her. Pushing her hand onto his chest, she laid it over his heart, and he felt the steady beating of it as she looked into his eyes.

"This is not the way it's meant to be, Kristian," she muttered. "Leave. Pretend you never came here. It's for the best. Please."

"Froggy, let me explain," he said.

The forgotten memories rekindled and rushed through her at the sound of his voice.

She lifted her eyes skyward. "Dear God, why now?" she muttered.

"When I got back from patrol, you were gone from Drancy. I couldn't find out a thing. I didn't know what to think. I'm sorry. Sorry that it's taken this long to find you."

She shook her head and pushed away from him.

"It doesn't matter how long it's taken, it's too late. Too much has happened, Kristian. How do you think I can leave here with you after going through all I've been through and seeing what I've seen? I have been to hell, Kristian, and I've made a pact with the devil."

"Can we leave the devil behind, Froggy? What do you say? I'll take you home to my folks. To the farm, it's safe there. This war can't go on for much longer. I've thought everything through, you see." He took her by the shoulders and turned her round again to face him, tilting her chin upward so that she had to meet his eyes. "Take my name, it will help to keep you safe, then later?" He gave a shrug.

Despite herself and the awkwardness of the situation, she snapped, "Won't Sophie have something to say about that?"

"Ah, Sophie—" He gave a grimace. "We didn't go through with it."

"Look," she said, shaking her head and frowning, "I can't go with you. You don't understand. If I go with you, I'll destroy you. I swear I will."

Mueller gave her one of his lopsided grins, lifting his eyebrows, showing the gap between his front teeth, and she felt her heart lurch once more. "I'll take that risk, Froggy," he said.

"You don't know what you're doing, you don't know what it's been like, what I've seen, what I've done, how I've suffered. I'm not me anymore, Kristian. You don't know, can't know, how much I have learnt to hate you… all of you. Just go! Go now, please."

"Not without you," said Mueller, nodding. "I'll take my chance. We're leaving here together. I've an order for your release, a pass paper and special permission for us to wed. It's taken a lot of time and effort for people to get us special permission and I'm buggered if I'm wasting it all now. It won't be valid forever. Come on, my driver is waiting for us outside. I told him I'd be five minutes."

He took her by the arm and steered her out into the passageway.

"Have you any luggage, anything you need to collect?"

"Yes, there are several cases with all my belongings in," she snapped. Then, with a sigh, she said, "No. I have nothing."

As they left the room, she shook her head in disbelief. Her luck had held again. Instead of leaving with Otto to be little more than a prisoner, here she was leaving with Mueller, who thought that in a couple of days he could make everything alright. Well, let him try. She would take her revenge on him instead, by not letting him. Then the laughter began, as he led her through the passageways, through the corridors of the administration block and out onto the parade ground of the out command. He shook her arm once or twice and scowled at her, but that only made her laugh even more. It was going to be easy, she thought. She could feel his agitation already, and she wasn't even trying.

Parked outside was a black Mercedes. A tall young man in a Naval uniform was leaning against it, enjoying a cigarette in the sunshine. As he noticed Mueller, he threw the cigarette to the ground and saluted, at the same time opening the rear car door. Mueller returned the salute briefly and shoved Frances into the rear of the car. Climbing in beside her, he pulled the door shut and tapped the glass to order his driver away. The car drew forward through the huge eagle topped wooden gates of Dachau, leaving the horrors of the camp behind. Only for Frances it wasn't that simple. The spectres clung to her, mind, body, and soul, and she was fearful they would eventually destroy her.

In silence, they passed through a couple of small homesteads, and then out into the open countryside. Mueller undid the neck of his shirt and loosened his tie in the early summer sunshine. The car had become stifling.

"Let me know if you're in a draft," he said, opening a window.

Frances had curled herself into the furthest corner of the backseat of the car and, apart from briefly looking back at the compound as they sped away, had kept her eyes focused on the window beside her. Her head was in turmoil and her thoughts were confused. Why him, why now? Why not Otto? It would have been so easy to destroy him, to hurt him, to kill him even. There would be no guilt. But this was Kristian sitting next to her, looking so… She had loved him once, had carried his child. He shouldn't have come. It shouldn't be him beside her, making things so difficult. Her mind was racing. She looked out of the window to help her think, and her eyes fell upon the beauty outside that was freedom.

"Where are we going?" she asked.

"Munich," Mueller replied, "We're booked into a hotel. There's a change of clothes waiting for you and a good meal. You look as if you could do with both."

"Could we stop for a while? Just for a minute? I'd like to stand outside. I need to take all this in." She turned to him. "Is that alright?"

He gave her a brief smile and nodded, then tapped the glass. "Pull over, Rittershausen."

The Mercedes pulled up on the side of the road, opposite a gateway which led into a field. The gate was half open and there were fresh prints from cattle and plough in the soft earth. Frances jumped out of the car and crossed the road and leant for a while against the gate. She closed her eyes, enjoying the feel of the fresh air on her skin. Then filling her lungs with it, she gloried that it was untainted with the smell from the ovens, or the stink of beer and sex from the bordello. This was freedom. Fresh and clean. She heard voices born upon that air. Laughing children and the deeper tones of the adults working the land.

Mueller watched from the other side of the road. After the initial shock of the change in her appearance, he was rediscovering her again. The amber almond-shaped eyes and the wide mouth were still the same, but the beautiful crowning glory of her hair that he loved so much had been taken away and there was even less of her than before. She had taken on an ethereal quality; her skin had become translucent, and the freckles had faded almost to nothingness. There was a fire in her eyes, though, which belied her delicacy, and the utter ferocity of it troubled him.

The sound of the women and children caught his attention. Working the land without petrol, he thought, would be an arduous task, and he wondered how his own parents and neighbours would cope with the shortage of fuel. It was virtually impossible to get hold of unless you wore a uniform. His ears, still astute from listening out for enemy aircraft, picked up the sound of a car on the road about a kilometre away. He looked across the road to Frances and wondered if she was ready to leave. She was kneeling in the grass, touching it with her face, running her hands through it like a child. He left her. There was no hurry. What could a few more moments matter?

The oncoming car sped past them and then screeched to a halt twenty yards or so further on. The rear door flew open and a man wearing the black uniform of the SS leapt out. He was shouting, not at him but at Frances, who was scrambling to her feet in confusion. Mueller crossed the road to her side as the stranger approached.

"What's going on, what are you doing here?" The stranger questioned her, then as he noticed Mueller and his insignia, he gave a smart salute.

"Von Liechtenstein, Sir. I have an order here giving me custody of this woman."

Mueller gave a sniff before continuing. "I've no idea why you should want this woman to be given into your custody, but I'm afraid you're too late. Unless she says differently, she's leaving with me." He turned questioning eyes onto Frances, who throughout the exchange had stood mutely beside him. Her expression made him uneasy.

"You missed the name," she said. "This is Otto von Liechtenstein."

Mueller nodded slowly, "Otto eh!" he drawled. "The same Otto who threatened you and your family and drove you from Paris?"

"Oh, come now, what fabrication is this?" snorted the man.

"Otto can do much better than that, can't you, Otto?" Frances felt the vomit rise from her stomach as she imagined herself back on the floor with Otto straddled across her. She fought to control herself. "This is also the Otto who raped me five nights ago," she said through clenched teeth.

Mueller looked at her in disbelief. She stood calmly holding Von Liechtenstein's eyes with her own, until he shifted awkwardly and said, "Rape? What rubbish you are talking!" He turned to Mueller. "You're a man of the world. You know what these French women are like, Korvetten Kapitan. Now why would I be here if it were rape?"

"I don't know," Mueller growled, "Supposing you tell me."

"Oh, she was willing enough and promised me more, that's why I'm here," Otto said with a sneer.

"Liar!" snapped Frances. As Otto took a step towards her, she backed away towards the safety of the car.

"You dare speak to me like that. I could take you back and make sure you never get out!" he threatened.

Mueller despised all that the SS stood for and on top of that, Frances said this man had raped her. His lip curled. "Bravo, you're good at intimidating women," he said.

"Look," said Von Liechtenstein, "I don't know what your interest is in this woman, if any. Suppose you just get into your car and drive off. There's a good fellow. There's plenty more whores to be had. What's so special about her, anyway? Take it from me, she's a cold bitch."

Frances looked on as Mueller grabbed Von Liechtenstein by the collar and drew his face to within inches of his own. "I'll tell you what's special about her. She's going to be my wife." He gave Von Liechtenstein a shove, sending him sprawling onto the road like a drunkard. Otto Von Liechtenstein pulled himself to his feet and faced Mueller with a look of pure hatred.

"Oh no, I'll not lose her again, not to you or anyone else," he said, as his hand went to the holster, lying on his thigh. Mueller was quick to see the danger, and as Von Liechtenstein drew the pistol, he kicked it from his hand. Then rushing in caught him on the side of the head, with a well-aimed right hook. Von Liechtenstein reeled against the blow, but quickly recovered enough to hurl himself back at Mueller, knocking him to the ground.

Frances looked on as Otto Von Liechtenstein, driven by the quest for her, fought as a demented soul. She saw Mueller take several hard blows before his superior physical fitness gained him the upper hand. A punch to the guts, winded Otto, doubling him over, buckling him up, so that a resounding left uppercut sent him crashing to within inches of his pistol. His fingers curled and uncurled, grasping madly for the grip, but he wasn't quick enough. Frances saw her chance and grabbed it first and levelled it straight between his eyes.

"Go on, Frances," he taunted, "you may as well." As she pulled back the trigger there was a click, and the smile on Otto's face faded.

"For God's sake, Frances, don't be a fool," yelled Mueller. She wheeled, immediately redirecting the pistol at him, and as he looked into her eyes, he was afraid of the madness he saw there.

"You too," she sneered, "a small revenge for the thousands that have burned in your ovens. You'll both burn in hell." Unsure which man to shoot first, she paused, giving Rittershausen just enough time to cross and grab her arm, forcing the muzzle of the pistol skywards as it discharged into the air.

There was a silence, giving them all the time to think.

Rittershausen had shaken the pistol from Frances's grasp, and she had fallen to the floor. Von Liechtenstein was still suffering from the winding Mueller had given him, and Mueller was dabbing at some blood which was running from his nose.

"Christ, Froggy," he eventually managed to say. Then retrieving Von Liechtenstein's cap, he emptied the pistol of its bullets, and threw them back at him. "Get out of here now, you heap of shit!" he spat.

Otto Von Liechtenstein pulled himself to his feet, dusted off his uniform and walked back towards his car, visibly shaken. Just before getting in, he turned to Mueller, top lip curled back. "She's a madwoman," he said, casting Frances a quick look. "You're welcome to her."

"Thanks," said Mueller to himself as the car sped Otto away. Then, with a painful grin, he slapped Rittershausen on the back. "Thanks, Rittershausen."

"You're welcome, Sir. Can't stand those SS bastards."

Mueller nodded in agreement, "Me neither."

He crossed to Frances, who was seated on the ground, rocking back and forth. Her eyes were staring blankly, and her breaths were coming in gasps as her mind played over once again the time she had been raped by Otto Von Liechtenstein. The man who had once been her friend.

Mueller was unsure what to do. He called her name and was shocked as her hands flew above her head to protect herself, as she cowered away from him. Through all the horrors on patrol she had managed to keep herself together and he was finding her present behaviour difficult to watch. He decided against showing her the pity he was feeling.

Grabbing her by the arm, he yanked her to her feet, calling her name and shaking her hard until she met his eyes. "You can stop this nonsense." he chided, "I know you, Froggy, you'll not let some pile of crap push you over the edge. Anyway, you still have me to deal with, don't you? Come on. Stand on your feet. A good rest in a good bed is what you need." He wiped his knuckles across his nose, shifting another drop of blood. "A good rest is what we both need, huh?" She straightened up, meeting his gaze.

"Why don't you just leave me here?" she asked.

"Oh, come on, that's much too easy. Besides, how are you going to destroy me from a distance? You are still intent on destroying me, I suppose?" he taunted.

Shaking her arm free, and frowning, Frances walked to the car and got in. "I am," she said, as Mueller climbed in beside her.

"Well, Froggy, my girl," he said, "who am I to spoil your fun?"

Chapter 2

Propped up in the corner of the back seat, as far away from him as she could get, she had tried to stay awake. He had offered her his shoulder, with an assurance that there would be no charge, but she had refused him with a disdainful glance. Then, as her tiredness had progressed, she had gradually flopped away from the window towards him, and he had moved closer to her, so that her head could rest against him. As sleep overcame her completely, she turned herself into him, laying her head on his chest, as she had many times before, and he felt the warmth of her body and smelled the familiar scent of it.

Looking down at the head lying against his chest, Mueller was reminded of a time on UBA some sixteen months or so previously. The chips were stacked against them then, as they appeared to be now, but they had pulled through, hadn't they? He pulled his fingers gently through Frances's hair as she slept, wondering why on earth she had cut off the long tresses he loved so much. He wanted to talk, to straighten things out in both of their minds, but she was clearly worn out.

He nodded to himself; a lot of water had passed under the bridge during the last months. She had clearly changed, and he supposed he had too. Whether the relationship they had so briefly but passionately experienced could be rekindled remained to be seen. He had made her a promise in Brest, though, and he would do his best to keep it. At least they were both alive, and there was something to be said for that. But what of the chemistry between them? He felt it. Not at first and not all the time, but now and again. Like when he watched her by the field, and as he did now, as her head lay nestled against him, and he listened to her gentle breathing. Ah well, time would tell.

But then what of her? What did she feel? There was an anger in her, as there had been when they first met. This time, though, the anger was somehow different. It was a private, dangerous anger, all sealed up, bubbling away just below the surface. A time bomb, ready to detonate at any moment, and he didn't think she'd give a damn who was in the way when it did.

The rape, he supposed. He wished he had killed that bastard Von Liechtenstein. Things were bad when you wanted to kill the blokes on your own side. Well, things were bad, weren't they? Only those shite-filled megalomaniacs in Berlin wouldn't admit it. Donitz knew. He was the only one worth his salt. A good man who knew how to look after his boys. At least old Adolf had the sense to recognise his worth and had made him Grand Admiral.

Donitz saw his tiredness before he would admit it to himself. "Too many patrols, Kristian, my boy," he said. "Give me the word and I'll get you a posting on shore." He'd refused at first, always psyched up for that next patrol, but Donitz had badgered him, knowing that a man's judgement could become impaired, or that maybe he would crack altogether when the pressure was on. On top of that, he was the son of a very dear friend.

He was allowed a last patrol after his return to Brest with Frances, and then Donitz's suggestion had become an order, and the command of UBA had been passed to Paul Werner on his recommendation. He'd pleased Donitz and relieved his parents by accepting the change in his circumstances with no further argument. Training Officer for would-be Kapitans of Under Water Boats, stationed at Kiel. Up ranked, to Korvetten Kapitan and awarded the Cross Swords to go with the oak-leaves and knight's cross. That had all happened over a year ago, when all the news of Frances had dried up with the death of her aunt. Something else, he was going to have to break to her when the time was right.

After exhausting all the available networks, he'd almost given up on finding her. He'd definitely not forgotten her. She was unforgettable. What they'd had together for that short time had been something he'd never experienced before. It was special. Special enough for him to break it off with Sophie Heyne and risk the wrath of her father and the Party. He shook his head as he thought of Sophie. She hadn't really cared when he had told her he wanted to call the wedding off. Later he found out that she'd up-ranked herself and had been dating a General. Ah well, he should have known better than to expect a girl like Sophie to remain celibate. Yes, a lot of water under the bridge. People had changed, circumstances had changed, the whole bloody war had changed.

On his return to Brest from that last patrol, things had been looking up for the Reich. The U-Boat Kapitans were enjoying a second happy time as the wolf packs devoured allied convoys. To top it all, Donitz, the old dog, had replaced Raeder as C-in-C of the German Navy, and it had looked like the Battle for the Atlantic had been just about won. Then in a few short months everything had changed again, and the U-boat arm had suffered a ridiculous number of casualties, forty-one just in May alone. Thankfully, his old crew and Werner were not amongst them.

Donitz had recalled his boys and temporarily, the battle in the Atlantic was halted as work at the Krupp's factory at Kiel was stepped up. Replacement boats were made, along with other would-be technical solutions, that in the new post he had found himself very much part of. The new boats were fitted out with heavier anti-aircraft armaments and a new homing torpedo was given the go ahead. Unfortunately, it hadn't behaved as well in a battle situation as it had done in trials.

* * *

They were soon on the outskirts of Munich; the streets were busy as the city was preparing for the big Party rally that was to take place in several days' time. Glancing down at Frances, he thanked God they would be long gone by then. He shook her gently, thinking it was a shame to wake her, and was taken aback by the speed with which she came around.

"What, what is it, Zahlappel?" She looked at him, eyes wide. "Where? Kristian?" and then she gave an enormous sigh. "I'm out. I'm out, aren't I? You came. I remember. You stopped the car, and I got out to breathe in the scent of freedom. And now we are here." She frowned. "Otto."

"Hey Froggy, you're free. Forget Otto. See, the Regina Palace Hotel."

The Mercedes pulled up outside the opulent building and Rittershausen stepped out from behind the driver's seat, opened the door and saluted. Mueller ducked out of the vehicle and took Frances's arm to help her out. As she took in the hotel's grandeur, she recoiled back into the safety of the car.

"I can't go in there," she said, noticing all the uniformed men.

Mueller tugged her arm. "Course you can. You're with me. Come on."

She fought against him as he pulled her out of the car, and they pushed their way into the busy foyer of the hotel, awash with all manner of people, who turned and looked at the strange couple making their way to the desk. Mueller, wearing a dust covered jacket with a sleeve torn from the scrap with Von Liechtenstein, and Frances, with her hair unfashionably shorn, grey skinned and wide-eyed, wearing clothes that could only be described as outdated. Noticing the looks they were getting, she made a grab for Mueller's arm, and he supported her through the crowd.

"Suite Twenty-Three," he informed the clerk, who looked over his spectacles with ill-concealed horror at the state of them both.

"Will you be dining, Sir?" he asked Mueller.

"I'll have something sent up," Mueller replied. "Could you get my jacket cleaned and mended?"

"Certainly, Sir," said the much-relieved clerk, as he handed over the keys to their suite.

The pair made their way up the wide staircase to the second floor, and then along the corridor. Mueller stopped at the door to one of the rooms.

"Here we are, suite twenty-three," he said, turning the key in the latch and opening the door. "Well, what do you think?"

Frances entered the room and stood silent for a while, taking in the lavish décor, the silk brocade and gilt. There were heavy armchairs, and an oak bureau topped with a large vase of roses, and a couple of decanters filled with spirits. Over on the other side of the room was a chaise, covered in rich fabric, and by the window there was an elegant dining table upon which sat a silver candelabra.

"I'd almost forgotten there were such places," she breathed.

Mueller steered her through double oak panelled doors, which opened into an equally elegant bedroom, and from that a gleaming white and gold bathroom. "I've been busy," he said. "I hope you approve." He showed her the bed. "See?"

Laid out on it for her inspection were several articles of women's clothing. A few sets of silken underwear, a day dress and jacket in lightweight oyster coloured wool and a full-length evening gown in deep blue satin, trimmed with even deeper blue georgette. Starved of such luxury for so long, Frances inspected each item. She picked up a set of silken underwear and laid it against her cheek, rekindling the memory of its smoothness. Next, she ran her hand over the day dress, feeling the quality of the fabric and breathing in the scent of its newness, whilst Mueller watched her, a smile tugging at his lips.

"I thought there was a war on," she eventually said.

"As always, you can get what you want if you try hard enough," Mueller replied. "Try them on. I had the evening dress taken up. I hope it's right. We will need to get you some more shoes tomorrow."

Desperate to rid herself of the trappings of Dachau and aching to dress once again in the fine clothes to which she'd been accustomed, she took up the oyster dress and a set of undergarments and stockings and retired to the bathroom.

Mueller sat on the side of the bed and, as he waited, he prodded at the side of his face and winced. Ah well, he thought, some things never change; she'd caused him trouble since the day he'd set eyes on her. When the door from the bathroom finally opened, she stood framed in the doorway, still wearing the clothes from Dachau.

"No good?" he asked, disappointed. "They don't fit?"

"Yes, they fit. Look, I can't…. These things, they're too good."

"Too good. What's that supposed to mean?"

Frances shook her head. "I shouldn't be here. It's a mistake."

Mueller patted the bed beside him. "Come here, Froggy, we need to talk."

She walked away from him, through the doors of the bedroom, into the lounge and over to the window, and looked out onto the busy Munich street. Mueller followed her.

"Frances," he repeated. "We need to talk."

Keeping her gaze fixed on the window, she muttered, "Do we?"

"You know we do." He watched her staring out of the window, refusing to meet his eyes, and changed tack. "Before anything, I'm going to get us something to eat. I'm starving, and you look as though you need a decent meal." He crossed the room and rang for room service. "Two Steak Diane, vegetables, some sort of sweet, I'll leave that to you, and a good bottle of Gewurztraminer." Replacing the phone, he said, "Your turn to sample good German wine. How about a brandy while we wait?" He poured two large ones from the decanter on the bureau and passed one over to her.

Frances took it from him, sniffing it first, and then she took a large gulp which made her eyes water.

"Well, if you want to talk, let's get on with it now." She shot him a glance. "What do you want to talk about? The filth and suffering at Drancy, or maybe the atrocities of Auschwitz or Dachau? I'm an expert on the lot."

The ferocity in her voice took Mueller aback. "Calm down, Froggy, for goodness' sake, I haven't got a clue what you're talking about."

She turned on him. "Haven't you, Kristian? Do you really not know? Isn't it part of the Party policy, mass destruction? Aren't you all in on it?" Her voice had become a strangled cry as she tore at her hair. "Oh God, how can I live with what I've witnessed?"

He moved towards her to calm her, but she backed away from him.

"Frances," he said, "you've been through a great deal. I know things have been tough for you—"

"Tough, is that a joke? They're killing people."

"Wars do."

"Innocent people, Kristian."

"Look, I know, we've talked of this before, haven't we? Civilians getting caught up. It's the state of modern warfare. There have been some dreadful air raids back at Kiel that I've been caught up in. Look at Cologne; right across Germany, the Tommies are sending in their bombers."

"No, you're not listening to me. This is not warfare that I'm speaking of. This is mass murder. These people aren't caught up... I don't believe that you think it's accidental. They're rounding them up, sending them to camps. Women, children, old people by the thousands, and you are trying to tell me you know nothing of this?"

"Gypsies, Slavs, Jews, for re-education or work, yes of course I know," interrupted Mueller.

"No! No! No! Not education, extermination. They're killing them. Yes, the gypsies, yes, the Jews and the Russians, French and Poles and those that aren't. Those whose only crime has been to oppose or offend in some way."

Seeing how wound up she was, Mueller tried to steer her to a seat at the table. "Look Frances, you're excitable. It's understandable."

"Get off me," she yelled, "It's not understandable. The things I've seen I'll never understand, and God knows, neither will I ever forgive."

Once again, he took her by the shoulders to calm her, and once again, she shook him off. "Forgive, Froggy, forgive who?" he asked.

"The German people, you, humanity, God, me even. I don't bloody know."

Chapter 3

Some of the food must have stayed down in her stomach, for when she woke, she was feeling much stronger and greatly refreshed. Mueller had closed the door to the lounge and pulled the curtains over the windows, so she had no idea what time of day or night it was or how long she had slept. She pulled the covers up to her chin, closing her eyes for a while longer, enjoying and remembering the luxury and warmth of sleeping in a good bed again.

She could feel some of her old energy returning coursing through her body. Stretching, she pulled herself up into a sitting position, listening carefully, head on one side, trying to make out if Mueller was in the lounge, or whether he had gone out.

She thought back to their last conversation the night before. She should be revelling in the enjoyment of it, the way she'd needled him and got a rise from him, but she wasn't. Was it possible that they, he, were unaware of what was going on in the camps? She had experienced two, Auschwitz and Dachau, but there was talk from inmates of many others.

At first, Mueller had accused her of lying, and she had accused him of being guilty of those crimes, as was the entire German population. He had then tried to excuse her behaviour by saying she was tired, worn out, her mind was playing tricks on her; nightmares, he'd said, no more than that.

She told him of Ruth, the children, the gas chambers, and the crematoria. Of Mandel and Grese, the orchestra and of Mengele and his sick experiments for the good of humankind. Then, like Otto had done, he charged her with being a madwoman, crazy. Was she? Had they beaten her after all? It was hard to believe now that any of it could have happened, as she lay in a proper bed in a suite of rooms. It was all so very civilised.

Through their shouting, they had scarcely heard the knock on the door which had heralded their meal. Mueller had answered it, hurling the door back on its hinges in his frustration and anger, frightening the young woman who wheeled in the trolley and who timidly asked if there was anything else they required.

"No!" snapped Mueller, then, recovering his composure in the presence of a third party, he apologised and taking the trolley from the woman, repeated, "No, thank you."

Closing the door behind the girl, he stood for a while, tugging his fingers through his hair, and rubbing at his chin as she had seen him do so many times before when he was deep in thought. Then he had turned on her, giving vent to his anger.

"Well... aren't you going to eat? There's decent food going to waste here."

"Aren't you?" she snapped back, and he set his mouth into the straight line that she remembered so well and indicated his awkward mood.

"I'm past it after all that," he said, grabbing the wine from the ice bucket and pouring himself a glass. Then he crossed the room to the window and looked out at the street below.

She had wished she had resisted the food just to show him. She did doubly so now, in retrospect. But this was food, the good food that had been so long denied her, and how she had savoured the smells, and how her mouth had watered. And so, she sat down and helped herself to meat and vegetables and a large glass of wine.

Slowly at first, to remember every forgotten taste. The steak cut easily, and the vegetables were cooked the way she liked them. A state of war, but a perfect meal. It was unbelievable.

Then, as she ate, she had wondered where the vegetables had come from, perhaps the gardens at Dachau. How many people had shed their blood that she might enjoy this meal? She had taken another few gulps of wine, and it was then that her stomach had rebelled. She remembered throwing back her chair and just making it to the bathroom. She should have known, as on the occasion at Mengele's, that her body was no longer accustomed to rich food and alcohol. Or maybe it was her guilt that had made her vomit.

Weakened, she had sunk to her knees, head over the pan of the toilet, sweating, and eyes streaming from the effort of throwing up. She vaguely remembered Mueller being there. He held her hair back from her face, rubbed her back and mopped her forehead with a wet, cool towel. That was all she remembered. He must have carried her through to the bed.

Now she swung her legs over the side of the bed and padded across the carpet to the bathroom in her underclothes. As she walked into the bathroom it was hard to say which of them was most taken aback. She was met by the sight of Mueller standing naked, except for a towel round his waist. He was mid shave. She wanted to turn and leave, but the sight of his body stirred beautiful memories, and so she stood rooted to the spot, staring.

Mueller recovered himself and smiled at her through the remains of his shaving soap. "You look better. How are you feeling?" he asked.

"Alright… Look I'm sorry, I didn't know you were in here."

"I've finished anyway," he said, grabbing a flannel and wiping his face. "You've had one heck of a sleep."

"How long?" She wished she could wrench her eyes away from him.

"About twenty hours. You passed out. I got a doctor in to look at you. Exhaustion and malnutrition. Plenty of rest and good simple food, and no alcohol."

Mueller took a couple of steps towards her. She hadn't moved from the bathroom, and he wondered if she was about to apologise for the night before. She looked so frail; he felt an overwhelming urge to just hold her. Reaching out, he gently stroked the side of her face, finding her gaze and holding it. He didn't notice her flinch as he pulled her towards him.

Part of her, the treacherous part, wanted him to kiss her but she fought to keep her mind clear and twisted from his grasp. "Don't ever touch me," she spat. He took his hands off her and stepped back, looking totally bewildered.

"My mistake, I'm sorry," he apologised, and clearly embarrassed, pushed past her, and left the bathroom.

She slammed the door behind him. How dare he touch her after all she had told him? How dare he think she could possibly be interested? Though she had to admit that her body had played traitor, and interested it was.

***

Fully refreshed after a bath, she felt able to face another meal, though this time she was determined to take her time and eat only a small amount. She opened the doors to the lounge to find Mueller listening to the wireless. The latest broadcast of Josef Goebbels, singing the praises of the Fuhrer's latest victories. He looked up as she entered and switched it off.

"Bleeding propaganda. Who do they think they're kidding? We're struggling on every front," he snapped. "I see you're hungry then?"

"How do you know?"

"You'd hardly be coming through just for my company, now, would you?"

Deciding that the question required no answer, she asked, "How long are we staying here?"

"A couple of days. I've arranged the registry office for tomorrow morning if you're up to it."

"Need we bother with that?" she asked.

"I'm thinking of you. It's best in the circumstances. There's always someone prying, even in our little town. You'll be safer." He gave a sigh. "And my mother will be more accepting. You can always say later that I forced you into it. You'll find German marriage surprisingly easy to get out of. Then again, maybe this war will save you the trouble, Froggy."

"What's that supposed to mean?"

"I mean that the way things are going, a lot of us won't be coming back. That at least should make you happy," he said, finding her gaze and holding it with his own.

"Yes," she said, "Yes it does."

"Christ, Frances, you've become a hard bitch."

"Yes, I suppose I have. I've had to be."

"Perhaps, but not now. It's over for you."

"No, you see, that's what you don't understand. It will never be over for me. I've seen too much. You know, often in Dachau we would hear screams in the night. Experiments, taking down a man's temperature to see how low they can get it before he died. I wonder how low that is, Kristian? Then they would look for ways to warm him up."

"Listen to you, Frances. How do you know all of this? I suppose you were all kept informed of what was going on, were you?"

"Oh, you'd be surprised by the networks. Desperate people can think of many ways to keep in touch. Not to mention the girls."

"I bet you will though," said Mueller sarcastically. She chose not to hear and continued.

"Do you know they took two girls from our hut one night and used them to warm up some poor bastard, who they'd more or less frozen to death? Science, Kristian, do you think, or some sort of sick floor show? They said it may help save pilot's lives, or even sailors. What do you think?"

"What I think is that I've heard enough of this," said Mueller. "It isn't doing us any good at all."

"Really, Kristian? Well, let me tell you it's doing me a great deal of good. Have you ever wondered what became of my hair? Remember how you loved it? Soles of slippers for U-Boat crews. Did you have a pair, Kristian? Was the hair chestnut? Perhaps it was mine."

She turned back the sleeve of her dress. "Look, tattooed like beasts. Not allowed to be people anymore, allowed no feelings other than shame."

Alone that night, Mueller paced the room, unable to sleep on the damned couch she had assigned him to. She gave him no peace; she had made him listen. Made him bear witness for the sins of his countrymen. She told him of beatings, killings, torture and experiments and she told him of the children.

He found that for his own peace of mind he had to deny the truth of much of what she had told him. It was far easier to believe it was just the wonderings of a mad woman. Otto had called her mad. Perhaps that was the truth of it. Her behaviour over the last couple of days had been... odd, and there was some doubt in his mind as to what she would have done if that gun had not been removed from her hand by Rittershausen.

He decided that time was what she needed. It would give balm to her wounds, real or imagined. He worried that she might never truly heal. He had to get her away from Munich into the countryside, back to the farm away from the war, if there was such a place. Maybe then she would stand a chance.

** * **

That night as Frances tried to sleep, the spectres came in their hordes. Just as she was dropping off, she heard the whistle blow, and the kapo shout, "Zahlappel. Out, out! It's your lucky day, there's a selection. Get up, you pieces of shit."

She sat bolt upright in bed with her arms wrapped around her head and her legs pulled up in front of her, shivering. Alone in the darkness, she tried to block out the memory of the horrors she had witnessed and endured, both at Dachau and Auschwitz. She wondered what had become of the girls in the orchestra and Miriam. Knowing what had become of Ruth and her baby. Then once again she was filled with guilt, as she sat in a comfortable bed, in a first-class hotel with a full stomach. She took some deep breaths to calm herself and tried to fill her mind with music to fight off the unwanted apparitions. It was going to be a long night.

Chapter 4

As the registrar announced, 'You may kiss the bride,' he thought to himself, what an odd young couple.

They'd been silent in the waiting room, not even communicating with their two witnesses, a young sailor, and a young woman. The couple were nervous. That was clear, and that was understandable, and not unusual. Marriage was not an affair to take lightly. Most young couples were nervous, but most young couples touched and teased, joked together; even in these war-torn times, marriage was still a time for happiness. These two young people, though, had stood stiffly throughout the brief ceremony, eyes steadfast on him, never on each other. They had each made their oath quietly and without feeling, and he couldn't help wondering why.

The man Mueller, a Korvetten Kapitan, well decorated, tall, and good looking; a catch for any girl. And her? Pretty enough, he thought, though too thin for his taste, and French. Ah, the Kapitan should have chosen wisely. A good broad hipped, hardworking Fraulein would have served him better.

* * *

As the ceremony had ended, Mueller turned and kissed his wife briefly on the brow, stepping back as though he had been scalded.

"Congratulations, Korvetten Kapitan," said Rittershausen.

Mueller nodded. "Thanks, Rittershausen. Look, you can get off. We'll walk back to the hotel, I think. Perhaps you could give Fraulein Crohn a lift, huh?"

Rittershausen saluted, "Yes, Korvetten Kapitan."

"By the way," said Mueller, "You can go back to Kiel tonight. I've finished with you for now. We'll make our way to Cologne by train, or as near as we can get." Rittershausen saluted again as he left with Magda Crohn.

Mueller and Frances walked out onto the busy Munich Street, bustling with comings and goings, preparing for another parade. They walked past the Fuhrer Haus, which made Frances's skin crawl in recollection of her visit, little more than a week before. There were guards outside, and the Nazi flag draped the entire building. As they approached it, she stood rooted to the spot until Mueller gently took her elbow and moved her on.

Her mind was in a whirl. She was supposed to be taking revenge and here she was married to Kristian. Once upon a lifetime ago, it was what she had dreamed of, a life with him. Now she had no idea how that life would pan out. She was after all married to a man who was her enemy. A man she should be destroying. She had almost laughed aloud when the official had asked her if she was free to marry. Truly, she hadn't a clue if she was. Kristian was speaking to her. "What?" she asked.

"I said, how about a coffee. We need to get you an ID card sorted, too. We'll have to contact Berlin."

She nodded, giving his words some thought before she replied, "Kristian, I'm not sure I want a coffee."

"What's wrong with coffee?" he asked.

She shrugged. "It doesn't feel right for me going into a coffee shop and sitting down and socialising with a load of… you know."

"Germans? I won't tell anyone; it can be our secret. It's real coffee. Come on." He took her arm and hurried her to a small cafe a little further on, in a road running parallel and next door to a jeweller's shop.

He found them a table by the window, where if she was to continue with her sullenness, he could at least amuse himself by watching the world go by. They sat opposite one another, she with her head down until they delivered the coffee, then she raised it up, and asked, "How did you find me?"

"With great difficulty, Froggy," he replied. "I visited your aunt again but…." He trailed off. He didn't want to be the one to tell her, not now, not today. He looked down at the table, damning himself for the mention.

"I know she's dead, Kristian. He told me, Otto. He was responsible."

"I'm sorry, I-I liked her." He caught her gaze for a moment. "Verdammt! I wish I had killed that bastard, Otto." In consternation, he shook his head and swept his fingers through his hair.

She asked again. "So how then?"

"Simon."

"Dieter? You are still in touch with your old crew?"

"No. Paul, of course. We write. He's commander of the old tub now. Dieter Simon just turned up out of the blue. My God, he had enough acne for the entire Hitler Youth." Frances smiled, remembering the youngest member of the crew on UBA who had developed quite a crush on her over the weeks of the patrol. Mueller continued.

"If the crew hadn't been on leave, and Simon hadn't taken his girl to the cinema and seen a news reel of a camp called Auschwitz, where it seemed everyone was having a jolly good time listening to the orchestra—" Frances exploded.

"That news reel was bloody propaganda, Kristian; it was a setup. Those people having such an enjoyable time are probably all dead now." He tried to take her hand across the table, but she snatched it back from him, almost upsetting the coffee cups, and glaring at him through her amber eyes.

"Hey calm down. It doesn't matter, propaganda or not. Simon recognised you and spent the rest of his leave, not with his girl, but looking for me in Kiel. The rest was relatively easy. Karl Donitz opened a few channels for me to that place Auschwitz, and we eventually tracked you down to Dachau. I'm sorry that things weren't sorted out a little quicker. Then perhaps the whole sickening episode with Von Liechtenstein could have been avoided."

"And I'd have been perfectly alright of course, is what you are thinking, isn't it?" She picked up her coffee cup. It was late morning, and the restaurant was picking up trade for lunch. As they sat, the place crowded out and Mueller sensed her uneasiness.

"Shall we go?" he asked.

"I'd like to, but the coffee is so hot."

He rested his chin on his hand and smiled at her. "I'll tell you what, you can leave the coffee as long as you promise to have dinner with me tonight."

She shrugged. "I have no choice, do I? We share a room, remember?"

"I don't mean in our room, Froggy. I mean downstairs in the hotel restaurant."

She raised her eyebrows. "Why?"

He tried to take her hand again, but she quickly withdrew it from his grasp. "Well, it's not every day I get married, you see; dinner at least would be nice," he said.

She was quiet for a moment, relishing the thought of a good meal in pleasant surroundings, where she could feel part of humanity again. But her fellow diners would all be German. How could she so easily dismiss her promises? But her life had taken yet another turn and it had to be for the better. Just for that day, she decided she would put the promises on hold; it was after all her wedding day.

"Alright," she said, giving him the glimmer of a smile, "perhaps it would be nice."

"Good. Now let's get you back to the hotel. A couple of hours of sleep for you, I think. Remember what the good doctor said."

A picture of Mengele shot through her mind. Oh, Kristian, she thought, I will never forget what the good doctor said, neither will I ever forget what he did.

They made their way back to the hotel through the busy streets side by side, almost relaxed in one another's company. As they entered the foyer, a female voice rang out clearly.

"Kristian darling, what on earth are you doing here? Much too serious a scene for you, I'd have thought."

A tall, curvaceous young woman was making her way towards them. Admiring glances followed her. As she reached them, she grabbed Mueller around his neck and planted a sensuous kiss on his lips, which he did little to resist, much to Frances's chagrin.

"Sophie, how are you?" Mueller gave the woman one of his most charming smiles, and pushing her away from him to arm's length, held her by the shoulders, so that he might get a better look at her in all her glory. "You look wonderful."

To her annoyance, Frances had to admit to herself that the woman did indeed look wonderful. Dressed in a lemon suit with matching hat, with her blond hair thickly braided and pinned up, the damn woman oozed style.

"Sophie, I'd like you to meet my wife. Frances, this is Sophie, an old friend." The woman was visibly shaken. She turned to scan Frances with her China-blue eyes, which reminded Frances of Maria Mandel's.

"Friend, darling?" Sophie retorted, holding out a finely tapered, white gloved hand with such aplomb that Frances was unsure whether to shake it, or bend at the knee and kiss it. She shook it briefly.

"So, you're the lucky girl who got him in the end," said Sophie, giving Frances a close inspection. Frances gave her a weak smile. "He got away from me, didn't you, darling?" Sophie continued, draping herself around Mueller. "You know I've always regretted that."

Mueller laughed. "The devil you have! You've never given me a second thought until today."

"You're wrong, Kris," she purred, "there's been no one as good as you."

"I bet you looked hard to find someone, though," Mueller replied, giving her a suggestive smile.

Sophie laughed charmingly. Pushing back his cap, she traced the lines etched around his eyes and mouth with a gloved finger. "We had some good times, though, didn't we?" she said, slyly glancing at Frances.

"You bet we did," nodded Mueller. His eyes swept the woman's perfect features while he kept half an eye on the effect it was having on Frances. He saw that she was flushed but was unsure whether it was from embarrassment or anger.

"Well, if you'll both excuse me, I'll get the key and meet you upstairs, Kristian." Her tone was brittle. Anger thought Mueller.

"No need," he said. "I'm coming now. Sophie, it's good to see you. Maybe we'll bump into you again before we leave."

"I'm sure you will, darling, I'm staying. How about dinner tonight? We'll eat out, shall we?"

"Well...." stuttered Mueller, "The truth is we only got married a few hours ago. We thought we would eat here tonight."

"Here? Perfect. What time? Shall we say about eight in the bar?"

Mueller sighed. He knew Sophie Heyne well enough to know that to argue was useless, and besides, he found her company delightful. Maybe, he thought, she would even cheer Frances up, though from the look on her face he doubted that. He kissed Sophie briefly on the cheek. "Right, eight. We'll see you at eight."

As he went to the desk for the key, Frances made her way to suite twenty-three alone. There was no way she was going to eat dinner with Sophie Heyne. She had taken an instant dislike to the woman. Those clothes she wore were unmistakably French. She wondered where the hell she had got them from, and who the hell she thought she was, behaving that way with Mueller and him enjoying every minute. He was just moments behind her, taking the stairs two at a time. He arrived at the door to their suite with an ear-splitting grin.

"Fancy that..." he said.

"Well, you obviously do!" snapped Frances.

"You know who that was, though," he continued, completely unabashed.

"Of course, I'm not stupid. That is the woman you should have married. Why didn't you, anyway?"

Mueller gave a sniff. "Perhaps she went off me," he said.

"Oh, I don't think so, not judging by the way she was climbing all over you!"

"Careful Frau Mueller, I might almost believe that you're jealous."

"Huh!" grunted Frances, and Mueller raised his eyebrows at her.

"Come on, you're tired, go and have a lie down."

He opened the door to the bedroom and drew the curtains across the window. "Do you want something to eat?" he asked.

"No, I'm still full up from breakfast."

"Sensible girl, you'll enjoy tonight more."

Frances gave an audible sigh. "Look, there is no way that I'm going to sit at a table with that woman," she said.

"You promised, remember?" he reminded her.

"I promised to have dinner with you, not her."

"Ah come on, Froggy, I tried to explain. It would have been downright rude—" Mueller began.

"And since when have you given a damn about being rude? You can't have changed that much!" Frances interrupted.

Refusing to rise, he continued, "I'm not going to argue with you, not today. Go and have a rest, eh?"

"Will you be here?" she asked.

"I must go out for a while. There's something I need to do."

"I bet there is!" she muttered.

Mueller left the room, shaking his head.

* * *

The sound of a trolley being wheeled into the room and the sound of curtains being drawn back woke Frances from a fitful sleep. She found Mueller pouring her a coffee. He handed a cup to her.

"Come on, sleepyhead, just time for a nice warm bath."

"I'm not going, Kristian, I'm staying here," she said awkwardly. Mueller sat on the side of the bed. His mood since bumping into Sophie was positively light-hearted, and it irked her.

"We'll see." He found her gaze and gave her one of his gap-toothed smiles. "Oh, I've got you something. It's in my jacket pocket." He strode into the lounge and returned with a small package, which he handed to her.

"What is it?" she asked.

"Open it."

"I don't want it, whatever it is. I don't want anything from you," she complained, trying to hand back the gift. Mueller pressed it back into her hand.

"Just shut up and open it," he said. Overcome by curiosity, Frances undid the wrappings to reveal a jewellery case. "I saw it this morning in the window of the jewellers by the cafe," explained Mueller as Frances opened the case. He took it from her and removed a heavy gold gate bracelet. "I had some links taken out." He placed it around her left wrist, concealing the tattooed numbers. "I thought if it fitted tight…."

"You thought that if it fitted tight, no one would see these," snapped Frances, shaking her wrist free and knocking the bracelet to the floor. "What's wrong, Kristian? Do the numbers embarrass you?"

Mueller was taken aback. "No, no, I thought…"

"Well, they don't embarrass me either. They might embarrass Sophie though, eh, or the people at the next table."

Kristian gave her a look of pure exasperation. "I left you here to sleep, and went out to get you a gift, and yes, I thought maybe you would be happier if those marks were covered up."

"You're wrong. I don't want them covered. I want them there as a constant reminder of what they did."

He threw up his hands in resignation. "Alright, alright, forget the bracelet. It was a mistake. It seems I must get used to the fact that I can do nothing right. Wear it or don't wear it. Wear it on your right wrist or not at all. I really don't care, you see."

He stood to leave and then reconsidered. "Look, can't we be civilised for tonight at least? Have a bath, put on the blue gown for me and come to dinner."

"I told you no!" she shot the reply with a toss of her head. "Why do you want me there, anyway?"

"I want to show you off."

"Huh, you'll have Sophie there for that. Why don't you have a nice little dinner for two?"

"Right," said Mueller through clenched teeth, "I can see I'm getting nowhere with you. Sod you, Frances, that's exactly what I'll do. All this so-called bloody suffering hasn't mellowed you, has it. I'm going to the bar! I've honoured my promise to you. I've got you out of Dachau. Tomorrow I'll look into getting you back to Paris if that is what you want."

"Damn you, damn!" she shouted as she heard the door close behind him, leaving her alone in the suite.

Why did she feel so angry? After all, she didn't really care what he did, did she? It was that bloody woman who annoyed her. She was making her look a fool. The staff of the hotel would all be talking. It would be common knowledge that she and Kristian had married that very morning. They'd even used their hotel maid as one of the witnesses.

Angry, she leapt out of bed and stood on the bracelet which dug into her foot. She shouted out, "Fuck!"

Stooping down, she picked it up, measuring the weight in her hand. It was beautiful, and it was a lovely gesture to go out and buy it while she slept, for whatever reason. She held it on her wrist for a few moments whilst she thought things through. She'd made promises to the girls at Dachau and at Auschwitz, but this was Mueller, not Otto. He had honoured his promise as he said and was now going to arrange for her to return to Paris. Is that what she wanted? What was there for her? An occupied city. Did she still have friends there? Perhaps. But Aunt Edie was dead. And then there was Otto who told her the night of the rape that he had commandeered her home in Neuilly the one she had shared with Steven. Maybe then seeing the war out with Mueller's parents was the better option. She left the bedroom for the bathroom and, placing the bracelet on a shelf, she ran herself a bath.

While she was waiting for it to fill, she found a pair of nail scissors and painstakingly snipped away at her hair, trying to get it into some sort of shape. Next, she cut in a wispy fringe, which she felt softened her still too gaunt features. After that, she luxuriated in the warm bath, though not for too long. She was running out of time.

She rubbed at her skin as she dried herself with the towel, trying to give it a healthy glow. With the wash, her hair appeared to have regained some of its old bounce and shine. Pattering back through to the bedroom, she donned clean underwear and took the blue gown from its hanger. He had said he had it shortened for her, another kind thought. And he'd gone out and bought shoes for her too. She slipped into the dress; the length was perfect. She was pleased with the way the georgette trimming around the neckline accentuated her bust, drawing the eye from the rest of her scrawny body.

There was a knock on the door. Expecting Mueller back with an apology, she checked her appearance in the mirror and was disappointed; the dress made her appear faded in comparison. She shrugged; she had done the best she could. She made her way to the door, wondering if he had forgotten his key and was doubly disappointed when she opened the door to find Fraulein Crohn, their young maid. The girl smiled at her.

"Have you finished with the trolley, Frau Mueller?"

"Yes, come in. It's in the bedroom."

"Your gown is lovely; I suppose you'll be joining the Kapitan in the bar. I noticed him there on my way here."

"Yes, thank you, I will, Fraulein Crohn."

"Magda," the girl introduced herself.

"Magda." Frances smiled and nodded at her. "Magda, can I ask you something?" The girl nodded. "This gown, the colour, it makes me look very pale, don't you think?"

Magda put her head on one side and looked at Frances for a few moments.

"The Kapitan says you have been unwell. Maybe a little makeup?"

"The truth is," lied Frances, "I've come away without any. I don't suppose—"

"Just a minute, it's in my bag downstairs," said the girl, smiling and running out of the room. She returned in no time.

"Here, look, mascara, shadow stick, lipstick, the lot. I love it. First thing I do when I'm off duty."

Frances smiled at her enthusiasm. "May I?" she asked.

"Anything you like," the girl offered.

Out of practice, Frances made sure she applied the makeup with care, trying to keep the look as natural as possible. Her brows were naturally shapely. She coloured them very lightly and then applied a couple of layers of mascara to her eyelashes, wetting the brush and rubbing it into the palette, relieved that Magda had chosen brown and not black.

"This red lipstick is the latest shade …" Magda suggested taking one from her case and offering it to Frances.

"Not with my hair, I don't think, but maybe if I rub a little into my cheeks …. There, what do you think?"

Magda shook her head slowly and smiled. "You look lovely, Frau Mueller. Like a woman should look on her wedding night."

Frances slipped on her shoes and checked the mirror one last time, pleased with the reflection that smiled back at her. She then checked the clock: three minutes past eight. Grabbing the bracelet, she placed it round her left wrist, and with a conspiratorial wink, she smiled her thanks and held the door open for Magda to push the trolley through. Making her way to the top of the stairs, she thought she liked Magda Crohn, which caused her a definite dichotomy of feelings. She put the thought to the back of her mind, enjoying the feeling of being in control of a situation for the first time in an age. Running down the stairs and crossing the foyer towards the bar, she was aware of the many admiring glances that were coming her way, not caring from where they came. What would they have thought if they had seen her a week ago? What would Mengele think if he could see her now, or Otto? And damn him, most importantly, what would Mueller think?

The bar was off to the left of the desk and was full of people enjoying a cabaret act. Through the smoky atmosphere, she could make out the sparsely clad form of the woman who was singing in deep guttural tones, accompanied by a small band. Then, as her glance swept the room, she saw Mueller. He had his back to her, seated at the bar with Sophie, who was laughing across his shoulder. Frances thought the woman looked dazzling and terribly sophisticated in the black close-fitting gown she was wearing. As she watched, Sophie pitched forward on her stool and Mueller threw his arms out and caught her. Perfectly positioned, she slipped her arms around his neck and gave him a lingering kiss. Frances couldn't move as she watched the two of them. She watched as Sophie whispered in his ear and she watched as he pitched back slightly on his stool. He was laughing. She watched as they laughed… together.

They were laughing about her; she knew it! Running back up the stairs and along the corridor, she wondered why she had even bothered. She struggled with the key in the door in her anger, and once inside the suite, she grabbed at the buttons down the back of her dress, tearing them apart. Oh, she would have her revenge on him all right. She wiped the makeup from her face and grabbed the bracelet from her wrist, dashing it across the floor, then once in bed she drew the covers up to her chin, and told herself none of it mattered. She would sleep until morning.

Sleep though, evaded her. She tossed and turned and watched the hours pass on the clock. Midnight came, and she heard footsteps outside in the corridor. Certain it was Mueller, she flew out of bed, dropped the latch on the door, and then listened, disappointed, as whoever it was walked on past.

Back in bed, she watched the clock approach one. The bastard, she thought, tonight of all nights. He was making her look a complete idiot. She grabbed the internal telephone, rang reception, and heard the sleepy voice of the night-clerk ask if he could be of service.

"Could you put me through to Fraulein Sophie Heyne's suite, please?" she asked. The night clerk asked her if she was aware of the time. "Yes, yes, I'm aware of the time. I know it's late, but it's important that I speak to her tonight."

"Very well… very well," said the voice of the night-clerk. There were a few clicks from the phone and then some seconds later, she heard the sleepy voice of Sophie.

"What is it?" she drawled.

"It's Frances Mueller. I believe you have something of mine. I want to speak with my husband now!" demanded Frances.

There was a pause, then the woman's voice at the other end of the phone cooed and moaned with pleasure. "Ahhhh, darling, he's much too busy to speak with you. Maybe… Ahhhh… maybe later, yes?" Furiously, Frances replaced the receiver with a slam.

She tossed restlessly, woken at three a.m. by the sound of someone tapping at the outer door. She lay quietly listening until the tapping stopped, and a few moments later she heard Mueller's hushed voice, and the sound of a key being turned in the lock. Enjoying the fact that he couldn't get in, she got out of bed and walked into the lounge to listen. She heard the key turn back and forth a few times and then the voice of who she assumed to be the night manager.

"It would appear you're locked out, Korvetten Kapitan… Your wife must have dropped the latch by mistake."

Unable to resist the temptation of further embarrassing Mueller, she grabbed a robe, opened the door, and said, "It was no mistake."

She watched as Mueller coloured ever so slightly and turned to the other man. "Thanks, sorry to trouble you," he said.

"No trouble, Sir." The man winked and left.

As Mueller walked into the room and closed the door behind him, he chided her. "Christ Froggy, that was a bit childish, wasn't it?"

"Childish? Yes, I suppose it was compared with what you've been up to," she snapped.

Slinging his jacket over the back of a chair, he turned to face her. "And exactly what am I supposed to have done now?"

"My God Kristian, you've got some gall, or maybe you were so far gone that you didn't even know that I phoned her."

Mueller's face creased. "Sophie!" he burst into laughter. "You think I've been with Sophie."

"Oh, I know you've been with Sophie!"

"You know, do you?" he said, raising his eyebrows, "You really are jealous of her, aren't you?"

"Jealous? Why would I be jealous? No!"

"If you feel so strongly," continued Mueller, "why didn't you come down to dinner?"

"I did, and I saw you kissing her, you bastard. You could have waited a day."

"Why, what difference would a day make? That ceremony meant nothing to either of us, did it? You made it quite clear you have no interest in me, Froggy. Sophie does, you see."

Mueller turned away from her and poured himself a brandy, smiling as he heard the bedroom door slam.

It was dawn before she slept, falling into a deep sleep from which Mueller had to shake her awake at 10:00 a.m., offering her bread and coffee. She came round abruptly, remembering the humiliation and the insult of the previous night, and smashed the proffered cup from his grasp, wondering not for the first time how the hell he looked so good and awake after a couple of hours of sleep on a small couch.

"Keep away from me, Kristian," she warned.

Mueller made a grab for her wrists and firmly pushed them onto the bed, holding them there. "Look," he said, "I don't know whether it makes any difference to you, but I did not kiss Sophie, and I certainly didn't spend the night with her."

"Liar!" she spat, "I phoned her, and you were there all right."

"Says who."

"Says her. That woman!"

Still holding her wrists, Mueller dragged her up from the bed.

"Right, come on. Me and you are going visiting."

Frances shook her hands free. "No, no, I can't."

"You can and will. I want to sort this out. We'll get to the bottom of it."

"Bottom of what? How the hell do you think I can face her?"

"Froggy, you're going to have to find a way because I'm going to clear my name, you see."

Calling his bluff, Frances got herself dressed in the oyster suit and combed her hair. Magda had kindly left the lipstick from the night before; she pinched her cheeks and applied a little to them, rubbing it well in, before lightly colouring her lips. When she looked in the mirror, though, she was disappointed. Her eyes were dark and puffy, and her hair hung lamely around her too narrow face, instead of in its usual wayward waves. She walked into the lounge and found Mueller drinking coffee and reading a newspaper.

"Look, I've been thinking, there's really no need for this. If you say you weren't with her, then I believe you," she blustered.

"The devil you do." Mueller scowled at her. "You won't believe me until you hear it from the horse's mouth."

"Don't you mean the whore's mouth?" she suggested, as Mueller stood and taking her by the arm, dragged her from their suite, slamming the door closed behind them. Then along the corridor and up more stairs, not caring about the amused smiles and glances that came their way. Upon arrival at room thirty-eight, he rapped on the door urgently. From the other side of the door came the voice of Sophie.

"Who is it?"

"Me, it's me, Kristian. Open this bloody door!"

Two chambermaids giggled from further up the corridor, and Frances felt herself colour under their gaze.

"Kristian darling," uttered the languorous voice of Sophie, as she opened the door and stood resplendent in a white bathrobe and towel, thrown turban style around her wet hair. "So, you changed your mind, fed up with the little drab already, are you? Where have you left her, asleep?"

"I'm here," said Frances, moving into view from behind Mueller, leaving Sophie for once stuck for words.

"What games have you been playing, Sophie?" Mueller asked.

"Games? Darling, do you really need reminding?" purred Sophie seductively. Aware of the two chambermaids still listening, Mueller pushed his way into the room, pulling Frances in behind him, and closed the door.

"Look, I haven't got time for all of this. Why did you do it, Sophie?" snapped Mueller.

"Do what? What have I done?"

"Pack in playing the innocent. You told my wife that I was with you last night."

"But we were together, we had fun, didn't we?" Frances twisted and spluttered in Mueller's grasp. He shook her wrist and held it fast.

"For a drink in the bar, and that was all. You told Frances I was in your room."

"Oh, did I? I don't remember."

Mueller raised his voice. "Why, Sophie?"

Sophie pouted and great tears dropped from her eyes and rolled down her cheeks.

"Please don't shout at me, darling, I don't like it. It was a joke, that's all. I was bored."

"Oh, for heaven's sake," snapped Mueller, "What on earth did I do wrong to get mixed up with you two?" He threw Sophie his handkerchief and turned to Frances. "Satisfied?"

She nodded mutely and followed him from the room back to their own, as Sophie dwelt for a while on the woman married to Kristian Mueller.

She had referred to her as a drab but had to admit that she was far from it. The woman was petite and feminine, and made herself feel big in comparison. Too thin, perhaps, but her skin was perfect, and if her hair hadn't been unfashionably short, and she'd worn a little makeup, then she had to admit that Frances Mueller would be quite lovely. And those eyes.... those eyes would burn any man.

* * *

Mueller sank into an armchair with a sigh and turned to Frances, puffing out his cheeks and exhaling loudly.

"You really thought I had, didn't you? You think that little of me, then?" He shook his head. "Do you really think I could do that to you, Froggy?"

Frances shrugged. "After what I've seen and been part of, I believe anyone is capable of anything."

"So, what became of good and evil, then?" asked Mueller. She turned and looked away from him.

"There's no such thing. There are only men," she muttered.

"And you believe we are all capable of committing the atrocities that you've spoken of?"

"Yes!"

"Then no wonder you hate me," he said tiredly, laying his head back in the chair.

Frances turned and faced him. "Can we go from here?" she asked. "I couldn't bear to bump into that woman again."

Mueller gave another audible sigh and nodded. "We'll pack after lunch. So, is it back to Paris for you, or into enemy territory?"

She considered her choices for a while, though truly she thought she didn't really have a choice. Go back to Paris to an occupied city or stay with the Muellers in a place that so far had remained reasonably untouched by the war. At least that is what Kristian had told her.

"I'll stay with you for now," she scowled, "the enemy."

Chapter 5

The train continued its monotonous journey into the heartland of Adolf Hitler's war-torn Third Reich. The first few hours had been in daylight, and Frances found she could look out of the window of the compartment and appreciate the countryside in the first throws of summer glory. She also appreciated the bombed-out factories and fragments of the railway line that had fallen victim to the R.A.F. bomber raids.

Mueller pointed out various places along the way, often remarking on their industrial significance. He also told her of Cologne, the nearest city to his parents' farm, and how it had fallen victim itself to a raid in forty-two, leaving forty thousand people homeless. Cologne, though, said Mueller had made a remarkable recovery. The people there refuse to be defeated.

At the start of their journey, they had been alone in the compartment, but now it was filling up, and Mueller felt it wouldn't do to talk of defeats any longer. Two SS officers looked in on the compartment, and seeing the black uniforms, Frances felt a sea of panic rise inside her. She had been arrested by men like these and it was the SS who ran Dachau and Auschwitz. Men like Taube and Mengele and Otto, of course.

As the two officers slid open the door to take their seats, she grabbed Mueller's arm, digging her fingers deeply into his flesh. He gave her a questioning look, seeing her panic and understanding it. The two SS gave them both a nod, then turned to load their luggage into the racks above the seats. Frances turned to Mueller and shook her head frantically, standing up and making to leave. Mueller stood too and took her hand firmly in his. The two SS had seated themselves and from their talk, it appeared that they were on leave.

"Are you on leave, Herr Kapitan?" one asked Mueller.

"Yes, yes, I am," Mueller replied, "but if you will excuse me for a few moments, my wife needs a little air." Which in truth was no lie, as Frances had become pale and clammy and appeared to be struggling to breathe. He slid back the compartment doors and, supporting her with his arm, took her out into the corridor and walked her along to the nearest door, opening the window slightly and securing it with the strap.

When he turned, he found Frances leaning against the side of the carriage, looking decidedly faint. He took her by the shoulders to support her, and finding her gaze, asked, "Are you alright?"

"No, I'm not alright," she began, then she hushed her voice and continued. "I can't go back in there, Kristian. I can't go and sit with those men."

"Hey, of course you can. You're with me."

"But they'll know I'm not German. They will arrest me and take me back."

"Not being German is not a reason to arrest you. Calm down. These men are on leave. We are going back into the carriage to continue our journey."

"No, please don't ask me to. I can't." Mueller looked deep into her eyes.

"Frances, I promise you will be safe with me. I won't let anything happen to you." She shook her head. "It will look much more suspicious if we don't return to our seats and leave our luggage there," he continued. "Please, take my arm. We will go back, and I will tell them you have been ill."

Although hesitant, Frances thought that Mueller may have a point. She made her way back to the compartment holding on tightly to his arm, fighting to control the nausea she was feeling. As he slid open the doors, they were met with smiles from the two officers.

"Ah, here you are," said one.

"Are you feeling better, Frau?" asked the other. Frances kept her head down and gave a brief nod.

"My wife is recovering from an illness," Mueller offered in explanation, thinking by rights he should have substituted the recovering with suffering. He helped Frances into her seat and seated himself close beside her, pulling her head onto his shoulder. "She needs to sleep." The two men gave a nod of understanding.

"Far to go Herr Kapitan?" one asked.

"Yes."

"Going home?" asked the other.

"Yes."

"Where might that be?"

"Near Cologne." Mueller's answers were clipped. He was not in the mood for chit chat.

"Ah Cologne, a long journey. You won't be there until morning."

"No."

"Wouldn't be surprised if we have to change trains. The R.A.F. are playing havoc with our railways."

They're good at questions, thought Frances, faking sleep. Along with other things that is. Stupidly she stretched and yawned, and they turned their attention onto her.

"You'll be looking forward to getting home, Frau." She sat up and nodded, frightened to speak in case her accent gave her away, and they took her back. She looked to Mueller for help. He took her hand and gave it a squeeze.

"We got married just yesterday. This will be my wife's first visit to my home, you see," he said.

Both men spoke together, "Congratulations."

One of them, the smaller of the two, continued, "Where are you from, Frau, this neck of the woods?"

"Really gentlemen, if you please, my wife is tired. She hasn't been well, and we have been on this train already for five hours. She needs to sleep, and so do I." Mueller pulled Frances's head down onto his shoulder and then placed his cap on his head, pulling the peak low down over his brow, thus preventing any further questions. The two SS looked at each other and shrugged.

* * *

The jolting of the train shook Frances to full consciousness, and she sat up. Mueller, she thought, looked sleepy. Hardly surprising, she felt worn out herself. He was pulling his hand through his hair as he looked questioningly at one of the SS who had opened their compartment door and was half hanging out, listening to the commotion taking place outside on the platform.

"Well?" asked his companion.

"Not far out of Frankfurt, the lines are down round Mainz. Looks like we'll have to backtrack to Bebra."

"Sod it!" said Mueller. "That's going to add a few more hours onto our journey." He turned to Frances. "It'll be morning now for sure before we make Cologne."

She felt cramped and hot, and the nearness of the two SS unnerved her. She wanted to ask Mueller what was going on but was too frightened to speak.

Whistles blew, warning of the imminent departure of the train. They had coupled its engine to the other end during the wait. More whistles, shouting and slamming of doors, until finally the engine itself blew, and the pistons slammed into action, throwing those who were standing, forwards off their feet.

"Off we go again," said someone.

"About time," said someone else.

"Still," said one of the SS in another attempt to engage Mueller in conversation, "at least we don't have to change trains."

"Not yet," said Mueller, "Not yet." He wondered just how much damage had been done to the rail network and thought perhaps it might have been more sensible to have braved the autobahns.

Daring to talk in the commotion, Frances asked what time it was. "Coming up ten thirty," said Mueller. "Why don't you close your eyes again?"

She shook her head. "I need to stretch my legs."

"Are you hungry?" Mueller asked.

"Thirsty more."

"Come on then, let's see if we can find the dining car. We can stretch our legs at the same time." Frances nodded her agreement. At least the hated black uniforms would be out of sight.

They made their way with ease to the diner, which despite the late hour, was busy serving young officers of the Wehrmacht, travelling home for a spot of leave. Many had already found female travelling companions, and there was a party atmosphere on board. Mueller found a quiet table in a corner and ordered two coffees.

"Do they know about me?" Frances asked him.

"Eh?"

"Your parents. Do they know about me?"

Mueller nodded, "A little. It was Pap who suggested I ask Donitz for help. They are good friends and go back a long way. Served together in the last war."

"And what do you think your parents will make of your wife with her tattooed wrist and her shorn hair?"

"That, Froggy, is up to you, but I'm telling you now, lay off them. They are good people and don't deserve any hassle from you. This damn war has given them enough of that already."

"German, aren't they?" she muttered.

"Lay off them," Mueller repeated, fixing her hard, with one of his well-remembered looks. He shook his head, holding her with icy eyes. "So, you want revenge for all that you tell me you've been through, and maybe that's normal, but if you have to take some ridiculous revenge then take it on me, alright?"

Frances snorted, "The sins of the fathers, hey? Are your shoulders broad enough, Kristian, do you think, to carry all the guilt?"

Mueller cast her a look and yawned. The train was pulling into a station for a short stop. "What about if we get some fresh air?" he suggested.

She nodded, and they made their way to the nearest door. Mueller released the strap on the window, leaning out to open the door latch from the outside. As the train stopped, he jumped out onto the platform, not offering Frances his hand. Not giving her the pleasure of refusing it, as she had in the past. He made his way to the end of the platform, and because she didn't know what else to do, she followed.

"Nice night," he said, looking skyward. "Starry night, sleepy town—" He was cut short as the sirens wailed. For a second, everyone was still, and then they ran in every direction. Frances started running back towards the train, but Mueller caught her arm and pulled her back.

"No, this way quickly!" He clambered through the wire surrounding the station, dragging her after him.

"Where are we going?" she yelled against the sound of the sirens.

"Away from here," he shouted back, "away from the station and the train. Didn't you see the munitions train in the siding? That's what they'll be after. Come on, Froggy, quicker."

Within seconds, they could hear the hum of the approaching aircraft. Mueller made for the nearest houses, which were set around three sides of a square, with the main part of the town at the far end. He followed a young soldier and his girl into one of them, through the kitchen and then down the unlit stairs into the cellar. They found it was already crowded with thirty or so people, all doing their best to reassure each other. Doing their best to control their own secret fears.

Mueller pushed Frances to the far end of a wooden bench and sat opposite her, between an old woman and a young mother nursing an infant. Their eyes stared hopefully up at him, and he nodded, wishing he could tell them that the bombing unit would fly straight past, but his sixth sense, and the knowledge of the munitions at the station, told him it was their turn.

Like the roaring of a hurricane, the engines approached, and they heard the first explosions. The old woman moaned pitifully, and Mueller put his arm around her, hugging her to him for comfort.

"It's alright, mother," he murmured. At that moment, the lights went out and automatically people cowered low, arms folded over their heads in the darkness.

"I'm afraid," Frances heard the old woman say, and Mueller's gentle reply.

"There's nothing wrong with that. You'd be a fool not to be."

Somewhere in the cellar, a baby cried, and the mother crooned softly to it.

As her eyes became accustomed to the dimness, Frances picked out the silhouette of Mueller. He had an arm around the women on either side of him now. She could make out that he was watching her intently, though she could not see him clearly enough to recognise the look on his face. She needed him and felt an overwhelming urge to cross to him and crawl under his arm, so that he held her close as he had on UBA all those months ago. They thought then that they hadn't a chance. She wondered how much against the odds it was to survive what seemed a certain death for a second time.

The bombing continued in waves, drawing near with its infernal roar of destruction, moving away, and then approaching yet again. Hearts hammered frantically, so hard that the beat was felt in the head, denying all other sensations.

Occasionally they heard the furling flak, and then bombs screamed down yet again, blotting out its sound. Suddenly the grill in the room's ceiling was lit by a sharp light, which hung in the sky. There was an intake of breath from many of the folk in the cellar.

"Target light," Mueller muttered.

Then once again the bombs thundered to earth, as hell loosed itself onto the town. Falling as a blanket, the bombs caused enormous explosions, which shook the house to its very foundations. Someone in the cellar switched on a torch, lighting the air thick with plaster and mortar from the many cracks that had appeared on the wall.

For a while there was silence, a minute or two to recover, then there were shouts and whimpers and cries to God, as a fresh wave of attack began.

Through the grill, the sky was lit blood red, as explosives and incendiaries rained down upon the condemned town. Phosphorus spurted fountain-like, and people scurried, searching for nooks and crannies, desperate to hold on to their lives. But to hide was useless. The flames licked hungrily, as in the inferno, asphalt, stone, trees, and people all went up together.

In the cellar, the soldier spoke. "We're going to die here. We're trapped like bloody rats. Well, not me, I'm getting out!" He climbed the stairs with his girl on his heels and pushed on the door, immediately slamming it shut. "Christ, the whole place is on fire up there. No way out that way." He returned to the cellar and made his way to the grill. "Hey, you, boy," he said, "come over here." A young lad, wearing the uniform of a Hitler Youth, crossed to him. "Right, get on my shoulders and pull that grill back. Let's see what's going on out there."

The boy clambered up onto the soldier's shoulders and pulled on the grill. Suddenly he lurched backwards, throwing the soldier off balance, so that he fell into the people behind.

"What the—?" the soldier complained.

"No way out there," the boy sobbed, "the whole square is ablaze."

Another bright light lit the sky just above the grill, warning of the return of the bombers.

"My God, we're off to hell," someone shrieked near to Frances, causing her spine and jaw to go rigid. She thought her heart and head would burst as both heaved with each beat. She saw that Mueller's eyes were still on her and as the cellar lit momentarily, she saw his face set like stone, his jaw tight, and his mouth thin lipped, as he fought to control himself like her, like the rest of them.

For two solid hours, incendiaries rained down onto the streets, onto houses, onto bank clerks, shop girls, soldiers, mothers, children, bakers, office workers young and old, fat, thin, good, and bad. Then the bombing stopped, and for a moment everyone in the cellar was silent.

Mueller was the first to move. He gently shook the two women from his arms.

"Where are you going?" the old woman asked, making a grab for him.

"I'm going to find us a way out of here, mother." He turned to Frances. "Frances, come over here."

"I've told you there's no way out! We're all going to roast," the soldier shrieked.

"We'll see," said Mueller. "Get over here and give me a lift up to the grill."

"You're bloody mad!" snapped the soldier.

"Maybe," said Mueller, "in which case you'll be well rid of me. Now come on, give me a lift, and that's an order."

The soldier bent down so that Mueller could climb onto his shoulders. He then pushed the grill outwards, relieved that it moved so easily, and hauled himself out. Removing his jacket, he threw it back down into the cellar to Frances.

"Here, soak this in the water butt by the stairs, and then get your arse up here." Petrified by the thought of climbing out of what she thought was the safety of the cellar, Frances still did as Mueller instructed. She pushed his jacket into the butt of water, then once soaked through, she passed it up to him. Seconds later he dragged her through the grill and up into the wrecked and burning square.

"Where?" she gasped, seeing no way out.

"Straight across."

"Into the fire? No, Kristian." Mueller quickly looked into her eyes; his gaze was steady.

"You're not going to give up now, Froggy, surely, are you?" he said.

"I can't, I can't breathe. The heat. Let me back into the cellar, Kristian, please."

Giving her no further time to panic, he placed the jacket over both of their heads and shoulders. Half carrying, half dragging, he took her straight across the square, moving quickly, not faltering, so that the fire couldn't get a hold. The other side of the square was more open, and it was a little easier for them both to breathe.

"Right, Froggy, you wait here." he instructed.

"Why?"

"I'm going back to get them out."

"No, you can't."

Mueller turned to her as he soaked his smouldering shoes in a nearby water tank, in which the water itself was near boiling. "You can't go back," Frances screamed at him. "I need you to get me out."

Mueller's laugh was harsh. "You know, just for a minute I thought it was me you were worried about." He threw his jacket into the water, then back over his head. "Don't you move from here," he ordered, and then he was lost to her, back into the flames.

Within minutes, he was back again, with the old woman in his arms. She was crying and clung to him like a child as he tried to put her down. "It's alright, Old Mother, get out of here now, and make for an open space. Go now."

"Bless you, son," she muttered. "Don't go back again. None of them will leave that cellar. They're all too scared, but I knew you would get me out."

Mueller smiled at her encouragingly, "Get out of here, go on." As she shuffled off, he dipped his shoes and jacket once more into the trough.

"No!" screamed Frances, grabbing his arm, shaking it. "Not again. You heard what she said. She told you no-one else will leave that cellar."

"I've got to try. Maybe my going back again will convince them." He shook himself free of her and once more she lost him in the fire. A few minutes passed, then another few. Frances screwed up her eyes, searching through the smoke and flames, but she could see no movement. She panicked. He'd lost his bearings in the smoke. Perhaps he was— She refused to think that.

"Sod him!" she said aloud. It was getting hotter. A great blazing cyclone hung over the town and was moving towards her. She watched as people stumbled, unsure of which way to go, and she seemed to be the only person standing still. She didn't like it. It was foolish. She must move, but to where? Anywhere!

She crossed the street to some large houses, seeking shelter from the heat, but flames were licking through the windows and doors of the buildings, fed by air flowing in from chimneys and corridors. Then, as she walked past one house, she got caught up in a terrific draught, which grabbed first at her clothes, then dragged her towards the open door from which the fire leapt out. As it drew her towards it, she saw its infernal beauty.

From inside the house, she could hear screaming. She tried to pull back against the draught and was aware that she was losing the battle. All the time she was getting weaker, slowly being drawn closer to the house, to the inferno. People were nearby, and she tried calling out to them, but the words wouldn't come out, and her voice was dry and thin and anyway they had their own troubles.

The screaming was close now, and as she looked around her for the source, she suddenly recognised that it was she who was screaming. She was going to die. She'd become a mark on a page. A statistic when the final death toll was taken. Just as her strength left her, she felt a grab on her arm. Mueller was blackened by the smoke, his breath rasping. Summoning the last of his own failing strength, he grabbed out with the other hand at the iron railing running along the front of the house and swung her round out of the driveway. "Shit!" she heard him gasp.

She fell to the floor, and he dragged her to her feet again. Not far away, delayed action bombs were exploding, adding to the breadth of the fiery cyclone, bringing it ever closer.

"I thought I told you to stay put," he barked.

"You were gone for ages— I thought—"

"Alright, alright, you panicked, I understand. Come on, there's no time. Let's get out of here. There's a sign to a park back there."

Clinging to each other for support, they made their way towards the open space. People fell in front of them, and Mueller bent to help them to their feet, only to see them fall again. Gasping, suffocated by the heat. Lying like pieces of litter, were the bodies of people caught up in the bomber's path, hardly burnt, but shrivelled to the size of children. Everywhere the nauseating smell of burning flesh surrounded them, making Frances silently reminiscent. Only now it was German flesh that burnt, and devoid of all feeling, the thought struck her that it smelled no different to the flesh that burned in the ovens of Auschwitz.

By keeping around the edge of the worst of the fire, Mueller got them to the park. Others had made it too, though many had fared much worse than them. Eyes staring madly from hairless faces. Sexless, stone faced, they stood wrapped in wet sacks, bodies and faces swollen from horrific burns.

Mueller threw himself to the ground, exhausted, hoping for some relief from the cooling grass, but the ground had been baked in the heat, and it prickled his face.

"Well, did you get anyone else out?" asked Frances.

"No, I couldn't get an answer. That's why I was so long. If there was anyone in there, they wouldn't open the grill. I banged and shouted, but then the air got suffocatingly hot, and I had to get out. Froggy, I've got to go back again. There could still be people alive there. You'll be fine here for a while."

"Go back? They're dead, Kristian. For God's sake, let's get out of here," she screamed.

"Just once more. There are children down there, people who need help."

"They're dead. They must be by now. You said yourself that the air was suffocating. I want to get out of here." She pulled at his arm roughly until he sat up. "You're mad if you go back again. Those people are past your help. Please," she begged.

"I've got to try."

"No! if you go back then I'll not wait, I'll take my chances on my own."

Before Muller could answer, a little girl ran towards him clutching a teddy bear, eyes wide with terror and confusion.

"You've got to help them. You've got to," she shouted. "My mummy and daddy are over there."

Mueller pulled her down onto his knee. "Alright, sweetheart," he soothed. He struggled to his feet and lifted her up. "Where are they? Show me."

"God, why do you have to be such a hero?" Frances spat with venom. Frightened, the little girl cried as she clung onto Mueller's neck.

"You will come, won't you?" she sobbed, as he shot Frances a withering glance.

"Yes, yes, I'll come. The three of us will go. Come on."

They all made their way back to the outskirts of the park. Already troops had been called in from the nearest barrack, to help with the bloody aftermath.

"Over there," the little girl pointed, and Mueller looked across to where the corner of a road used to be.

"My God, it's a direct hit. Where were you?"

"Staying at my friend's house. When the bangs came, I ran away. I wanted my mummy."

"You were out during the raid?" The girl looked at him questioningly and he tried again. "You were out when all the bombs fell, when all the bangs came?"

The girl nodded. "I hid in the park; you will get them out, won't you?"

Mueller forced a smile and nodded back at her, "Yes, yes. I'll try, I will."

In the streets, cars were now adding to the chaos, as the petrol heated in the tanks to boiling, and then further to flash point. Crossing the road to the corner, Mueller saw the enormity of the problem. He looked around in desperation and noticed that a couple of hundred yards up the road, troops were digging for survivors. He put the child down, kicking out at the rubble, not knowing where to start.

"Can you tell me where the cellar is?" he asked her.

"Over there, over there," she cried out, pointing to a strewn heap of brick and concrete remains.

"Right, now I'm going to need more help," Mueller said. He bent over to her level and pointed to the troops further up the road. "You tell the army lads up there that I need their help."

The child ran as fast as she could towards the soldiers, as Mueller called Frances over to give him some help. She was sitting on a pile of debris, emotions completely exhausted, fighting to understand what it was she was or wasn't feeling. She looked on as Mueller tore at the rubble and thought that he must surely know it was useless, but still he continued, and she couldn't think why. She could barely think at all. She wanted him to stop. He had to. She would make him.

From down the road came a shout, and as Frances turned to look in the direction that the child had taken, she saw she had almost reached the soldiers. But they were running away from her and yelling. Frances couldn't understand exactly what they were shouting, but Mueller could.

Suddenly he was up and running towards the girl, who was standing bewildered in the middle of the road. The explosion rocked the entire area and Frances saw Mueller hurl himself to the ground, as an enormous crater appeared where the child had been standing. Then he was up again, running back towards her shouting, "Move, Frances! Go! There's a gas leak. This whole bloody street is going to go up."

He reached for her and dragged her after him. Away from the road, away from the centre of the town. They heard a series of further explosions but didn't stop to look back. Further on were a couple of parked cars and Mueller tried the doors of the first to find it locked. Not so the second, not only unlocked but ignition keys in the dash.

"Get in," he ordered. Frances leapt into the car as he started it up and made for the outskirts of the town.

Chapter 6

At first the journey was slow, as the road was full of people all intent on leaving the stricken town, and mostly on foot. After half an hour, they had left the masses behind, and found themselves in the open countryside. The road first climbed a steep hill, and at the top, Mueller pulled up on an area of flattened ground to the side of a small, wooded area. He sat for some minutes not speaking, staring blankly ahead of him. The dawn light cast shadows across his face, already blackened by the fire, accentuating the lines around his eyes and mouth and the scarring on his chin.

Frances also sat in silence, listening to his breathing, deep and regular. Then he wordlessly opened the car door, got out, and walked in amongst the trees. She watched him throw his arms around an old oak. He lay his face against the bark, as if in some way he could replenish his strength from that of the tree. Then he walked a little further, until he was looking down on the smoking remnants of the town, lit not only by the still raging fires but also by the sun rising behind it.

For a while, she left him alone with his thoughts of the night, knowing they would be as dark as her own. Then, leaving the car, she walked towards him, having an overwhelming urge to take his arm and lay her face against him, so that she could renew her strength from his. Aware of her approach, he twisted and kicked out at a tree.

"This makes you happy, I suppose, does it?" he snapped.

Frances was shocked. He'd turned on her, and angered by his outburst, she replied, "Yes, it makes me happy."

He grabbed her by the neck, forcing her head round so that she looked directly into the devastation below.

"No pity, Frances, no tears?" he asked. "Surely you've tears for the children, huh?" She struggled in his grasp, and he let her go.

"No, Kristian, I've no tears left," she said, "and if I had, I wouldn't shed them for your people."

He turned to her, holding onto her gaze for a while, eyes bloodshot. She was struck by the depth of pain in them.

"I should have left you where you were," he said.

"I told you that."

He turned away, wiping his face in one of his hands, rubbing hard at his eyes, wondering if by leaving her now, he would be doing them both a favour. He knew he couldn't, so he yawned and after a few moments asked, "Can you drive?"

"No," she replied.

"Well, you're going to have to learn, and now. I've a burn on my hand."

"Can I see?" she asked. "Show me."

He shook his head. "No, it'll be alright."

She reached out and took his hands, seeing him wince as she did so. Turning the palms upwards, the burns across the palm and fingers of his left hand horrified her. "From the iron railings?" she asked, remembering that he'd cried out. He nodded. "Why didn't you say something before?"

He sniffed. "And you'd have cared?" Ignoring him, Frances lifted her dress and tore at the lining, damning the expertise of the tailor who had stitched it so well, until she ripped a large section of it away from the rest.

"How on earth have you driven this far, and to dig in the rubble?" she chided, shaking her head. "This really needs cleaning, but at least if it's covered, it will protect it a little."

Mueller turned his face from her, as she bandaged his hand as best, she could. The events of the night had made him overly emotional, and he felt it wouldn't do for her to see that.

"There," she said, tucking the end of the material into place, "Do you think we might find somewhere to get a drink? I'm so parched."

He nodded, "We'll carry on up the road, and stop at the next village or whatever. We're going to have to trust ourselves to people's charitable natures. I've lost my wallet; it must have fallen out of my jacket. Of course, it bloody well fell out of my jacket! Are you going to manage to drive?"

She shrugged. "If you show me."

They made their way back to the car, and Frances took the unfamiliar position behind the driving wheel. Mueller explained the pedals to her and placed his good hand over hers to help her find the gears.

"Right, now turn on the ignition," he said.

"What?"

"Turn the bloody key!" The engine fired after a couple of tries. He pushed her hand forward on the gear stick as she depressed the clutch pedal. "Now," he instructed, "let the clutch out gently, and gently depress the accelerator with your right foot." The car suddenly lurched forward and cut out. "Christ Froggy, I said gently on the pedals," he snapped.

"Sorry, sorry."

"Never mind, we'll try again. Now turn on the ignition, depress the clutch and find first gear. Gently off the clutch, gently on the accelerator. Good, good girl, a little more on the accelerator. Left foot gently off the clutch."

"Is that better?" Frances asked him, as the car pulled forwards after a few awkward hops.

"It would be if you remembered to steer as well," he said, grabbing the wheel and steering them onto the road. "Bloody Hell, woman!"

She stiffened. "I can't do it. I want to stop, Kristian; I can't do it!"

"So, we just stop here then, do we? You're going to have to bloody well do it, aren't you!"

"No! not if you keep shouting. I can't. I won't!"

Mueller took a deep breath to calm himself. "Look," he said, "Just keep your foot on the accelerator and your hands on the wheel. It's easy. Come on. Clutch in second gear, now clutch out. Good, better." He bit his lip to prevent himself from snapping as the car moved slowly forward, jolting its way along the road. With the sun rising, they left the remains of a town and its people behind.

"We've got to travel west, away from the sun," said Mueller, glancing over the landscape. "Look over there in the distance, at the foot of that hill. There appears to be a farm. Let's head over that way and see about that drink."

Further along the road, they turned left onto a dirt track which led them down to a small farm, and they drew up in front of the closed gates. Mueller got out of the car to open them, aware of the signs of life from across the far side of the small yard, where cockerels were crowing their welcome to the new day, unaware of the horrors that it would hold for many.

Returning, he said, "We'll leave the car here. Switch the ignition off."

"What?"

He scowled at her. "Turn the bloody key."

As Frances turned the key, the engine gave an angry shriek.

"Turn the key the other way, Froggy," shouted Mueller. "For Christ's sake. Right is on and left is off. Don't you know anything?" He gave his forehead an anguished slap.

Frances switched the ignition off and sat in the car, head in hands, until Mueller made his way back to the car, opened the door and offered his hand to help her out.

"Sod off!" she snapped, refusing to take it.

"Come on. We're both the worst for wear," said Mueller. "Let's see if friendly folk live here, eh?" She made an awkward exit from the car, relieved that he hadn't noticed.

As Mueller lifted the latch on the gate and ushered Frances into the yard, an overweight sheepdog charged at them from its hiding place, tail wagging in joyful anticipation of some fuss, taking the whole of its rear end with it.

"Hello girl," said Mueller, bending down and patting her, "where's your master?" The dog barked an excited welcome, bringing forth a reprimand from inside the henhouse.

"Shut up, you daft old dog. What's up with you now?"

"Hello," shouted Mueller. "She's letting you know you've got visitors."

"Visitors, eh?" came the reply. A small wiry man in his late fifties ducked out of the henhouse and into the yard. "What can I do for you, young folks? My God, you both look as though you have been to hell and back."

Mueller nodded and took Frances's hand. "We have."

"Ah, got caught up in that lot last night, did you? I wondered when it would be our turn. Pretty bad then, huh?"

"Pretty bad," Mueller agreed. "We could both do with a drink. Water, anything."

"Sure, you could," said the man, slapping Mueller across the back. "There's a pump by the house. Help yourself." He glanced at Frances. "You could both do with a bit of a clean-up too, by the look of things. Get yourselves sorted and we'll see if we can find you something to eat."

"I can't pay you; my wallet fell out of my jacket sometime last night. All we have is what's on our backs," Mueller explained.

The man smiled. "Don't worry, son, there'll be no charge. Come on, we'll go and find the Missus. Looks like you've got a hand that could do with looking at too." He led the way across the yard and past a couple of pig styes, the dog close at his heel. At the end of the yard was a small grey stone cottage.

"Pump's over there, help yourselves. Dag," he called, "come on out here and bring a towel or two with you."

A couple of seconds later, the door opened and a buxom middle-aged woman, clutching a couple of pieces of towelling, joined them in the yard.

"My wife, Dagmar," said the man, "I'm Eduard Schtunn." He shook Mueller firmly by his good hand.

"Kristian Mueller and this is my wife, Frances," he said, taking Frances by the hand and drawing her forward.

The woman also took Mueller by his good hand and gave it a firm shake, before putting her arm around Frances's shoulders and giving her a matronly hug.

"My, my," she clucked, "you kids look worn out. Clean up a bit, and then when you're ready, come on in. Eduard, shall I get your breakfast early?" The man nodded.

"And mind it's a big one," he said, slapping her across the rump as she went back into the house. Mueller smiled at the man's familiarity in front of guests and Eduard grinned back. "I'll finish in the henhouse and then join you soon. A few more eggs could do with gathering if we're going to have a feast."

Mueller gave the farmer a nod as he left. Then he stripped off his shirt and tie, giving an involuntary shiver in the early morning chill. Grabbing the handle of the pump, he gave it a few sharp tugs until the water flowed. As it did so, he ducked his head beneath it, rubbing hard at his face and neck with his good hand.

"That's better," he said, grabbing a towel from Frances. "Come on, Froggy, your turn, get that dress off and stick your head under the pump."

Frances scowled as she removed her dress, and then waited while Mueller yanked at the pump handle again. After a deep breath, she stuck her head briefly under the running water and, gasping from the cold, grabbed the towel.

"I was hoping I'd left all of this behind me," she said, quickly drying herself off and stepping back into the remains of her ruined dress.

As they entered the farmhouse kitchen, they were greeted by the wonderful aroma of fried ham and eggs, which Dagmar was cooking on the range.

"Sit, sit," she said, gesturing with a smile to the old pine table laid out for breakfast. They seated themselves just as the farmer returned. He joined them at the table, instructing his wife to get a move on with the food. "There's starving folk here, woman," he teased.

Mueller breathed in the smell of the food. "I haven't smelled anything this good for a while."

The farmer nodded. "It has its compensations living in the country. Are you city folk? You're not from round here. Kriegsmarine, aren't you son?"

Just as Mueller was about to answer, breakfast was dished up, and over the meal he told them of his post in Kiel, their recent marriage, and their nightmare journey towards his parents' farm.

Frances sat in silence, eating her meal slowly and wondering if in a few years she would look as worn out as her hosts. Simple folk these. What on earth would she have in common with Mueller's family? She would at least be safe, he'd said, and for that she should be thankful. She glanced at Dagmar's hands gnarled, red and roughened, hardly the hands of a virtuoso.

The men talked of the war, and Frances noted Mueller was much more guarded in what he said. The couple told them of their two sons, both away fighting in the Wehrmacht.

"Well," said Eduard, as he rose from the table, scraping back his chair over the flagstone floor, "it's all very well and pleasant sitting here chatting and passing the time of day, but I've got a dozen cows out there that are looking to be milked."

Mueller rose from the table with him. "Please, carry on. It's time we were on the move. We've still a good long journey ahead of us."

"Not until I dress that hand for you," said Dagmar, "and have you got enough petrol to get home?"

Mueller nodded and returned to his chair, letting the woman remove the make do dressing from his hand, wincing as she carefully peeled it back from the places it had stuck.

"Have we got enough petrol?" Frances asked.

Mueller puffed out his cheeks thoughtfully. "Hopefully, yes."

"Well now, I think we may have a little we could spare." Dagmar smiled at him as she tied the clean dressing in place. "Why don't you stay a while and have a sleep? Look at you both. You're worn out." Frances shot a hopeful glance at Mueller.

"If I'm to drive, you need to be wide awake," she said.

"Hmm… Well, perhaps a couple of hours then," he agreed.

Dagmar led them to a small, neat bedroom, and an old bed covered in a homemade throw. "Old but comfy," she smiled. "Let me get you some clean linen."

"Please don't go to any trouble. We'll be fine just lying on the top. It's warm enough," said Frances.

"Well now, if you're sure, I'll leave you both to have a good rest." She left, closing the door gently behind her.

Frances sighed, collapsed on the bed, and closed her eyes, thinking she could sleep forever. As Mueller took a pillow and put it on the floor, she sat back up. "What are you doing?" she asked.

"I thought—."

"Kristian, you're exhausted. There's room here for two. Like I said, you need to be alert if I'm to get you home."

He watched her as he removed his tie and then joined her on the bed, lying back with a sigh. Exhausted, he was asleep in seconds. Likewise, she quickly followed.

* * *

Propped up on his elbow, Mueller watched Frances thoughtfully. She had curled herself into his body as she had in the car when they journeyed from Dachau. This time she was clinging to his arm as she slept. He wondered if she had read his thoughts from earlier when he had toyed with the idea of leaving her. Perhaps she was making sure that he couldn't slip away. He knew he couldn't. He yawned and she moved beside him.

"What is it?" she asked sleepily.

"Nothing, didn't want to wake you up." He glanced down at his arm. She saw, and made to remove her hand from him, but he grabbed hold of it firmly. "Can we have a truce, Froggy? I'm so tired of all this fighting, you see," he said, looking into her eyes.

"So am I," she nodded, looking down, avoiding his gaze. She was tired of fighting too, for the time being at least. She agreed, "A truce is a good idea."

Still having hold of her hand, he lifted it from the bed and studied it. "I'd forgotten how beautiful your hands are," he said. Then, glancing down at his watch, he suddenly swung himself off the bed, exclaiming, "My God, it's midday. We've been asleep here for almost four hours."

She yawned. "Four hours really. Do you feel any better?"

"No, do you?" he asked.

She shook her head. "Time to go though, right?" Mueller nodded.

"Time to go. I don't think we'll relax until we're home." Speak for yourself, thought Frances.

There was a gentle knocking on the door.

"I heard you chattering," Dagmar's voice came from the other side, "I thought I would bring you a hot drink." Mueller pulled the door open, and Dagmar stepped into the room. "I suppose you'll be eager to set off," she said, passing each of them a mug of steaming coffee.

"Thanks. We still have a way to go," said Mueller, giving her a winning smile.

"Now, when you are ready, come through to the kitchen. The toilet is out the back." Dagmar looked from one to the other and sighed. "It doesn't seem two minutes since Eduard and I were youngsters, and so in love with each other. Just like you two, eh? And I'll tell you a little secret, we still are. We haven't aged at all in each other's eyes." She turned and left them with their coffee. As the door clicked shut, Mueller gave Frances one of his boyish grins.

"What?" she asked.

"I'm worried about that woman's eyesight," he said.

"Just seeing us through rose-coloured spectacles, that's all," Frances replied with a lift of her eyebrows.

* * *

They found Dagmar in the kitchen. She pointed to a cloth wrapped parcel on the table. "It's not much, but there's bread and cheese for your journey." They both took a fond farewell before going to find Eduard in the yard. The man produced a petrol can, which he pushed into Mueller's hand.

"I can't take this," said Mueller. "I know how short you must be."

"Sure, you can. Take it, son," he replied. "I'd like to think someone would take care of my boys if they were in your situation. We won't be needing much petrol here, and if we get stuck, we still have a horse and cart."

"I'll make sure I get some money back to you," Mueller promised, as Frances gave the man a kiss on the cheek before she and Mueller walked down the drive.

"Have a safe journey," shouted Eduard, as they climbed into the car.

Frances sat for a few moments, her thoughts retracing the last few hours. She had been shown kindness by an elderly couple who had made it their business to look after two young people they didn't know from Adam, who had turned up on their doorstep with not a penny to their name. She had been given warmth and sustenance. These people were good people. They were also German.

"Right, are you ready?" asked Mueller, cutting into her thoughts.

"Are you?" she countered, raising her eyebrows. Then starting up the engine, and finding first gear, she let out the clutch and kangaroo hopped for some way up the drive as Mueller blasphemed beside her.

Chapter 7

By mid-afternoon, their journey was almost complete. Frances had found Mueller's silence difficult at first, it was unlike him. He had spent the time privately questioning himself as to whether he had been instrumental in sending the young child in Bebra to her death. Aware that her behaviour during the raid had been unpleasant, Frances assumed that she was the cause of his melancholy, and fearing a caustic reprimand, she had kept quiet, only speaking to check on the finer points of her driving.

They travelled over many kilometres of open countryside, through villages and towns. The autobahns were well-constructed and as yet reasonably unravaged by war. They eventually reached the outskirts of the bombed-out city of Cologne.

"See, Froggy, see? That's what your lot have done." She threw him a look which he chose to ignore. "Cologne was a beautiful city once," he continued. "Still, at least the Cathedral has sort of survived. Paul and I had some great times here." He puffed out his cheeks and exhaled. "I think we'll keep out of the city. Not much left to see, anyway. Take the next road on the right and carry straight on. You know, I bet you we could have found somewhere serving food in that old shell. If we had money to pay for it, that is."

"And would you want to go into the city the way it is?"

He shrugged. "Perhaps not. Remember it the way it was, eh? Nearly home anyway."

"How much further?"

"An hour or so. I meant to ring the folks to let them know we were on the way, but I think we'll surprise them."

"Looking at the state of us, I think we'll certainly do that, Kristian. Don't you think you should warn them though?"

"About you?"

"Hah, very funny. But really, we don't want to catch them at an inconvenient time. They might want to get things ready."

"Nothing to get ready. They're expecting us sometime."

Frances spent the rest of the journey imagining what it was going to be like, spending the rest of the war living in a small farmhouse with two elderly people she didn't know, who belonged to a race she abhorred. She'd decided there would be no pretence from her. Despite agreeing to a truce with Mueller, and despite his threats regarding her treatment of his parents, she thought it better they should know from the start which way the land lay.

Her mind then took her to wondering what would happen if Germany lost the war. How would she fare with allied troops? A half French, half English woman married to a German. Worse still, what if the Russians should break through from the East? Would they even bother to listen to her explanation? She decided if that were the case, then Mueller had done her no favours at all by wedding her and bringing her to his home.

And then, what if Germany should win? Where would she go? Would they let her out of the country to return to Paris? And if they did, what would she be going back to? An occupied country no better than when she left it. Maybe England then. She had relatives there, or at least she had. Once upon a time, a lifetime ago.

"Stop here," said Mueller, bringing her back to the present. She hit the brake a little too hard, and the car came to a screeching halt, drawing a grimace from him.

She looked at him and lifted her eyebrows. "What?"

"We're here now," he said, nodding his head and fixing his eyes on her. "I want to remind you that these are good people. If you have something to say, then you say it to me. Do you understand, Froggy?" She decided the question didn't require an answer, just a scowl.

They drove on for half a kilometre, and it was worse than she had even expected. Around the corner stood a tiny brick cottage surrounded by lots of open countryside. Nicely kept, she had to admit. Mueller suddenly made a grab for the wheel.

"For goodness' sake, concentrate, will you? I told you next, right up the driveway. That's Anna's house by the way."

"Who is Anna?" she asked.

"You'll soon find out."

He turned the car across the deserted road and onto a wide, shale covered driveway, which crackled as the tyres of the car ran over it. The drive stretched between a long, winding avenue of evergreens with far-reaching fields beyond. There had been a sign as they'd turned, which, because she had been taken unaware, she had been too slow to read.

About another quarter of a kilometre further on, the drive broadened out and wound to the left, leading up to a large house with paddocks to the side, in which grazed large Hanoverian horses.

"Schonen Felder, home," said Mueller, sitting forward in anticipation. "Pull up just in front of the steps."

Frances froze to her seat. This was not at all what she'd expected. The house stood tall and commanding. Steps ran from the drive to a wooden plant covered veranda, which appeared to encircle most of the house. The stone of the building was palest grey, white almost, and it stretched upwards for three storeys, ending in a red gabled roof. Around the middle floor was a balcony which, she would find later, could be accessed through a glazed door leading from each of the front bedrooms.

"Well," asked Mueller, "do you like it?"

Frances bit her lip. "You said you were farmers," she muttered.

"We are."

The front door had opened, and Frances caught a first sight of a stylish middle-aged woman, who stood for a moment, before making her way towards the car. She was tall and slender; her dark hair was drawn back in a chignon, which emphasised her narrow chin. Frances noticed Mueller had set his jaw before opening the car door and standing before the woman, who had locked her eyes on him hungrily. Similar eyes to his, Frances noted, but devoid of the depth of colour, making them seemingly hard. As the woman reached Mueller, she threw her arms around his neck, and Frances saw him stiffen in her embrace as she kissed him on both cheeks.

"Mutti," he said simply, stepping back from her.

The woman reached up and ran her hand down the side of his face. "Look at you, Kristian, you're filthy. Where have you been? And what have you done to your hand?"

"Oh, it's nothing much for you to worry about. Where's Pa?"

"Where do you think? More to the point, where's this wife of yours?"

"Froggy, come on out," shouted Mueller, turning back to the car.

Frances wished she could disappear. She felt thoroughly foolish. He had told her that his family were farmers, and then brought her back to what amounted to a small mansion. She'd felt in control and superior whilst she had expected a hovel housing worn-out people. Now she had nothing to berate him for. He walked round to her side of the car, opened the door, and levered her out from behind the wheel. She frowned at him as he led her towards his mother and introduced them to one another. "Frances, Mutti."

Frances looked into the cold eyes of Freya Mueller, and returned her stare, until the elder Frau Mueller finally extended her hand. Having no alternative, Frances took it briefly. She saw Freya Mueller stiffen and give her son a questioning glance. Thankfully, they were all saved further embarrassment by the arrival of a tall, distinguished man, wearing a straw homburg, and followed by a couple of bouncing retriever dogs. Frances immediately recognised the familiar features of Kristian in this man's face, though they were much heavier, particularly around the jaw. She rightly assumed the man to be Mueller's father, Peter.

The two men grabbed each other's hands warmly, and slapped one another around the shoulders, and then Peter Mueller took his son in an embrace, as the dogs leapt round both sets of legs. Peter stepped back and surveyed his son through bright grey eyes, and as he did so, he nodded to himself, a smile playing at the corners of his mouth.

"My God, son, what the hell have you been doing? You look dreadful!" Turning to Frances, he asked, "Is this the effect you have on my boy?" Then he gave her a warm smile and ushered them both towards the open door.

"Come on, you look as though you could do with a clean-up and a good rest, both of you. I'll get your bags."

"No need," said Kristian, bending down to pet the dogs. "We haven't got any. We got caught up in a raid at Bebra, lost the lot. My damn wallet too."

"Ah, well, never mind the baggage."

"But just look at the state of them both, Peter," said Freya.

"At least they are both safe," he said, giving them another warm smile. "Bad raid, huh?" His son nodded and Peter turned to his wife. "Freya, sort some food out for these children. Is Anna still in the kitchen?"

"Yes, yes in a moment," replied Freya. "First, they must see their room."

The front door had opened onto a large reception hall, from which opened several other rooms. A winding staircase with white barley twist spindles and an oak balustrade twisted upwards centrally from the hall.

At the mention of their room, Frances shot Mueller a warning glance.

"I've had the front guest room redecorated," continued Freya. "Come on, both of you, come and see if you like it."

She led the way to the first floor, swiftly climbing the stairs, and paused outside a white, panelled door on the left side of the landing.

"Mutti..." began Mueller, "I think I ought..."

"Not now, Kristian, look," she said, pushing open the door into a recently decorated room. Frances's gaze swept over her surroundings. There was a large bed covered in a white, heavily embroidered throw and the furnishings in the room were of antiqued pine. The walls had been freshly decorated in the palest lemon and blue, which she found tasteful.

"Well, children?" Freya asked with a smile, looking from one to the other. Neither of them answered. Frances looked at the floor with embarrassment. "You don't like it?" asked Freya Mueller, eyebrows raised in astonishment.

"No, no, it's lovely, Mutti, isn't it, Frances?" said Mueller.

"Yes, lovely," Frances replied weakly.

"Well then?" questioned Freya.

"Well then," began Mueller, and for the first time, Frances noted with glee that he really was embarrassed. "I'll be sleeping in my old room, Mutti," he said.

"Kristian, I know how much you love your room, but really, it's hardly the place—.

Mueller had stiffened. "I said that I would sleep in my room," he repeated.

Freya gave her son an incredulous look. "But why?" she asked. Silent until now, Peter Mueller butted in.

"Never mind why, Freya, your son has told you he wants to stay in his old room. That's fine by us now, isn't it?"

Freya Mueller's jaw dropped open as if to speak, and then closed again, as she looked first at her son, then to her daughter-in-law, who was still looking at the floor, and then to her husband. She finally nodded her agreement.

"Now," continued Peter, "we will leave you two alone to clean up and have a rest while we sort out some food for you." Freya's eyes lingered on her son as her husband guided her back down the stairs.

"Kristian, you need your mother to look at that hand!" he shouted as they descended.

"Don't worry, I'll see Anna; she can sort it," Mueller shouted back. Then he turned to Frances. "Well, that was some bloody home coming."

He pushed her into the room and closed the door on the dogs, who attempted to follow.

"What did you expect? Isn't it better that they know from the start?" she said.

He sighed. "I'd have preferred a couple of hours' peace maybe, and a good meal first. My mother is upset, I can tell you, though I don't suppose, Frances my dear, that you care, do you?"

She looked him in the face. "No, Kristian, no, I don't."

Mueller shook his head. "Well then, I'll leave you to rest. Your bathroom is over there." He pointed to a door opposite her room. "I'm up on the next floor should you need anything. Far right of the landing."

She nodded as he closed the door. Once left alone, she fell back on the bed, kicking off her tattered shoes and enjoying the feel of the clean bed linen. She saw that at the far end of the room was a large window, part of which was a glazed door, standing partially open. It allowed the late afternoon sunshine in, which painted dancing, watery sunbeams on the wall, and across part of the wooden, rug covered floor. She got up from the bed and made her way over to the window, wondering what lay beyond the house. Stepping out onto the balcony, the amount of land around the farm took her aback. They were in what she thought of as the industrial heartland of Germany, not that many kilometres from Cologne.

Her window looked out onto the front of the house, but from the balcony she could see partially around to the side, towards the back. There was a large lawn rolling away towards a well-stocked garden and winding paths. She struggled to see it completely but could make out flower beds, and here and there stone benches and statues stood. Beyond the garden were the fields, full now of ripening crops and surprisingly horses. More distantly the fields became black hills, which eventually gave way to the forest. Not at all what she had expected, she had to admit.

She made her mind up to take a long overdue bath and then she thought she would rest. She had to make her mind clear to enable her to think. It would have been so much simpler if he had taken her to a hovel, which at every opportunity she could have thrown back in his face. Here it looked as though she would want for nothing, apart from her freedom, and to rid herself of Germany and of all it stood for.

* * *

"Froggy, Froggy, are you awake?" she woke to a gentle knocking, and Mueller's hushed voice from out on the landing.

"Yes, I am now," she replied coldly.

"We're about to have dinner. Are you ready to join us?"

"No. Look, couldn't I have something in here? Couldn't you bring me something?"

There was a pause, and then the handle of the door twisted and was pushed open to reveal Mueller, cleaned up and in casual clothes, as she'd never seen him before. He'd shaved, and his hand had been freshly dressed. She was sitting up on the bed and once again she wantonly stared at him, as she mentally kicked herself for not having locked the door. Instinctively, she drew the towel in which she had fallen asleep, tighter around her body.

"I'm sorry, I thought you would be ready," he apologised.

"I've nothing to wear, have I?" she snapped, annoyed by her body's response, and even more by the smile that had appeared at the corner of Mueller's mouth, as he took in her state of undress.

He raised his eyebrows at her, "No! Of course, you haven't. I'm sorry, you should have said before. Well, if that's the only reason you want to eat in your room, we can easily remedy it."

"No!" said Frances, too late. He had closed the door and disappeared.

A minute or two later, he reappeared, with a couple of dresses slung over his arm. "Here, they'll be a bit on the large side, I'm afraid. See which one fits you best. They're Mutti's."

"Well, I didn't think they were yours, Kristian. Look, I don't want your mother's clothes. I don't want to join you for dinner. I want to stay here." Mueller gnawed his lip and fixed her with a look.

She threw her legs over the bed and stood up, grasping the towel around her body. "Damn you!" she exploded, grabbing the dresses from his arm.

"Be polite, Frances, that's not too much to ask, surely, is it?" he asked, as he left the room. Then, just as she was about to step out of her towel, he reappeared, head stuck around the door. "I'll take the key just in case and wait for you on the landing."

"No need to wait. I'm not a child. I can make my own way down!"

"Don't be long then, or we will be in trouble with Anna. She doesn't like her food going to waste."

She made her way down to the dining room, cross with herself for being nervous and even more so for being hungry. She wished she had the strength to refuse dinner, but the smell of good food pervaded the house and her nostrils, making it nigh on impossible for her to ignore the ache of hunger in her belly.

First, she wondered whether to knock, and then telling herself it was stupid, she took a deep breath and pushed the door open. Freya was already seated at the table; she looked up briefly when Frances entered the room but that was all. Kristian and Peter were leaning at either end of a charcoal marble fireplace, on which sat a huge vase of fresh flowers. The men straightened up as she entered. She'd surprised them, that was obvious, and by their reaction, they had clearly been talking about her. Kristian, she thought, would have been making excuses for her behaviour when she needed none.

"Ah Frances," Peter Mueller gave her a smile, "you look refreshed. Can I get you a sherry?"

She frowned; she knew she looked dreadful. The dress that suited her the least was the one she had chosen. It was too long and hung on her too thin body. The bright red fabric clashed dreadfully with her hair, making her skin take on a sickly hue.

The meal, as she intended, was a disaster. The talk had been mostly trivial at first, all the Muellers, it seemed, being ill at ease in her company. She wondered what Kristian had been telling them. That she was a madwoman, perhaps.

It was Peter who attempted to break the ice. "My son tells me you have your origins in Paris."

"No, I have my origins in England," she replied.

"Ah yes, England, but you have spent most of your life in France."

"After my father died, yes, I went to live in Paris."

"Ah, with your aunt."

"Who's dead now. They questioned her. German soldiers. She had a weak heart. I was told her death was unfortunate. Who for the most, I wonder?" From across the table, Kristian was giving her warning glances and she saw that Freya had noticed too.

Not understanding what she was talking about, and not having a clue what else to do to clear the atmosphere, Peter Mueller cleared his throat and continued.

"You know, Frances, back in my youth, I visited Paris several times. Is it still the beautiful city that it was?"

"Beautiful? Now that would depend. Last time I was there, it was somewhat marred by a multitude of German uniforms. An occupied city loses its beauty somewhat, don't you, OUCH!" she cried out as Kristian kicked her shin hard beneath the table.

"Enough, Frances," he warned.

Throwing back the chair, she fled up to her room, and there reproached herself for feeling foolish and guilty, but mostly for still being hungry.

* * *

Sometime later, just as she was considering going to bed, there was a gentle knock on the door. Thinking it would be Kristian, she ignored it.

"Frances, it's Peter," came the voice from outside on the landing. "May I come in, just for a moment?"

Frances was sitting by the open doors to the balcony. She turned away as she heard him enter the room, not wanting him to see that the tears were still falling. He crossed the room to her side and touched her gently on the shoulder.

"Frances, Kristian has been telling us some of what you've been through. It's hard for us to—"

"Believe?" she cut in.

"No, my dear, accept. It will take us all time to get along, Frances. We can wait, I want you to know that. Here, I've brought you a sandwich. Kristian said you have eaten nothing since this morning. You must be starving." He put a tray with a sandwich, cake, and a mug of warm milk down on a small table next to the bed and quietly left her.

That brief conversation had made things so much worse. She found herself liking the man. What about her promises to take revenge? Here she was, wantonly wanting one Mueller and liking another. What about Freya though? She'd not yet decided about Freya. There was something cold and detached about her, even in her dealings with Kristian.

Chapter 8

"When I heard; I couldn't wait. Where is he, still in bed? Ah well, newlyweds. I suppose it was expecting too much for him to be up at this hour."

Freya Mueller put her arms around the early morning visitor and gave her a warm hug. This was the girl who should occupy the room upstairs. She should be lying next to her son. She had always wanted it so, and for many years, it had looked as though she would have her way.

Sara was the daughter of her close friends and neighbours from the next farm, the Kohls. Both being of a similar age, Kristian and Sara had grown up together and were inseparable, so that a close bond had formed between the two families. That close bond had remained, but as the children had grown, each had gone their own way, particularly Kristian, first to university, then into the Kriegsmarine, and then to war.

Neither of them had been involved in a meaningful relationship that she knew of, and she had even questioned Kristian about his feelings for Sara, just as the war had broken out. He'd laughed when she'd mentioned it.

"Marry Sara, Mutts? We are much too good friends for that."

Well, perhaps he was right, thought Freya, but a good-looking girl like Sara shouldn't remain unmarried.

Sara was shaking with excitement, and her eyes sparkled. "Well Aunty Freya, spill the beans. What's she like?"

Unable to think of how to answer, Freya stumbled over her words. "I... I... You'll have to see for yourself, Sara. Kristian is breakfasting. I'll get him."

"No need, Mutts." Hearing the commotion, Kristian and Peter had ended their breakfasts and made their way to the hall. Kristian took the girl in his arms and hugged her fondly.

"And what brings you here, I wonder?" he teased.

"As if you didn't know."

He set her away from him and grinned at her. "I suppose the whole damn town knows my business, eh?"

"Just about, but don't put all the blame on me. Your mother was so excited she couldn't keep it to herself for a moment. Well, aren't you going to introduce your wife to your greatest friend? Where is she, upstairs?"

"Sara, She's in the guest room, just a minute. I need to talk to you."

Too late. Kristian looked on as Sara rushed up the stairs and opened the door to his wife's bedroom. He shrugged at his parents. "Best to leave them to it, I'd say."

* * *

Frances jumped around as the door opened and a tall, well-built young woman confronted her, dressed in riding breeches and an open-necked cream shirt. A headscarf partially covered her dark hair, and after an initial look of surprise, the woman smiled, showing strong white teeth.

"Sara Kohl," she said, grabbing Frances's hand in a firm grip. "I'm from the next farm. If there's anything you want to know about Kristian, then ask me. I know the lot."

Frances's jaw dropped open, causing Sara to laugh aloud. "Don't worry," she said, "we grew up together. We were best pals until he discovered there were girls other than me on the scene." Frances watched, as the woman thought for a moment. "We're still best pals, I think," she said.

Sara threw herself down onto the bed, still smiling, and there was something about her that reminded Frances of Miriam. Maybe it was her forthright manner.

"It's Frances, isn't it?" Sara asked.

"Yes, Frances Meyer."

Sara laughed again. "Mueller, my dear," she corrected her.

"Of course, I forgot. I haven't got used to the idea yet."

Sara pulled a face. "Married to Kristian; I wouldn't be at all surprised if you never get used to that."

Despite trying not to, Frances laughed out loud, and there was something in the sound that stirred her. For the first time in an age, the laugh was one of humour, not irony or sarcasm, and she liked the way it made her feel. She liked the way Sara made her feel too. There was something wholesome and strong about Sara, which somehow made her feel safe.

"So, what do you think of the farm? Do you like it here?" Sara asked.

Frances shrugged. "I don't know. I haven't really had a chance to see much yet. We didn't get here until late yesterday afternoon, and I was so exhausted with the raid and all…"

"You got caught in a raid?"

"Hmm, somewhere round Bebra? I think that's what Kristian said. We lost everything."

"Thank goodness for that," said Sara, and seeing Frances's puzzled look continued. "That dress you're wearing is not one of yours, I take it?"

"Not really my colour, is it?" Frances said with a grimace.

* * *

As Sara tripped down the stairs, she was met by three people at the bottom who looked at her and one another in disbelief. She grabbed Kristian round the neck and planted a firm kiss on his cheek.

"Oh Kris, I'm so happy for you. She's delightful," she said, hugging him. "I'm going home, but I'll be back in less than an hour to take your wife shopping in town. Be a dear, and see if you can sort her out a bicycle, will you? Unless you want to run us in, of course."

None of the Muellers were able to think of a word to say. As she crossed the hall to leave through the kitchen, Sara turned back to Kristian. "You'd better not be stingy, by the way; stylish clothing is costing a great deal of Reichsmarks these days." With a bang of the door, Sara Kohl left.

"Do you think she got the right room?" Kristian asked his parents wryly.

"Overnight metamorphosis, do you think?" suggested Peter Mueller, rubbing his chin.

Kristian shook his head. "Too easy."

"Yes," snapped his mother. "She'll be up there hatching some nasty little plot."

"Really, Mutti," said Kristian in mock alarm, "that's my wife you're referring to. Ah well, to the lion's den," he said, giving his parents a twisted expression as he climbed the stairs. He knocked on Frances's bedroom door and when she opened it and invited him in with a smile, he was completely baffled.

"Am I too late for breakfast?" she asked. He shook his head. "Good, I'm starving."

"Froggy, what are you up to?" he asked.

"Nothing, I'm hungry."

"Why this sudden change? You're different this morning."

She shrugged. "I don't know. Perhaps I'm just looking forward to going shopping." She paused and flopped down on the bed. "It seems a lifetime ago. The last time I went shopping was in Paris, before...." He watched her as she became thoughtful for a few moments. Then she turned to him. "Meeting Sara this morning, so full of life, just getting on with things. It made me think how I just want everything to be normal again. I know it can't be, not yet, but I want it to be, even if for now I must pretend. I can go with Sara, can't I?"

Mueller sat down beside her, intending to take her hand, but aware that even still she shied away from him. "I think that's what most of us do, Froggy, pretend. For a few days at least, while I'm away from the fighting, I try not to think too much about the bloody war. You should try it. It's easy here. And of course, you can go shopping on condition that you let me show you round the farm first."

"I won't have time, surely. Sara said she would be back in less than an hour."

"The garden and stables, at least then."

"Stables?" Frances questioned.

"Of course, stables."

"All of those horses in the field then—"

"Are ours? That's the main money spinner. Pa's a horse breeder like his father before him. We have some of the finest Hanoverian blood stock in the country. Do you like horses?"

She thought for a while. "I think so…. We used to have a pony and trap when I was a child back in England. I can remember being fond of the pony. Amber, that was her name."

Mueller stood up and gave her a thoughtful smile. "Amber, like your eyes, huh?"

She found his gaze and held it. "Yes, I suppose so," she said.

"So, can we pretend then, Froggy, for the sake of our sanity?" She nodded.

"It's easy to pretend in a place like this."

"Come on then, what are we waiting for? One whistle-stop tour of the Mueller estate coming up, with special attention to the stables. Come on, Froggy, get a move on."

He led the way downstairs, through the hall and into a large sitting room, which opened out onto the gardens that Frances had seen from her window the evening before. He whistled to the dogs, and standing out on the veranda, he motioned with his arm for her to join him.

"See," he said, pointing, "these fields right over to the woods are ours. Sara's family owns the farm that joins our land, you see."

"Do they breed horses too?" Frances asked.

"No, they keep one or two for interest, but they're mainly crop farmers. They have a few cattle and hens like us. It takes a war to make you realise how lucky you are. No shortage here, though we must make a percentage payment to the Reich. Well, what do you think?"

The air was clean, and in the early morning summer sunshine, everything had a healthy new greenness about it. "It's not what I expected, Kristian," she said.

"In a good way, I hope."

She looked up at him and gave the glimmer of a smile. "Yes, in a good way."

"Come on then," he said, "I'll show you the garden. My Granddam planted most of it. At the end of the lawn down there is a formal affair, but my favourite bit is up that path to the right."

He grabbed her by the wrist and pulled her towards some evergreens on the right side of the lawn, and it didn't occur to her to remove her hand from his, as she was so caught up in his boyish enthusiasm. An arch had been cut into two of the trees and a black wrought-iron gate had been erected, which squeaked as they pushed through into a much smaller paved area surrounded with beds of flowers, all threatening to break into bloom.

Frances gasped with delight as it took her back to the cottage garden of her childhood in the mid county of England. Those heady happy days when she was a child and war didn't enter into a game of pretend. Rosebuds were almost in bloom, delphinium, hollyhocks, and lupins stood proudly at the back of the beds, while central there were a variety of daisies, geraniums, and graceful nodding columbines. To the front were pinks and pansies and the remains of the clumps of aubretia. She walked among the beds for a while, as Mueller stood and watched her, not giving her long before he ushered her on again.

"Froggy, this way. We'll go to the stables. There's a drive round the side of the house which leads down to them too."

They threaded their way along the narrow winding paths, until they reached the far end of the garden where there were benches and a small summer house, which stood in front of a tall brick wall, shielding off the working farm from the house.

Mueller opened the old wooden gate onto a well-laid gravel drive. On either side of the drive were paddocks where horses grazed lazily, hardly bothering to look up at them as they both crunched their way along the path to the stable block.

The stables comprised of fourteen loose boxes laid out in two rows of seven, around a paved yard. At the near end of the yard stood another building, which Mueller explained housed six stalls, a tack room and a large storage space for hay and straw.

"Come on," he enthused, striding off across the yard Frances followed him over to the first box. The head of an enormous chestnut stallion watched them approach, nostrils splayed wide, showing the whites of his eyes. "Bismarck." Mueller turned to her with a wide smile. Along with his obvious excitement, he seemed to Frances to be more boyish than ever. He slapped the animal on the side of the neck affectionately. "Come on, Froggy, come and meet him."

Frances stood her ground; the animal was immense and not at all like the gentle pony of her childhood. "Is he safe?" she asked.

"He's good mannered enough, usually," Mueller replied, continuing to rub at the animal's arched neck, pulling at his ears and forelock, and gaining a snort of approval. As Frances approached, the animal turned towards her and widened his eyes and nostrils still further, flattening his ears back against his enormous head.

"He doesn't like me," she said nervously.

"He hasn't met you yet. Come on, don't let him know you're scared. He'll pick up on that, you see. Here, stroke his nose." Mueller took Frances's hand in his and stretched it towards the horse. Just as she was about to touch him, the animal kicked the stable door with all his might and threw back his head. Frances jumped back in alarm and Mueller burst out laughing.

"You pig! You knew he would do that," she accused.

"No, I swear," said Mueller through his laughter. "He's usually gentle, I promise you."

"Who are you trying to kid?" Frances swung round to see Sara Kohl walking across the yard. She had changed out of her riding breeches and was wearing a pale blue dress. "There is no way I would ever trust that horse. He's Kristian's, for a start," she said, joining in with Mueller's laughter. "Well, are you ready, Frau Mueller?" she asked.

Frances was tempted to tell Mueller just what she thought of his bloody horse, but the thought of a shopping trip was uppermost in her mind. She was going shopping for clothes, something for herself. Maybe when she changed into something new and clean, she would feel the filthy vestiges of Dachau and Auschwitz fall away from her. Then, as she thought about it more, those thoughts changed and were not of shopping but of going into a strange town. An enemy town. She panicked. What if they arrested her? What if they sent her back to Dachau, or worse?

"Look, Sara," she said, "I don't think I'll go after all, if you don't mind."

"Not go? I thought you were looking forward to it," said Mueller, with a shake of his head. Frances turned her back on Sara and appealed to him.

"I don't feel well. It wasn't a good idea," she muttered.

"Froggy, you've put Sara to all of this...." He stopped for a second or two and fixed her with his eyes. Moving her out of earshot of Sara, he said, "You're afraid, aren't you?"

She nodded. "I don't think I can do it. How can I cycle through— For me, this is an enemy country."

Aware that something was wrong, Sara had moved further away, giving them a chance to talk in private.

"Look, give me a few minutes and I'll run you into town in the car if there's petrol. Sara's right, you need clothes and I need a new uniform before I go back. If I can get one made in time, that is. What do you say?"

What she wanted to say was, how will I manage when you are not here? When you have gone back to continue your battle against everything I love? I will be left with people I don't know and am not sure I can trust. She knew he would just tell her she would be safe and not to worry and so what she said was, "Couldn't you just get me something like you did before? The things you got me were fine. Please Kristian." Mueller placed his hands on her shoulders.

"You'll be with Sara, Froggy. Our town is small and safe. Everybody knows everyone else. Our family and Sara's are held in good stead. You're my wife, that's all anyone needs to know." Mueller nodded encouragement and turned to Sara, "Hang on, Sar, I'll run you in."

"What about your hand?" shouted Sara. "Are you able to drive?"

"It's well-padded enough. Take Frances back to the house. Let me have a quick word with Alf."

Leaving the two women, he walked off in the direction of the farm with the dogs at his heel. Sara took Frances by the arm and led her back along the gravel drive to the house. She didn't ask any questions and Frances was thankful for it. As they neared one paddock, Sara stopped and pointed.

"See that blue roan over there?"

"What's a blue roan?" Frances asked.

"The dark grey mare."

"Yes."

"Now, she's well worth your meeting."

"Oh no Sara, I've done all the meeting of horses I'm going to do for one day."

"This one's different."

"Hmm, and so was the last one."

Sara laughed and walked over to the paddock fence, clicking her tongue until the horse looked up from its grazing. "Come on, Majesty," she cooed. "Come on, come and meet Frances, good girl."

The mare took a couple of steps, faltered slightly, and then continued across the paddock towards the fence, stretching her neck across to be petted. "Come on, Frances, come and see," Sara encouraged. Frances shook her head, staying put.

"She's a bit fat, isn't she?" she shouted.

"Pregnant. Only a couple of more weeks to go. I'm surprised Kristian didn't bring you to meet her first. She and he have a bit of a thing going. They're crazy about one another."

Frances took a couple of steps towards the fence, expecting the horse to throw back her head as Bismarck had done, but it fixed her with liquid brown eyes, and gaining confidence, she crossed to Sara's side.

"See, Frances, this is a soppy mare if ever there was one. Come on, give her a pat. She'll love you for it."

With hand outstretched, Frances tentatively rubbed the side of the blue grey face, and the horse rewarded her with a gentle wicker. "I think she likes me," she said.

Sara nodded and tickled the mare's muzzle, making her curl back her top lip in a horsey grin. Both women laughed. "You do it," Sara coaxed.

Frances cautiously put her hand out towards Majesty and stroked her nose, wondering at its velvety softness, and enjoying how the animal nuzzled against her hand, asking for more.

"So, I see you and Majesty have met."

At the sound of Mueller's voice, the mare pulled away from Frances and trotted the few yards along the fence to meet him, surprising Frances with its doglike devotion.

"Well, are you two ready?" Mueller enquired, rubbing at the horse's neck.

"I could do with something to eat," Frances admitted.

"Take her round to see Anna, will you Sar? I'll bring the car round to the front of the house."

As he watched the two women walk away, Mueller turned back to the mare. "Well, old girl, what on earth do you make of my wife?" he asked.

Chapter 9

Frances was buzzing with the thought of a shopping trip and spending time with another young woman. Mueller's mood had lightened, because for the first time since she'd left Dachau, Frances appeared to be behaving like a normal human being. And Sara was just Sara, a steadfastly loyal friend. She was genuinely pleased for Kristian and determined to make a friend of Frances, too.

There was a short spat over who should drive between Kristian, who pointed out that he knew the roads around the town, so his driving made more sense, and Frances, who wanted to further hone her skills. The three of them were high from the company of one another, and it was Sara who started things off by asking Frances what it had been like for eight weeks on a U-boat, with only the company of almost fifty men.

Frances gave the question some thought. "I suppose the best thing about it had to be the whales."

"You saw whales?" Sara asked, eyes wide.

"Yes, it was wonderful," she replied, "and the worst bit had to be the toilet. One toilet between almost fifty, Sara. Can you imagine?"

"Erghh, do I have to?" asked Sara, as Mueller joined in from the driver's seat by mimicking a female voice.

"I suppose you have a bathroom on this ship, don't you?"

"I hadn't a clue where I was. I woke up tied down to a bed as naked as the day I was born," Frances explained.

"Naked?" shrieked Sara.

"I had a cover over me."

"Naked, Kristian?" Sara shrieked a second time.

"She'd have caught pneumonia if we had left her in wet clothes. That's what Hengst said, anyway. We took every care to do things decently. At least Paul said he did." He turned to Frances and gave her a cheeky smile.

"Paul did it. Paul removed my clothing. I thought Hengst or even you. Paul, did it?" questioned Frances.

"I could hardly give myself all the best jobs now, could I?" teased Mueller. "We thought Froggy must have been from a fishing vessel, Sar, but her silk underwear was a bit of a giveaway."

"You discussed my underwear?"

"Oh, I should think the entire crew discussed your underwear, Froggy. I should think they jerked off thinking about it."

"Kristian!" Frances sat with her head in her hands, filled with embarrassment as Sara and Kristian collapsed into fits of laughter.

"I reckon Paul did. There was a bit of grunting going on from his bunk on a couple of occasions."

"Kris, I think we had better stop. I think we are really upsetting Frances," Sara said with concern, noting that Frances had turned a bright red and was silently dying from embarrassment. Mueller looked at her sitting flushed beside him and carried on with the taunt.

"Don't worry about her, Sar, she's as tough as old boots. Ask her what the first thing she ever said to me was."

Sara leant forward from the back seat, tapping Frances on the shoulder until she turned round and then she raised her eyebrows in question. "Well?" she asked.

"I haven't got a clue what the first thing I said to you was, Kristian," Frances said, still flushed.

"Fuck off, Kapitan, that's what she said. I was shocked." Mueller laughed gleefully, which caused Sara to giggle, and Frances to eventually concede and join in with the laughter, too.

Desperate for revenge, Frances said, "Ask him about the time he hit me and all the other nasty things he did?"

Sara was clearly alarmed. "You hit a woman, Kristian?"

"It was that or put a bullet between her eyes. She only sung the bloody Marseillaise while we were under attack." Sara laughed again, and high on the sound of her laughter, the other two, despite themselves, joined in, too.

"Would you really have shot me, Kristian, if I had done that again?" asked Frances. "You threatened me with it."

Mueller went quiet and thought for a while and then gave a sniff. "Well, thankfully, you didn't put me to the test, did you?"

"But if I had," she pressed. He nodded, giving the question some thought.

"If you had, and I had, then I would have been full of regret, Froggy."

"Ahh, well, that's nice to know," said Frances, fixing him with her eyes.

"And what about you? Would you have shot me the day we left Dachau, if Rittershausen hadn't taken that pistol you were pointing at my head off you?" Mueller retorted.

Frances didn't respond to his question; she was lost in thought and muttered, "Otto was there. You and Otto had a fight. It's all become a bit hazy." She sighed and was quiet for a moment, recovering herself, biting on her lip, wondering what other unpleasant memories she had locked away in her head. She would have to deal with them later when they decided to make themselves known. "I suppose if I was holding the pistol like you say I was, then I meant to use it. So, if Rittershausen hadn't taken it, I suppose I would have." She threw a glance his way along with a smile. "I probably would have regretted it later though."

"Oh, that's alright then," said Mueller.

Sara looked from one to the other. "Jesus, you two have got a very odd relationship." There was an awkward silence for a few moments until Mueller chuckled and Frances laughed with him. Then Sara joined in, thinking they had set her up.

As they drew into the town, Mueller said, "Right, I've got to see old Fritz to see if I can get a new uniform made. Where do I leave you?"

"Central," Sara ordered.

❉ ❉ ❉

Mueller dropped off the women and arrangements were made to all meet up for a coffee two hours later.

Sara took Frances to two women's wear shops. A couple of hours soon passed, and Mueller's money was quickly spent. The choice of goods had been surprising, and Frances found it amusing that she was buying mostly French goods at grossly inflated prices.

"So, all you need now is something to wear tomorrow evening." Sara said.

"Why? What's happening?" asked Frances.

"Oops, I forgot to mention it earlier. Dinner at ours, tomorrow night."

"Won't one of the dresses I've just bought do?"

"Formal," said Sara. "We always make a point, particularly since this war broke out. We like to pretend everything is normal for a few

~ 79 ~

hours. Come on, I know where there's a place that specialises in clothing for short arses."

"Petite," shrieked Frances, "I'm petite, Sar."

They crossed the town square still laughing and found the shop up a side street.

"Well, this is one I've never been in," Sara said with a chuckle as she pushed the door open. The assistant met them. "We need an evening dress, well she does," Sara explained.

There was the choice of only two dresses in Frances's size, and she thought she would settle for the cheaper one, which fitted her reasonably well but wasn't particularly flattering.

"Now try the other," Sara ordered.

Frances shook her head. "I can't. Look at the price of it."

"Try it on. Look at the colour of it. It lights you up." Sara smiled and held the dress up in front of Frances, who puffed out her cheeks.

"It is lovely, isn't it?" she said, touching the fabric of the dress, which was dark steel grey satin, overlaid with fine sheer silk of the same colour. The satin stopped above the bustline and dipped into a heart shape which covered the breasts, leaving the arms and shoulders and decolletage covered by the silk alone. The bodice was decorated with beading from the breast area down to the waist where the skirt draped in soft folds of satin overlaid with silk. Frances put it on and stepped out of the dressing room to show Sara and the assistant.

"Perfect," nodded Sara. "Come on, Froggy, that's the one. Turn round."

"I beg your pardon," said Frances in mock alarm, turning to give Sara a view of the dress, which was backless, "It's bad enough when Kristian calls me that, so don't you dare start."

"Come on, have a look at yourself in that mirror," Sara ordered. "Just look at those eyes. My God, you could kill with them." Frances put her head on one side and then the other, enjoying the reflection of herself in the dress. She turned to the side so that she could see how the fabric of the dress dipped down in folds from shoulders to waist, leaving her back naked. She swung around with a giggle, making the folds of material splay out.

"Kristian says I have wolf's eyes, Sar," she said. "I'm not sure that it's a compliment." She swung around in the dress again and then stopped and sighed. "Sara, I can't have this. It will use up all the money Kristian has given me, just about."

"If he gave you money, then you are meant to spend it, Sillyhead. Come on, take it off, and let's get it packaged up. We are late for that coffee already."

Admitting defeat rather too soon, Frances returned to the dressing room to take off the dress, and whilst she was doing so, Sara paid for two jet combs and asked that they be put in the bag along with the dress.

"Sar," Frances called out from the changing room. "Can you pass me one of the dresses I bought earlier?" Sara passed her one of the many parcels. "I can't wait to get out of Freya's dress and be myself," Frances said from the changing room. And at that moment she realised that she did, for the first time in almost two years, feel like herself. In an enemy country, in an enemy town, alongside two people she should despise.

* * *

The two women hurried across town, completely laden down with purchases. Sara strode out towards the coffee shop and Frances struggled to keep up.

"Sara, stop a minute, will you?" she shouted, "I want to ask you something."

"What?" asked Sara, waiting for Frances to catch up.

"The scarring on Kristian's chin, how did it happen? He won't talk about it."

Sara hesitated, looked at Frances and took a deep breath. "Ah, no, it's not spoken of."

"And?" Frances encouraged, and Sara thought she should know. She was Kristian's wife.

"It happened the day his sister died; you know he had a sister?" Frances nodded. "Well, on the day she died, Kristian went out and saddled up his father's horse. Great mad thing it was. He just wanted to get away from everything and everybody. We both had had the measles, and he thought he was to blame for passing it on to Karin. God, he was only eight." She shook her head in recollection. "That horse was gigantic. They found Kris sometime later. The horse had thrown him onto some barbed wire. He was lucky it hadn't taken his eye out. Peter was furious, what with the death and all, and the worry of Freya, of course. Kris told me he got one hell of a beating once the doctor had stitched him up."

"What worry of Freya do you mean?"

"She went to pieces. Understandable I suppose after losing a child."

Frances thought back to the loss of her own child and had some sympathy for how Freya must have felt. "So, what happened?" she asked.

"She locked herself away and became a recluse for months. Kristian was devastated. He and Freya had always been so close; they adored one another. Or so he thought."

"I knew there was something going on between them." said Frances, "Kristian scarcely looks at his mother."

"It was sad. He sat outside her room like a puppy for days. He mourned not only for Karin but for the loss of Freya too. It was Anna who eventually took him under her wing. I don't think he has ever forgiven Freya. He said she left him when he needed her most and she did it because he had given Karin the measles that killed her."

* * *

The drive back was like the drive into town, full of laughter and banter.

"So, how are the rest of the Kohl family?" Kristian asked.

"Good," she replied.

"And mine, Sar. How have mine been? Is Pa managing the farm?"

"Seems to be and the horses are still selling well even though there is a war on. I think Aunty Freya felt disappointed when she found out that the big Sophie Heyne wedding was off." She patted Frances on the shoulder from the backseat. "Oh, sorry, Frances. Do you know about Sophie?" Frances turned around.

"Oh yes, I know all about Sophie, Sara. In fact, I've met her."

Mueller butted in, "She's jealous of her, Sar."

"Huh!" Frances shot back.

"Come on, tell me, what's she like then?" Sara begged.

Mueller nodded towards Frances. "She'll tell you."

"Well," said Frances thoughtfully, "tall, curvaceous, blond, stylish, domineering and a complete cow. She was all over Kristian. It was sickening, and he loved every minute."

Mueller briefly took his eyes off the road and looked over his shoulder at Sara. "Jealous, Sar, I told you."

"Not without cause, I think," said Frances. "Kristian went on a walkabout one night and I thought he was with her, so I phoned her room."

Sara let out a scream of laughter. "What on earth did you say?"

"I said I thought she had something of mine, and I wanted it back." Sara couldn't contain her laughter and there were shrieks from the back of the car.

"Did you really say that?" asked Mueller.

"Yes, yes, I did."

He glanced at her. "You really did care, then?" Frances shrugged and turned away from him, then muttered to herself, and giggled.

"What was that?" asked Mueller.

"If I show you mine, will you show me yours?" she repeated for them both to hear. "It was you, Sar, wasn't it?"

Sara and Mueller collapsed into peals of laughter, so much so that Frances feared the car would be driven off the road. "Come on, Sara," she spluttered, "I want your story. It's your turn now. How old were you both?"

* * *

As they drew up on the drive of Schonen Felder, Peter and Freya, who had watched their approach from the house, met them at the door.

"Well?" asked Peter as Frances stumbled inside under her purchases. "Did you manage to spend all of my son's money?" He took some of the parcels from her and gave her a huge smile. She smiled back at him, eyes bright.

"I wouldn't have believed that in two small shops, the entire Paris Haute couture collection was hidden away."

Peter grimaced. "You have spent all of my son's money."

"Not quite," said Mueller, following her in. "I was left with enough to buy this." He took her packages from her, placed them on the floor and handed her a violin case. She stood rooted to the spot, staring down at the case laying in her hands.

"Kristian, I can't take this," she said, trying to push it back into his hands.

"Of course, you can. Late wedding present." Frances shook her head. "I know it's not what you're used to…" apologised Mueller, as she opened the case.

She took out the violin, caressing the body, and weighing the bow. "It's a Roth," she stated to herself. Then, turning to Mueller, she continued, "They're fine instruments. They're getting an excellent reputation." She shook her head thoughtfully. "There's such snobbery about instruments, you know."

Placing the violin beneath her chin she lay her cheek against it, enjoying the feel of the varnished wood, cool and smooth against her skin, then shaking her head once again, she placed it lovingly back in its case and put it on a side table in the hall.

"Won't you play for us, Frances?" asked Peter. Frances shook her head as the memory of the night she had played for Adolf Hitler came flooding back, along with the other horrors of that night. Being told that her beloved Aunt Edie was dead and being raped by Otto Von Liechtenstein.

"The last time I played was for your Fuhrer. I can't play anymore. I just can't," she said, as she fled upstairs to her room, leaving them all staring after her.

"It was a very generous thought, Kristian," said Freya. "Its's not your fault that the girl can't appreciate an expensive gift." Mueller glared at his mother as Sara took his arm.

"She'll come round, Kris; you'll see."

Mueller gave her a half-hearted smile. "I think that might have been a mistake."

"Oh, she'll be fine. I like your Frances," said Sara. "By the way, I almost forgot to say, you're all invited to dinner tomorrow night. Mutti and Pop said it's high time they saw Kris, but I think they just want to check Frances out. We have some elderly relatives of mother's staying from Munich. A chance to get dressed up, eh, Freya?"

Chapter 10

Could you live through the atrocities, see, hear, smell, touch, be part of the things that she had been part of and remain unaltered? And yet the face that had looked back at her from the mirror in the dress shop, the day before, had been her face, the same face. Somewhere surely there must be a mark on it, a mark of the suffering from all that she'd endured over the past months, and yet she'd seen none.

Her hair was growing back as wayward as ever. It touched her jaw now. The amber eyes had still flashed through the frame of dark lashes and her brows were still arched. She touched the skin of her face, smooth and elastic. Maybe her cheeks were a little more sunken than before, perhaps not. She was scarcely a week out of Dachau and already the greyness had vanished from her skin and was taking on a healthy glow.

She let the towel drop to the floor and lay back on the bed, running her hands across her breasts and finding them still small and firm. Looking down, she could see that they tilted upwards slightly. She stroked downwards towards her waist and hips, assessing the contours of her body, pleased by the feel of her body, as her hand slid over her long waist and curved outwards across her buttocks to her slender legs.

No! There was nothing to show except for the number tattooed on her wrist. She'd come through it all physically unscathed. She had survived. She was a survivor, and now she was learning to live again. Learning to anaesthetise her mind.

She walked across the bedroom floor to the wardrobe and took out the dress she'd purchased the day before, ready for that evening, and held it against her. She was again pleased with the effect. Yesterday, she actually enjoyed herself. Now in the solitude of the room, she wondered how many had died in the gas chambers at Auschwitz during those few hours that she had done that. How many would die of starvation or typhus at Dachau, whilst she sat down to dinner in a few hours' time with a family of Germans?

Yes, she was learning to anaesthetise her mind, to rid herself of dark thoughts. Only often it didn't work, and she found herself wracked with guilt again and again, like now.

The nights were the worst. Lying in bed alone, she often missed the sound of others breathing and the forgotten comfort of a good bed sometimes kept her awake.

Stupid! Kristian had told her when she had mentioned it to him. You're stupid to feel guilty for being one of the lucky ones. Against all odds, she had survived, but for what? For sleeping with the enemy. And now she was being given time to dwell upon her treachery, or maybe as the orchestra girls and the girls in the bordello had believed, she had been given this time to become a small instrument of revenge. She had been so sure that was the case when she had left Dachau, but in a few short days with Mueller, she was starting to have doubts. Otto? Maybe. But Kristian? He and his family had been so kind. She couldn't hurt anyone at Schonen Felder, not even Freya. She didn't want to. They were no more part of the madness that had grabbed hold of the world than Edie, Steven or Jaques had been. They were just people swept up in the tide of war, doing their best to survive it.

She sighed and laid the dress down on the bed, thinking back again to the day before, when Kristian had reminded her, she had pointed a gun at him. She had almost buried the memory of that, and it bothered her, scared her even. Perhaps she was mad after all.

Putting on her underclothes, she thought about these black moods, and how much she hated them. They'd creep up on her from nowhere, filling her head with the things she so desperately wanted to forget. Making her heart boom in her chest wall as she sweated and gasped for breath. She had never been a morose person. She was a lover of good times and needed the stimulation of others round about her, like Sara and, God damn him, Mueller. Since arriving at his home, she was seeing other facets of his character. She already knew the commander, the leader, counsellor, philosopher, and the lover. Lately she had seen the dutiful son and had glimpses of the boy, and they all fascinated her.

He'd been more than fair to her. Since the encounter in the hotel bedroom, he had made no sexual advances, and she'd been fair on him, not mentioning her internment since setting foot in his home, though she had to admit she had been obnoxious during that first meal.

She wondered how much Kristian had told his parents about her, and what they really thought. Freya Mueller didn't like her; of that, she was certain. A mother's jealousy? Perhaps. A woman who played a violin and belonged to an enemy nation wouldn't be many mothers' idea of the perfect daughter-in-law. Peter though, had been gentle with her and kindly, doing his best to put her at her ease and once she had allowed the initial barrier to fall, she had found him so very easy to like.

"Frances, get a move on. We're due at the Kohl's in fifteen minutes."

Kristian's voice from the landing drew her attention to the clock, seven fifteen, and she had begun her toilet before six. She hurriedly completed her dressing, and then began on her face, a little shadow, lots of mascara and a touch of lip colour, all bought the day before. Tonight, she would forget her promise to the girls. It was proving harder to keep it each day she spent with Mueller. Tonight, she would allow the anaesthetic to work, and she would enjoy herself, as she had when she had shopped. She deserved that surely, didn't she?

She descended the stairs to the accompaniment of laughter from below. Peter and Kristian were sharing a joke whilst Freya Mueller was looking in a mirror in the hall, putting the finishing touches to her hair, which was swept up in a complicated pleat.

"You look stunning, Freya," she heard Peter say to his wife as she walked down the stairs to join them. Kristian and he were wearing dinner suits, and Freya Mueller was wearing a black evening gown. Freya did, Frances had to admit, look stunning. She had walked away from the mirror to her son and was trying to adjust his bow tie, seemingly against his will.

"I'm so sorry. I don't know where the time has gone," Frances said, giving them all an apologetic smile. Kristian stepped away from his mother and as he turned to Frances, his jaw dropped slightly open in surprise.

"Well, it's obvious to me where the time went," remarked Peter. "You look wonderful, my dear. What do you say, son? I'd say we are a couple of lucky chaps."

"She'll do," nodded Kristian, as a slow smile crept across his face and into his eyes, which gave Frances a warm glow inside. "Can you fix this damn tie for me, Froggy?" he asked.

She walked over to him, reaching up to his neck, taking the ends of the bow tie in her fingers, feeling the warmth from the closeness of his body.

"Lift your head up," she ordered, knocking him under the chin. "How on earth do you expect me to sort it while you're looking down?"

"I can't take my eyes off you. You do, as Pa said, look wonderful," he muttered.

She smiled back at him, holding his gaze for a moment. "You don't look bad yourself, and you'll look even better when this tie is sorted. Now hold your head up and keep still."

Once Frances had sorted out the tie, Peter Mueller offered his wife his arm and led the way through the front door to the car, which was parked just outside.

"I'll drive," he said. "You youngsters sit in the back and relax, enjoy yourselves. It's about time you did."

Kristian went to the back door of the car and opened it for Frances, giving a slight bow as she climbed in. Making to the other side of the car, he clambered in beside her.

The drive to the Kohl family's house was short and uneventful, apart from the tremendous awareness of the closeness of Kristian that Frances felt. They'd not seen each other all day, as he and Peter had been busy in Bonn on some sort of business. As she sat beside him now, she had an overwhelming urge to touch him, but shied away from making a move. As they neared the Kohl's residence, he reached across and took her hand in his. She rubbed her thumb across his knuckles, and he gave her hand an answering squeeze.

* * *

Eva and Gunter Kohl, it turned out, were very likeable people. They were both outgoing and amusing, and from the moment Frances arrived at their home, they did their best to put her at ease.

"Come in, come in, my friends," Gunter, a plump jolly looking man, said with a smile, opening the door wide and taking Freya into an embrace. "Just look at you, woman, you never age, you're still a beauty." He turned to Frances. "So, you're the girl who has won the heart of young Kristian," he said, taking her hand and kissing it, "and I can see why. What do you say, Eva? This girl is gorgeous, isn't she?"

Frances felt the blood rush to her face and before she could recover herself, Eva Kohl took her into a warm embrace, and hugged her.

"You're as lovely as Sara said," she said, giving Frances a warm smile, and then ushered them all into the hall where they were met by the Kohl's visitors.

They were the second cousins of Gunter's mother and were on their way up north to visit other relatives. Being elderly, they had stopped off for a couple of days with the Kohls to break up their journey. The visitors greeted the Muellers with a Heil Hitler before a handshake, and Frances glimpsed Peter Mueller giving his son a quick look. It soon became obvious that Frank and Ina Braun were active members of the Nazi Party and admired and venerated their Fuhrer. Both tried to steer the conversation around to the war efforts whenever they could, and Frances, as an outsider, was aware of the embarrassment felt by the Kohls. She gravitated away from the rest of the group with Sara but caught sight of Kristian walking away from Frank Braun mid-conversation. She wondered what the man had said to him to cause such a reaction.

Ina Braun grabbed him firmly by the arm as he walked past her. "I was hoping to see you in uniform tonight, Korvetten Kapitan." Frances overheard her remark. "All of those decorations I've heard about, from Sara and Eva. Oh, I do like to see a man in uniform."

She saw Kristian give the woman a forced smile. "Then I'm sorry to disappoint you. I do my best to forget about the war for a while when I'm on leave," he said.

There was an intake of breath from Ina as her husband walked over and joined her, catching the end of Kristian's comment.

"Damn it, man, a good German shouldn't forget for a minute that there's a war on," he snapped.

"Then sorry to disappoint you again," returned Kristian. "I'm obviously not a good German." And with that, he walked away and joined Sara and herself on the other side of the room.

Sara raised her eyebrows as he approached, and he apologised to her.

"Come on, Kris," she said, giving him a broad grin and keeping her voice down, "Well said, I think. We've had it all afternoon."

Sara launched into a full-scale description of what the last few hours had been like in the Kohl household, stopping mid-sentence as she noticed neither Frances nor Kristian was giving her the attention, she thought she deserved. She saw that their eyes were locked on one another.

"You know you can touch each other," she said. "Maybe just hold hands or something." She looked from one to the other and shook her head as Kristian took Frances's hand with a smile. "Anyway, what do you think of the dress, Kris? It's beautiful, isn't it?"

"It is, Sar," he said, looking at Frances. "It's exquisite." Frances felt herself blush and quickly turned to Sara.

"I haven't thanked you for the combs. They are lovely," she said, touching her hair, which she had swept away from her face with the combs.

"I'm glad you found them. I thought they'd be the finishing touch, and they are. You look marvelous."

* * *

Dinner was served, and Frances found herself seated at an oval table in a large dining room, much like the one in the Mueller's home. To her left was Peter Mueller, and to her right, Frank Braun. Kristian sat opposite her, with Sara on his right and Ina Braun on his left. The rest of the diners comprised Eva Kohl next to Peter, and then Freya and Gunter. She found she couldn't take part in much of the conversation happening during the first course, as most of it was about relatives and mutual friends and acquaintances of the families. The wine flowed and one or two amusing stories were told, and then other conversations began as the main course was cleared away by the Kohl's housekeeper.

She was unsure who started it, but she heard Dachau mentioned. Her spine went rigid, and she sat up with a start. In an instant, her mind took her back there, and the rest of the conversation seemed to come from somewhere else. Somewhere distant. She was aware of Freya's voice, trying to find out how long it was that the Brauns had lived in the town of Dachau.

"Virtually all our married life," she heard the voice of Ina Braun. "It's an interesting town, isn't it, Frank? The fortifications and the castle, of course, with Frank being in the paper industry it's perfect."

"Are you aware what's going on there?" Frances heard a voice say and noticed all eyes were instantly on her. She had spoken her thoughts without being aware of it. Kristian had been having a conversation with Sara and had missed the mention of Dachau, but he could see that something was troubling his wife.

Frank Braun had turned to her; his beady eyes were studying her more closely. "Do you know our town?" he asked.

Frances had to concentrate hard on what the man was saying. Her brain was playing tricks, and her head was swimming with the memories of the horrors she had witnessed. A pulse was tapping frantically in her forehead, and she was struggling to fill her lungs. She moved her lips to speak, but the voice she heard seemed unnatural, and far away, and yet she knew it as her own.

"Yes, I think you might say that I do. There are things going on there. Are you aware?"

Frank Braun gave her an understanding smile. "You mean Prittlbach, my dear. It's not actually in the town. Prittlbach, er, well it's a little way outside."

Her voice rose in volume. "So, are you telling me you are unaware of what is going on there, at Prittlbach?" There was silence from the other diners. Kristian watched as Frances leant towards Frank Braun and fixed her eyes on him. Braun sat back in his chair; clearly, he found the fire in them disconcerting.

"Frances," said Kristian and his voice held a warning. Too late, Frank Braun was answering her.

"Well yes," he began, "certainly we know. There are no secrets. It's a place where enemies of our Reich are imprisoned, that's all."

Frances's eyes bore into Braun. "Women, priests, children even? They are marched through Dachau; the trains stop there. That's correct, isn't it?"

Dachau. Kristian straightened up. Someone had mentioned Dachau. Shit! He thought, there was only one way this conversation was going to go. He tried to gain Frances's attention.

"Frances, this is not the place," he said. Her eyes were unwavering and stayed on Braun.

"We see one or two," said Frank Braun defensively, in answer to her question. "Now and again, perhaps."

"One or two hundred perhaps, hey?" shot Frances.

"But they're mostly gypsies or homosexuals, convicts and such," said his wife.

Kristian watched in horror as Frances pulled off her bracelet to uncover the tattooed number on her wrist and thrust it under Braun's face. He drew back from her and looked at it in horror.

"Oh look, French women even. My only crime was to be married to a Jew." Frances leant forward in her chair towards Frank Braun, holding his gaze. "Does it sicken you to be sitting at a table with the wife of a Jew?"

Ina Braun turned towards Kristian. "But I thought..." she began weakly.

"Yes, you're right," he said, rising to his feet. "Frances, stop now, before you say something that we will all regret." His voice was icy.

"I'll stop when I've finished. They need to know!" she said through gritted teeth. "They mark you and treat you like animals. There is a place in Poland called Oswiecim, or Auschwitz, as you people call it. They kill people there by the thousands. Are you aware of that?"

"It's not our affair," said Ina Braun, as Kristian cut in.

"I must apologise for my wife; she is recovering from an illness."

Frances stood, throwing back her chair, now fixing him with her eyes, which flared at him across the table. He was making excuses for her; they were at fault, and he was excusing her.

"Don't you dare apologise for me," she spat, "There's no recovery from what I've seen, what I've experienced, and the sickness is yours. It belongs to you all. It's not mine."

Kristian held Frances's eyes with his own. She was receiving the look that told her not to take things any further, but she had lost control and was reveling in their discomfort. He pushed his chair back and made his way round the table to his father's side and took her by the arm.

"Enough now, Frances, we're going home. I'm sorry, I apologise again to you all for Frances's behaviour."

Frances yanked her arm free from his grasp. "No! Don't you touch me ever. I'm not going anywhere, because I haven't finished. I haven't told you about the child."

"I've heard it all before, Frances, you've told me of the children. That's enough. We are leaving."

Her voice rose. "You're not listening to me. I said child, not children. Your child, Kristian."

There was a gasp from the others in the room and Mueller took a step back, looking at her with disbelief.

"What's the matter, Kristian?" she taunted. "Didn't you know that sort of thing can happen?"

Kristian's brain was racing. He could feel the veins in his temple thudding as she continued. "Don't you want to know what happened to your son?" She twisted in his grasp as he half carried, half dragged her towards the French window, which opened out onto the Kohl's Garden. "Don't you think his grandparents should know what happened to him?" she screeched and caught sight of the shocked look on the faces of those seated round the table, particularly Freya and Peter Mueller. Kristian carried her through the doors and out onto a paved area, down several steps, and into an orchard. And there he let go of her and she fell to the ground.

"Stop now, Frances! I am fed up with your damn stories." He walked further into the orchard for privacy, and Frances pulled herself to her feet and followed him. Standing under a large apple tree, she spoke, and he thought how pitiful she sounded.

"The doctor was going to let me carry to full term. He was going to let me. He said he would deliver my baby himself. I could have held him. They said he would have taken him away, and I know he would, but I could have held him, at least for a while. I could have let him know I loved him, at least for a minute or two, couldn't I?"

He turned away from her as she continued. "Only Miriam, the girls, my friends. They didn't think it was right. They kicked me. They didn't think it was right that I should give birth to some Kraut's bastard."

Kristian swung round. "Is that how you think of me then, as just some Kraut? Is it?" He stood for a moment, shaking his head, and then made a grab for Frances and shook her. "Is it?" he repeated and pushed her away. He saw a look of utter confusion sweep across her face as she put out her hand towards him, which he chose to ignore.

"My God, I really should have left you at Dachau," he spat, moving further into the orchard as Frances slumped to the ground and sat for a while with her head in her hands.

After a while, she stood. Unsteady on her feet, she followed him and tried to take him by the arm, but he shook her off again.

"You're angry with me, Kristian. I'm sorry. I've said things, haven't I? It just happened. The things I said just came out. I couldn't stop them."

As he turned, she put her hand to her head. She stood wide-eyed and silent, looking thoroughly lost.

"You know, you are unbelievable, Frances," he said, pulling his hands through his hair. He was aware of his father watching from the steps near the house. "Take her home, Pa," he said, "I'll walk. I need the air."

* * *

The journey home, though short, seemed to Frances to take an age. The atmosphere in the car was decidedly icy. She was filled with remorse for the way she thought she must have acted in front of Sara, who had shown her friendship, and Sara's parents, who had welcomed her into their home. She must have behaved despicably towards Kristian too, who the day before had been so generous, and even worse, towards his parents. She remembered someone mentioning Dachau during the meal, and that she had questioned them, and maybe told them things. Perhaps she had lost control? She must have done because she'd mentioned the baby, their son. That was the last thing that she remembered, apart from Kristian's anger in the orchard.

On arrival back at the Mueller home, she attempted to retreat up the stairs to her room, to dwell on her guilt alone, but was stopped dead in her tracks when Peter Mueller called her.

"Frances, one moment please." She turned and saw that Freya was standing beside him, devastation written on her face. The thought crossed her mind that it was the first time she had seen the woman show any emotion.

"The child, Frances? Was there a child?" Peter asked gently.

"A child?" she said. "No, of course not. I made the story up. I'm sorry." And with that, she made for the seclusion of her room to mull over the agony she had felt and caused over the last few hours.

* * *

The Muellers stayed up until their son got home. Between them, they tried to find out what had happened that night, to make Frances behave the way she had. Freya suggested she believed the girl might even be mad. Kristian refused to discuss the matter, only telling them of his decision to cut short his leave and return to Kiel.

Freya pleaded with him, and used her maternal art of persuasion, so that finally he agreed to stay on, not for himself or Frances, but for his parents. It was the beginning of June and the war had taken a turn; things had not been going well for Germany for some time. An allied invasion was expected, and if it happened, he knew that this could well be his last leave for quite a while.

* * *

A knocking on the bedroom door woke Frances the following morning. She had not slept well, tossing, and turning in a guilt-ridden slumber. She had told herself she had every right to behave the way she had, but failed to convince herself that it was so. It was unforgivable to mention the loss of her child in public like that. She now had a double helping of guilt to contend with. The guilt of survival and the guilt of her outburst which had affected others and ruined what should have been a pleasant evening.

She had lost control and said things she had no intention of saying. It was easier for them all, she decided, if they thought she had made it all up, especially the loss of her child. She would carry that burden alone. There was a knock on the door for a second time.

"Come in," she called weakly, hoping that Kristian had come to check that she was alright or even, she thought, to apologise for his anger.

It surprised Frances when Anna, the Muellers' cook, came in with a breakfast tray. "What's this?" she asked. "Have I overslept?"

The woman was stiff as a rod and gave her a severe look. "You're not wanted down there," she snapped.

Anna put the tray down on a table near to the bed and walked across the room to open the curtains, leaving Frances to digest her last statement.

Anna had worked for the Muellers for over thirty years. They were good people, like part of her family, and it was upsetting her to witness the problems that this young woman was causing them, particularly Kristian, whom she adored. As she walked back towards the door, she turned.

"Why did you have to come here? We were all fine until you arrived."

"I didn't ask to come," Frances shouted, as Anna slammed the door shut behind her. Then she jumped out of bed and ran to the door, wondering if they were going to confine her to her room. She twisted the doorknob, and she was thankful that the door opened. It seemed that they just didn't want her company. She thought maybe they had done her a favour; it would have been difficult to face them all over the breakfast table, anyway.

She looked around the room, which bore the devastation of the night before. She had thrown her dress down on the floor and kicked off her shoes close by. She was still wearing her underwear, and the remains of the makeup, which she had so carefully applied the night before, was smeared across her face and her pillow. On top of that she had a thumping headache. She groaned.

* * *

It was later that morning that the Mueller household received the first of two visitors. Hans Stahl was chief of the gestapo unit in the town. Prior to the war, he had been the manager of the bank patronised by the Mueller family, and for that matter, also by the Kohls.

Following the incident, the night before, the Brauns felt it was their duty as good members of the Nazi Party to report Frances to the authorities. The Kohl family had tried to dissuade them but had failed: they knew that if they tried too hard, then the Brauns might think that there was something more to hide.

Stahl decided it sufficed to take Peter Muller on one side and caution him regarding his daughter-in-law's behaviour. After all, the Muellers had been good customers. He knew they had friends in high places, and that their son was feted as a war hero. A reprimand was certainly sufficient, as one never knew when or how the war would end.

The second visitor was Sara. Too late, she had set out to warn the family of Stahl's visit and to apologise for what she viewed as the treachery of the Brauns. She also wanted to return Frances's bracelet. Still visibly shaken by the unpleasantness of the night before, she spoke to Peter, refusing to exonerate Frances's behaviour for any reason. Her loyalty lay with Kristian, who had made himself scarce since breakfast. She decided as she left to go in search of him and suspected that he may well be in the walled garden, a favourite haunt of his, when as a child, he was upset.

Sara didn't find him there. Instead, she found Frances seated on a bench, nestling amongst the shrubbery. At first, Sara remained unnoticed. Frances was so deep in thought that Sara decided to leave her. Just as she was about to go, Frances sensed someone's presence and looked up. Seeing Sara, she was filled with embarrassment and was unsure which way to react. She stood and took a couple of steps forward. What she needed was a friend, but Sara halted her with a raise of her hand.

"Keep away from me, Frances. How could you do that to him? You'll not be seeing me again." And with that she turned and left, leaving Frances with a feeling of utter loneliness, which even the beauty of the garden could not assuage. She needed to talk, but there was no one now who would listen. Even the dogs ignored her.

The mare, Majesty, she'd not judge her. She made her way to the end of the garden and through the gate. Looking across the gravel path to the paddock, she could see that someone was with her. At first, she panicked, thinking it was Kristian, but then the figure moved and came into view, and she saw it was just the boy who worked on the farm. She'd noticed him a couple of times and decided he offered her no threat. She crunched her way across the pathway towards the fence and as she did so, both the mare and the boy looked up.

"Hello, I was wondering how Majesty was doing," she said.

The boy doffed his cap. "You'd be the Kapitan's wife." Frances nodded, and he continued. "I work here with me grandad."

"I know, I've seen you."

Delighted because she had noticed him, the boy rewarded her with a dopey grin, which in turn made Frances smile back at him.

"Well," she asked, "what's your name?"

"Willie, Willie Moser."

Frances held out her hand across the fence, and the boy shook it warmly, whilst Majesty made known her displeasure at not being part of the conversation by butting the boy in the rear. They both laughed and Willie gave the mare's ears a gentle tug, as Frances had seen Kristian do.

"She's my favourite," he admitted.

"Mine too. So how is she today?"

"Won't be long now," said Willie. "Could be anytime." Frances heard a call from nearby.

"Willie, what the bloody hell are you doing? There's work here to be done."

"That'll be me granddad," said Willie, eyes wide. "I reckon I'm going to be in trouble for nattering too much." He climbed the fence.

At the gate by the farm buildings stood Willie's granddad Alf, a small wiry man, who Frances understood had worked on the farm for some forty years, except for a short break in the trenches during the Great War. He was gesticulating at his grandson to get a move on.

"I think I'd better go, Frau Mueller."

Frances nodded, "I think you had. See you, Willie."

The boy ran off towards the farm. She called him back. "Willie, have you seen Kapitan Mueller this morning?"

"Yes, he was down here early on. He's taken Bismarck out. Got to go, Frau Mueller."

Frances turned her attention back to the mare, who was nuzzling her arm across the fence.

"Well, at least you still like me," she said, throwing her arms round the mare's neck.

"Why don't you go in with her?"

She turned to find Peter watching her from the driveway. He walked across to join her. "Go in the paddock with her. She's a stickler for company."

"Would that be alright?" she asked.

"Of course, it is. The gate is at the far end of the paddock, or better still, climb the fence. Come on." He leapt the fence with surprising agility for an older man and held out his hand to assist her. She landed awkwardly, causing Majesty to back away slightly.

Peter walked over to the horse, rubbing his hands expertly over her back and flanks.

"Willie said the foal could come any day," said Frances.

"The sooner the better for this old girl, I reckon. That's one active foal in there, big too," said Peter. "Have you felt?" Frances shook her head. "Well, come on then, come here."

She walked to Peter's side, and he took her hand firmly in his and stroked it over the bumps in the mare's belly.

"Can you feel the foal push against your hand?" he asked.

"Yes," she said, "yes I can." Remembering the wonder of her own baby moving inside her, she felt a kinship with the mare.

"It doesn't seem to be in a very good position yet. It could do with being a little further down," Peter remarked. He still had hold of her hand and, putting his other hand on top of hers, and holding it there, he said, "Frances, this has got to stop. Not only are you harming Kristian and goodness knows the rest of us, but you are also destroying yourself with this behaviour of yours. You know, I think there is something inside of you that's consuming you. You can't live with hate, my dear; it will eat you alive."

She felt herself go hot with embarrassment and gave an awkward nod, raising her head to face him, blushing with guilt and shame.

"I didn't ruin the night on purpose, Peter, believe me. I was looking forward to the evening. Things just seem to happen sometimes; I don't understand why. There are triggers, I think. It can be a word, a sound, a smell or even someone's gesture, and it initiates a response in me which I no longer seem able to control." She put her hands to her head. "I'm back there in the camp, feeling it, smelling it," she paused and raised her eyes to his, "and I'm worried that I'm going mad. Am I going mad, Peter, do you think?

Peter rubbed his jaw thoughtfully.

"And yet I saw you come in from that shopping trip and you were happy and as normal as the rest of us, whatever normal is, of course." Peter gave her a smile and, finding her gaze, held on to it. "So, what happened on that morning that was different do you think?"

She shrugged. "I don't know. What?"

"Ah no, Frances, this has to come from inside you." She thought back to the morning two days previous and shrugged again.

"I was with Sara and Kristian, but I was with Sara and Kristian last night too, wasn't I?"

"Kristian has told me...." Peter stopped, not knowing whether to proceed.

"What? What did he tell you?" Peter Mueller exhaled with a sigh and gave her a steady look.

"That you also lost control when there were just the two of you. You told him things, back in the hotel in Munich."

Frances thought for a moment and shook her head. "No, no, I think that was different. I was aiming my anger at him then. I knew what I was doing. I wanted revenge, I wanted to hurt him. I made a promise, you see, before I left Auschwitz, and again when I left Dachau. These memories, and the triggers are different, they take me back there." She thought for a moment. "It's different, it's beyond my control, and it frightens me."

Peter lay a comforting hand on her shoulder. "So, think back again to two days ago, and remove Sara and Kristian from the equation." Frances shook her head and was thoughtful for a while.

"Well, I was shopping. I was relaxed and happy. I haven't been that for an age."

"Go on."

"I was— doing. I was busy?"

"Yes," said Peter, nodding, "You see what I think is, if you can keep yourself busy, then maybe you can keep the bogeyman at bay. So come on now, tell me how you would usually have filled your days before all of this happened to you?"

Frances puffed up her cheeks. "Pfff... that's easy. I would practise for a good five hours at least, and more leading up to a performance."

"So, there you are. You need to play, do you think? Maybe?"

"No, I can't, Peter, really, I can't, not now. I don't know when." She shrugged. "Perhaps never."

"For a while then, until you can, you just need to find other things to fill in your time. It will help you, I'm sure. You won't dwell on all the dreadful things that are filling your head."

"What can I do, though? There's nothing else I know apart from music."

"Well, you have this mare here that you seem to have taken a shine to. And how about I make a promise to you that before this war is over, I will turn you into a fine horsewoman?"

Frances forced a laugh. "Oh, please don't promise that. You'll be condemning us all to many more years of bloodshed."

* * *

Following the conversation with Peter Mueller, Frances stayed at the paddock for quite some time, until her body told her she needed to eat. It was mid-afternoon and she had neither eaten nor had a drink since the night before. She was dreading dinner, knowing that because of her anxiety regarding sitting at the table with the family, she would scarcely be able to eat anything, anyway. She decided to see if she could sneak into the kitchen from the garden and at least grab some water.

Walking back through the garden, she looked through the kitchen window and was relieved to see that Anna wasn't there. She went in to see if she could quickly grab something to eat and drink, and then leave unseen. She saw freshly baked bread on the table; the smell filled her nostrils, and she salivated in anticipation of eating a piece. As she placed her hand on the loaf to rip a chunk off, a voice stopped in her tracks.

"Thief!"

She turned to find Anna scowling at her. She had not considered that the woman might be in the pantry and so out of view from the window. Not knowing what to say, she stood rooted to the spot, stuttering over some sort of apology and blushing, as Anna glared at her. Then the woman's face softened, and she shook her head slowly and sighed.

"So, when did you last eat, child? You didn't touch your breakfast, and as far as I know, you had nothing for lunch. I suspect you're hungry, aren't you?"

Frances tentatively raised her eyes to meet those of the woman and nodded. "I could do with a drink of water please, or a coffee."

"Well now," the woman replied, pointing around the kitchen, "there's the sink and the tap. Here are cups and glasses, and there is a pot of coffee percolating on the stove."

"I can help myself?"

"Of course, Frau Mueller. Did you think I was going to slap your hands?"

"I thought you were going to slap more than my hands this morning," said Frances. The woman came close to giving a smile.

"Ah, well, I have worked in this house for many years and these people are my family. You hurt them, and that makes me angry. I am especially angry when you hurt my boy, Frau Mueller. But perhaps I was a little hard on you this morning, yes?"

"Frances. Anna, please call me by my name."

"We'll see, shall we? Go on, go, and sit at the table, but keep your paws off my bread. I will get you that coffee. Go! Sit!" she instructed, wiping her hands down her pinafore.

Frances sat at the large pine table in the Mueller kitchen, which she noted was spotlessly clean and well organised. She received the coffee with thanks, together with a slice of fruitcake, and took her time drinking and eating, watching as Anna went about her tasks, finding some sort of comfort in it. Perhaps, she decided, the woman wasn't quite as terrifying as she had first thought. She was mulling over Peter's advice about keeping busy and decided to see if she could use her art of persuasion on Anna.

"Anna, will you show me how to cook?" she asked.

Anna turned from her task and raised her eyebrows. "You think I've got time for that then, Frau, do you?"

"Well, no," said Frances thoughtfully, "but if you were to show me how, I could help you, and that would give you more time, wouldn't it?"

"Ah, would it now? And how much cooking experience do you have?"

"Not much. It's so easy to eat out in Paris. There are cafes, bistros, and restaurants everywhere. Or you can just go to the patisserie."

"I see," said Anna. "So, no cooking experience, huh?"

"I can make a salad."

Despite trying not to, Anna cracked a smile. "And you think that's cooking, do you?"

Frances gave a shrug and thought for a few moments. "I can cook eggs."

"Ah, so you can make a good omelette then. Well, at least that's a start."

"No," said Frances, shaking her head, "I can only boil them." Anna gave a harsh laugh. Crossing to a drawer, she took out a knife and then put a bowl of potatoes in front of Frances. "Well, there you go. Let's make a start. You can peel these."

Frances attacked the potatoes with gusto, completing the task in no time. She put the peeled potatoes in front of her teacher with a smile.

"Done," she said. Anna cast a practised eye over the bowl.

"Hmm, but next time more potatoes and less peel, yes?"

"Ah, so not so good?"

"Like I said," replied Anna, "next time more potatoes and less peel."

"So, there can be a next time then?" Frances asked. A smile played on Anna's mouth and Frances returned it. "So, can I come and spend time here?"

"Whenever you like."

"And can I have my dinner in here instead of with the family?"

"So that's what this is all about, is it? Don't you think you should join them?" asked Anna.

"Not now, not while Kristian is so cross with me. And Freya doesn't like me either."

"Freya doesn't like many things and maybe she has just cause," said Anna.

* * *

Over the following couple of days, Frances became increasingly attached to Majesty and Anna, sharing her time between the two. Even though the weather was poor for June, she spent a great deal of time in the paddock, sometimes just sitting and watching the mare, and other times grooming or petting her. Mostly though, she just talked, off-loading all of her guilt, both for surviving the camps, and for the way she had behaved since getting out.

Once or twice, she bumped into Kristian when he was on his way to or from the stables and she wished he would stop, even for a few moments, for Majesty's sake. The animal was confused because he was staying away from her. She recognised his footsteps and would whinny a greeting, but he would hurry past with just a nod and scarcely a glance.

She rarely bumped into him in the house, too, as she had decided to take her meals in the kitchen. Kristian was up much earlier than the rest of the household and had breakfast alone, then like the rest of them, he would grab a sandwich from the kitchen as hunger struck. On one such occasion, she was helping Anna when he came inside looking for food. He grabbed hold of the cook encircling her waist from behind, giving her such a scare that she threatened to take the stick to him, as she had used to do when he was a child. He didn't notice Frances until it was too late, having then to acknowledge her, or risk Anna's wrath.

"Frances."

"Kristian, could we talk?" she asked. He shook his head.

"Nothing to say." And with that he was gone.

* * *

Since her outburst at the Kohl's, Frances felt ostracised, at least by Kristian and Freya. She knew the family all met at certain times of the day in the study to listen to their Fuhrer or Goebbels make one of their propaganda speeches. Coming downstairs one time, she heard Peter's raised voice from the study. She stopped to listen, thinking that maybe they were discussing her.

"You're a fool, Kristian, if you get mixed up in it," she heard Peter shout. Then he dropped his voice, so she went like a child to listen at the door. "Do you think any good will come of removing part of the cancer? They'd just replace him with fat Hermann or maybe even worse."

She then heard Kristian speak but couldn't make out what he said and concluded that he must be at the far end of the room.

"It's too soon," Peter continued. "When the strike is made, the whole of the diseased tissue must be removed. Promise me, for God's sake, Kristian, that you will have nothing to do with this."

There was another mumbled reply.

"Have they got anything on you?" a pause, "Well, thank God for that. Keep away! If you mix yourself up in this, then I doubt that even Karl Doenitz could get you out. I doubt he would even want to. His loyalty to the party doesn't seem to waver; the man must have changed from the old days. Look at what happened to young Oskar Kusch, and that was only a month ago. Just for making his thoughts known, they shot him, and him a brilliant young Kapitan. Keep quiet, Kristian. You don't know who's listening, son."

She dwelt on what she had heard for some time, but because she could make no sense of it, she eventually let it go.

Chapter 11

"Froggy, when you're dressed, come down to the study, will you?" Frances turned over lazily to look at the clock. It was just gone eight a.m. and already the Muellers had received an early morning telephone call, which had interrupted her sleep. And now there was Kristian, calling her down to study. This was the first time in days, ever since the Kohls' party, that he had spoken to her. All she had received prior to this morning had been sharp glances. As she dressed, she tried to think if June 8th was a day of any special significance.

As she reached the bottom of the stairs, it surprised her to see Mueller's staff leaving the study. Alf, Willie, and Anna and the two men who helped run the farm were looking thoughtful. She called out good morning, but they appeared not to hear her. Hearing her voice, Kristian opened the door.

"There's something you need to know. Come in," he said. She quickly tried to assess his mood but couldn't.

"What is it? What's wrong?" she asked, noting that his parents were there too. He pointed to a chair.

"Sit down." She sat on the chair nearest the door and Kristian continued. "Two days ago, Frances, the Allies landed."

"Where?"

"Normandy, the bay of the Seine."

"The Allies are in France. What's happened?" She couldn't keep the excitement from her voice.

"As far as we know, they have already taken Bayeux, Douvres, Ouistreham… our troops are being reinforced and there is heavy fighting in Caen."

"Yes!" Frances gave a whoop, then, suddenly aware of what the news meant to the other three people, she quickly apologised. "I'm so sorry, I wasn't thinking," she said.

"Empathetic as ever, eh," Kristian bit.

"I'm sorry. But surely this means that the war will soon be over," she said, casting a glance at Peter and Freya, and then looking back to Kristian.

"Do you think we will just lay down our arms without a fight?" he asked, and then he gave a sigh. "Some of us might like to, Froggy, but there will be those in Berlin who will want us to fight to the end, you see." He nodded. "There's a great deal more bloodshed to come, I'm afraid."

Peter Mueller rubbed his hands across his worried face and stood up to leave. "Ah well, despite what's going on, I still have a business to run. Alf and I have a meeting in Bonn." He slapped his son on the shoulder and then crossed the room to his wife and kissed her on the cheek. "We should be back early evening, but don't keep dinner back."

"Just a minute," said Freya, "I'll come with you, Peter." She turned and her face lingered upon Kristian, and Frances noticed that it was even more careworn than usual.

The pair left the room, leaving Frances and Kristian alone.

"Happy?" Kristian sniffed.

"I am, of course I am. Do you think…"

"What? Do I think the Allies will beat us back?" he asked. She nodded.

"We'll have to see, won't we? Now, if you'll excuse me, I have things to do."

He turned his back on her and messed with a few papers on the desk, leaving her to feel dismissed, like a schoolchild. She called into the kitchen to grab some bread and sausage and a coffee and chatted about the news with Anna briefly, trying not to sound as elated as she felt. Then she made her way to the stables to give more thought to the importance of what she had learnt.

The weather that day was poor for June; it was poor for any month. She fought her way up the gravel path to the paddock against a sheet of rain. Screwing up her eyes against the deluge and drawing the wax jacket closer about her, she scanned the field for the mare but failed to find her. She made her way quickly to the gate, wondering if by any chance the animal could have escaped, but she saw that the gate was firmly shut. Ah well, she thought, Willie would know what was going on. Perhaps he had brought her in out of the rain.

She eventually found the boy in the yard going about his tasks, mucking out the stables and paying small heed to the weather.

"You're late," he called to her when he saw her, "I thought when you didn't show up first thing that the weather was keeping you off. Must be hell for them that's fighting. You've heard the news, I'm guessing."

"Yes, Willie, yes I have heard the news, and yes, it must be hell," she replied, taking shelter in the stable where he was working.

"Well, I suspect I'll be going me self soon."

"What on earth are you talking about? You're just a child."

Willie pulled himself up to his full height and puffed himself out, making her smile. "I'm near fourteen," he said. "I wonder where I'll be posted."

Frances knew the boy was part of the Hitler Youth and as such had been well schooled in warfare, but the thought of mere children like him being expected to fight sickened her, so she refused to be dragged any further into a conversation regarding fighting, and quickly dismissed the thought.

"Where's Majesty, Willie?" she asked.

"We brought her in first thing. She's showing all the signs." He gave her a grin. "I thought you were going to miss it. She's over in the stalls."

Frances ran along the side of the paddock to the long barnlike building that housed the stalls, tack room and feed. Even though there was no door to close on the building, it felt warm when she entered and smelled of sweet hay and straw, which were stacked along one wall opposite the stalls. At first, she thought the stalls were all empty, but then she heard laboured breathing coming from the far end of the building. She found Majesty lying on her side. The mare tried to lift her head, as she heard her approach, but she struggled with the effort and let her head drop back down with a snort.

"Willie, Willie come quick," shrieked Frances as she ran back to the doorway of the building. The boy appeared from one of the stables, bolting the door and ditching his pitchfork. He ran across the yard to join her, and they both ran to the end stall where the horse lay.

"She's having difficulties, Frau. I'll try to get her up. You go back to the house and get the Kapitan," he ordered.

Frances ran out into torrential rain, not feeling it, and fought her way to the walled garden and back to the rear of the house and into the kitchen. Anna was stitching the ribbons onto Kristian's new uniform and looked up with surprise as Frances ran through the kitchen without a word.

"What is it, Frances?" she shouted after her. Frances stopped and ran back.

"Kristian, where is he? Is he in?" she asked quickly.

"As far as I know, yes, try the study. Is everything alright?"

"Yes, no! I don't know," Frances shouted over her shoulder.

Bursting through the door to the study dripping wet, she found Kristian, as Anna had suggested, seated behind his father's desk, reading some mail, and drinking a coffee.

"Thank goodness," she panted. "Quick, Kristian, the stables. Majesty is having her foal."

He refused to meet her eyes, not even bothering to look up, giving an audible sigh. "My God, is that all? I thought at least the Allies had reached the farm," he said.

"No, you don't understand. She's in trouble."

"Froggy, this is Majesty's third foal. She has them with no trouble at all. She'll be fine."

"But she's lying down, and Willie is trying to get her up." She crossed to the desk and grabbed his arm, pulling on it. "Please, Kristian. You must come."

He sighed again. "Alright, just give me a minute to finish my coffee, huh?"

She grabbed the cup from his hand. "No, now!" she said.

"Now. You want me now?"

"Yes."

He gave a nod, and a scowl. "Then I suppose I'd better do as I'm told."

He followed as Frances ran through the house and back through the kitchen, where he grabbed a jacket to keep off the worst of the rain. "Anna, tell Mutti I'm down at the stables if she wants me. We're having a drama, it seems," he said with a shrug and some sarcasm, as he closed the door.

He just caught sight of Frances scurrying off through the gate into the garden, and he followed her, shaking his head. She reached the barn before him, and it wasn't until he saw Willie's face anxiously peering from the doorway that the thought occurred to him that there might be something wrong after all. He lengthened his stride and shouted, "What's the problem, Willie?"

The boy ran to meet him. "I can't get her up, Kapitan, I've tried. There's something wrong."

Mueller hastened his step to the far end of the barn and found the mare still lying down on her side. Frances was kneeling beside her head, stroking her muzzle. "See, I told you, didn't I?"

Dismissing her reproach, he turned to Willie. "How long's she been like this?" he asked.

"Hard to say exactly, Kapitan, I ate my breakfast in here with her and she seemed ok. Then I set about cleaning out the loose boxes." He indicated Frances with a nod of his head. "It was Frau who found her, about half an hour ago, I reckon."

"How long's she been sweating?"

"Since I tried to get her standing."

Mueller knelt beside the mare and ran his hand down her neck and flank. She snorted gently, comforted by his presence. "Willie, you run up to the house and get my mother to phone Manstein. Tell her to get him out here as quick as he can. I'll try to get her up."

"Who's Manstein?" Frances asked, as Willie left at the double.

"Veterinary," Mueller grunted.

"But she's going to be alright, isn't she?"

Mueller was non-committal. "Let's just see if we can get her standing, shall we?"

He moved round to the front of the mare and pulled hard on her head collar, geeing her up and shouting encouragingly. At first the animal pulled against him, showing the whites of her eyes, then suddenly she swung her head over and pulled herself up onto her knees.

"Yes," roared Mueller, "Come on, come on, girl, good girl, you can do it." He called Frances to take over at the front end. "Hold her head up, don't let her roll back over." Then he went down the rear end and slapped the horse's flanks. "Come on, Majesty, come on girl, up you come." With an enormous effort and a loud groan, the mare rose to her feet.

"She's up!" shrieked Frances.

Mueller nodded. "We've got to keep her up now. This birth will be a lot easier for her with a little help from gravity you see." He took some handfuls of hay and rubbed the sweat from the animal's body, then taking the pail from the corner of the stall, he filled it with fresh water for her to drink. "Where the bloody hell has Willie got to?" he complained.

Frances ran the length of the barn to the doorway and stared across the stable yard towards the house.

"He's coming now."

The boy ran into the building soaking wet and panting. "Well?" demanded Mueller. "Is Manstein on his way?"

"Couldn't get him, Kapitan. Wife says he's on another call."

"Shit!" Mueller walked away from the stall and thought for a while, then exhaled loudly. "Right. Willie, get me a clean bucket of water and plenty of soap. Looks like it's down to us, huh?"

Frances turned to him wide eyed. "What are you going to do?"

"I'm going to see if we can get this foal born. If she's left much longer...."

"What?"

"Let's just see, shall we?" Mueller said, stripping down to his waist and soaping his hands and arms. "Willie, you stay down the business end with me. Froggy, you hold her head steady and give her lots of encouragement. Are we ready?"

The other two nodded as Mueller took a deep breath and gently inserted his hand inside the mare, who snorted and stamped.

"Easy, old girl. Hold her steady, Froggy," he instructed, as he withdrew his hand. Willie looked at him questioningly. "Foal has got its head back. It'll never be born like that; it needs pulling round. Get me a rope, Willie, not too thick. Maybe if I can attach it to the foal's muzzle, we can get some leverage and pull the head around. I need to check first, though, on which way to pull. We need to get that right."

"But won't that hurt it?" asked Frances.

"I'll try to be gentle, or maybe you have a better idea, have you?" he snapped.

Feeling foolish, she watched as he made a small noose with the rope and once again gently felt inside the mare with his hand. He ran his other hand over her flank, speaking gently to her, as the mare snorted her approval. Then very carefully he inserted his other hand, which held the rope, continuing to speak the mare's name, shushing and crooning, calming her with his words.

It seemed an age, and in fact it was some minutes before exhausted, he announced, "That's got it!"

"What now?" asked Frances, rubbing at Majesty's ear.

"Now we get a hold on that rope and try to manipulate the foal's head forwards. We need to keep Majesty relaxed, and that's down to you." He inserted his hands again. "Willie, take the slack off the rope, and pull very gently when I tell you to," he instructed. The boy nodded. "Good, that's it. I can feel the side of the head, easy now."

Deciding that she had had enough, the mare lurched forwards onto her knees, throwing Frances off balance, and then fell onto her side. They were back where they started.

"For Christ's sake! Shit! Now look!" Mueller stepped back, holding the rope limply in his hands.

The mare had sweated and lathered up badly again, and her breathing had become laboured. Mueller rubbed her down once more, then knelt beside her and took her neck in his arms. Laying his head against hers for a while. He then sat back and gently tugged her forelock. She whinnied softly and pushed her velvet nose into his belly. Mueller stayed in that position with her for some time, and then with a nod and a sigh he said, "OK, old girl, you've had enough. Maybe we can still save this foal of yours, eh?" He stood up. "Willie, go to the house and get a shotgun and cartridges. Frances, you get back up to the house with Willie and stay there," he instructed.

"What are you going to do?" she asked him. He turned away from her and didn't answer. He knew she didn't really need telling.

"No, Kristian," she screamed, "No, you can't."

He saw Willie look from him to Frances. "Go to the house, Willie, and get me that gun," he repeated.

"Is there no other way, Kapitan Mueller?"

Mueller shook his head. "No, Willie, not that I can see. I can't do any more. The mare has had enough."

"I'll get the gun, but do I have to stay?" asked the boy.

"No Willie, of course not." The boy left, making for the house. Mueller turned to Frances. "You go too. Now!"

Frances fixed her eyes on him and held his gaze. "How can you? I thought she meant something to you."

"The animal is in pain, Frances; we've done all we can. Please go. Don't make this any more difficult."

She refused to leave, and he watched as she knelt beside the mare. It seemed an age until Willie returned with a shotgun, which he passed to Mueller along with a couple of cartridges. Mueller loaded up the gun and then looked down at it, lying in his hands, unable to meet the gaze of either of his companions.

"It's because I care, you see. I've seen men suffering, begging to be shot. There have been times...."

Frances leapt up and grabbed his arm, pleading with him. "Please Kristian, please, just try one more time." He shook his head and then shook her from his arm. Running over to Majesty, she threw herself in front of her. "Well, you're going to have to shoot me too," she said, stiffening her jaw and giving him a scowl.

Mueller raised the gun and pointed it at her. "Well, that wouldn't be a bad idea, would it?" Then, despite the situation, he shook his head, and a smile tugged at the corners of his mouth. "You know what, this is the first time I've ever known you put something before yourself, Froggy," he said.

"Please, Kristian," she pleaded.

He blew his cheeks out and exhaled, looking over at Willie whose face was wet with tears. Turning away, he walked the length of the building, back towards the doorway, and there he stood for a while, thinking, leaning on the door frame. Then he made the walk back to the end stall, snapped the shotgun open and removed the cartridge, casting his eyes over both Frances, who was stretched across the mare in some ridiculous attempt at shielding her, and Willie, who stood with large tears dripping down his face.

Mueller chewed his lips, looking from one to the other. Then he shook his head and said, "Well come on you two, enough of the bloody dramatics. We'll give it one more try, eh?"

Not quite trusting him, Frances asked from her position in front of the mare. "Really?"

"Yes, really, Froggy. Now come on, we're going to have to get her up again if this is going to work."

The three of them encouraged the mare with renewed determination. There were plenty of calls of "Come on, Majesty," "Please, Majesty," "Please get up," "Don't give up, Majesty," "Majesty, please," "Come on, girl," "Hup!" Finally, Mueller took the mare's head collar from Frances and gave the horse a firm spank on the rear. Her ears went back, and her eyes rolled, and with an exhausted groan, she finally pulled herself to her feet once more.

Mueller thrust the lead-rope into Frances's hands and quickly soaped himself up. Then he began once again to try to get the rope noose around the foal's nose. The time dragged on, and the mare's discomfort grew. She stamped the ground and snorted, swaying her rear end, and almost knocking Mueller to the ground. "Got ya!" Mueller said suddenly, after a twenty-minute struggle, which seemed to them all much longer. He turned to the other two and gave them a brief smile and a nod. He knew he would have given up if it hadn't been for them. "Right, Willie," he said. "Let's try again. Take the slack out of the rope. Froggy, you'd damn well better hold her steady."

"I will, I will," she said, holding the rope tightly with one hand and caressing the mare's face with the other. She said a silent prayer as Mueller inserted a hand once again inside the mare to pull the foal's head round.

"Right, easy old girl," he said, "Willie, pull ever so gently when I say." There was a short pause, and Frances struggled to breathe, she was so anxious. "Right, now, Willie, good, good," said Mueller, then he exhaled loudly, and removing his hands, he stood back, nodding and smiling. Willie nodded too, with a beam that threatened to split his head in two.

More comfortable at last, Majesty gave a snort of approval, as Frances, down at the front end of the mare, asked, "Have you done it?"

Mueller stepped back where she could see him, sniffed, and nodded, and with relief, Frances gasped, feeling she could breathe again. "Should be plain sailing now. It's down to Majesty, but I think perhaps we should give her a bit of a helping hand. What do you think, Willie?" asked Mueller.

The boy, still beaming, nodded back. Mueller gave the horse another rub-down and a few hearty pats. "Right, old girl, ready for the last stage, then?"

This time, Mueller easily tied the rope onto the foal's front legs, which were now lying in an excellent position within the birth canal. "Right, Willie this is it, this time we both tug," said Mueller. "Give her plenty of encouragement, Froggy. Now!"

With a chorus of, "Come on, Majesty," "Keep it up," "You can do it," and similar exclamations, with a plop, the foal was born. Mueller immediately dropped onto his knees to remove the rope from around the legs of the new-born, and the remains of the birth sac from its mouth, better enabling it to draw its first breaths. Frances and Willie looked on in wonderment, as they witnessed the miracle of birth.

"It's a colt," Mueller exclaimed, smiling, "I hope he'll be a blue roan like his mother. Well done, Majesty," he cooed, standing, and giving the horse a rub of her muzzle, tugging her ears and forelock.

"He's black," remarked Frances. "won't he stay black?"

"Blue roans are born black or very dark grey. Hopefully, when he sheds his first coat, he'll be like his mother, you see," Mueller explained.

"It's a fine colt, Kapitan," said Willie with a smile.

"Didn't he hurt himself falling like that?" asked Frances, leaving Majesty to lick the rest of the afterbirth from her foal, which was already trying to struggle to its feet.

"He had a softer landing than some," said Willie through an ear-splitting grin.

 "I think it's time I took a bath," Mueller declared, looking down at the state of himself, covered in blood and afterbirth. With a last look at Majesty and her foal, he grabbed his shirt and jacket and walked off towards the house.

After he'd gone, Willie and Frances moved several bales of straw, seated themselves comfortably, and watched Majesty, who was already recovering from the trauma of a difficult birth, and was welcoming her foal with licks and nuzzles.

Chapter 12

"Ah, so you are still here. I thought this is where I would find you. You're missing dinner."

Frances turned to look behind her. Her gaze found Mueller freshly changed, leaning on the doorway of the building, watching her.

"I have no idea what the time is," she replied. "Have you all eaten?"

He shook his head. "It's about 7:00, why don't you join us? That's if you want to, of course."

Her heart leapt, it was the first time he had suggested they spent time together since the Kohls' dinner, but how could she tear herself away from this foal and its mother's joy? "I can't leave them, Kristian; I could sit here all night," she stated.

"Well, I wouldn't recommend it, speaking from experience." Mueller walked the length of the barn and joined her on the bales. "So how is our newcomer?"

"I think he's doing fine. Do you know, he has even been over to me and introduced himself, and Majesty is so proud of him?"

"He's a splendid colt. What are you going to call him?"

"Me?" she asked.

"The little chap probably wouldn't be here if it weren't for you. He certainly wouldn't have a mother."

"But it was you who did the hard work."

"True, but he's yours, anyway."

"Mine?"

He nodded. "For now. You can take care of him for me. I've been recalled early. I've been waiting for the right moment to tell you."

"Recalled, but why, when?"

"You know yourself that things aren't going too well, for us that is. I'm to report back to Kiel the day after tomorrow. Then, I don't know." He leant forward across the wooden bar of the stall towards the foal.

"The day after tomorrow, so soon?" she questioned.

"What's the matter, Froggy? I thought you'd be glad to see the back of me."

"Well, I'm not," she said, leaning forward to join him. He glanced at her and shook his head. "And what's that supposed to mean?" she asked.

"It means I don't think I will ever fathom you out. A few days ago, you as good as said you hated me, now you don't want me to go… Anyway, what are you going to call this foal of yours?"

"I don't know, something beautiful, when I can think." She lay her hand on his arm, and she felt him flinch, ever so slightly. "I really don't want you to leave, Kristian," she breathed.

He turned to look at her, holding her eyes for a fleeting moment. Then quickly he turned away, clicking to the horses to cover his chaos. There existed a long silence between them, yet each was crying out to the other, begging to be heard. It was she who broke it.

"I thought you were wonderful today," she said.

"Not bad for just some Kraut, eh?" He kept his head down, refusing to meet her gaze again. He was quiet for a moment and then exhaled. "I think it's time for dinner, Froggy."

As he pulled himself to his feet, she grabbed his arm a second time. "Don't go, Kristian."

He turned his eyes on hers, looking deep into the molten amber of them and asked, "What are you trying to say to me?"

She reached up and touched his hair with her fingers and traced the lines around his eyes and the corners of his mouth. Drawing closer to him, she pulled his head down towards her and kissed him, briefly at first, savouring every sweet memory that stirred inside her. Then, as her kisses became more lingering, she felt him respond. His mouth softened beneath hers and finally his lips parted and became more demanding.

Pushing her back into the sweet-smelling straw, he lay beside her, encircling her waist with his arms and pulling her close. "Are you sure?" he asked, his voice thick with emotion. She answered him with another kiss. He pushed himself up onto one elbow and looked down at her. "I thought I'd lost you," he said.

She shook her head, "No. I've always been here."

"Then why?"

"A feeling of guilt, I suppose, and a promise to some friends. I've struggled to keep that promise, and I don't want to keep it anymore, Kristian. I want you."

He kissed her, pulling her up, so that they were both on their knees facing one another. He placed her fingers on the buttons of his shirt and slowly toyed with those on her blouse, stopping from time to time to kiss the hollows of her neck and throat, or to cup her breasts, whilst she rediscovered the firmness of his body.

They both jumped at the sound of a bicycle being thrown down to the ground just outside. Mueller got to his feet, and hurriedly did up the buttons of his shirt, making for the doorway to give Frances more time to gather herself together. He was only a little surprised to find Willie on his way in, clasping a flask, a blanket, and a large pack of sandwiches. The boy grinned at him.

"I asked my Mutti if I could stay the night," he said. "I figured it would be as well, after what the mare has been through."

"Did you now?" said Mueller, blocking his way, "Frances, it's Willie, come to babysit for the night," he shouted. "Now go back outside, Willie, and stand your bike up against the wall. Someone could have a nasty accident tripping over it."

Willie ran back outside to sort out his bicycle as Frances pulled herself out of the straw, flushed with embarrassment at being caught in a compromising situation. The boy scarcely gave her a second glance. He made his way back towards the stall and into what was going to be their love nest. He raked the straw into a bed and threw his blanket down, ready for the night.

"We'll leave you then," said Mueller, looking at Frances, unable to prevent a smile from creeping across his face.

"OK Kapitan, any problem and I'll come up to the house and get you."

"You do that, Willie."

As they crossed the stable yard, both Frances and Kristian burst into laughter. Catching at Frances's arm, Mueller pulled her to him. "Well, now what?" he asked.

She shrugged. "Back to what is supposed to be our room," she suggested.

He shook his head. "No, I couldn't, not the first time. Not after the way things have been."

"Why not?" she asked.

He looked at her sheepishly. "Well, it's a bit obvious they'd know."

"You're embarrassed about your folks," she said and giggled.

"Too right I am. From what I recall, I will have a problem keeping you quiet."

It was her turn to be embarrassed, and she found she was blushing and so looked at the ground as they carried on walking. He took her arm and, stopping, turned her round to face him, drawing her close.

"Looks like we are going to have to wait."

She breathed into his shoulder. "But I don't want to wait. Let's not wait, Kristian, there must be somewhere we can go."

"Froggy, it's going to be a fine day tomorrow. How about I get up early and beg a picnic lunch off Anna? There's a place I can take you to."

"But you're leaving. We've so little time."

"We can have the whole day together. The folks will know, I'll tell them, give them time to come to terms with the way things are, and then we can have the entire night together, too."

She pouted at him. "I want you now." He nodded.

"I know, don't you think I feel the same, but surely after all this time we can wait until morning. Until we're on our own, huh? Free from any interruption."

"No, I can't."

"Right, madam," he said, sweeping her off the ground and into his arms. "I know somewhere we can go." He began running back to the stable yard.

"Where?" she shrieked with laughter.

"Bismarck's loose box. He won't mind."

The laughter turned into a scream as she kicked out, unsure whether he was joking, but he didn't put her down until he reached the stable, and there he flattened her against the wall next to the door with the weight of his body.

"Well, we could go in here, Froggy, if that's what you want, or we could have a quick screw behind some shrub in the garden, huh? I reckon we deserve better than that, don't you? Let's make it special. I want it to be special."

"Alright, you win," she said weakly, her hand caressing the side of his face. "Perhaps you could come to my room in the night, do you think?"

He pushed some stray hair behind her ear and nodded. "We'll see. Come on, we are going to be in trouble with Anna. We're late for dinner. Join us tonight, Froggy, don't go to the kitchen."

"Only if you give me one more kiss," she teased.

He nodded. "One more kiss."

***

The mood in the Mueller household that evening was, for the first time since Frances's arrival, one of relaxed optimism. Kristian had needed to explain little to his parents, as it was obvious to all that encountered them that evening that the relationship had taken a U turn. Even Freya was prepared to be forgiving for her son's sake and made a further attempt to welcome her daughter-in-law into the family. Peter's business meeting had also gone well too, and he'd made it back early enough for dinner. The night took on a celebratory atmosphere, and it was late before Frances got to her room. She left Kristian and his father in deep conversation and knew that they would be there for some time yet.

She lay awake for a while wondering if he would make his excuses to his father and come to her room after all, but he didn't. Lying in bed now, she thought back over the happenings of the day, smiling to herself. Korvetten Kapitan Kristian Mueller, Knight's Cross with Oak Leaves and Crossed Swords, had fought shy of making love to her in his parent's home. There were so many facets to him, many still to be discovered, each one she found more endearing than the last. Small wonder she couldn't resist him. His charms were countless.

Chapter 13

The next day dawned as Mueller said it would, extremely clement. After the storm of the previous day blew itself out, there was a promise of a fine day to come.

Frances sighed as she languished in bed, wishing Kristian was beside her. She'd been remembering their lovemaking from the past, which could still make her squirm between the sheets. She glanced at the clock: nine thirty. They had let her lie in, probably they had slept late too. She pulled herself to a sitting position and stretched, shaking off the remains of her sleep. Today, she decided her life would take a turn for the better.

* * *

"Kristian Mueller, put me down!" shrieked Anna in mock horror. "You're not too old for me to take the stick to you. Just remember that."

"How could I forget?" winced Mueller. "I still have the marks to show for it."

"Yes, and you deserved every one, as I recall."

He carried on swinging her round until her head was spinning, and then he put her down, dizzy, onto the floor.

"Now," he said, "Are you going to help me put this picnic together or do I have to give you more of the treatment?"

"Umph! This war is turning your head. The sooner it's over, the better."

"Amen to that."

"Fancy coming home with that wife of yours," she complained. "French! Now why couldn't you have found a good German girl to keep you in your place?"

"Frances has been through a great deal, Anna. Anyway, I thought you liked her."

"Yes, as a matter of fact I do, but many people have been through a great deal, as you put it, Kristian, but they don't go around behaving as she has done."

"Hmm, by the end of this war, I think we will find many people behaving strangely. We're lucky out here. You can remain reasonably untouched, you see."

"Lucky? Yes, I suppose we are." She paused. "And just what do you expect to take on this picnic? Out to impress, are we?"

"Yes, as a matter of fact," he said, disarming her with a boyish grin. She rubbed her hands down her pinafore.

"Then we'd better see what we can do."

As she ferreted around in the cupboards and larders, she thought about the changes the war had wrought on him. She had always had a huge tender spot for him, from the moment he had been born, just upstairs. He had been such a bright child, full of fun and all too often devilment for which she had taken the stick to him many times. But the war had wreaked its changes on him as it had on many, she supposed, and he now had a dark, brooding side to his nature, which had hitherto been unknown. He'd never spoken to her much about what it was like on patrol, in one of those underwater boats. He'd never mentioned the war to her much at all, but she knew that on the rare occasions when he was back home, he and his father had sealed themselves up together and talked into the dark hours.

He had a carefree air about him this morning though, and it pleased her to see the boy in him again. She grudgingly supposed it was something to do with the young woman upstairs. Well, talk, or at least think, of the devil. The door opened and Frances walked into the kitchen.

Anna thought she had never seen her look so lovely, not even on the night of the Kohls' party when she was all dolled up. Her skin that morning had taken on a healthy glow, and her amber eyes held a bright spark. She was wearing a cream crepe dress covered in blue flowers. It had a sweetheart neckline and short sleeves and buttoned down the front, belted in self- fabric around her tiny waist. She watched as the girl smiled at Kristian coquettishly.

"Well, is the picnic still on?" she asked.

Picnic be damned, thought Anna. The way they were looking at each other left her in no doubt as to what they were going to get up to. She thought they would pay little heed to what was going into the picnic basket at all.

"We're just seeing to it, aren't we, Anna?" Kristian replied, and then he walked a couple of steps towards the girl, tentatively reaching out and gently stroking the side of her face and her hair. Then Anna noticed more subtle changes in the girl, like the way she coloured ever so slightly and lowered her eyes as he touched her. It pleased her to see that the girl was clearly in love with her favourite boy.

"Can I help?" asked Frances.

Kristian shook his head. "Too many cooks, eh, Anna? Anyway, it's my surprise. Go down to the paddock and see that foal of yours for a while. I'll come down when everything's done."

Anna watched as the girl then stood on tiptoe and brushed his cheek with her lips, then she was gone, leaving him wantonly staring after her.

"Chop, chop!" she interrupted his thoughts, "There's a picnic to get ready."

* * *

It was late morning by the time he made his way down to the stables. Frances was keeping a lookout and waved as he approached, armed with a large picnic basket.

"How are they both?" he asked, clicking at Majesty and her youngster.

"Fine. Willie said he will put them out to pasture for a few hours. Where are we going?"

"I'm taking you out to pasture too," he teased. "You see those hills over there across the fields?

"In the distance?"

"A few fields away, that's all. It's up behind the Kohl's house, it's where I would go when I was a lad. A pleasant walk will do us good. Do you need anything from the house?" She shook her head, and he took her hand. "Come on, then, my girl."

He'd called her my girl. She knew she would never be anyone else's.

He led the way back across the stable yard and shouted out farewell to Willie and his grandfather, who were sitting in the sun eating their lunch, then he turned right onto a track that led across the first of the fields. Frances had to break into a trot to keep up with his long strides.

"Don't walk so fast, Kristian, I can't keep up," she complained. He stopped and waited for her.

"Short arse." He grinned at her, and she felt herself colour again under his gaze.

They continued their walk for a while in silence. It was enough to just be together; words would almost have spoiled it. Eventually, she asked, "What will happen when you leave?"

"You'll stay here, Froggy, like I said."

"No, not to me, to you. What will happen in Kiel?" He shook his head and blew out his cheeks.

"I wish I knew. We've had some heavy raids there already."

"You will be alright, won't you?"

"Of course, I will. I'm indestructible. I thought you knew that."

They continued walking, and she watched as he chewed on his lip, deep in thought. Eventually he said, "It's the kids I feel sorry for. We're sending them out with next to no training. They haven't got a clue how to command or even what to expect, some of them. The shits in Berlin gave them the order to ram enemy shipping if all else failed."

"What do you mean?" she asked.

"Back in May, just before I found you. Thankfully, they all had more sense. I worry about our lads, about Paul. So far, they've been lucky. They were sent off to the Med, you know. It's about time they scrapped the old girl and gave him a nice new shiny tub. There's been lots of improvements, Froggy."

"How?"

"Roomier for a start."

"Really? Well, that's a good thing."

"And they have a schnorkel, so they can stay down for as long as they like. Proper submersibles now, underwater attack, the lot. Adolf should realise that he can win the war with them. Donitz knows." He glanced at her, noticing the wide smile on her face. "I'm talking too much, aren't I? I'm sorry," he apologised.

"No, you're not. You don't talk enough."

He stopped walking and raised his eyebrows at her, holding her gaze, and then suddenly he grabbed her around the waist. "That, my dear, is because I am a man of action." He planted a firm kiss on her lips. "No more talk of war," he said, holding her tightly and lifting her so that her feet were off the floor. "Today, Froggy, is made for love." Then he dropped her to the ground and stood over her.

"You've done that before, Korvetten Kapitan Mueller, I seem to recall," she said, as he took her arm and pulled her to her feet. Once up, she struck out at him, kicking him in the shin, racing off across the field at a run, laughing as he clutched his injured limb.

"Right, you just wait, my girl," he called after her, dumping the picnic basket and running after her, catching up easily and making her shriek with laughter as he prolonged the chase to the end of the field at which lay a small coppice.

He pulled her through the trees into a clearing which was surprisingly high up, and she was met with superb views across the fields beyond.

Unaccustomed to the exercise and still bursting with laughter, she had to take some deep breaths as she struggled to ask, "Is this all-Mueller land?"

He pointed in the direction they had just come, sweeping his arm across acres of land. "All this is but look," he said, guiding her to the other side of the coppice and pointing, "Just down there is Kohl land. See, there's the house at the bottom of the hill, probably about two kilometres away. And over there, look, you can just see the outskirts of the town."

She nodded and wandered off across the clearing and then stopped to take in the view. Turning to face him, she said, "I feel so dreadful about Sara and her family. Do you think they will ever forgive me for the way I behaved?"

He turned her around and placed his hands on her shoulders, laying his cheek against hers. "Oh, I should think they have already. They won't hold a grudge; they're good people."

"Why hasn't Sara been to the house then? Oh, Kristian, I really have completely messed things up, haven't I?" She leant back against him, turning her face to the sun as he wrapped his arms around her waist and planted a kiss on the top of her head.

"It will all be fine you'll see. Are you hungry?" he asked.

"I'm just enjoying the feeling of you holding me. I've missed this. Missed you." She sighed. "But yes, I think I could eat something."

"Then I'll retrieve our picnic while you find a good place for us to sit."

She watched him walk back across the clearing, his long legs covering the distance in a few strides, and then he was through the trees and lost to her view. A good place to sit for us, she thought. What he really means is a good place for us to lie together, to have sex. She suddenly felt ridiculously shy about being alone with him in such a place, but before she could dwell upon it, he was back walking towards her, smiling; the sunbeams breaking through the trees, picking out golden glints in his hair. She was shy no longer and ran to him and pushed her way into his arms.

"Hussy," he teased, eyes crinkling. "Champagne?"

"Champagne?" she squealed. "I can't remember the last time."

They found a lush area of grass, dappled in shade, growing in front of a tree, and it was here that they set about unpacking their picnic. Fresh baked bread, sausage, cheese, cake, apples.

"It's good?" questioned Mueller, laughing at her wide, eyed stare.

"As good as any picnic in peacetime."

"Like I said before, it has its advantages being a farmer, you see."

"Or a farmer's son." She smiled.

"Indeed. Or a farmer's daughter-in-law."

He popped the cork on the champagne and poured a couple of glasses, offering her one which she drank down greedily.

"It's rather warm, Froggy," he apologised.

"I don't care, it's still champagne."

They ate for a while in almost total silence, each aware of what the meal was leading up to. Mueller watched her toying with her food, finding difficulty with his own.

"Was this a good idea, do you think, coming here?" he asked.

"Of course, it's beautiful," she replied, eyes downcast.

"You're not hungry, though, are you?" She looked up and shook her head. "Me neither," he said, fixing her with a sky-blue stare until she coyly looked down, thinking desperately of something to say which wouldn't sound stupid. Her mind was racing.

"It doesn't matter though, does it, the food? It's lovely here."

"Mmnn." He stretched out his hand and stroked her shoulder. "Lovely. So, I got it half right then?"

"What?" she asked, raising her eyes, and coming face to face with one of Mueller's most wicked looks.

"What about if we forget the food?" he suggested.

She felt her heartbeat soar and leap into her throat, making her swallow before she could reply, "I think that would be a wonderful idea."

Chapter 14

What a performance she had given, and like a fool, he'd fallen for it. He should have realised it was all a pretence. Yet another way to get to him. Part of her plan to destroy him, to take revenge for the things she'd seen, the things she'd suffered. And what of those things? Were they a pretence too? Just things that her twisted mind had made up. The horrors, the atrocities, all in her mind. Thought up to fill him with guilt, the bitch.

He'd frightened her, though, and that had made him feel good, at least for that moment. He lashed out with his foot and sent the entire picnic crashing towards her. He saw the shock on her face, and she cried. What a show! She even made some attempts at an explanation for her behaviour.

He had told her that enough was enough. That he had had enough! She had made a fool of him, had led him on, and then at the last minute had told him that it was a mistake. He wondered if that had happened with the man Otto. Maybe he deserved some sympathy after all. Perhaps she had deserved what she had got. The way she had made him feel, the way his temper had soared, had given him an understanding of how that kind of thing could happen. So, he had turned and left her mopping up her crocodile tears.

Today was to have been a special day. He had tried to make it special for her, for them both. Today he had allowed himself the inanity of wearing his feelings on his sleeve. Well, never again! Not for her, not for anyone. Romance, love, call it what you will, had never been for him. He didn't need it, and he didn't want it!

* * *

Maybe, she thought, if he had said anything other than those words, then things might have been different. They would have been different! There had been a desperation on her part at first, during the preliminaries of their lovemaking. He slowed her down, caressed her, kissed her. First her lips, then her breasts, brushing his lips down across the flat of her belly, until she had cried out for him to enter her. And, as he did so, he had uttered those words into her hair with a sigh.

"God, Frances I've waited a long time for this."

She froze. Suddenly it wasn't him, but Otto who was straddled across her. She had pushed him away and turned her mouth from his and cried out.

"No! Please don't." First, she had felt his body tense and then he withdrew from her.

"Frances, I thought you wanted this," he said. She saw the confusion written on his face and answered.

"I, I do, but…?"

"But what?"

"Not now."

"When then? I'll be gone tomorrow, remember?" He rolled onto his side, fighting to re-button his fly, and then sat up and chewed on his lips, thinking. "Is this part of your ridiculous plan for revenge?" he suddenly asked.

"No, no. Kristian please, I just need a few minutes, that's all," she begged. "Just give me a few minutes."

"For what? So you can make a fool of me a second time?" He nodded at her and laughed, but there was no humour in it. "I'll not play anymore of your stupid games, Frances; I've had enough of them."

The tears had started to well up in her eyes and her throat had tightened. She found herself unable to speak to him.

He didn't wait. He didn't give her time to explain. She wanted to tell him that it would be alright. To give her a few moments, and it would be alright. She had hurt him, injured his pride, she knew that. And he had frightened her with his anger, kicking out at the picnic. Plates, glasses, food, hamper, and all. And then he had left her. Striding off to God knows where. Leaving her there with the pieces of what was to have been a special day scattered around her.

The tears, the first she had wept since they'd struck him down at the prison in Brest, fell from her eyes in a deluge. She cried for Ruth and her child, and all the thousands that had died at Auschwitz. She cried for the suffering of those at Drancy and those that had been part of the cruel experiments at Dachau. Her lost friend Miriam, her child, and mostly she cried for them; for Frances and Kristian, who had it not been for this war would never have met, and who, because of the war, didn't stand a chance.

It was sometime later that she recovered enough to think about what she should do. She wanted to make things right, but she knew him well enough to know that on the rare occasions when his mood was black, it was safer to stay away until he had calmed down. Time was short, tomorrow he would leave, and any chance of a reconciliation would leave with him. Maybe his parents would help, but how could she explain what had happened to them?

Sara, she would know what to do. She knew him better than anyone. She decided to make her way to the Kohl house, praying that Sara would be there.

Swollen eyed, tears still falling, she made her way across the fields to the Kohls, scarcely noticing the folk in the fields, who looked up questioningly from their tasks as she passed. The Kohl's woman answered the door and, po faced, directed her to wait in the hall while she went in search of Sara. She looked up as she heard footsteps.

"Frances, what on earth has happened to you? You look dreadful." And at the sound of a sympathetic voice, the tears started all over again, so that she was unable to relate the tale.

"Come." Sara took her by the arm and steered her into the lounge to her mother, who was seated near the French doors, reading.

"Sara, Frances?" Eva rose from her chair, crossing the room to them. Sara shook her head, indicating to her mother that she had no idea why Frances was in such a state.

"Sara, get a coffee, sweetened. Frances, come now, and sit here by me and tell me what has happened for you to be so upset and in such a state." Eva Kohl took control of the situation, her years of nursing coming into play. "Right, my dear, now take some deep breaths and then try to talk me through what has happened to cause your distress."

"It happened again. Like the night I was here. I am so sorry for what happened that night," sobbed Frances. "I spoilt your evening."

"Frances, it's all water under the bridge. Please don't stress yourself over that, it's all forgotten," said Eva, taking her by the hand.

"It was going to be such a special day today, and it happened again, and I've wrecked everything."

Sara returned to the room with the coffee and seated herself on the other side of the couch. Frances found herself between mother and daughter.

She told them of the day before, how she had learnt that Kristian had been ordered back to Kiel, and how she had kissed him and told him she didn't want him to go, and of how much she had wanted him. Of Willie ruining everything, by turning up at the stables where they were somewhat compromised, which made them all smile along with Kristian's reticence in spending the night with her under his parent's roof, which made Sara laugh outright, resulting in a warning glance from her mother.

Then she told them of the beautiful start to the day, how he had organised a picnic with champagne, and they'd walked and talked and chased across the fields to the clearing. Of how neither of them had been able to eat because of what was uppermost in both of their minds. She spoke of the kissing and caressing and how she had begged him to make love to her, and how he had sighed into her hair, and she told them how very much in love with him she was.

"And then, when we, when he…. you know," Sara and Eva nodded their understanding as Frances continued. "He said I've waited a long time for this. And that's what he said when he raped me. And then it wasn't Kristian anymore, it was him."

There was an intake of breath from both women. "My God, Frances, are you saying that Kristian raped you?" Sara asked in disbelief.

"No! No! of course not. Whatever made you think that Sar? Kristian would never do that!"

"You just said he raped you, my dear," said Eva, casting a look at her daughter.

"No, not Kristian. No, that was Otto." Sara took Frances's hand.

"Frances, who the hell is Otto?"

"My friend Otto. Only, well, he's not my friend anymore. It was at the Reichstag when I played for Adolf, with the men from Dachau."

"When was this, Frances?" asked Eva.

"Probably a little more than a month ago now. I don't know exactly. I'm afraid I've lost the ability to keep track of time with any accuracy."

"My God, Frances, I'm not surprised you freaked out. Kristian should have shown more restraint," said Eva.

"No, you mustn't blame Kristian. I thought… I love him so much; I wanted him so much. I thought it would be alright, and it would have been, you know. I lost control, got confused, forgot where I was, what was happening. But I think if he had given me time. Well, I think it would have been alright. He thought I had engineered the whole thing; you see. It's my fault. I have said some dreadful things to him. Told him some dreadful things. I felt at first when he found me that I needed revenge, not just for myself but for others. I see now that revenge is an ugly thing."

Eva patted her hand. "Does Kristian know about this Otto?"

"Yes, he knows Otto was the reason we left Paris. And I told him that Otto raped me the day we left Dachau; Otto turned up too, isn't that odd? That was the first time I lost it. Do you remember when we went shopping, Sar, and Kristian said I had a pistol? It's all so confused in my head. I sort of remember a fight, of being there but not really being part of what was going on."

"My God, I'm surprised Kristian didn't kill this Otto," said Sara.

"He told me he wished that he had. I could tell you both such tales. But that's the trouble, isn't it? It all sounds so far-fetched. I wonder if anyone will ever believe it all really happened. Is still really happening."

"What a dreadful coincidence, though," said Sara thoughtfully, "that Kris used the same words as Otto."

"Huh!" Eva interjected. "A coincidence. Do you really think so? I'll tell you what I think, and that's that men are born with one or two stock phrases implanted in their heads that they think every woman wants to hear."

Both Frances and Sara burst into laughter. Frances's laughter hovering on being hysterical. Sara grabbed her and planted a kiss on her brow. "See Froggy, you're laughing."

"Of course," Eva continued, "I can only speak of German men."

"Well, you've clearly had a very romantic time with Pops," Sara said through her laughter.

"I won't comment on that, Sara. Seriously though, Frances," said Eva, "I think you have been traumatised by what has happened to you, and that is why you are having flashbacks and these peculiar things that are happening to you. It happened during the last war with soldiers in the trenches. I came across it many times when I was nursing."

"Traumatised? So, does that mean that I'm mad, Eva?"

"No, it just means that a part of you is reacting in a certain way when something jogs an unpleasant memory inside of you. Like today, like with the Brauns." Frances frowned and shook her head.

"But will it go?"

"Perhaps. For some it does, and for others maybe not completely. What you need are coping mechanisms. You said earlier that you thought you would have been able to control the last one, which is very positive. I think understanding what is happening to you could make an enormous difference, my dear. Now I am going to call Peter and ask him to pick you up. What you need is a good sleep, my sweet.”

Eva left the room to make the call, leaving the two girls together and Frances turned to Sara, grabbing hold of her shoulders.

“I must find Kristian, Sar. Where would he go? Do you have any idea?”

“I wouldn’t be at all surprised if he wasn’t out looking for you at this moment. He’ll have calmed down. He doesn’t hold on to his anger for long.”

“No, I think this was the last straw. He’s put up with so much from me and I’m not sure he has ever had any deep feelings for me, anyway.”

“That’s rubbish. He married you and brought you here, didn’t he?”

“That was because of some man thing about giving his word, repaying some sort of debt, because he screwed me. He’s never mentioned feelings, you know, ever.”

“Have you?”

“I … I have, yes.”

“Lately?”

“Perhaps not lately. I’ve been so intent on wallowing in self-pity and hatred, haven’t I? And now I’ve destroyed the thing that’s really the most important. Oh! I’m so tired, Sar, so very tired.”

“Here,” said Sara, “put your feet up and close your eyes until Peter gets here.” She stood up, fluffing up a cushion at one end of the couch and lifting Frances’s legs up, fussing until she gave in and lay back, closing her eyes, immediately drifting towards slumber.

“It’ll be alright, Froggy, you’ll see,” Sara said softly as she left the room.

* * *

Peter Mueller arrived about half an hour later and was waved into the hall by Sara’s father Gunter. Sara and Eva joined the two men in the hall and Eva took Peter to one side.

“Peter, Frances arrived here in a dreadful state. I don’t know how much she has told you, but I believe the poor girl is traumatised.”

“Kristian has told us some of what she says she has been through but, well at times her behaviour has been... You saw for yourself, Eva. What would you call it? Difficult?”

“From what she has told us today, I would say understandably so.”

Peter Mueller shook his head. "What exactly has she told you, Eva? What do you think has happened to the girl?"

"The worst thing that could happen to a woman short of being killed, Peter, I would say."

"She's been abused, is that what you are saying?"

Eva Kohl nodded. "And not long ago. A matter of days before Kristian found her."

"Well, that explains a great deal, don't you think?" Peter said. He then filled them in too, informing them that Kristian had returned home and had immediately taken a car and driven into town. "He was in one hell of a temper and wouldn't tell us where Frances was."

"What time was that?" Sara asked.

"About five, I'd say. How long has Frances been here?"

"A couple of hours, maybe."

Peter Mueller shook his head. "We were hoping things would take a turn for the better. They seemed in such high spirits last night, and this morning when they went off together. What on earth happened?"

Eva Kohl raised her eyebrows. "Two young people, Peter, what do you think?"

"My God! Why couldn't Kristian be more sympathetic? He has pushed that girl into a… a liaison before she was ready. I am ashamed of him, Eva."

"Shush now. I shouldn't think Kristian pushed her into anything that she didn't want."

Eva and he made their way into the lounge with Sara and Gunter following. They found Frances dead to the world, curled up on the couch. Peter touched her gently. She reacted instantly, leaping up, eyes wide, repeating the number tattooed on her wrist and shocking them all. Then she recovered herself as she became aware and questioned, "Peter?"

"Frances, sit down, girl. Eva and Sara have told me some of what happened. I am so sorry. Sorry also for my son's lack of empathy and respect. He had no right, no right!"

"Please Peter, you're wrong. Today was my idea. Kristian is not to blame. He's been completely understanding. Never pushed me, always gentle. I thought… well, no matter what I thought."

He patted her hand as she sat down beside him. "This explains a great deal though, doesn't it, about what we talked about the other day in the paddock?"

She swept them all with a gaze, seeing the concern written on all their faces, because they understood she had suffered the physical indignity of rape. She wanted them to know, wanted them to have some understanding. Smiling at them, she shook her head and muttered.

"It's strange, isn't it how you think that someone forcing themself on me, taking my body, raping me, has caused what Eva calls this trauma? Let me tell you that in Auschwitz they raped us daily. Oh, not our physical bodies but our minds and souls, that's what they raped, repeatedly, over and over again. That is where this trauma has come from. But you can't accept that any of it could have happened, can you? Because it's outside any normal person's comprehension, and I understand that. So, I forgive you all for it."

She left them speechless and wandered over to the French windows, looking out onto what was a glorious evening.

"I think we need to give much more consideration to what Frances is saying, Peter," whispered Eva Kohl as Frances turned round from the window.

"This was to have been a beautiful day. I must make things right with Kristian before he leaves. Can we go home now, Peter?"

Chapter 15

Freya's first reaction was to totally blame Frances. She considered her unsuitable for her son. He needed someone steady and dependable, like Sara. It was not until sometime later, after a chat in the study with Peter, and a long telephone conversation with Eva Kohl, that she gained some insight into what her daughter-in-law had been through. Kristian had mentioned only wrongful arrest and internment, no mention of abuse or cruelty. She thought about it, wanting to believe that like the baby, it was some delusion of the girls, but Eva had more than half convinced her that maybe it was all true, and she was angry with Eva for that. It had been so much easier to believe that Frances was insane. Now she was being forced into considering the sanity of her homeland.

It was late, and still there was no word from Kristian. Peter talked the women into turning in for the night.

Sometime after midnight, they all heard a car draw up noisily in front of the house, and a couple of lads delivered Kristian home. They were on leave from the Wehrmacht and banged on the front door, quickly drawing away with a crackle down the drive before Peter could get to the door. He opened it to find his son propped up against the wall beside the door and just caught sight of the car speeding away up the drive.

Taking him under the arm, Peter steered Kristian into the hall with difficulty, taking most of his weight as he appeared unable to stand. Frances and Freya met on the landing and looked on with concern as Peter did his best to haul his son, who was having a problem focussing on them, up the first flight of stairs.

"He is alright, Peter, isn't he?" asked Freya, full of concern.

"Nothing wrong that sleep won't cure," he replied with a groan, as with a last effort, father and son made the final step.

Kristian pushed his father aside and reeled slightly before grabbing hold of the top of the banister to prevent himself from falling.

"I'm plastered, Mutti, smashed out of my skull." He gave her a drunken grin.

"Really, Kristian," Freya began, "I thought...."

~ 134 ~

"You're not going to lecture me, Mutts, are you? Shit! Surely a bloke deserves a drink... could well be dead...." His eyes caught sight of Frances. "Ah, there she is, look... my wife." He tried to focus on her, pointing his finger roughly in her direction. "I've been telling the lads about you. Bloody cock teaser, I told them, that's what you are."

"Kristian, for goodness' sake, watch your mouth, that's enough," warned his father. "Come on, let's get you to your room."

"Pffff, my room and my lonely little bed. Destined for that forever, am I, Frances, huh?"

Peter grabbed him under the armpit and tried to drag him to the flight of stairs that led to the next floor of the house, but Kristian stood fast, and without cooperation, it was hard to move him. He stared at Frances, trying hard to keep his eyes focussed on her, and then he turned his attention to his father.

"Pretty, Pa, isn't she, my wife?"

Peter Mueller nodded, "Yes Kristian, yes, Frances is very pretty."

"Hmm, I think so too. Got wolf's eyes, so you have to watch out though, Pa. Dangerous you see." He swung his gaze back to Frances briefly and then back to his father. "Bloody beautiful, that's what she is, isn't she, Pa?"

"Yes, Kristian, very. Come now, we will talk about this in your room."

They got to the bottom of the stairs leading up to the third floor and Kristian's room. He turned to cast another penetrating glance at Frances. Wagging a finger at her and shaking his head, he said, "You know what the trouble is with her though, Pa?"

"Suppose you tell me while we go up the stairs, son." Kristian nodded, and they took the first couple of steps and disappeared from the women's view. They heard, though.

"Look, but don't bloody well touch. Look, but don't bloody touch, hey Froggy?"

Blaming Frances for the state of her son and pushing to the back of her mind all that she had recently been told, Freya turned on Frances.

"Satisfied?" she said, turning her back and making for her room.

Frances woke with a start. Sod it, she thought. Why is it that when you are desperate for sleep it alludes you, and when you're desperate to stay awake you fall into a heavy slumber? She pulled her hand through her hair and rubbed her eyes. The sleep might have been heavy, but it had been fitful too. She had a thumping headache, and her eyes were still swollen from all the unaccustomed crying of the previous day.

She had intended to get up with the lark, to make amends with Kristian for the day before. She had even thought about sneaking up to his room in the night, but decided against that idea, as she didn't think that he would be in any fit state to be forgiving. Surely there would still be time. She knew that despite the skin full of drink he had the night before, he would be up early. There would be things he would want to do before he left, such as visit the stables, or even the Kohls.

She looked at the clock: 8:15 a.m. Hardly lark time but early enough to bathe and try to look something like presentable. Last night he had said that she was beautiful, and she didn't want to disappoint him on this, his last morning at home. She knew it could be months until she saw him again.

Briefly, the thought crossed her mind that she might never see him again. Germany was taking a bashing from the rest of Europe and on the Eastern front. There was an actual possibility that she could lose him. No! As quickly as that thought came, she dismissed it. She could not, would not, think of that possibility.

She bathed and dressed quickly and drew back the curtains, letting in the morning sunshine. Today was going to be another fine day. Looking out into the garden, it surprised her to see Kristian, already in uniform, speaking with his mother. She was about to move away from the window when she saw Peter join them. He took his son firmly by the shoulders and spoke to him for some time. Then she saw Kristian look briefly up towards her window and shake his head. He then walked back towards the house, followed by Freya.

Until that moment, she had not seen Freya clearly. Now she recognised the grief on the woman's face and realised that she had little time to spare. She fled from her room and down the staircase as Kristian was crossing the hall with a suitcase, heading towards the kitchen.

"Right, Rittershausen, ready when you are," he called.

She heard the reply from the kitchen, "Yes, Korvetten Kapitan." The young driver appeared at the double and disappeared out of the front door to the parked car. She wondered if Rittershausen had driven from Kiel through the night.

She watched the farewells in the hall from a couple of stairs up, standing back, not wanting to impose, waiting her turn. First, Kristian gave Anna a hug, and then took his father by the hand. The two men held each other's gaze until Peter Mueller broke it and grabbed his son in a firm embrace. Freya was standing back a little, dabbing her eyes with a handkerchief, desperately trying to keep control of her emotions, and not quite succeeding. Kristian chucked her under the chin as you would a child. "Come on Mutts, it will be all over soon, you see." She nodded and tried to smile at him through her tears.

"Promise me you'll be careful, Kristian. Please don't do anything silly."

"I'll be fine," he said, stepping away from her. Frances noted that there was no embrace.

He then ushered his parents and Anna towards the front door, and it was only then that Frances realised she was not on his list of farewells.

"Kristian, please, I have to speak to you." Her voice echoed across the hall, and he turned towards her, mock surprise on his face, as though he hadn't known that she had been waiting. She took the last couple of steps down, but as she did so, he turned from her and stepped outside to the waiting car.

She ran after him, calling out, "No, Kristian, please wait."

Chasing through the front door and across the veranda, she caught up with him as he bent his head to step into the Mercedes. She grabbed at his arm and pulled at it until he straightened up and looked down at her with something like pity on his face.

"What is it, Frances?" he asked tiredly.

"You can't just go," she sobbed.

"That's exactly what I'm going to do. The play has finished, Froggy, the final curtain has come down, and all the lines have been spoken."

She struggled to speak through her tears. "No Kristian, please don't go, not yet. Hold me, please, just for a minute."

He took out a handkerchief from his pocket and wiped the tears from her eyes, rolling into a ball and pressing it into her palm. "You must be so tired of all this acting, surely," he said quietly, and then he sighed and blew out his cheeks. "I don't want any more encores. I'm finished."

And with that, he was in the car with the door shut, giving the order to "Drive on."

The car crackled its way down the drive slowly, picking up speed as she cried out for it to stop. Cried out for him.

Chapter 16

The evening of July 20th, 1944, Brest

The mess hall was full. Every available officer had suddenly been called to attend a meeting, and each now was brimming with a mixture of confusion and anger. The reason was that Command had just received news that someone had made an attempt on the life of the Fuhrer.

Kristian Mueller gazed around at his fellow officers and wondered if any of them felt like him, that it was about time someone had a go at removing the sick fool, the one who had brought them now to the brink of defeat. He wished he were back with the old crew. At least there he would have been safe to give vent to his feelings. Best to trust no one here, he decided. You just didn't know who your friends were these days. Things had changed in Brest alright. It had come as quite a surprise when, within two or three weeks of returning to Kiel, he had received new orders to take him back there.

He had guessed that there would be quite a few changes, and he hadn't been wrong. Unlike some he was under no misapprehension as to how well Germany was doing. On top of the Allied landings on the north coast of France, there were the added setbacks in Greece. Rumania had joined the Allies; German forces had withdrawn from Rome and the Soviet armies were making a powerful offensive. And still the forces remained loyal, still thinking that Germany could win. He gave some thought to what the poor bastards who had been involved in the plot against old Adolf were going to be put through. An involuntary shudder ran through his body as he remembered the conversation a few weeks ago, when his father had warned him not to have any involvement in any such plot.

***

Deep into her practice time, the knocking on the door of her room irritated Frances. At first, she tried to ignore it, hoping that whichever member of the household it was who was trying to gain her attention would give up and wait for her to finish the sacrosanct daily five-hour session of practice, which had begun on the day Kristian had returned to Kiel.

She had felt utterly bereft on that day, as she watched the car crackle its way up the drive. It was taking him away from her. He had not given her the chance to make amends and had told her it was over, that he wanted no more of her. Struggling with her own emotions, she had eventually followed a tearful Freya and Peter back into the house. Kristian was her reason for being there, and now she was left with two people who, she thought, would probably prefer she was not there at all. Her own grief was private, and she felt she was encroaching upon theirs, so she crossed the hall to take herself to her room, catching sight through her tears of the violin case. It was still on the hall table, exactly where she had put it a few weeks before.

The familiar shape drew her towards it, as to an old friend, and as she opened it and took out the instrument, she breathed in the familiar scent of the wood. Putting its silky body to her chin, she found immediate solace. About half an hour later, the Mueller residence resonated to a heart-rending rendition of the Massenet Meditation, which drew Peter, Freya, and Anna to the bottom of the stairs to listen, with jaws dropped. As she played the final note, she remembered what Steven had told her all those years before, that she needed to play with more emotion, that being technically brilliant wasn't enough, and as she dried the instrument off from her fallen tears, she finally understood what it was that he had meant.

And so, along with the horses and Anna's kitchen, five hours' practice had become a much-loved part of her routine. Now, though, there was someone interfering with it. She snatched open the door to find an apologetic Anna.

"You need to go down to the study, Frances; Peter needs to give you some information."

She felt the blood drain from her; It had to be news of Kristian, but there was Anna calmly telling her that Peter needed to give her information, so surely it couldn't be bad news. She lay the violin on her bed and asked Anna if there was a problem, but Anna only repeated that she should go to the study. She left her room, running down the stairs and across the hall. Peter was listening to the radio when she knocked on the door. He turned it off as she went in.

"Ah, there you are. The music sounds wonderful, by the way. Come on, come on in and sit down." He ushered her to a chair.

She could tell that there was something bothering him. "What is it, Kristian, is Kristian alright?"

He nodded. "Yes, for the moment. There has been a plot to assassinate the Fuhrer, Frances, which I am afraid has failed."

She thought back to the conversation she had partially heard between father and son.

"He's not part of it, Peter, is he? I listened in at the door on a conversation you were having with him a few weeks ago. I know I shouldn't have, but I thought you were discussing me."

"Did you now? Then you know Kristian swore he wasn't mixed up in any plots."

"I struggled to hear some of what he said, but he isn't, is he? He was telling the truth, wasn't he?"

"Yes, I am fairly sure he's clean. They will have nothing on him, no worries on that front."

"But there are worries on another front, then?" she questioned.

"He's been ordered to Brest. We received a letter today. He must have sent it just before he left Kiel, so I am thinking he will be there already. He's been assigned another U-boat, Frances."

"They're putting him back out on patrol?" Her eyes were wide with disbelief.

"It looks that way. He obviously hasn't been able to tell me any details, but I suspect that with the way things are going, there will be some sort of big push."

"Did he send me any message, Peter? Did he mention me at all?"

"No, my dear, I'm sorry, no, he didn't."

"I see." She felt the tears prickling. "Can I go now?"

"Yes, yes, of course. Don't forget the riding later, huh?"

"No, of course not." She felt the tears flowing and turned away from him, making for the door. "I'll meet you at the paddock after lunch, then," she said, as she closed the door behind her.

* * *

Well, thought Mueller, Donitz the old dog still believed in the ability of his U-Boat boys to wage war in the channel and hamper the Allies. But to wage a war, you needed boats and men to sail them, and so they had recalled him to Brest, where he found there was neither. The once bustling Naval College lay almost deserted, dormitories lay empty, as did many of the pens. Fitting mausoleums, he thought, to those already gone.

Things in the town had changed, too. He found himself with his pockets full of francs but with nothing to buy in the shops, and with the Allied troops getting ever closer, the friendliness of the French was suspect. He thought of Frances and her very French total disregard for any of their feelings. She had given a victory whoop when he had informed her of the Allied landings. He shook his head, wondering what she thought was going to happen if the Allies made it into Germany. There was certainly no guarantee of safety now in Brest, and a curfew had been imposed, making sure that the Kriesgsmarine boys were promptly back to their quarters for the night. Madame and her girls would find their trade extremely hard hit. Thinking of the girls had made him think of Frances again, and he smiled to himself. She had done him a favour by totally putting him off women, for the time being at least.

The remnants of the great U-boat fleet had been laid to rest at Brest, Lorient and St Nazaire and plans were made for their defence. At Brest, the Naval College was to be the centre of it. The flotillas were dissolved, and preparations made. It was decided to try to get what remaining boats there were to La Rochelle or Norway, but veteran Kapitans that used to command veteran boats were scarce. Most of the training now was for the new schnorkel-fitted boats, which were supposed to be vastly superior, although in the months they had used them for fighting, their success had been questionable.

In June alone, twenty-two U-boats had been lost, with only five Allied cargo ships and two destroyers being lost. Mueller reckoned it was hardly because of a fault with the boats but due to the lack of training the young men who manned them were receiving. He had been hoping to try his hand at commanding one of these new crafts, but due to his previous expertise, instead he found himself assigned to one of the few remaining Class V11C boats. Ah well, he thought, at least they have decked the old girl out with a schnorkel.

By the end of July, things had rapidly deteriorated, and orders came for the U-boats to be evacuated. As the American Allied Forces moved in, the evacuation became more difficult, almost impossible, as destroyers surrounded the port of Brest, sealing off the U-boat escape routes. The U-boat force went to earth in their bunkers, and despite heavy shelling during the first part of August, the remaining few boats remained intact.

Various American units were advancing along the northern shore towards Brest and Donitz gave orders that all functional U-boats should make an exodus towards more Southern ports such as La Pallice and La Rochelle. From these two bases, he thought they might be able to continue with their war.

Mueller agreed with the decision. It made sense that only a complete idiot would attempt to get through the Allied offensive and into the Channel. He was somewhat aggrieved, therefore, when they singled him out to be that idiot. He received new orders to ferry half a dozen engineers over to Norway, which was to become the new U-boat centre. It hardly helped when Command reassured him, they had chosen him, as they thought he was the one person who had some sort of slight chance of getting through. Now that's a bloody poisoned chalice if ever there was one, he thought. He knew he was going to have to get through destroyers, aircraft, and mines, and with a young crew who probably had absolutely no idea of what was waiting for them.

His orders had told him to leave at his discretion. His discretion, though, told him not to go in the direction they had pointed him in at all. And so, he found himself explaining to his green crew the dangers of their mission, that they probably would not be able to break through the British blockade, and if they did, they would take the long route along the western coast of Ireland and up around the northern tip of Scotland. Then he ordered that no one should leave the boat and they should be on alert, ready to leave port at a moment's notice. He shook his head as he watched the young fools, who were clearly excited by the prospect of leaving. They thought they would escape the trap, and not be humiliated by death on land. The bonus was to serve under such a renowned Wolf as himself. At least keeping them on board would mean they would not be able to inadvertently let on that they were due to leave. The fewer people who knew, the better, he thought.

As in the old days, news somehow leaked out about his mission, and he found himself on the eve of his departure fighting off all manner of people looking for a way out of Brest. Colonels from the Wehrmacht, along with their mistresses, civil employees, collaborators, all offering him huge bribes if he would find them a place on his boat. A way of escaping that now certain defeat, the fall of Brest. He stood his ground and had none of it.

* * *

Frances woke from a deep sleep to find she wasn't alone. Freya Mueller was in the room with her, standing beside the bed gazing through her hard blue eyes, making her feel like a child caught in the act of doing something wrong, and maybe she had been.

She sat up on the bed and launched into some sort of idiotic apology. "I'm so sorry, Freya, I haven't done this before. I just felt the need to come here. I don't know why. I haven't touched anything."

Freya shook her head and fixed her with a stern look. "Frances, I know you have been coming in here regularly, and today, you have touched at least two things: the submarine toy and the photograph of Karin and Kristian. I know exactly where I put them yesterday after you moved them. I know everything about this room."

Frances felt herself colour under Freya's scrutiny. "You're right, of course. I'm so sorry. I come in here to be near him, to lie on his bed. I can smell him; I can feel him here. I should have asked permission. It won't happen again."

Freya sat on the bed beside her and surprised Frances when she took her by the hand.

"And why do you think you need permission to go anywhere in this house, Frances? This is your home, isn't it? For as long as you want it to be."

The two women held each other's eyes momentarily until Frances looked down briefly and then, lifting them back to search Freya's face, whispered, "Mutti?"

Freya Mueller nodded and then turning threw her arms wide open, and replied, "Daughter."

The two women embraced one another, tears running down both of their faces.

"I think you love him as much as I," Freya said, smiling through her tears. "We'll come here together and sit and talk. I can tell you all about my son, and you can fill in all the bits I don't know. As long as it's all decent, of course."

"I'd like that."

"Well then, that's what we will do. It seems for the moment, at least, I have lost a son but gained a daughter."

"He will be back, Freya; I know he will. You just see."

_* * *_

That day Freya and Frances formed a close bond which as time passed became closer still. Freya became a mother again and Frances a daughter. They both found that the other was a good listener, and over time, they were able to unburden themselves by discussing some of their darkest thoughts.

Freya spoke in depth of the loss of her daughter Karin and how badly it had affected her. She told Frances that in her darkest hour she had wished herself dead. "It was Kristian who saved me," she said. "Had he not been here, I would have had nothing to live for."

"He needs to know that Freya. He thinks you shut yourself away because you blamed him for Karin's death," Frances told her.

"He said that?" she asked.

"No, Sara told me but surely you knew."

"Yes, I suppose I knew but knowing is different than being told. If you are told there is a problem, there is more chance of you doing something about it. I suppose I pretended I didn't know. It was easier to deal with and I didn't have to blame myself. They should have told me. I have lost my son, Frances."

"No, no. Freya. Please don't look to blame anyone, yourself especially. I keep telling myself now that all that happened to me was through no fault of mine. Bad things happen to good people all the time. Maybe it's how we deal with it that is important."

"But I dealt with it all so badly, Frances. I locked Peter out and Kristian, though I never meant to. I now have a husband who sees me as weak, and I have totally lost Kristian."

"No, you haven't. He's still there. You just must talk to him."

"When the time is right."

"Most definitely wait until the time is right."

Tears gathered in Freya's eyes.

"What if I don't have the opportunity, Frances? What then? How will I cope with that?"

"You will speak to him. I know you will. Anything other is not open to discussion."

On one occasion whilst talking to Freya of the dreadful things that she had witnessed and experienced, and the evil that had pervaded those in Auschwitz and Dachau, Frances reached a conclusion that was to be the start of her healing process.

"You know the evil in those places, it rubbed off on us all. I don't think anyone could survive there for any amount of time and not be affected by it. People, good people became capable of carrying out atrocities and I don't mean just the guards, Freya. It was all about survival there. I had believed that in those circumstances I would have done anything to stay alive; now I'm not sure.

Others saw my leaving as an opportunity for me to take revenge, and I wanted to, goodness knows I did. I promised I would. I told myself it would be easy. I wonder about that now."

She took Freya's hand and looked into her eyes. "I had a pistol in my hand the day Kristian found me at Dachau, did you know?" Freya shook her head. "There was a fight. Otto and Kristian. It's all a bit hazy but Otto's pistol fell out of his hand, and I grabbed it. I had the perfect opportunity."

"You should have shot him," said Freya.

"Maybe. I believe I meant to. But I faltered and Rittershausen grabbed my arm and I shot into the air. For a split second something, some feeling, prevented me from using that pistol on Otto, and thank goodness, because if I had, I'd have used it on Kristian, too."

"But you didn't," Freya said, squeezing Frances's arm.

"No. Because I couldn't have lived with the guilt. It would have been my guilt; I would be to blame. It would be something I had done to myself. I see that now. That's the difference. All this shame and guilt I have been carrying is not of my doing. It's been loaded onto me by circumstances, Freya. And now I see that, I can start to let it go. What I was part of is not my fault, and it's not my fault that I survived, it's my strength."

Chapter 17

August 1944

How do you find a needle in a haystack? How could he find a safe course through the immense tonnage of Allied shipping surrounding the way out of the harbour at Brest, and pouring all over the Channel? Kristian Mueller knew he had one big problem. It was magnified by having a young, inexperienced crew that he didn't know from Adam, and six very nervous shipyard engineers. Tommy was making matters worse by broadcasting on their wavelengths and suggesting that they sail out under a white flag and give themselves up. He admitted to himself that seemed to be the most sensible option, and if he had been given a choice, he thought that's what he would do. He decided that the time had come before anyone should lose his nerve, himself included.

He went in search of the young chief, Frennsen. He had given the officers leave to go into town and found him in a small bar with a couple of petty officers from a different crew. The man had already impressed him by having the same regard to detail as his old chief on UBA Klaus Zeitler.

He gave Frenssen a friendly pat on the shoulder. "I thought I might have to go to the brothel to find you, Chief."

Frenssen gave a smile. "No, Korvetten Kapitan, not me. I'm a married man." Mueller ruminated on the information. The man didn't look old enough to be married.

"Any family, Frenssen?" he asked.

"Yes, sir, two."

Somehow that information made everything much worse, as Mueller wondered how many more of his young crew had children, wives or sweethearts waiting for them to return.

"Can I get you a drink, Korvetten Kapitan?" Frenssen offered.

"A beer then, but a quick one. We need to get back on board; there's work to be done. Let's get those batteries charged up, Chief."

* * *

The next morning, they slid surreptitiously from their pen, stern first, before it became light. The same fresh vegetables as in the good old days filled every available space on board, but Mueller couldn't help thinking that all similarities to the good days ended with the vegetables.

Only a handful of men were out on deck, just enough to handle the wires. There was to be no band, no fond farewells, and no escort vessel to give the game away. If they were to fail on this patrol, there wouldn't be anyone left in Brest to weep for them. And yet the sea breeze that lashed at Mueller's face was the same and it made the blood pulse through his veins as it did in the good old days. He was ready for action.

"Set course 280 degrees," he ordered.

The boat swung her bow around so that she was sailing headlong into the waiting blockade, offering them as small a silhouette as possible. Then came the wait, until the water was deep enough for them to dive. Until then, everyone on board prayed they wouldn't be noticed. Mueller said his own private prayer too, that he wouldn't be responsible for making any wrong decision that would lead to these fifty or so young men not returning to their loved ones.

Dawn streaked the sky.

"Clear the decks. Chief, take her down." Mueller closed the hatch and dropped down into the control room. Many of the crew along with the engineers had crammed themselves into it. The bow of the boat dipped as it made a graceful dive into the depths, and the excitement on board was palpable.

"Do you think they've seen us, Kapitan?" asked one of the engineers.

"They don't need to see us to know we are here," Mueller replied. "Now we keep quiet."

It wasn't long until they picked up the high-pitched whirring of the torpedo boats which crisscrossed above them, dropping grenades and depth charges at random, frightening the shit out of all of them. The order to keep quiet was quickly forgotten as men cried out like frightened children.

Mueller gave his next order. "Run silent, stay deep." And then working on intuition alone, he set course so that they were heading towards the northwest coast of Ireland. At low tide, the chief rested the boat on the sea bottom, some 80 metres down. They were forced to sit it out, whilst above them several destroyers circled, stopped, sounded, and dropped their charges, repeatedly making their boat buck and rear, throwing them into submerged rocks. Every man's nerves were on a knife edge and Mueller prayed again that he had got things right. That the ebb and flow of the current would give them the movement they needed to lift them over the uneven ocean floor. Seven hours later, the current reversed and headed out to sea, taking them with it. Gradually the whirring of the propellers above receded, and they realised with immense relief that they had made it through the Allied blockade.

The stench on board was unbearable: oil, grease, sweat, urine, and vomit; it was time to put the schnorkel into operation.

"Take her up to fourteen metres, Chief, switch on the engines," Mueller ordered.

Frenssen gave the order for the mast to be erected, and the valve on the schnorkel opened, allowing a rush of fresh air into the hull of the vessel.

Mueller was impressed. To run submerged on diesels that sucked in fresh air gave an entirely new slant on submarine warfare, and one to their benefit. He couldn't help feeling though that it had all come a little too late. If only those in Berlin had listened to Donitz and produced more of these boats at an earlier time, then the outcome of the Atlantic war could well have been very different, he thought.

"Korvetten Kapitan," the radio operator interrupted his reverie.

"What is it, Morgan?"

"Latest losses, Sir, from headquarters."

"Well?"

"U.B.V and U.B.G both lost in the Med."

"Whose boats?"

"Not sure."

"U.B.G is Kern's boat, isn't it?" cut in Frenssen, "and I think that U.B.V is the boat that Paul Werner had not long been assigned to."

Mueller felt the blood drain from his face. "Werner? Are you sure?" he asked.

"Fairly certain, Korvetten Kapitan."

"Shit! What do you know about the crew members, Morgan?"

"All hands lost, Sir."

"Shit!" he exclaimed once more. "The lot of them?" He received an answering nod from Morgan and so quickly took himself away from the control room, making for his berth, drawing the green curtain across for privacy. For the first time since his sister Karin had died, Mueller wept.

A couple of days into their assignment, the weather became inclement. Freak gales for August whip lashed the surface of the ocean; they struggled to make any headway and the schnorkel was difficult to use. On top of that, the valve became jammed in the closed position, quickly establishing a vacuum. As the diesel engines sucked all the air from the hull, every man was left gasping for breath.

The young chief acted immediately and gave the order to dive so that the schnorkel head was below the surface, in a vain attempt to loosen the sticking valve. Following that vain attempt, he ordered men to lower the schnorkel bearing mast. They agonised over the handles of the winch against the pressure of the water above them. Next, Frenssen gave the order to raise it again. Suddenly it drained noisily, and sea water spewed into the bilges as the float cleared with a crack, sucking fresh air back into the boat.

Mueller felt extreme pain as an eardrum burst and he swallowed madly to try to equalise the pressure in his ears. All around him, men fell to the deck plates, hands clasped over their heads, crying with the pain that was written on their faces. Within the hour, the valve had stuck again, and he had to make the choice between carrying on below and risking suffocation or surfacing and facing likely attack and destruction from some Allied aircraft.

Having little time to deliberate, he gave the order to surface and made for the Irish coast. Once there, hopefully they could hide in one of the many small inlets whilst one or two repairs were carried out. They surfaced and opened the hatch, cursing for once the hunter's moon, as this time it could well be themselves who became the hunted.

A couple of hours later, they reached the safety of the tip of the coast of Ireland, their only problem having been a reconnaissance plane, which they were almost certain hadn't seen them. As planned, they found a small inlet, a short distance along the west coast and Mueller set a course which took them into the shallows, and there they nestled among the cliffs in relative safety.

Mueller wanted the repairs carried out on the schnorkel in double time, in the hope that they might escape into the open sea before dawn broke. As it was, the repairs were completed a little later than he would have liked. He gave the order and the bow of the boat swung out and headed for the open sea. The sun was rising, shooting red streaks across the land behind them. As Mueller took up a position on the bridge, his knowledge of past assignments and the danger of being close to the coast made him uneasy. He would remain so, until they were further out and in water that was deep enough to allow them to dive.

"You men keep on your toes," he ordered, referring to the watch. "The rest of you down below, except you two, Kurtwiel, Ehmke, man the guns and, for God's sake, stay awake! Watch out for enemy aircraft."

He raised his glasses to his eyes and swept the sky, praying they would be out of the shallows before some keen-eyed young pilot could spot them. He was surprised and doubtful when some fifteen minutes or so later one of the lookouts gave the alarm. Round the southern tip of the inlet, scarcely a mile out, an Allied destroyer lay in wait. It was useless to go below; the water was still too shallow for them to dive. They would be caught only semi-submerged, and depth charged to Christendom.

"How did they know we were here, Korvetten Kapitan?" asked one of the watch lads.

"Must have been the plane initially."

"But to find us in the dark?"

"Hmm, Tommy has some sort of tracking device we can't pick up on our wavelengths. He's been sitting here for a while just waiting for us, you see," said Mueller.

"Has he seen us yet, do you think, Sir?" asked a second member of the watch.

"Possibly not, but he knows we're here alright. Both engines half power." He heard his order repeated down below until it got to the engine boys.

The engines spluttered as they lost power, and the boat slowed down, giving Mueller precious moments in which to think, though he knew already what his plan had to be. He silently cursed, knowing that there was only one way out for them, that they had scarcely a chance of making it, and that the lives of his crew were his responsibility alone.

Below, the men were hushed, waiting for his next order, praying that it would be the right one, hardly daring to take a breath. In the quiet, someone started to weep and suddenly the destroyer let them know they had been spotted by delivering a barrage of shells which forced Mueller into action.

"Watch, get below, full power ahead." He wanted as few men on the bridge as possible, the shells from the destroyer were getting dangerously close. Their only chance now was to run for the open sea, and there to dive and try to outmanoeuvre the destroyer under the water.

Mueller stayed on the bridge, and through gritted teeth gave the order, "More power! Verdammt, more power!" knowing that there was none to be had, and all the time the shells came dangerously closer.

The gunners were making a token gesture by firing at the destroyer, but their gun power against her made little impression. Without warning the bow of the boat suddenly leapt high in the air, throwing Mueller off his feet and into the rails. He cursed as the boat came to rest with the bow dipping slightly at a downward angle.

There were terrified cries from the young men below. "We're taking on water."

"God help us."

"Sweet Jesu."

"We're going to die."

Mueller knew that this time the game was up. They were finished.

He shouted down the voice tube, giving the order, "Abandon ship." An order he had never given before and had prayed he never would have to.

Making his way over to the main hatch, he held out his hand to help his men in turn as they fought to climb up the ladder from below. Most of them were scarcely into manhood and he saw the fear on each of the faces as they climbed out onto the deck plates. He felt their fear, too, and knew it was time to end all hostilities, then at least these boys would be picked up by the destroyer. There was a shout from one of the crew to get off quick, as from across the Irish coast came a Sunderland plane. It circled above them and then opened fire. Bullets tore into the metal casing of the boat and men screamed in agony as their flesh was torn from their bones and bones were torn from their bodies. Most chose the option to dive into the sea in a scramble to save themselves from the gunfire of the circling Sunderland.

"Bastards!" howled Mueller. "All of you, NOW! Get overboard, save yourselves!"

The remaining members of the crew threw themselves into the sea as the plane swept round for a second attack. Frenssen had taken Mueller by the arm. "Come on, you too, Sir." Mueller shook his head and made for the guns.

"Go!" he yelled the order to his chief, "I've got some unfinished business here. Those bastards could see we had ceased our attack." He made a grab for the guns and swung them round, aiming at the cockpit of the plane. "This one's for you, Paul," he spat.

He let go of a few rounds of ammo just as the plane fired along the casing, and as the bullets reached the gun placement, he felt a shattering, hot pain, searing into his left thigh as his leg gave way beneath him. Pulling himself up on to the guns, he cried out from the agony but was determined to finish the aircraft. He didn't need to bother. His previous attack had shattered the cockpit, blinding the pilot who sent the plane crashing into the ocean.

The destroyer renewed its attack on a boat that was visibly sinking. The bow was now dipping at an angle of twenty or so degrees. Despite his fear, Frenssen had not abandoned his Kapitan. Officers of his class were scarce. His commander was wounded, and their boat was about to go down; he acted.

Mueller was directing all his anger at the destroyer. Anger over the loss of his comrades, of a failed relationship, of a failed mission and a failed war. He had failed. As far as he knew, the boys on board had cleared the area around the boat and the destroyer was moving in for the kill. He fired on it indiscriminately, challenging it, unaware that his shots were falling well short of the target.

Frenssen grabbed at him a second time, and Mueller tried to shake him off, but weakened by his exertions at the gun and by the loss of blood, he failed.

First, he demanded that Frenssen leave him, claiming a Kapitan's right to go down with his boat. When that failed, he became abusive, forcing Frenssen to apologise before landing an uppercut to the jaw, which knocked him unconscious, giving Frenssen the break he needed to get him off the vessel before it sank. He pulled Mueller's head back and kicked off his heavy sea boots, before kicking off his own. Then he swam away supporting Mueller, as quickly as he could. The boat was in its death throes, and as it went down, it would create enough turbulence to drag men down with it. They got clear just in time, as the destroyer delivered a shell which hit the casing of the sub midships and broke it into two. As she sank, the boys in the water gave her a cheer, and Mueller, scarcely conscious, lifted his head just enough to see the last few feet disappear into the deep.

"How are you, Sir?" asked Frenssen.

"Striking a superior officer, Frenssen: I could have your arse for that," Mueller muttered weakly, and then lost consciousness.

Chapter 18

Late August 1944

"Come on, up you get." Peter Mueller extended his hand to help Frances up from the ground.

"I don't understand what I did wrong this time," Frances complained, taking his hand, and pulling on it to help herself stand.

"You just need to grip more with your thighs and give the horse her head as she makes the jump. If you hold her back, she'll make a mistake. You must trust her to get it right."

"I don't know why I have to go over those silly jumps anyway; they're only forty odd centimetres high."

"Like I said, it's to get you used to trusting the horse."

"I do trust her. It's me I don't trust. I'll never make a good horsewoman, Peter," said Frances with a frown as she scuffed her way across the menage to Majesty's side. She took the reins in her hands and, after giving the horse a pat, led her back over to Peter.

"Come on then, get back on," he ordered. Frances pulled a disgruntled face, and he answered her with a huge smile. He reminded her so much of Kristian at times.

"Can you at least give me a leg up please?" she asked.

"Only if you agree to do what we talked about yesterday."

"I can't not hold on. For goodness' sake, I fall off when I do." Peter grabbed her bent leg and hoisted her back onto Majesty's back.

"Trust, Frances," he said looking up at her seated-on Majesty. "Now use your thighs to tell her which way to go. Let go of the reins, cross your arms, and kick her on. Let her walk around the circle."

Frances did as he asked. She crossed her arms, casting Peter Mueller a withering look, and kicked Majesty on. The horse had done it all before and keeping to the edge of the menage she walked around the circle.

"Now kick her on a little more. Good. Well done. Now sitting trot."

Frances felt the power of the horse beneath her as it lengthened its stride and broke into a trot. She fought to maintain her balance with her arms crossed, as she was bounced around in the saddle all the way around the circle.

"Relax, girl," shouted Peter.

She completed one round of the circle and took the reins, pulling Majesty to a standstill as Peter walked over. "See you did it, well done. Go and ask Willie to take her tack off and I will see you back at the house." He walked over and opened the gate to the menage, closing it behind, as Frances and Majesty made their way back to the turnout paddock.

After leaving Willie to untack Majesty, Frances made her way to the back of the house. She opened the kitchen door and found Anna as usual making the days bread.

"Enjoyed that did you?" Anna asked, giving her a broad grin.

Frances gave her an answering scowl. "No, I'm rubbish." She grabbed a coffee from the pot on the range and sat down at the table with a groan. "Anna, my backside is killing me. I do believe Peter is a bloody sadist. If I don't leave the stables with at least a limp, he feels he's failed me."

"I don't know why you want to ride those animals anyway," Anna replied.

"You know why."

"I can give you plenty more to do here if you just want to keep busy."

"Yes, I'm sure you can but, I want to do it for... you know. When he comes home, I want to be able to do all the things he enjoys with him. I have so much making up to do." She took a sip of her coffee and felt the now accustomed tears spring to her eyes. "He hasn't mentioned me in any of his letters, Anna."

Anna crossed the kitchen and wrapped her arms around Frances's shoulders, in a warm embrace. "Come, child, dry your eyes. No man is worth the river you've wept these past weeks."

Frances looked up and met Anna's eyes. "Not even your favourite boy?" she asked.

"No not even my favourite...."

The door was thrust open, and Freya was framed in the doorway.

"Frances, there you are. Come. There is news."

"Of Kristian?" Frances leapt to her feet, all pain and tears forgotten.

"No, not of Kristian, of France. We are listening to the news in the study. Come. You too if you like, Anna."

Anna wiped her hands down her pinafore and all three women made their way to the study, where Peter had managed to tune the radio in to a broadcast.

"What is it, Peter?" Frances asked.

"Paris has been liberated, Frances." It took a few moments for the news to fully sink in.

"When?" she asked.

"A couple of days ago. Brussels too it seems." He turned the tuning knob on the radio causing it to screech until he found the latest German news. Goebbels was spouting his usual propaganda, referring to the latest German miracle weapons that were causing apocalyptic damage to the Allies. "Damn fool," snapped Peter. "The only forces causing apocalyptic damage are the Allies, for God's sake. Look at Berlin and Cologne and goodness knows how much more damage the RAF will do to our cities before this war is over." Freya moved to his side and put a hand on his shoulder and gave it a rub. He looked up and gave her a weak smile.

"What are you thinking?" she asked.

"I'm thinking it's time to throw in the towel my dear. I always thought the coalition between Russia, the United Sates and Great Britain would fall apart. I always thought there were too many conflicting beliefs. But it seems I was wrong, they're as strong as ever. Perhaps it's time to surrender. It's certainly time to get rid of the madmen who are running and destroying our country. If they have their way, there won't be any German males left for you girls."

"What do you mean?" asked Anna.

"I've heard talk of a Volkssturm Militia."

"A what?" the three women asked in unison.

"They are saying that all males between sixteen years and sixty and who are not serving in the regular Wehrmacht will be called up to defend our country. It will be run by the Party they say, not the Wehrmacht, which in itself is a worry."

Freya threw her arms around Peter. "Then thank goodness you are sixty- two. I couldn't bear them to take you away, as well as Kristian."

"There's been no mention of this militia on the news, at least if there has, I haven't heard it," Anna said.

"It's not been generally talked about as yet," said Peter, "But take it from me it will happen."

"So, our Great Reich will be relying on babes and old men to save it," said Freya. "What on earth will become of us, Peter?"

"Sadly, my dear that will depend on the madmen I fear," he replied.

* * *

In her bed that night, Frances thought back over the weeks since Kristian had left for Kiel. He would be in Brest now, she thought, or even back out on patrol. That thought troubled her. As Peter suspected, the dreadful reaction to the traumas she had suffered had lessened since she had found ways to keep busy. The riding with Peter, the cooking with Anna and the talks she had with Freya had all helped, and it was also heavenly to be holding a violin again.

Could she turn her life around? Here? Now? She had survived the camps and was now living what amounted to a good life, with people she would at one time have thought of as the enemy. She had made promises some months ago and had found she couldn't keep them. It crossed her mind that fate could seek to punish her for that.

Chapter 19

Mueller learnt from his captors that he had been in the water for about three quarters of an hour before being picked up by the enemy destroyer. He could remember little about being in the water, apart from feeling morbidly tired and wanting to just let go. If Frenssen hadn't held on to him, he was certain he would have thrown in the towel and delivered himself to the deep. Fifteen of his men had been lost, including four of the six shipyard engineers. He had no idea what had become of the rest of them, and he knew that because he had carried on with the attack, they were lucky that any of them had been picked up.

Because of his wounds, Mueller had found himself hospitalised and back in France, though he couldn't find out exactly where in France. He was left on the ward to recuperate for a few weeks. The wound to his thigh was not good. He had lost a great deal of blood, and his femur was shattered. He was patched up well enough though, by a confident and experienced doctor, and the nursing was nothing he could complain about either. All in all, he was being treated well. The nurses often spent the time of day with him, though they would not give him news of the war or information of his whereabouts. They denied him any useful information.

When awake, most of his thoughts were of Schonen Felder. He wondered if his family were still managing to stay reasonably untouched by the war, and whether they had been informed of his failed mission and his whereabouts. During those thoughts of home, he was unable to keep thoughts of Frances out of his head. He dwelt on whether it had always been on her mind to play him for the fool as she had.

When their relationship had first begun on board UBA, he felt he had the upper hand. He had always been able to read a woman. But not her, and not now. She had tied his emotions into knots, so that he didn't know whether he was coming or going, never mind what she was thinking or feeling.

Late one morning, whilst having such thoughts, a young French nurse ordered him into a wheelchair and pushed him along stark corridors, eventually stopping in front of an office door. She knocked on it smartly.

"You can leave me now," he said curtly. He was embarrassed, and annoyed that when coming face to face with the enemy, as he surely was going to, he was having to rely on a woman for help.

"I most certainly cannot leave you, Korvetten Kapitan Mueller," she replied crisply, leaving him no room for argument.

Before he could dispute the fact any further, a British officer opened the door. Mueller set his jaw and pushed himself to his feet, fighting to stand, grimacing from the pain. The man extended his hand, taking Mueller by surprise.

"Colonel John Franklyn," the man introduced himself and grinned through a heavy moustache. "Please, sit down, old chap, before you do yourself some more damage."

"He probably has already," complained the nurse, pushing Mueller firmly back down into the wheelchair.

"It's alright, nurse, you can go now. I can take care of Kapitan Mueller, and I promise to return him to his bed after we've had a chat," said Franklyn. He wheeled Mueller into the office and pushed him over towards a large desk at the far end of the room. Then instead of seating himself behind it, as Mueller expected him to do, he drew up a chair close to him.

"This is cosy," jibed Mueller.

Franklyn chose not to respond; he had been in the army for a good while and had a good understanding of what it must feel like to be taken prisoner. "Drink, cigar?" he offered.

Mueller wasn't expecting that. He didn't know exactly what he had been expecting, but it certainly had not been the offer of a drink and a cigar. He was immediately on his guard and slowly nodded, setting Franklyn with one of his looks.

"You'll get nothing from me," he said.

"Well, I don't suppose there's anything you can give us we don't know already, Mueller," replied Franklyn. "Look, this is run-of-the-mill stuff, no need to feel threatened. I question all of you officer Chappy's, it's common form you know. To be quite honest, we already know a good deal about you all, anyway." He held out the box of cigars. "Here."

Mueller took one, thinking that the man Franklyn seemed to be a decent sort. He would have to wait and see though. He was after all the enemy. Franklyn leant forward with the lighter.

"And a drink, Kapitan. What can I get you?" he asked.

"Brandy, thank you."

"So, Korvetten Kapitan, I understand that you and your men were picked up off the Irish coast."

Mueller nodded as he took a long leisurely drag on the cigar, savouring it before exhaling.

"I don't suppose it's any use asking you what your mission was," continued Franklyn.

Mueller thought for a moment and decided that telling the truth was hardly going to damage the German war effort. After all, the engineers involved were dead, or captured, like himself. He hoped that if he cooperated, then Franklyn would give him information in return.

"I was trying to get a few shipyard engineers to one of our new bases in Norway."

"From where?" asked Franklyn.

"Brest."

"Good God, man," said Franklyn with surprise, "How the devil did you get through our blockades?"

"With difficulty," Mueller said wryly. "We'd have made it too if it hadn't been for our damn schnorkel giving us problems."

Franklyn thought for a moment and then rewarded Mueller with another grin. "Well, Kapitan, it seems you've passed the test. Your story ties in nicely with the one that your men have given us."

"My men, you've questioned them? Where are they?"

"Long gone, I'm afraid. They'll be well settled into some camp or other by now. Another few weeks and you'll be off, too."

"To a camp? Behind wire?"

"Now we can hardly have you making a nuisance of yourself on the streets now, can we?"

"You'll not keep me behind wire," snapped Mueller.

"I guess that could well be the case. But look, Mueller, if I were you, I would just accept things the way they are. You've survived the war this far, and it can't last much longer."

"What makes you so certain?"

"We've made tremendous advances; your lot are on the run, I'm afraid."

"Just in France?" asked Mueller, hardly surprised by the news.

"On all fronts, old chap. You know that your man Choltitz has surrendered Paris?"

Mueller shook his head lamely. It was all much worse than he thought, and he wondered what damage they had done to that beautiful city.

"When?" he asked.

"End of August."

"Bitter fighting?"

It was Franklyn's turn to shake his head. "Old Adolf gave the orders for the lot to be destroyed; thankfully Choltitz disobeyed."

"Well, thank God for that, at least."

"You know Paris then?" Franklyn asked.

"No, not well. One or two visits, but my wife is from Paris, you see."

"You're married to a French girl," remarked Franklyn. "That must have caused you one or two problems."

Mueller nodded, unable to prevent a smile from creeping across his face. You can say that again, he thought.

"Do you play chess, Kapitan?" asked Franklyn.

"Not for some time, but yes."

"Jolly good. How about a game now then? I get bloody bored to tears here, I can tell you."

Mueller nodded his acceptance; after all he should make the most of his time in hospital. Soon they would put him behind the wire. Franklyn moved his chair back and placed a small table between them for the board. For the next three hours, both men forgot about the war and drowned themselves intellectually into the game.

Mueller impressed Franklyn: he watched him closely before each of his moves. The man didn't rush anything, thinking each move through, and the consequences each would have. Despite being an adequate player, he felt he was being toyed with, and that Mueller could have drawn the game to a close by winning whenever he chose to. And then suddenly there it was, he was the winner, and Mueller had made a move which could only be described as thoughtless.

Mueller gave a sniff. "Well, there you are, Colonel. Well, played, I had forgotten how enjoyable a game of chess could be."

Franklyn stood and moved to the back of the wheelchair. "Right, old chap, we'd better get you back to the ward or that nurse will have both our heads. I'd like another game or two, Mueller, if you're up for it while you're here," he said, manoeuvring the wheelchair out into the corridor and making back for the ward.

Mueller nodded. "Haven't got much else in my diary."

"Tomorrow then, early evening. Only next time don't let me win, eh? We're winning the bloody war, you know, so I don't mind losing to you at the odd game of chess."

Mueller grinned. He liked Franklyn. "I'll look forward to it, Colonel. By the way, can I write a letter home to let my family know I'm still alive?"

"You can certainly do that, Mueller, though whether it will ever reach your home, God only knows."

"And where should I tell them I am?" Mueller asked.

Franklyn gave a sharp laugh and said, "Good try. Just tell them you're in hospital. They'll be happy to know you're still alive, I should think."

Chapter 20

September 18th, 1944.

The day Brest fell to the Allied troops, they transported Mueller to a prisoner of war camp. He'd foolishly hoped the camp would be a British one, and Franklyn had hinted that it could be. He was handed to French guards though and herded onto a cattle truck with thirty odd other men, who had received some sort of injury and were now considered fit enough to be incarcerated.

He sat himself in the corner of the truck and considered his travelling companions. Men of the Wehrmacht mostly enlisted. He was the only naval man amongst them. At the start of the journey, a few of them had talked of escape, but they'd all been threatened with serious reprisals should even one of them get away, and so they found themselves guarded by their own comrades. He would bide his time and talk to no man of his plans. He would make no friends, it didn't do. He figured if he had no relationships, then whatever happened, there would not be any guilt. This was war, after all, and people got hurt. That's what he'd told Frances many times.

Frances! He shook his head and gave a humourless laugh inside. Wouldn't she just love to see him now? He could almost believe that she had wished this upon him. He'd bloody well make sure he got back home just to wipe the smile from her lovely face. He thought back to the day he'd left. She had cried out to him, begged him to hold her. Another of her tricks? He shook his head to rid her from his thoughts. It didn't work and he wondered if she would still be at home if he made it back. There was nothing to keep her there. Rightly or wrongly, he'd made sure of that.

During the first weeks he had returned to Kiel, her letters had come fast and furious, and he'd returned them all unopened. Then she had stopped writing. He wondered now what those letters had said. He had driven away leaving her, so his parents had said in their letters, distraught. Had she been? Wasn't it all an act? She had taken up her violin the day he left, they told him, and the music she had played had left them all bereft. He wondered how much thought they had given to how he had felt, and then felt guilty for thinking it. He wondered how they were all coping. What was the latest news of the war that they had received through the radio transmissions? Were the messages from Fuhrer headquarters still of outstanding victories, or did they think it was now the time to tell the truth?

"Pfennig for them?"

A man stood before him, somehow keeping his balance, as the truck trundled along the bomb torn road. He wore the uniform of a Kapitan in the Wehrmacht, and Mueller guessed he was perhaps five years his senior.

He met the man's steady gaze. "Eh?"

"I've been watching you deep in thought. What are you thinking about? A way out?"

Mueller was immediately on his guard. He held onto the man's gaze. "Would I tell you if I were?"

"Not if you're a sensible fellow." The man gave a broad smile and held out his hand. "Eddy Fackler. Fancy a travelling companion, at least?"

Mueller refused the offer of a handshake but nodded to the space beside him. "If you're hard-up, sit here, but I warn you I make lousy company."

The journey was slow and by the end of eight hours the cart stunk, and Mueller had found a new friend in Eddy Fackler. They disembarked at a station. Mueller had been trying to monitor any station or village signs that they passed and reckoned they were not too far from Paris. French guards prodded them into two lines of officers and enlisted men together and then they were force marched some three miles outside the town. By the end of the march, Mueller was relying on the skinny frame of Fackler for support, the wound on his leg having reopened.

The camp was just a transit camp, temporary. It was vast, crude, and totally uninviting, hardly Geneva Convention. A series of cages, each containing inadequate shelters, the whole being encircled by a barbed wire wall and machine-gun watch towers. The men from the truck were separated into officers and enlistees, issued with food tickets, and then assigned one of the cages, each of which housed hundreds of prisoners.

Mueller had found in Fackler a like-minded spirit and the first thing the two of them did was to take a stroll around the perimeter of the cage looking for weaknesses which would give rise to ways out. They were disappointed. There was nothing obvious. Escape would not be simple. They discussed bribery. Fackler had hung on to his watch, but the guards appeared to be beyond reproach. The prisoners they were guarding had an enormous debt to repay, and a watch certainly wouldn't do. They would take their pound of flesh for sure.

Chapter 21

October 1944

"My God, my God. Freya are you there?" Peter Mueller made a noisy entrance, slamming the door on the ravages of the outside world in a vain attempt to leave them behind him. It was late evening and Freya was ready for bed. She wrapped a gown around herself and made for downstairs. As she passed the front bedroom Frances stuck her head out.

"What on earth is going on, Freya?" she asked.

"Just Peter, home late, that's all. I do wish he would tell me if he wasn't going to be back for dinner."

"It's unusual for him to be back this…." Frances's comment was cut short as Peter shouted for his wife once again.

"Freya, where the devil are you?" The two women looked at one another. It was unusual for Peter Mueller to raise his voice except at the dogs. They made their way down the stairs and found him pacing up and down in the lounge.

"What on earth is wrong?" asked Freya, taking his arm, and leading him to one of the couches. She sat him down and herself beside him. Frances took the chair across from them.

"I've had some day I can tell you," he said.

"Please do. You'll be waking the Kohls up if you make much more noise," said Freya, patting his hand.

"I don't think I'll be going to Bonn again for some time, my dears," he said addressing Freya and Frances. "I think it's time to put business on hold for a while."

"What's happened?" Frances asked.

"Aachen is what's happened. There's one hell of a battle taking place there. I'm surprised we can't hear it here. It started a few days ago, so I guess the wind has been blowing in the wrong direction. I bumped into Fritz; you know." Freya shook her head. "Yes, you do. Fritz, God, what's his damn name?" His hand tapped the arm of the couch in agitation.

"Fischer," he said eventually. "Fritz Fischer, he lives just outside Duren." Freya still shook her head. "Well never mind if you know him or don't know him, it only matters that I do, and I bumped into him today."

Frances smiled as Freya said, "Well done. So, bumping into Fritz Fischer is why you are making such a noise."

"For goodness' sake, woman." It was unusual, Frances thought, for Peter to snap at Freya. Something had clearly upset him. She decided it was best to ask him outright.

"Peter, what's happened today? I have never seen you so worked up." He whipped his eyes to her; she could see the anger in them. As he looked his eyes softened. He took a deep breath and sighed.

"We have the war on our doorstep," he said, "Our beautiful city of Aachen will be torn down by the American Allies. Our troops are no longer the Nazis, though thank God for that. They are now just German soldiers fighting to protect their homeland."

"And perhaps it's about time," muttered Frances and immediately wished she hadn't. As Peter turned his tired eyes upon her, she felt herself flush.

"Perhaps it is, Frances," he said. "If defeat is the only way to prevent thousands more deaths and bring my son back home, then I for one will relinquish what little patriotism I have left." He gave a sardonic laugh. "The stupid thing is that Aachen could have been saved. Fritz told me that Von Schwerin, who was commanding the Panzer division, was all for leaving the city to the allies. He could have saved it and its people. Of course, our illustrious madmen in charge had him arrested." He pulled his fingers through his hair. Just like Kristian, Frances thought. "Where on earth will this all end?" he sighed.

"Shall I get us all a coffee?" Frances suggested, looking for an excuse to leave the room.

"Oh, please," said Freya.

* * *

October went from bad to worse at Schonen Felder, and as the month deteriorated, so did Peter's temper. The battle in Aachen resulted in the German troops refusing to surrender and the American commander carrying out what had been his ultimatum. The city was bombed to the ground. For three days Aachen was shelled by American troops and bombed by their air force. By the end of the battle, on October 21st, eighty seven percent of Aachen had been destroyed.

Three days following the fall of Aachen, Peter Mueller was working in the study with the Volkemfanger radio playing classical music in the background, when he was interrupted by Freya, clutching the day's newspaper and clearly in a state of shock.

"Whatever is wrong? You look ashen, Freya." He crossed the room to her and placed a protective arm around her shoulders. "Come, sit down."

"Have you seen it? Do you know about this atrocity?" she asked, waving the paper in his face.

"I've been busy, so I haven't got round to looking yet." He led her to a couch near the fireplace and seated himself next to her. Freya placed the newspaper on her lap and pointed to a photograph on the front page.

"See, Peter, see what happened at Nemmensdorf three days ago? Those Russian brutes have raped and murdered all these people, and some were only children. We are not safe here anymore."

A shudder ran through Peter as he looked down at the photograph of the corpses of women and girls with their dresses pulled up as if they had been raped and left there.

"What are we to do, Peter?" Freya asked through the tears which had started to fall.

"Nothing for the moment, my dear. It's unlikely that the Russians will get to us before the Americans or British do. We must pray that remains the case. I suspect that fool Josef Goebbels will use this to his advantage. He will use it to terrify our people into putting up greater resistance and will spread even more hatred. I don't know about you, Freya, but I am beginning to feel my age. I am so tired of all of this."

"We need Kristian to come home," said Freya.

"Yes, my dear we do." They placed their arms around one another and found solace in the nearness of one another.

Chapter 22

After almost two months in the camp on little more than starvation rations, Mueller decided that if they were going to make a break for it, then it had to be soon. He could see that Fackler's cheeks were now hollowed out and knew that his own would be the same. The filthy remnants of their uniforms hung on them, so that they were little more than a pair of walking scarecrows. They both knew that if they left things much longer, they would not have the strength or the energy to escape. Also, the condition of Mueller's leg was worsening, there now being several oozing sores.

They had spent the last few weeks sitting for most of the day in a corner of the cage, talking and loosening the soil with their bare hands and a small spoon they had hidden about them. Mueller learnt that Fackler originated from Nuremburg. He had married his childhood sweetheart, but she had died in childbirth, leaving him with a daughter to bring up.

"So, the child is in Nuremburg with your family then?" Mueller asked.

"Hah, would you want your child to be brought up in Nuremburg, Mueller?"

"No."

"No, too bloody right. She'd have been a Nazi before she could walk. No, she is with Annalise's family just outside Berlin."

"Do you see her? Does she have a name?" Fackler sighed, and Mueller felt his friend's sorrow, plus a little guilt for possibly asking too many questions.

"We named her after her mother, and yes, I see her, though not often enough because of this bloody war."

As they dug and talked, they developed their plan to escape.

Their plan was that when the time came, they could remove the loosened soil easily and slip under the cage and into the corridor between theirs and the next cage. Using this route over the last few nights, they had taken it in turns to snake and push their way across the floodlit ground to the first perimeter fence, a barbed wire roll. Finding a position mid-way between two gunners and in the shadow of a post, they had bent and twisted the wire with their bare hands until they bled, and they reckoned they now had space enough to wriggle through.

On this day, they had both taken up their usual position in the cage's corner, watching the antics of their compatriots with interest. Intelligent men, Germany's best. Many were now reduced to little more than animals, relying on their instincts to stay alive. Mueller was glad he had found a friend in Fackler. They kept each other sane. There were few of the others he would trust. Men would thieve and lie for an extra crust, and as well as these men, there were still the fanatics and the deviants.

Often Fackler would curse the French for their maltreatment, and Mueller would tell him the tales that Frances had told him of the place Oswiecim. Like him, Fackler found its very existence difficult to accept, never mind the list of atrocities she had said had taken place there.

"No," argued Fackler, "civilised people don't behave like that towards one another."

"What about our treatment here?" Mueller argued back. "A few weeks ago, I thought all I had to dread was barbed wire. Look around you, Eddy. We're all becoming animals just like she said. Don't you think they would kill us if they thought they could get away with it?" He sighed. "God, I'd rather be put to work than just bloody idling here. They might at least give us more food, eh? Perhaps we should ask for a transfer. What do you reckon? Bastards!"

Fackler was still thinking over Mueller's comments about Frances. He blew his cheeks out. "What the hell did you get involved with that woman for anyway? You should have left things alone when you got back to Brest from that patrol. Instead, you made some bloody stupid promise and look what you've ended up with."

Mueller shrugged. "You're right, I should have had more bloody sense, shouldn't I? My God, I bet she would love to see me now though, eh? No need for her to take revenge, these bastards have done it for her. Well, it stops here. I've done more than my bit as far as she is concerned."

A small group of men halfway across the cage caught his attention. They were newcomers and wore the black SS uniforms, which were still clean, and under a thin layer of dust, boots were still shining. One of them seemed familiar to Mueller, and he wracked his tired brain for recognition.

"Otto!" he snarled, making a bid to stand up, but Fackler's arm restrained him.

"What is it?"

"There's a man over there. There's something I need to ask him."

Fackler was worried by the look on his friend's face. He didn't know what Mueller wanted to ask the man, but he knew for certain that one way or another, he would get an answer. He could see the chance of escape evading them if he didn't step in. The Froggies would have no truck with fighting, and Mueller would find himself in solitary and all their efforts would count for nothing.

"Leave it alone, Kristian!" he warned.

"The devil I will! I told you I need to talk with the man."

"Talk to him?" questioned Fackler. "By the look on your face, I'd say you want to kill the bastard." Mueller averted his gaze and Fackler knew he was right. "Have that talk to him tonight, Kris, away from prying eyes. How about we both talk to him together, eh?"

* * *

Fackler showed himself to be a smooth talker and conned Von Liechtenstein. He told him that there was a prisoner of some importance who wanted to speak to him in private, regarding a serious matter that he thought a man of his calibre could help with. "The arrogant arse hadn't suspected a thing," Fackler told Mueller. "I said this important officer had clearly already recognised the talent in him and there might be a bit of money to be made."

Later that evening, Mueller waited for them behind one of the shelters. There was some cloud cover. It was dark and cold. Very few others were out, most having already sought some night-time shelter. The compound was only dimly lit, the only bright lights being from the sentries' searchlights which constantly swept the camp perimeter.

Expecting to meet up with a high-ranking party member, Otto was visibly taken aback when confronted by a bearded wild man who demanded to know the truth. The pent-up anger and the remnants of a naval uniform were the giveaway.

"Mueller," he smirked, "don't tell me everything in the garden isn't rosy."

"You might say that" hissed Mueller. "What I want to know is what you had to do with that. Did you or didn't you rape my wife?"

"Oh, so you are now doubting the lady?" parried Otto. "I told you she's a madwoman."

"Maybe. So?"

"Why should you believe what I tell you?"

"Your side of things. Come on, that's all." said Mueller.

Otto gave a harsh laugh. "Oh, I think it's going to be much more fun if I keep you in the dark. Let you guess what happened, eh?" He turned and began to walk off. Mueller leapt on his back and toppled him to the ground and the pair rolled around in the dirt until Mueller managed to get to his feet and yanked Otto up with him.

"I should have killed you when I had the chance," he spat.

"Leave it, Kris," said Fackler, putting a hand on Mueller's shoulder. "He's shit, he's not worth it."

Mueller was beside himself with anger. Fackler could see the tautness in his body which appeared to be in danger of snapping. As he made another move towards Otto, Fackler gripped his shoulder hard.

"Let the bastard go Kristian." Mueller looked at him and nodded, and Fackler relaxed his grip as Otto walked away. After several steps, he turned and with a sneer said, "I gave it to her hard, Mueller, and enjoyed every thrust. She did too."

In an instant, Mueller was on him again. "Just one, you bastard, just one," he muttered, as he extended his fist into Otto's sneering face.

Otto Von Liechtenstein reeled against the blow, stumbling back towards a shelter, and as he fell, he caught his head on an iron post. Momentarily, Fackler and Mueller froze, then Fackler approached the recumbent body. The seriousness of the injury to Otto's head was obvious from the plentiful amount of blood which had already pooled beside him. He knelt and felt for a pulse. "Christ, Kristian," he said, "the bastard's dead."

That is why they were forced to escape before they were ready. They had to get out before the body was found. Luckily, no one from the shelter bothered to even come out to see what the racket was. They probably would rather not know, thought Mueller, who felt a transient guilt, not for Von Liechtenstein, but by the thought that someone, somewhere, probably loved the bastard, or at least depended on him.

Fackler said that from the sound of things Otto had deserved to die anyway, and so between them they dragged the body to the shithouse.

"A fitting place for him," Fackler said.

There they propped him up with his trousers round his ankles, hoping he'd not be missed until morning, and that anyone took short in the night would think the body was just part of the shithouse furniture.

Now they had to go. The camp commandant was not a man to be trifled with. There had been a movement in the shadows and maybe it was dark enough for them not to be recognised, but Mueller thought they shouldn't take the chance. The commandant would enjoy making an example of them.

They both knew that the escape attempt was a little too soon, that they were not quite ready. At first, Mueller tried to talk Fackler into letting him give himself up. That way at least Fackler would be safe, but Fackler insisted they were mates, and that they had both acted together. They then both decided that it was better to be shot than strung up as murderers.

The first part was easy. They had prepared their way well, over the last few weeks. After shifting the soil to the side and squeezing under the compound fence, they snaked their way across the hundred metres to the first perimeter fence, and the huge spiral of barbed wire. The gap in it was just enough, and they pushed their way through that easily. Now they had to make their way to the outer fence, again across some hundred metres of open land. The outer fence sentry towers were set midway between the inner fence towers so that now, there were towers closer together. They adopted the same plan to go midway between two towers and belly their way across the gap to the outer fence. They thanked God that it was a dark and overcast night. For the seconds that the searchlight beams were directly on them, they froze and lay low until they passed over. Then they writhed and squirmed a few feet more towards their goal.

Even though the air was icy cold, by the time they had covered the hundred metres, they were dripping with sweat. Once they had made it to the outer perimeter fence, again, they lay low, catching their breath and desperately trying to formulate a plan. Given a few more nights, they would have loosened the earth here too and replaced the turf, then when the time had been right, they could have simply removed it, slipped underneath the fence, and crawled away to the safety of the woods, which were some five hundred metres away from the camp. As it was, there was no time for this. Removing the turf and enough soil with only their hands as tools and in frozen conditions was several nights' work. They had to move fast and put as much ground as possible between the camp and themselves before dawn.

"There's only one way out as I see it," said Mueller.

"Over the top," agreed Fackler. "Those guards would have to be blind not to see us."

"Go back, Eddy. You'd be a fool to come along. Go back and tell them about the body and about me."

"Not bloody likely. I thought we'd already had this conversation. I'm not getting this far and then turning back. Like I said, we're mates, aren't we?"

"You're a madman, Fackler," said Mueller with a shake of his head.

"Takes one to know one, Mueller."

Once they had recovered from the rigours thus far, they crept along the fence until they were once again between two sentry towers. There they lay and calculated the time for the searchlights to sweep their entire arc. They estimated they had about thirty seconds of shadow, an impossible feat to climb a thirty-foot fence and make it across barbed wire and down the other side, but the time for choosing had gone, and besides, they had no choice.

Chapter 23

He must have half dragged, half carried Fackler for an hour at least, before he found he had been carrying a dead man. God knows how they had got out of that compound without being spotted, thought Mueller. The Froggies had been none too alert, that was for sure. They were some metres out towards the woods before they heard the alarm that signalled their escape.

Immediately, the guards from the watchtowers opened fire, and they were caught in the beam of the lamps. It was too late to flatten themselves onto the floor. In a matter of minutes, the dogs would be out, so they sped towards the protection of the woods in some crazy zig-zag path. They almost made it as well. Then Fackler cried out in pain as bullets ripped into his body.

For a while, he carried on running like some headless chicken, then a couple of metres from the woods, he fell, and Mueller had to drag him into the cover of the trees. Already he could hear the dogs.

"Leave me here," Fackler begged, but Mueller shook his head.

"Like you said, we're mates, aren't we, Eddy?"

He threw Fackler's arm around his neck and hoisted the man onto his feet, and as Fackler groaned in agony, he damned himself for not being more careful, though he knew the time for care was long past. He had no clue in which direction he was heading. It was enough that it was away from the camp, the dogs, and the body of Otto Von Liechtenstein. The dogs, though, were gaining, and he thought that surely it must be all over, until by pure fluke he heard running water, and making towards the sound, found a fast, running brook. He slid down the bank, dragging Fackler with him into the icy water. At first, he had struggled to maintain a foothold on the slippery bedrocks with Fackler's feet dragging behind. He changed his tactics, bending forwards, throwing Fackler across his shoulders in a firefighter's hold, wincing from the extra weight on his injured leg. He knew that to lose the dogs, he would have to keep to the water for some distance. A well-trained tracker would not give up easily.

And so, he had stuck to the brook for a good hour, relaxing slightly, as he heard the pursuing hounds grow more distant. Only as the brook threatened to leave the cover of the woods did he drag himself and Fackler up the opposite bank, and it was there that he had rested for a moment and found that Eddy Fackler was dead.

Now it was Fackler's corpse that could well be his undoing. He could bury it in a shallow grave and cover it with leaves, but the dogs would soon sniff it out and then they'd know in which direction he'd travelled. He could double back on himself, but then there was the chance of having his scent picked up even sooner. His judgement had to be instinctive as it had been in the past during battle. He had no time to think about his limited options.

He dragged Fackler into some thick undergrowth and paused only to pull down his eyelids, resting his hand briefly on his friend's brow, quickly murmuring a prayer, guiltily removing the watch in case he could trade it for food somewhere. Then he was off, heading towards the faint light of the rising sun, eastwards, towards his home and what was left of the war and his broken relationship. Along with those thoughts was the other, which was uppermost in his mind, how that day he had lost a good friend.

***

Five days into his journey, he knew that his strength was ebbing. He had been lucky in shaking off the dogs and was certain that he was no longer being pursued. He kept to the open fields only moving at night, using the stars as guides, circling towns, and villages, relying on the many small farmsteads to find food. There he would steal food in the dead of night, raw eggs, pigswill, milk. By day, he sought cover in ditches or hedgerows; once he was lucky enough to find a deserted farmhouse and he'd had the luxury of a roof over his head for several hours, until the need for food drove him on again.

At one point, he thought of heading towards a town and trying to pick up a railway line, but he was still unsure of his whereabouts and what he could be heading into. Then the weather changed for the worse, and icy rain bit into his flesh, making his breath rasp, sapping his strength still further. He knew that if he stayed out much longer without proper food or rest, then the wintery weather would finish him.

The next night he searched the countryside for a homestead with no immediate neighbours, far removed from village or town. He was lucky;

he found a small farm and decided to explore it. There was a dim light shining from the curtained windows of the old stone house, and just across the yard was a henhouse and a barn.

From inside the house, a sharp-eared dog barked, and he chastised himself for not taking a dog into consideration. He, of all people, should have known better. He heard a man cursing, and he flattened himself against the wall at the corner of the house as the door opened. Just for a moment, he thought that the game was up. Any dog worth its salt would, in his present condition, sniff him out in no time. But the man came to the door with a shotgun cocked, and thankfully, without his dog. He was middle-aged and strongly built and he let forth a torrent of abuse which Mueller, despite the situation, admired.

"Come out, you snivelling bastards, where are ya? Come out and face me, you bloody fuckers, or do you only pick on defenceless children?" The man stood still, his head on one side, waiting to pick up any hostile sounds. "Bloody crap heaps, sod off! Leave us alone!" Then he turned on his heel and went back indoors, still cursing.

Mueller made his way quickly across the yard, keeping to the shadows, moving as quickly as his leg would allow. The dog barked again, and he heard the man reprimand it. He made for the barn, pulling back the old doors just enough to admit him. Over in one corner of the barn was a pile of hay, just as he had hoped. Half a dozen cows, a sizeable number he thought, for a small farm, occupied the rest of the space. Outside, he guessed there would be a couple of pigsties, as well as the henhouse. He found an old bucket and set about milking the nearest cow; she yielded her milk willingly enough, and he knew it had been some hours since she had last been milked, which meant the occupants of the house were likely to be early risers. As he milked, he planned.

He would rest for a few brief hours, and then, well before dawn, he would raid the henhouse. It had been in his mind to look for more substantial food in the house, but the dog had put pay to that. He was utterly exhausted and knew he had to rest. Looking around the barn, he wondered if there was a place that he could risk hiding for the daytime, too.

There was a ladder at the far end which led up to a hayloft and desperate for rest and warmth, he knew that he would have to take the risk. Just one day, he thought, that's all he needed, just one day to get his strength back. He lifted the bucket to his mouth, savouring at first the sweet taste of the warm milk, then he drained it back.

* * *

"Wake up, you pile of crap!!!"

The sharp shock of a metal toecap in the ribs should have brought Mueller round with a vengeance, but worse than the pain of the kick was the throbbing of his head and the burning in his chest. His eyes flickered weakly, encouraging a second kick, which prevailed upon him to open his eyes with a groan. He stared down at the muzzle of a shotgun.

"On your feet!"

The man behind the shotgun was the same thickly set man who had cursed from the farmhouse the night before. "You owe me for a few eggs, I'm thinking!" Mueller tried to pull himself up. He didn't like the look on the man's face. He made it first onto his knees.

"Get up!" the man continued.

"Papa, he's ill, can't you see?"

Mueller strained his eyes, trying to focus on the position that he judged the voice to have come from. He pushed himself up onto one foot, fighting the dizziness that overcame him. He vaguely saw a girl standing a few feet from the man. Then he collapsed back into the straw.

Chapter 24

Aware of movement, the girl turned her head and visibly jumped as she realised Mueller was watching her. His brain was working overtime, trying to remember what had happened. The man and the girl in the hayloft. So, he hadn't pulled the trigger on the shotgun.

"How long have I been here?" he asked, his voice rasping in his throat.

"Eight days," she answered.

He tried to lift his head from the pillow, but the effort was too great. "Have you been here all this time?"

She gave a slight nod. "Most of the time, between chores on the farm."

"Ah yes, the farm. And the man?"

"My father."

"I thought he was going to put a bullet through me."

"Don't judge him too harshly."

"I'm not judging him at all. I probably would have put a bullet through me, too, you see. So, you have taken care of me all this time then?"

"I've tried."

Mueller forced the ghost of a smile. "I'd say you've made a pretty good job of it."

The girl blushed. "I thought for a while that you wouldn't pull through, or at least that you would lose your leg."

"And now what?" asked Mueller.

The girl shrugged. "I think your leg is safe, Monsieur."

"That's not what I meant."

"No? We'll see. I have some soup in the kitchen. I will fetch you some."

She walked to the door, and as it closed behind her, Mueller lay back and thought of the irony of the situation. She'd spent all that time making him well, only to deliver him over to the French authorities, who would no doubt hang him. Not bloody likely! He had to go. He looked around the room. His clothes, he thought, would be about somewhere.

The room was basic but clean. There was a set of drawers beneath the window; no doubt that was where he would find his clothes. He pushed himself up onto his elbows and waited for his head to stop swimming, then he sat upright and threw his legs over the side of the bed and onto the floor. As he tried to stand, the pain was intense, ripping through his thigh. He cried out once and collapsed as the door opened.

The girl was concerned. Hurrying across the room to a small table, she put the soup down. "What on earth are you thinking of?" she chastised. "You're nowhere near ready to be out of bed." She knelt beside him, checking the dressing on his leg, and he suddenly realised his nakedness.

"If you leave, I'll get myself back into bed," he said lamely.

"You'll need help," she said, then conscious of his embarrassment, she added, "Don't worry, I've seen it all before. Who do you think cleaned you up?"

"I thought perhaps your father."

"Pffff, he was all for shooting you, remember? Right come on." She put her shoulder under his armpit to help lever him to his feet. "Grab the bed post when I tell you," She ordered. "Now!"

Between them, they got him back into the bed. She hastily pulled the covers back over him and, meeting her eyes, he conjured up a lopsided grin. "You're just a kid," he said.

"I'm nineteen, Monsieur, and despite what you may think, I'm not some simpering virgin."

Mueller raised his eyebrows at her. "I think it may be time for introductions." He held out his hand. "Korvetten Kapitan Kristian Mueller," he said as she took it.

"Marianne Cousteau," she replied.

"Thank you, Marianne Cousteau. I think you have saved my life."

"And I think you need to rest, Kapitan Mueller."

"I'd rather talk, if you have the time, that is."

"Only if you eat your soup," she said, suddenly remembering the bowl on the table. She took it up and offered it to him. "Can you manage?"

He nodded. "If you hold the bowl for me. Yes, I think so."

She sat down on the bed holding the bowl, and as he slowly spooned down the soup, he studied her. She said she was nineteen, but she appeared younger. She was tall and broad shouldered; he noticed her hands were roughened from hard work, and her face had a rosy glow from being out of doors. Her eyes, brown and doe-like, were probably her best feature, giving her a gentle visage. He wondered what colour her hair was under the scarf tied gypsy fashion around her head.

Finishing the soup, he let the spoon fall back into the empty bowl and, with a sigh, lay back on the pillow. "Excellent soup. Did you make it?" She nodded, blushing again. "Where am I?" he asked.

"About twenty kilometres out of St. Dizier."

"That doesn't mean much to me. How far from Paris and in what direction?"

"About a hundred kilometres east."

"Well, at least I've been travelling in the right direction. How far from the border would you say?"

She shrugged. "I'm not sure. Papa would know. Are you from one of the camps?" Mueller nodded. "I thought so. You speak pretty good French. How come?"

Mueller forced a laugh, "Well, I know someone who would disagree with that," he said.

"Who?"

"My wife. She's French, you see."

"Where is she?"

"My home, at least that's where I left her, near Bonn. Cologne way."

She shrugged again. "You are trying to get back to her?"

"Do you know, Marianne?" he said thoughtfully. "I can't answer that. I just know I need to go home."

"But she's French, you said."

"It's a long story and I'm exhausted. Perhaps some other time. If there is another time. Have you contacted the authorities yet?"

"You can rest, Korvetten Kapitan Mueller. We won't be contacting the authorities," said Marianne. Dragging back the kerchief, she revealed her head, which had been brutally shorn, leaving her scalp covered in lesions. "The authorities did nothing to prevent this. They tarred and feathered me. They said I was fraternising. They wouldn't understand that I loved him."

Chapter 25

December 1944

Despite there being a war in Europe with bombing raids, shortages of food and death of loved ones, there was still some anticipation of the coming of that best of times, Christmas.

Frances had been so busy that she hadn't thought at all about Christmas, until an Adventskranz appeared on the centre of the table one night.

"What's all this?" she asked as she sat down to the evening meal with Freya and Peter.

"Christmas," said Freya. "It's December the first, Frances. I've been busy."

"I can see you have. It's beautiful, Freya." The advent wreath was made of sprigs of fir with four red candles set inside it, decorated with delicately made bows of ribbon in red and gold.

"She always makes a good one," said Peter, giving Freya a smile.

"I almost didn't bother this year; it somehow doesn't seem right to celebrate when we don't even know where Kristian is, or even if…"

"Don't say it Freya, please don't," Frances begged.

The door was pushed open, and Anna entered carrying a tray laden with the evening meal. Steaming vegetable soup, rabbit stew and dumplings. She noticed the look of misery on the faces of those round the table.

"Now what?" she asked, as she put the food on the centre of the table by the Adventskranz. Is there bad news that I haven't heard or been told of yet?"

"I was just saying, Anna, that it doesn't seem right to be thinking of celebrating Christmas when we don't know where Kristian is or what he's doing," Freya said.

"I can tell you exactly what he'll be doing," said Anna, "He'll be looking forward to Christmas. You know how much he loves it."

"It's all of your food that he loves," Peter said with a chuckle.

"Yes, and I for one am going to carry on as though he will be here. There will be Christstollen in this house as there has always been. And you, young lady," she continued, pointing at Frances, "will be kept very busy helping me cook. We have Zimsterne, Bethmannchen and Nussecken biscuits to prepare, as well as the stollen."

"Is there any chance of finding a goose this year do you think?" asked Peter.

"Only if you catch a wild one. I suggest we resort to one of the cockerels."

"There's one who attacks me when I go to gather eggs," Frances said. "Can't we eat him?"

"No, no. That's old Eigor," said Anna, "He's been around for years."

"Ahhh. We can't eat him if he's your friend, Anna," Frances teased, giving Anna a cheeky smile.

"Friend!" Anna squawked, "He's the most devilish animal we have on the farm, worse than that damn horse of Kristian's. No, we can't eat Eigor; he will be as tough as old rope. It will have to be one of the younger ones."

"Well, you decide which one, Anna, and get Alf to dispatch it in plenty of time. Don't forget it will need a few days hanging to get a better flavour," Peter said and was rewarded with a look from Anna that would have crippled a lesser man.

"You think I need you to teach me how to hang a chicken, do you? Have you any complaints to make regarding my Christmas cooking over the last what is it? Nearly forty years. Do I need a man's advice, Peter Mueller? I don't think so."

Peter felt obliged to make an apology.

* * *

As Christmas approached, Frances found that she was indeed kept busy in the kitchen. She didn't mind that too much, as the kitchen was one of the warmer parts of the house, and it smelled completely of Christmas every day. Anna had got to work almost immediately following the dinner, making the biscuits and stollen, with her help of course, though she did get her fingers slapped from time to time for helping herself to the freshly baked Christmas biscuits.

"You dare touch that stollen and it will be more than your life is worth," Anna warned.

During one of her chats with Freya, a few days later, Frances was relieved when the topic of her wardrobe was brought up. She had been wearing the summer clothes that she had bought on the trip out with Sara and Kristian all those months ago, and hand-me-downs from Sara for riding which were very much on the large side. She didn't like to ask for money to buy more.

"You need a winter coat, Frances," Freya said quite out of the blue. "In fact, I haven't seen anything at all warm on you. Have you nothing with long sleeves, or jumpers to wear?"

"No, just the clothes Kristian paid for when I got here."

"Well, here is something we can look at together, see," she said, producing a clothing catalogue. "Come here. Sit, look, buy."

"But I can't repay you, Freya. Really, I can manage in what I have."

"I don't want you to just manage, and you repay me by being here. I love our time together because I can talk to you about my son." She patted the couch beside her, and Frances sat. For a good couple of hours, they perused the catalogue, at the end of which Frances had a completely new wardrobe to see her through the winter season, and Freya hadn't gone without either.

"Early Christmas presents," Freya said.

"Thank you, Freya," Frances said thoughtfully. "Do you know one of the most beautiful and touching Christmas presents I ever had was when I was on the boat?"

Freya shook her head and smiled. "Tell me."

"On that Christmas morning, Dieter, the youngest of the crew, gave me a huge bunch of paper flowers that the men had made for me. They were beautiful. I was so touched."

"Kristian didn't come home that Christmas. I wish I'd known you were with him."

Frances nodded, hoping that Freya wouldn't want too much detail of the Christmas of 42. She thought she would get in first and said, "Don't ask me what we did, Freya, as I wouldn't want to embarrass us both, but it was a pretty wonderful Christmas."

* * *

Christmas Eve
Near St Dizier, France 1944

Kristian Mueller stamped his feet hard to remove excess water from his boots. He then wiped his feet on the mat before he opened the door and entered the farmhouse. Marianne was at the sink preparing vegetables for the evening meal. It was to be special, for today was Christmas Eve.

"Here," said Mueller. "I have your mistletoe."

"Ahh, you found some, well done," she said, wiping her hands down her skirt. "I wish the weather would cheer up for Christmas day. Will it, do you think?"

"The rain has set in I'm afraid. Where should I hang this?" he asked, referring to the mistletoe.

"Over the front door. It's to bring us luck. I think we could all do with a little of that."

Mueller opened the door just as Marianne's father Georges returned from sorting out the livestock. "All done?" asked Mueller.

"All done," he replied, "at least for now. I watched you walk across the fields earlier, Kristian. You're limping less by the looks." Mueller nodded.

"Definitely less painful. I can weight bear now, thanks to your daughter." He stretched up with his hand to hook the mistletoe over a nail above the door.

"That nail's been there since before I was born, Kristian. It could tell a few stories about the Christmases here," said Georges.

"Most of them good, Dad, I hope," Marianne threw in, as she joined them in the doorway to check that Mueller had done a good job of hanging the mistletoe.

"Perfect," she said. "It's going to be odd not going to mass this year, isn't it? I wondered if we should just go. Maybe people will have forgotten or at least forgiven us by now."

"It is the season of goodwill," reflected Mueller.

"Or not!" snapped Georges. "We will not risk it, Marianne. You're much too precious."

"I agree," Mueller said, giving Marianne a wink, and watched with a smile as a blush crept across her face. To cover her embarrassment, he said, "We have no tree. There must be a tree. Do you have decorations?"

~ 185 ~

"A few yes, if I can find them," said Marianne, joining in with Mueller's excitement. "They are in the cupboard under the cups and plates. Many are past their best though. I don't think we have bought any since Mama died."

"You find the decorations and I'll find the tree," Mueller said stepping back out into the rain. "And Georges, I will milk the cows and bed down the animals tonight. My Christmas present to you, now I'm getting stronger."

Georges' face lit with a huge smile; he couldn't remember the last time he hadn't tended his livestock before bed. "And after dinner tonight," he announced, "we will sing carols and drink brandy. Now go and find that tree, man."

* * *

It was well past midnight when Mueller heaved himself up from the table to go to his bed. He congratulated Marianne on putting together a wonderful meal, and it had been. Capon stuffed with chestnuts, green beans in garlic butter and sauté potatoes, followed by bouche de Noel which somehow Marianne had made and hidden from Georges and himself. To go with the brandy, Georges produced some crystallised fruits and nougat which Marianne loved and had known nothing about. It had been a very different Christmas, Mueller thought, but special all the same.

As he lay in his bed early that Christmas morning, he couldn't help wondering what would be served up at Schonen Felder later that day. He knew Anna wouldn't let a mere war get in the way of Christmas dinner. Later there would be goose stuffed with apples and chestnuts, roasted potatoes, and red cabbage, all followed by Anna's Christstollen and his favourite Bethmuchen, the biscuits he loved full of almonds and marzipan. There would be champagne if there was any left in the cellar and they would finish with chocolate and good German brandy.

He wondered how many would be round the table that night. Would the Kohls be there, with Mutti, Pa, and Anna? And her, Frances. Would she still be there? He lay back on his pillow, closed his eyes and imagined her sitting in the dining room, sipping champagne with his family around her. That thought sent a warm glow through his body, inviting him to sleep some more, and was the last thought he had until late morning.

***

Christmas Eve 1944
Schonen Felder

"Where on earth are they?" said Frances, stamping her feet against the cold and drawing her coat closer around her body. It was snowing and she was glad of the new coat and boots, part of the winter wardrobe that Freya had provided.

"Stop whingeing, girl. They'll be here when they get here. I've never known anyone so impatient," said Peter.

They were standing outside the church in town, waiting for the Kohls to join them for mass. Anna had refused to come, declaring that she had little interest in celebrating the birth of a son of God who was doing nothing to prevent the civilised world from blowing itself up.

"Frances, Aunty Freya." Frances swung around to see the Kohl family making their way towards them along with many others towards the church.

"Late as usual," Gunter apologised. "You must tell me how you get your two women moving Peter. These two have been in the looking glass for the last two hours."

"Well, they both look wonderful," said Peter, kissing Eva, and Sara on the cheek. After kisses all round, they made their way inside the church and found it already packed with townspeople.

"Where's Frances?" Sara asked, suddenly noticing that Frances wasn't with them. They all turned just in time to see her rushing out of the church. Eva immediately took control.

"Freya, Peter, Gunter, save us some seats. Sara, you come with me." The two retraced their steps and found Frances outside, sheltering under a large yew tree looking totally bewildered.

They walked over and joined her.

"Frances, what is it?" Eva asked.

"I saw the uniforms. There are SS in there. I can't come in." Sara placed her arms protectively around Frances's shoulders.

"Come on, Froggy, you'll be fine," she said.

"They are just men in uniform, home for Christmas," said Eva. "Frances, I promise, you are quite safe." Frances shook her head.

"I can't, Eva. What if…"

"What if what, Frances?" Eva asked.

~ 187 ~

"I don't know what. I just know I can't go in there."

"Yes, you can," said Eva and Sara together. They stood on either side of her and linked arms. Eva, looked steadily into Frances's eyes.

"Come, Frances, show them all, but mostly yourself, that this night you have finally beaten your devils with the help of Christ."

Frances stood for a moment, taking deep breaths. She wanted to run and hide but also, she didn't want to be the cause of another ruined evening. "Promise me we won't be near them."

"Most definitely we will not," Eva said. Sara leant across and gave Frances a kiss on the cheek.

"Come on, Froggy. You can do it," she encouraged.

Frances took a few more deep breaths, blew out her cheeks and sighed. Clinging to the hands of the other two women, she made her way back inside the church to find the others. She seated herself between Peter, who welcomed her with a warm smile, and Sara. The closeness of the other two helped make her feel safe. She had overcome the devils for that night at least, and it made her feel good.

The church had been decorated for Christmas. There was a large tree at the front by the lectern, on top of which was a light up swastika. The branches had been hung with glass baubles emblazoned with swastikas, eagles, and the hated SS insignia. Frances raised her eyebrows at Peter, and getting no reaction turned her attention to the service sheet searching through the musical items. She gasped and shook Peter's arm pointing to the new lyrics of Silent Night.

'Silent night, Holy night, all is calm, all is bright.
Only the Chancellor stays on guard,
Germany's future to watch and to ward,'

"Peter, I'm not singing that. I shall sing the lyrics that should be there," she whispered, just as the service began.

"When in Rome, Frances," he whispered back.

"I can't. It's wrong," she replied.

"What's wrong?" whispered Sara, joining in on the conversation.

"This!" Frances pointed to the new lyrics and Sara struggled to stifle a chuckle until her mother gave her a push.

"Shush," she said.

"When in Rome," Peter repeated. Frances cocked her head to one side and screwed up her face.

"For you then," she said. "But I'm not going to sing those stupid lyrics. I won't sing at all." He nodded.

"I'll settle for that, and I will probably join you."

"Me too." Sara whispered.

"Peter, what on earth is going on?" Freya asked.

"Shush," someone said from behind.

* * *

Following the service, farewells were said, and invitations given to the Kohls to spend Christmas day at Schonen Felder. Once home, it was straight to the dining room to eat the wonderful meal that Anna had prepared in their absence. An extra place had been set for Kristian, who was in their thoughts and conversation for the entire evening.

It was gone 3 a.m. before they retired, full of good food, good wine, and the warmth from the company they had kept that night. Frances undressed and slipped into her nightdress. She pulled back the heavy curtains to the French door that led out onto the balcony. Anna had shut them earlier to keep in some heat, and Frances soon found out why. She grabbed her coat and wrapped it around her, opened the window, and stepped outside. It had stopped snowing, and the sky was clear, lit by a bright crescent moon and a million stars. It was still, and the distant sound of battle reached her ears.

"Where are you, Kristian?" she whispered. "Are you looking up at the same beautiful sky this Christmas morning? I know you are. Please, please come home, my dearest love."

Chapter 26

It was into the end of January 1945 before Mueller felt anywhere near recovered; the situations dogging the German armed forces weren't so lucky and never recovered, despite an offensive aimed at recapturing Antwerp, which centred around Bastogne. Delaying tactics were all that the German command could hope for. The Battle of the Bulge, which had taken place over the Christmas period of 1944, achieved this, though at a terrific human cost.

There was further action around the port of Antwerp as, against heavy odds, the German 16th Army battled against the allies for eighty-five days, denying them the use of the port that they had captured in September. At this time, Eisenhower set out to clear the west bank of the Rhine of German soldiers. On the Eastern Front too, resistance was proving useless and by early 1945, the Russians had liberated Warsaw, and Budapest had surrendered.

The liberation by the Russians that was on the lips of everyone, though, was that of Auschwitz on January 27[th.]

* * *

March 1945

The sound of war hadn't abated for several days, and those at Schonen Felder were in no doubt that Germany was in its last throws. There was news of a large attack by American troops on the bridge at Remagen, and someone had reported American tank divisions heading for Cologne.

"There can't be much left of Cologne surely. I don't know why anyone is bothering. The place has been flattened. There're just a few poor civilians, that's all," mused Frances.

"It's a way into Germany for the Allies, Frances," said Peter. "They need to get across the Rhine and once they've made, it will be the end. There'll be no stopping them, I fear."

Freya Mueller had been in a state of panic for some time since she had read about Nemmersdorf.

"Are we safe here, Peter? Shouldn't we move out before they get here?" she asked.

Peter Mueller crossed the lounge and sat down next to his wife, taking her hand.

"And where do you think we should go, Freya? I'd say we are pretty much surrounded. Let's be thankful that it's the Americans who are on our doorstep and not the Soviets. We sit it out. It's going to be the end of Hitler, and the end of the bloody Nazi party. Things can only get better, don't you think? Chin up."

It was less than a week later, with the sound of war still being carried on the wind, that three American jeeps drove up the drive to the house, complete with eight GIs carrying rifles. It was getting on for lunchtime and Sara had turned up that morning, and she and Frances had wrapped up against the cold and taken a mug of ersatz coffee into the garden. Sara had been telling Frances about some of her and Kristian's childhood exploits. Frances never tired of hearing about what they got up to. It kept him alive in her head.

They both jumped at the sound of vehicles crackling their way along the gravel drive. It was rare now that there were visitors. Making their way to the front of the house, they arrived just as Peter came out with a shotgun. Freya, she noticed, was watching from the window.

"Girls, get inside the house," Peter instructed, but it was too late.

"Stay there please all of you. Sir, lower your shotgun please. You are quite safe. We don't make war on civilians."

The words were spoken in passable German, as a very tall, well-built young man jumped out of the front seat of the first jeep. He approached the girls and Peter, who had now lowered his gun. The man's eyes lingered momentarily on the women, and Sara in particular, before he covered the ground and stood before Peter Mueller.

"Leutnant Jack Burton, American 12th army," he introduced himself.

A worried Peter Mueller held out his hand, which Burton declined to take. "You speak German?" Peter asked the young man.

"Well enough, Sir. Please excuse any gaffs though as I'm not an expert."

"Can you tell us what's happening, Leutnant? All the gunfire?" Peter asked.

"There's a fight going on for the bridge at Remagen, Sir. Your chaps are putting up a bit of a scrap. We took Cologne a few days ago."

"You've taken Cologne?" Peter questioned.

"What little is left of it, yes."

"Are you requisitioning our home?" Frances asked in English, as she and Sara made their way over to Peter. Lieutenant Burton whipped his gaze to Frances.

"You're a farm, Mam, aren't you?"

"Yes, that's correct, we are a farm." Burton turned his gaze back to Peter.

"Can you tell me what type of farming you do here, Sir, and how much land you have?" Peter Mueller shook his head.

"My English isn't too good, Lieutenant, so please use German where you can, or perhaps if you have questions, you could put them to my daughter-in-law."

Burton turned to the women, and as Frances stepped forward, she thought she noticed a look of relief on Burton's face.

"Frances Mueller, Lieutenant," she said, holding out her hand.

He declined her hand too, "Sorry, Mam," he apologised, "Orders I'm afraid."

Frances gave him a smile and nodded. "So, is it likely that we will lose our home, Lieutenant?"

"It's unlikely, Mam. You are rather removed up here, and I think the farms are going to be left to continue as they are. There appears to be a huge food shortage in Germany." He turned to Sara with a questioning look and turned back to Frances.

"Is this lady your sister-in-law, Mam?" he asked.

"Ah, this is our neighbour and best friend, Sara Kohl," said Frances. "The Kohls have the farm next to us." Frances looked on as Burton gave Sara a wide smile.

"Pleased to meet you, Miss Kohl, is it?" Sara nodded and coloured up under his gaze but managed to smile as they held each other's eyes for a fleeting moment. Peter Mueller had been joined on the steps by Freya who, bursting with anxious anticipation, had plucked up enough courage to join her husband. Peter introduced her to Burton who gave her a nod before turning back to Frances.

"I need to see everyone's ID cards, please Mam, and have you any guns in the property, Mam, and any ammunition? Let's sort all of this before we get round to discussing the farm, shall we?"

Frances spoke in German, asking Peter about the guns and ammunition.

"Just two," he said, turning to Burton. "This one and one inside."

"Can you bring it out please?" Burton asked.

Peter Mueller disappeared into the house with Freya on his heels, returning quickly with a second hunting rifle and ammunition, which he passed to Burton.

"Thank you, Sir. I'm afraid we are going to have to conduct a quick search of the property. We will treat everything with respect, I assure you."

Frances looked at Peter, who nodded his understanding, and looked relieved, like her, that the young man in charge wasn't some sort of fanatic out for revenge. Burton gave orders to his six accompanying troops who went about their business quickly and thoroughly as the Muellers and Sara waited outside. There was a loud shriek from the kitchen.

"Anna!" shouted Frances, rushing indoors with Sara. They made it to the kitchen to find Anna brandishing her stick at a young GI, who had been trying to search her domain.

"It's alright, Anna. Let him go about his work. Peter knows. They are checking for guns," Frances explained. Anna screeched her reply.

"Well, he won't find any guns here but plenty of ammunition, yes!" She picked up the vegetables she had been preparing on the kitchen table and threw them with expert precision at the young GI, who did his best to dodge them. Frances approached Anna and wrapped her arms around her, giving the soldier a thankful smile for taking the attack in such good stead.

"Now, Anna, calm down, everything is going to be alright. These men won't hurt us. Have you got your ID card on you?" she asked.

"It's in my bag, in the pantry," she replied sullenly.

"Right, now go and find it." After giving Anna a hug, she grabbed her own ID from her bag and, seeing Burton outside in the garden with Sara and Anna, who was still in a rage, went outside to join him.

"It's a truly beautiful place you have here," he remarked to both women. "You must be English, Mam, the way you speak the language," he said, addressing Frances.

"Yes, well, half. English mother, French father. I lived in England until I was fourteen, then I joined my aunt in France."

"Is that where you met your husband, then?"

"It's a very long story, Lieutenant Burton, and I suspect you are a very busy man, but if ever you are passing and you have time?" Burton nodded.

The troops were on their way back out of the house after completing the search in a matter of minutes, assuring Burton that there were no other firearms on the property.

"Well then, a quick guided tour of your land, if you don't mind. Let's see what you are up to, shall we? Very impressive, mam, if you don't mind my saying, the way you can change from one language to the other without thinking about it."

"It's certainly proving useful today," she replied with a smile, changing back to German to speak with Peter who had brought his and Freya's identity cards to show Burton.

"Peter, the Lieutenant wants a quick look at the farm, come on."

"Perhaps I should go home and warn my parents of the visit," said Sara. It was the first time she had spoken, and Burton raised his eyebrows having a good understanding of what she had said.

"Ah, now, we don't want you giving any warning. Stay with us, Miss, and we'll give you a lift home." Frances translated back to Sara, noting her blush.

Frances, Sara, and Peter were loaded into the first jeep with Burton, and the vehicles made their way towards the stables and then out across the farmland.

Burton learnt that the Mueller farm was some ninety-seven or so hectares which classified it as large and that they gave a portion of it over to the breeding of horses. The huge Hanoverians impressed him. Frances led him over to meet Bismarck and explained that he was Kristian's horse and a bit of a bastard, which made him laugh. He told her he was from farming stock in Illinois, but mostly grew crops.

"We could do with some of your crops," she told Burton. "Since last autumn there's been a shortage of food here. I know that Peter is worried that it can only get worse. The occupied countries have provided a good deal of food for the last few years, particularly France and Denmark, and now, of course, that has stopped."

Peter liked Burton more, once he had found out that he was from farming stock, and with Frances's help informed him that German agriculture was in his opinion entirely inefficient. "With the coming of war, it has been difficult for some farmers to find labourers. Luckily for once," Peter said with a smile, "I have been forward thinking when others

haven't. I employed two elderly men to help on the farm along with Willie
and his grandad. I invested in some up-to-date machinery. A tractor, and
a harvester, and they have proved invaluable, and have given me more
time to concentrate on my bloodstock. You will want to see the ID cards
of my workers, of course."

Once back at the house, Burton thanked them for their time, and
Peter warned him that the coming harvest was going to be short. "A real
lack of decent seeds this year," he said, "There will be rationing I fear."
Burton nodded his understanding of what was going to be a very worrying
situation.

Peter and Frances gave a quick wave as Burton invited Sara into the
front of the jeep. As Peter walked back towards the house, Frances had
the thought that she could be missing an opportunity. Burton seemed to
be a good man. She called out for him to stop just as he was about to drive
off and ran over to the jeep. For the entire journey around the farm, she
had been thinking of a way she could make use of what amounted to be
enemy soldiers to help her find Kristian. The war was over now. Surely
there was some way of tracking him down. He wasn't dead, he couldn't
be. She could feel his life force running through her own body.

"Lieutenant Burton, have you any idea how I might find out the
whereabouts of my husband? Can you help me in any way? Please."

Burton gave a shrug, "I don't know, Mam. When did you last hear
from him?"

"Last August. He was injured and hospitalised. He wrote from
hospital."

"That's months ago. Have you heard nothing since then?"

"No, nothing."

"Where was the hospital?"

"Somewhere in France, he wasn't allowed to say where exactly. I
don't suppose he even knew. I do know that the Brits ran the hospital."

"Then that's where you need to start, Mam. There will be records,
I'm sure. It's my understanding that Germany is going to be split into three
zones, and while I can't tell you exactly where each zone will be, I'm pretty
sure you will fall into the American or British zone. Wait a while for things
to settle. That would be my advice. Now, I think we had better get Miss
Kohl home," he said, turning to Sara. "Do I need you as a translator,
Mam?"

"Well, if you do, I'm here, Lieutenant. The Kohl farm is smaller and
less complicated than this one. Sara's father speaks a little English, as does

Sara, so speak slowly and clearly and they should understand most of what you say. Oh, and Lieutenant?"

"Yes, Mam."

"Take good care of Sara, won't you?"

Burton gave her a broad grin and saluted. "Yes, Mam, I sure will."

Chapter 27

France, May 1945

As time passed, Mueller grew quite fond of them, the Cousteaus. For quite a while, Georges, the girl's father, had treated him with mistrust, but as he recovered his strength and showed himself willing to help on the farm, the man accepted his presence as a bonus. Mueller had always preferred the outdoor life and often wondered why he had read law. He flourished once he was fit enough to be outside, fixing fences and gates, tilling the soil, and helping with the livestock. The situation was perfect. Because of Marianne's involvement with her German lover, the Cousteaus had been ostracised by the surrounding villages and town, and there was little if any danger of being found out as no one ever visited the farm.

Once a week, Georges Cousteau had to travel to town for supplies and to sell his livestock or produce; the round trip took him almost a full day and he would return in the evening with news of the war. Then the three of them would sit down together and talk of how much longer the war could go on, particularly with Germany making such losses. During these times, Mueller would often speak of leaving, of making his way back to the border, and home. He would then allow them to talk him out of going. What good could come of it? The war was nearly over, the Nazis finished. Germany had lost. His going home would achieve nothing. He'd more than likely get captured, or worse.

It was following a trip into town during March that Georges returned with news that the allies had taken Cologne, and Mueller's talk of leaving ceased. He worried in his bed at night about how things would be at Schonen Felder but took solace in the fact that at least the Yanks had made it to Cologne in front of the Russians. On top of the news of Cologne, Georges also told him of the camps that were being liberated. He brought back newspapers with photographs of a place called Auschwitz that the Russians had liberated back at the end of January.

It sickened Mueller not only because of the wretchedness of the inmates shown in the photographs but because of the shame he felt for the way he had treated Frances. He had accused her of being mad, or of gross exaggeration. He became depressed, still working, but withdrawing from the company of the other two, unable to rid himself of thoughts of her suffering.

The occupation of Germany by the Allies also made him worry about the farm and how his parents would be coping. He knew his father was a sensible man and wouldn't cause any trouble that would put the family or workers in danger. Frances also filled his head. He had treated her badly; he knew that now. He could hardly deny it when evidence in the papers was slapped down in front of him. He supposed that by now she would be back in Paris, or maybe she had gone in search of relatives in England. He hoped that was the case. She would need support. There would be little of anything left in Germany apart from a beaten people who would struggle to even support themselves.

Recognising his depression, Marianne worried about him, and she would often turn up at lunchtime, seeking him out, armed with bread and cheese or cake that she'd made, along with beer or wine, and sometimes both.

On a fine day, she'd find somewhere for them to sit, and then encourage him to talk. He found she had a wonderfully calming effect on him, and with her there, he could speak of his home. He told her all about the farm and the horse breeding business, of his parents, of Sara and even Karin. He spoke of some of the modern equipment that they were using too, but not of his sham of a marriage, never of Frances. She belonged just to him.

During one such lunchtime, Marianne told him of her involvement with a young pilot stationed at St. Dizier airport. How she had met him when she'd gone into town with her father for supplies, and how they had struck up a conversation whilst she waited patiently for Georges to finish his business. She had told him where she lived, and he had driven out to find her on the farm and a relationship had developed. He would often take her into town, and that had been her downfall.

She told Mueller how very much in love they were, but the allied advance had forced him to leave. He knew she was pregnant, and swore that he would be back, and that they would marry. As the allies had advanced, he had been caught up in a skirmish and was badly wounded. A friend had posted his last letter. In it he apologised for not getting back, for being unable to keep his promise and he reassured her of his love. He asked that one day, when the world was back to normal, she would take their child to his home in Leipzig. On their next visit to town, she had been dragged from the cart and tar and feathered in front of her father, who had been made to watch. Several days after that, she miscarried.

* * *

By April, they had got themselves a radio by pawning Fackler's watch, and then the news came in thick and fast. News of the Russian Offensive towards Berlin, of the death of Mussolini, the unconditional surrender of Germany signed at Caserta, and finally on May 1st of the death of Adolph Hitler by suicide, the day before, in his bunker. Together with this news though there also came more reports of the liberation of camps and the sickening realisation for Mueller once again, that the atrocities Frances had told him of were not the wanderings of her sick mind but the realities of a sick world, worse, a sick race, his race.

Then came euphoria! A little over a week later, when Georges was on one of his trips to town, they learnt that the war had ended, and it was this euphoria that had thrown them together.

Georges was away and Mueller was working outside. Marianne was left at the house alone, preparing food. She had the radio on for company, and then there it was. The war was over, May 8th, 1945, a date to remember. A date to celebrate. She was eager to tell Mueller and rushed out to find him. She knew he would be in the barn, seeing to the livestock.

"Kristian, Kristian," she called. He met her at the barn doors, pitchfork in hand, with a worried expression on his face, wondering what the cause of all her shouting could be.

"Marianne?" he questioned.

She threw herself towards him, removing the pitchfork from his hands and throwing her arms around his neck.

"It's over, Kristian, the war; it's over."

He swung her around and they both laughed madly, hardly daring to believe the broadcast.

"It has to be right, doesn't it?" she said.

"Where was the broadcast from?"

"Ours, French."

He took her by the hand, leading her back to the house. "Come on, let's see if we can tune into the BBC."

They went into the kitchen and Mueller drew a chair up to the radio, leaning forward and turning the tuning knob backwards and forwards a little at a time, until they heard it, the BBC, and there was no mistake the war in Europe was over.

"See I told you, didn't I?" squealed Marianne. She leant over his back and kissed him on the cheek, and he turned to her and laughed.

"We should celebrate. It's a shame your father's not here," he said.

She walked round to the front of the chair, taking both of his hands in hers, pulling him from the chair to standing. "We can celebrate, can't we, without him?"

She pulled him towards her room. "Marianne, this isn't a good idea, you know," he argued. "Your father, he trusts me, you see."

"My life, Kristian, and he doesn't need to know. It's a good way to celebrate, isn't it?"

They reached the door of her bedroom, which was next to the kitchen, and she pushed down the latch and led him to her bed. While they made love, they could hear Londoners on the radio celebrating too, but in a different way.

After their lovemaking, she brought in a bottle of wine and two glasses and clambered back on the bed beside him, and he smiled and shook his head at her. She passed him a glass of wine.

"You needn't feel guilty, you know. I know exactly what I'm doing," she said.

He lifted his eyebrows at her. "God, Marianne, I'm almost old enough to be your father."

"But you're not, are you? And I'm so very fond of you, Kristian, you must know that surely."

He leant forward and kissed the tip of her nose. "And I you."

"What does Froschlein mean?" she suddenly asked.

"Frog, little frog, why?"

She laughed, "Really? You called it out all the time when you were sick, and still do sometimes in your sleep."

Mueller puffed out his cheeks and sighed. "Ah, it's my pet name for my wife, Marianne. Though why I should call it out in my sleep..." He shrugged.

She leant forward and kissed his cheek and they sipped at their wine, listening still to the celebrations from London, but then the tone of the broadcast suddenly changed.

"Full horror revealed of Auschwitz, as the worst of the German concentration camps. According to evidence, some sixty thousand inmates who were fit enough to walk were moved to other camps within Germany.

On questioning thousands of inmates left behind at Auschwitz due to their sickness, the State Commission compiled by the Soviets found that there was evidence of up to four million people having perished there between 1941 and early 1945."

Mueller turned to stone as the broadcast continued.

"The dead, it said, included citizens from the Soviet Union, Poland, France, Belgium, Holland, Czechoslovakia, Yugoslavia, Hungary, Italy, and Greece. The Commission described Auschwitz as the worst camp it had experienced. It found evidence of experiments carried out on humans of a revolting character. The few thousand people left behind were freed by the Russians. They also found 7 tons of women's hair, human teeth from which gold fillings had been extracted and tens of thousands of children's and adult's outfits."

He lay back on the bed with a groan, unable to speak, sickened by what he had heard.

"Kristian, speak to me. What is it? What's wrong? Please speak to me," Marianne begged.

He sat up again, unsure what to do, and pulled his fingers through his hair. "She told me about the hair, and I told her she was mad."

"You're making no sense. What hair, who did you say was mad?"

"Frances, Marianne. They took her to Auschwitz. She told me about it, and I wouldn't believe her. She told me about the hair, and I wouldn't believe her. You see, that's the kind of man I am. I turned my back on her when she needed me. Sweet Jesu." The sound caught in his throat and became a sob. She took him in her arms, and he continued, "It was so much easier, you see, for me, for us all, not to believe her."

"They took her to one of those camps and she survived?" Marianne asked.

He pushed away from her and sat with his head in his hands. "She must hate me, Marianne. She should hate me for the things I said."

"How, though? How did she get out?"

"I think her music saved her. Along with her pig-headedness. You should see her, Marianne. God, what a force she is at times." He gave a strangled laugh and shook his head.

She took his hand. "Tell me about her, Kristian, talk to me about her."

"I've just made love to you, and now you want to know about my wife?" He forced a smile and, taking her hand, gave it a squeeze. "You're some girl, you know."

She rubbed her thumb back and forth across the back of his hand. "Talk to me about her. Come on, I want to know her. She must be special."

He exhaled and thought for a moment and then nodded. "Special? Yes. She's small and neat. You have a word for it in French ...."

"Petite?"

"Yes, that's it. She's petite, a little over 1.6 metres, I guess. She's outspoken and obstinate. My God, she will fight her corner if she thinks she's right. She's awkward when she wants to be, and willful." He smiled to himself in recollection. "She's also clever, funny and incredibly talented."

Mueller told her how he and Frances had met, and they both laughed together over the stories he told. He then went on to the latest part of the story, since he had found her at Dachau, and of how Otto had raped her. Of their ill-fated attempts to make love. And he finished with the day he left Schonen Felder, and how once again he had turned his back on her when she needed him most.

"She asked me to hold her, just for a moment. I wouldn't, Marianne. I wasn't being cruel. Well, not entirely anyway. I knew there was a good chance I wouldn't make it back, and if it hadn't been for you, I would have had no chance, and wouldn't be here talking about it." He paused for a while, thinking. "Have you seen those shitty films in the cinema where the guy tells the girl to wait for him, even though he knows there's a bloody good chance he's going to get his head blown off? The day I left, well it was a bit like that, you see. I didn't want her mourning her life away. I thought it would be easier for her if she hated me, so I told her it was over. The whole damned lot." He was quiet for a while and she let him be, and then he sighed. "I killed Otto by the way. If they catch me, I'm a dead man."

"Hey," said Marianne, looking into his eyes, "he deserved it, didn't he?"

"Doesn't make it right though, does it? I make myself feel better by telling myself it was an accident. It was me who hit him though, and by God, when I did, I wanted him dead...." He sat for a moment deep in thought and she knew it would be wrong to intrude. After a while, he gave another sigh. "Anyway, come on, madam, up! The time's pushing on and I have work to do. Your old man will have my guts."

"I know," said Marianne, "I have a meal to prepare, but in a minute. Tell me what she looks like first."

"I've told you enough, haven't I?" he said, caressing her cheek and kissing the tip of her nose. "Too much."

"Come on, Kristian. I want to see her."

He shook his head, wondering where to start. "She has beautiful wayward hair." He cursed himself for mentioning her hair, but Marianne didn't seem to care.

"What colour?" she asked.

"Hold on, I'm thinking! It's somewhere between red and brown, like autumn leaves. Her nose is just her nose." He chuckled. "It's pretty and turns up slightly."

Marianne watched his face change. There was a constant smile as he thought about Frances, and he continued slowly with his description, imagining her, seeing her, painting a picture in words for Marianne to see her too.

"There are... I don't know the word in French." He ran his fingers across the bridge of his nose. "Across her nose, little marks."

"Freckles?"

"Freckles then. When she cries, I worry that they'll get washed away. They don't of course. Her mouth is quite wide, and she has a little pout sometimes when she's thinking or cross about something. There's a small dimple on her chin. But it's her eyes, Marianne. You've never seen eyes like them. Eyes that burn you. A wolf's eyes. They flame. Particularly when she's angry or passionate and then when she's not...." He was silent, lost in his thoughts for a moment. "Like after making love, they become glowing embers." He paused. "And they warm me...."

Marianne smiled at him, and he met her eyes and exhaled. "So, there you are, and there she is."

"You really love her, don't you?"

"Oh! There's the love word," Mueller said, eyebrows lifted. "The answer to your question, Marianne, is I don't know, because love is something that I've done my best to avoid. Am I feeling light and walking on air? Do I hear the birds sing everywhere I go? No, I do not. But I think about her every waking moment of every day, and also in the night it seems, so you tell me. If that is love, then..." He shrugged. "If that is love, then it's not what it's made out to be and I would gladly do without it."

Marianne held his gaze. "You'll never heal completely until you see her, you know," she said.

"I am healed, aren't I? And that's all thanks to you."

"You're healed physically alright, but I think you're only half healed. Kristian. Believe me, until you heal emotionally, you'll only be half a man."

He laughed aloud, "So are you saying, Marianne, that I'm not all there?"

She took his hand and kissed the palm. "No, but I think you need healing deep within yourself. If I could, I would heal that place for you, but I know I can't reach it. It's special for you and her, Kristian. For you and Frances."

"Hmm." He stretched and pulled himself up. She'd made him uncomfortable by getting so close to the truth. She had made him dwell on the feelings that he'd kept under wraps. "Time for work, I think," he said.

She stood too and took his face between her hands, making him look into her eyes. "I think I've opened a wound. I never meant to. I care too much to ever hurt you. Do you know what you should do? Instead of fighting your feelings, Kristian, try embracing them. It's much less destructive."

He took a step back from her and gave her a smile. "And where did you get all of this wisdom from, young woman?" he asked.

Later, when alone, he had thought over how it had taken Georges Cousteau some time to trust him. He had abused that trust now, and he hated himself for it. He had noticed the way Marianne had looked at him. How couldn't he? He had put it down to a childish crush as he was so much older than her. It had made him feel good all the same, and he hadn't been able to resist teasing her from time to time. Had he led her on, encouraged her?

Chapter 28

It was early summer when Lieutenant Burton made a return visit to Schonen Felder. The war was over, Hitler was dead and Germany, under the command of Karl Donitz, had made an unconditional surrender. This time Burton came alone. He drove up to the front of the house and, finding no one in other than Freya and Anna, went in search of Frances. He thought she was likely to be at the stables and found her grooming Majesty and her foal, who was now getting on to a being a yearling. As Burton approached, Frances heard his footsteps on the gravel path and looked up.

"Lieutenant Burton, good to see you." She waved. "Peter is in the barn, I believe."

Burton smiled as he walked towards her. "Mam, it's you I've come to see. I was wondering if you have any free time on your hands. We could do with your help."

Intrigued, Frances climbed the paddock fence and approached him. "Free time. What are you thinking? There's nothing I can do, surely."

"I think you could be a significant help in Cologne, Mam."

"Cologne, how?"

"The Military Government is trying to get things back to some sort of normality, although I guess that isn't the correct word, as normal is going to take years. Have you been there of late?"

"No, I never have. When I came here with Kristian, which would be almost a year ago now, we skirted round the city. The devastation even then was dreadful, and there have been other raids since then. There can be nothing left there, surely."

"Very little. A hospital thankfully, the remains of another, and the cathedral spires, of course. It's a sad place to see but we are trying to do what we can there. We could do with some good interpreters though, and well, to be quite honest, Mam, you immediately came to mind. It's rough there, I won't deny it, but safe enough, I think. If you could work at the Military Court, it would be a great help. What do you say?"

Peter Mueller had heard voices and was walking across the stable yard to join them. Frances explained what was going on and asked what he thought.

"It's up to you, Frances, of course. You would be helping to get the city back on its feet as long as it's safe for you to be there."

"Peter is concerned about my safety," Frances told Burton.

"We would make sure she was safe, Sir," Burton reassured him.

"If I say yes, Lieutenant, could we make some enquiries about Kristian?"

Burton gave her a smile. "I'll see what we can do. How about we try to find a list of the military hospitals run by the Brits in France, as a starter?"

"Do you think you can do that?"

"Shouldn't be that hard, Mam. So, what do you say? Have we got a deal?"

"We most certainly have," said Frances, rewarding him with a warm smile.

"Well then, I'll report back and get you timetabled for two or three days a week. You will get paid, of course, and we will have to get you there and back."

"Thank you, Lieutenant Burton, it will be good to feel that I'm helping somewhere, at least."

"How's Miss Kohl, Mam? Have you seen her?" he asked.

"Miss Kohl?" Frances gave him a knowing look. "I see her regularly, Lieutenant Burton. Maybe if you can let me have a timetable of when you need me, say the day after tomorrow, Miss Kohl may well be here then, and you can ask her yourself how she is."

A smile crept across Burton's face. "I will look forward to that Mam." He gave a salute and crunched his way back up the drive to his jeep.

"Frances, what on earth are you thinking of?" Peter admonished. "Sara's parents would be horrified if they knew you were encouraging that young man."

"Well then, Peter, let's make sure that they don't find out, shall we? Sara likes Lieutenant Burton, and he likes her, and stranger things have happened. Just look at me and Kristian."

Despite himself, Peter smiled. "Yes, my dear, just look at you." He grabbed her around the shoulders and gave her a hug. Both he and Freya had become very fond of her.

"Isn't it marvellous, though? Lieutenant Burton said he would find a list of the hospitals. We'll be able to find out where that last letter came from, Peter, and then get him home."

"Frances, stop, stop now. You must know surely that it's highly unlikely that Kristian will come home. Freya and I accepted it sometime ago. It's time, my dear, that you did too." Frances gave him a look of pure horror.

"No! No, Peter, I won't accept it! He's still alive, I know he is. I'd feel it if he weren't, and I don't. He's alive and we're going to find him. We will, I know we will."

Peter Mueller shook his head. "He'd have let us know, Frances. I know my son and somehow, he would have let us know. He would know how much we would be worrying, and he'd have got a message to us."

"You said yourself that it's unlikely, not that he won't come home."

Peter took her by the shoulders. "I think it's time we had a conversation that I've been putting off, Frances. I think you need to write to your bank, and do you have a solicitor?"

"Yes, of course, in Paris."

"Then you need to write to your solicitor and bank and let them know you are alive. You need to know what assets, if any, you now have."

She swallowed and asked, "Do you want me to leave here then Peter?"

He took her by the shoulders again and gave her another hug. "No, of course we don't. We've grown to love you as our own. You know that, surely. You can stay here as long as you need to, or want to, but you're a beautiful young woman with a life ahead of you. What I am saying is that you need to know what your options are. You mustn't waste your life. After all this killing, a life is so precious, Frances."

* * *

Two days later, Burton returned with a timetable of Court hearings for Frances and a big smile for Sara. Frances left them alone in the garden under the guise of going to get them all a coffee. Burton was breaking non-fraternisation orders, she knew that, but couldn't see that there could possibly be a problem for the two of them to meet at Schonen Felder on the days that Burton picked her up and drove her home. Burton had overcome the problem of potentially being accused of fraternisation with herself, on two counts; one she was working for the Military Court and

~ 207 ~

two she was a French National, not a German. Plus, boy, they really needed her help.

Frances thought she would never forget that first trip to Cologne. The journey to the outskirts of the city had taken no time at all, but then, as they got closer, they met with hundreds of people making their way into a place which lay in a state of complete devastation. Burton explained that the people were DPs, displaced persons either stuck in Germany with nowhere to go, or Germans returning after being evicted from other countries they had been working in, after Germany's defeat. Line upon line of ragged people, some with nothing. The lucky ones had sacks and bags, and hand-drawn or even horse-drawn carts loaded up with the pathetic remnants of their past lives. Burton informed her that about eighty percent of Cologne had been destroyed.

"Then what on earth do they think they will find here?" she asked.

"Anything they can get hold of; that's why the courts are busy. There's looting and stealing going on, and the black market is growing daily. Can you blame them, though? Look at them, for God's sake, they're starving and desperate."

As they entered the city, there was a growing stench of sewage, and something worse; rotting corpses which were still stuck beneath the piles of bombed-out buildings. The stink hung in the air, putrid. People, confused and fearful, were standing in large groups listening to orders given over the loudspeakers. There was little else to do. Groups of German men, mostly elderly, if fit enough, had been set to work shifting the rubble from the bombed-out buildings that had fallen onto the road. People queued for food supplied by the American army, thankful for any morsel they could get hold of, to stave off the starvation.

"I had no idea that it was going to be like this," muttered Frances, thinking back to the raid at Bebra. That had been horrendous, but Cologne had suffered night after night of attacks.

"No, and neither had we," said Burton, jolting her back from her thoughts. "That's the big problem. No one has thought about what to do after we had won the war. We put all our energy just into winning. We have no food to give to these people. We thought rather foolishly that they were going to be self-sufficient, but how could they be in this mess? It's a complete nightmare, to be honest. There's still no running water and no electricity and a shortage of fuel. Basically, Mam, Cologne, well, it's a shit hole."

"And surely, it's going to get worse too, isn't it? What on earth will happen in the winter?" asked Frances.

"I don't know. I try not to think about it. The lucky ones have been living in cellars for the last year."

They drove further on into the city over which the enormous gothic spires of the cathedral loomed and which beyond all odds had survived the bombing. Frances's thoughts wandered back to Bebra again. Had they endured further raids, she wondered? The people in Cologne were now living in conditions comparable to Auschwitz, worse in some ways because of the filth. No running water, sewage in the streets, rotting corpses, hardly any food and, worst of all, hardly any hope.

"Can you believe it?" said Burton. "They say there's getting on for 100,000 civilians living in this rubble."

Frances pulled on Burton's shirtsleeve. "Look, look over there." She pointed to a group of children throwing Nazi signs and propaganda leaflets onto a huge bonfire. A couple of troops were supervising them. They looked so undernourished, and their clothes hung on their backs. They were in no better state than those in the camps.

"We're not even supposed to speak to the kids, never mind the adults," said Burton. "Hardly their fault all of this is it? Poor little sods."

He drove into a square. "Ah, here we are. I'll take you in and introduce you. I'm sure you'll be looked after, and I'll pick you back up at 4:00 pm, Mam."

** * **

Over the next few weeks, the American Army made great leaps forward in Cologne, sorting out water and electricity and reinstating Konrad Adenauer as mayor of the city. He had been mayor for some years before the war but had been removed from office in 1933 by the Nazis. But now he was back, using his extraordinary skills to get some sort of order into the city, and the people were relieved to have one of their own taking charge again.

Frances continued to work her three days a week at the courts, and because she felt she was being of some use to the people, she enjoyed the work. At first there had been a problem finding judges as most of the old judicial system was run for years by the Nazis and the Americans were keen not to put Nazi Party members into seats of power. Eventually, they had to back down if they were going to use the best people for the job.

They needed to throw some of the responsibility of running the towns and cities back into the hands of the German people.

Burton informed her on the way back home one afternoon that there appeared upon questioning to be a total lack of Nazi Party members in the civilian population. Those that admitted to being members blamed the old regime and not themselves. The people, it seemed, were going to take no responsibility at all for the dreadful deeds of their Nazi government.

Burton also informed her on one of his later visits that he had news of Kristian, and he gave Frances a letter he had received from a Colonel John Franklyn, who ran one of the British military hospitals in France. In it, Franklyn informed Burton that he remembered Korvetten Kapitan Mueller very well and had enjoyed many games of chess with him, most of which he had to admit to losing. Mueller, he said, had made a good recovery from his wounds and had been discharged as fit to leave the hospital for a POW camp. He had hoped, he said, that Mueller would be sent to one of the British camps but unfortunately, he learned he had in fact been sent to a French one, as the British were refusing to send anymore prisoners back to the UK. He believed the camp was situated near Paris and sadly that was all the information he had.

"That's wonderful, Jack, isn't it? Now all we must do is find out which camps there are around Paris, and we can write and track him down. Maybe he has been released already. He could be on his way home even, couldn't he?"

Burton was a little more reticent. "I don't think it's going to be that easy. The French camps are notoriously bad by all accounts. The French want their pound of flesh, Frances. I don't think they will let many of their prisoners loose for some time yet, years maybe, but it's a first step, and it's in the right direction."

Frances refused to acknowledge that Kristian could possibly be in any danger in a French run camp. She also refused to be downhearted and rushed off to share her news with the Muellers and Anna. Kristian was fit enough to leave the hospital; the war was over, and he would be home soon. They would all be together. Everything would be fine.

Burton was hopeful too. He was on a mission to the Kohls' farm; he knew he would soon be leaving the district when the Americans withdrew from the British zone for their own. He wanted to speak with Sara's parents to see if they would agree to him calling on Sara whenever he had enough free time to make the journey.

Chapter 29

Summer 1945

The situation in Germany as described by Field Marshall Montgomery in his memoirs.

"The immediate problem that now faced us was terrific. We had in our area nearly one and a half million German prisoners of war. There were a further one million German wounded, without medical supplies, and in particular no bandages and no anaesthetics. In addition, there were about one million civilian refugees who had fled into our area from the advancing Russians: these and displaced persons were roaming about the country, often looting as they went. Transportation and communication services had ceased to function. Agriculture and industry were largely at a standstill. Food was scarce and there was a serious risk of famine and disease throughout the coming months. And to crown it all, there was no central government in being, and the machinery whereby a central government could function no longer existed.

Here was a pretty pickle.

I was a soldier, and I had not been trained to handle anything of this nature.

However, something had to be done and quick."

Following the Potsdam agreement, Germany was split into four, not three, zones as Burton had thought. The British Military and the other Allies took over the government of their zones in the late summer of 1945. In the British zone, most towns had some sort of military presence, and the town near Schonen Felder was no exception. A battalion of British troops took over its running at the beginning of August, under the control of Major Richard Forsythe. Gone was the friendly, approachable atmosphere created by the Yanks. The British wanted order. Reform or punishment was the order of the day. They feared a rise of Nazi-ism and came down hard on the German people, having little sympathy for them. As Montgomery said in his memoirs, they had trained none of the military to handle anything of a civilian nature, and so he treated the work that needed to be done as a military operation, totally devoid of people's feelings.

The British decided that the most important tasks were to restore law and order, prevent starvation, guard against spread of disease, find shelter for the homeless, keep young people off the street and start to build the economy.

* * *

At Schonen Felder, little changed. The British viewed the farmers as a necessity, as of course they were, and so they were pretty much left alone and encouraged to carry on with food production on the understanding that 20% it would be given to the Military Government. This was bad news not just for the farmers but for the civilians too. The farmers were used to giving up 20% to the Reich but in 1945 the harvest was particularly poor with a worry that the next year it may be even worse. The 20% that was given to the military would have gone a good way to provide the civilians with extra rations. They were of course in no position to complain; they were vanquished people.

With most of the German workforce being imprisoned in POW camps, there was a genuine worry about getting the harvest in, and so began Operation Barleycorn, which supplied the farms with POW labour to help. As Peter had told Burton, he had employed a couple of elderly farm hands prior to Germany's defeat and so he was in the enviable position of not struggling to bring in the harvest at Schonen Felder.

Operation Coalscuttle followed. The coal mines of the Ruhr district were reopened and were again manned by German POWs, who were happy to work for extra rations of food.

When the British took over their sector, Frances found herself moved from the court system in Cologne to the smaller court system in the local town. Jack Burton had suggested the move, pointing out that the British were unlikely to use up fuel getting her from Schonen Felder to Cologne twice or three times a week. With the work now being local, she could cycle the few kilometres to town. She had to agree that he was right, though she was worried that her cycling skills were less than proficient.

Her first day of work at the local Townhall did not go to plan. There were plenty of bicycles around Schonen Felder and finding one was not a problem. The problem was that she had scarcely ever ridden one before, apart from rarely, around the streets of Paris.

On that first day whilst riding from Schonen Felder to town she had taken a nasty fall. She was badly shaken up and the fall had left her knees and elbows bleeding and her stockings torn. She arrived half an hour late and bumped straight into Jack, looking out for her from the doorway.

"Frances, where have you been?" he began, and then noticed her grazed knees and torn stockings. "Ouch!" He winced. "What on earth have you done?"

"My cycling skills are none too good, Jack. I took a bit of a tumble. I think I'm going to stiffen up later." She screwed up her face, turned over the palms of her hands and showed him the grazes there, too.

"Do you need medical help? I can find someone, I'm sure," he said.

"No really, I'll be alright. I just need to go to the ladies' room and clean up. I think I'm going to be sore by tonight though."

Burton touched her lightly on the shoulder. "Right, off you go then. You clean up and I'll try to placate our good Major. Between you and me, he seems to be a bit of an ass."

"Jack, I am so sorry. I hope I haven't caused a problem for you. It's so kind of you to meet me here and do the introductions."

"Hey you are welcome. Just get yourself sorted. We are in the Major's office. Third door on the right up the corridor."

Ten minutes later, Frances walked into the room third on the right up the corridor and was met with a smile from a young private who introduced himself as Major Forsythe's secretary, Phillips. He beckoned her over to another door behind him, which carried the name of Major Richard Forsythe. She gave the door a knock.

A stern voice from behind the door said, "Yes come," and upon opening the door, she was met by a small wiry man with dark hair and a thin moustache who waved her inside and showed that she should sit in a seat next to Jack Burton. The man who she assumed was Major Forsythe positioned himself on the other side of a large wooden desk and gave her a severe look. She had the distinct feeling that she was back at school.

"Well, at least you've made it, eventually," he said.

"Yes, I'm so sorry. I had a fall on..." Forsythe didn't let her finish.

"Let's just get on, shall we? Mrs. Mueller, isn't it?"

"Yes."

"Now let's make it clear from the start that I can't abide shoddiness, and that includes being late. Lieutenant Burton, you can leave us. I'll let you know if we require any further information or assistance."

Burton stood up and gave Frances a look full of pity before saluting Forsythe and leaving the room.

"Now then," began Forsythe, "they tell me you are fluent in German and English, and from what I have heard so far, your English is very good. You speak with a slight accent, I notice, which isn't German." He paused, and she wondered if she should speak, but not wanting to annoy him anymore, she kept quiet.

"Well?" he continued.

"I'm French," she said. "Well, half French. My mother was English."

"My God, half French, half English and married to a bloody kraut." He shook his head. "I wonder where exactly your sympathies lie, young woman. Do you actually know?" Forsythe stood up and leant towards her across his desk.

Frances refused to be intimidated. "My sympathy lies with those who need it, Major. Where does yours lie?"

"Not with the bloody Germans, and that's for sure. In my opinion, we should shoot the bloody lot of them. That's what they deserve. If you're ready now, we do have a meeting with the krauts who are going to help us run this bloody town. They're all waiting in the court chamber and I'm relying on you to tell the buggers what I'm saying to them."

* * *

To say that Frances found working for Forsythe difficult was an understatement, and the working relationship between them quickly deteriorated. His hatred of the German people was consuming, and she could understand that. After all, hadn't she been there? It had taken her time to accept that to move on from the traumas she had suffered, she had to learn to forgive. That had been hard at times, and she felt even then she was still learning. Forsythe showed no sympathy at all for the local people who came to him for help. He treated her with disdain because she had dared to give her body to a German. She tried to break through the barrier he had erected and went to him first to ask if he could help her in her search for Mueller, which he flatly refused to do.

"Do you think I've got time for that sort of thing Mrs. Mueller?" he asked her. "How many of my own men do you think are lost?"

She frequently tried to get help for people from the town, who had approached her directly, thinking wrongly it turned out, that she might have the ear of the man in charge.

There was the young woman who was pregnant and struggling to feed herself and her small child on the paltry ration that she had been awarded. She gave most of her own food to her young child and found that her baby wasn't growing. This struck a tremendous chord with Frances, who had been in a similar position during her own pregnancy in Auschwitz. She had to put the woman's race to the back of her mind. First off, she decided, the woman was a mother, and her child was an innocent. When she approached Forsythe on the woman's behalf, he turned on her.

"Let me make it clear, Mrs. Mueller, that I don't care if the child, the woman, and the baby she is carrying fail to thrive. It's just three krauts less in the world, which, as far as I'm concerned would be a bloody good thing."

She tried again when she bumped into an elderly woman arguing with Forsythe's secretary, Private Phillips, who was given strict instructions that he, Forsythe, was not to be disturbed. The woman told her she had gone shopping in town and left her door open as she had done for years. She came back home to find two British soldiers ransacking her home. They had left through the back door as she came in through the front, but not before she had got a good look at them, and not before they had helped themselves to a few family treasures. In particular, the woman was upset that they had taken her father's gold pocket watch, which was of enormous sentimental value to her. Frances knew where that would end up. It would be worth a few quid to the perpetrators of the crime on the black market.

Incensed by the fact that army personnel thought they had a right to enter any person's home, Frances ignored Phillips's pleas to not disturb Forsythe. She knocked on his office door and entered before he could challenge who it was that was ignoring his orders. He was beyond angry when he found it was Frances and refused to give permission for the woman to identify the soldiers concerned.

"What does the woman expect? What a stupid thing to do, to leave your door open to every Tommy, Dick and Harry that might pass, and then to go shopping."

"These men, your soldiers, have entered someone's home and stolen personal items. Surely that makes them thieves, Major, doesn't it?" Frances argued.

"Mrs. Mueller, let me remind you, you are here as an interpreter. You are not here to play Madam Bloody Bountiful to enemy persons that turn up on the doorstep after a bit of sympathy and anything else they can get hold of."

Phillips lifted his eyebrows at her when she came out fuming. "Don't think too badly of the old boy," he said. "This war has just about broken him; he made a wrong call at Dunkirk, you know, and lost most of his men. He's never been the same since. They made him suffer the indignity of an office job."

"I don't believe he was any different before that happened," she replied. "The man is totally lacking in any kind of empathy. He shouldn't be in the post that's been given to him. He can't see any further than his hatred. These people are going through their own hell. Yes, they are the enemy, but it's time to put an end to the suffering on both sides, isn't it?"

The straw that broke the camel's back, although it was a heavily loaded straw, happened a couple of weeks later. It was the case of a fourteen-year-old girl who had been set upon by three young soldiers who were out on the town. They came across the youngster making the short journey back home after babysitting for a neighbour. It was just before the curfew. The men dragged her off the street to a lonely lane and molested her. They ran off and left her as her screams alerted a local couple. They found the girl in a state of shock and helped her make her way home to her mother.

Mother and daughter turned up at the town hall the next day. The girl, still seriously distressed, sobbed uncontrollably in Forsythe's office, whilst the mother berated him. Not having a clue what the woman was saying to him, he sent for Frances, who told him in no uncertain terms what had happened and demanded that the men be brought to justice.

"Goodness knows what would have happened if that couple had not come along. That child would probably have been raped by all three of your men," she snapped.

"There's a bloody war on," Forsythe had snapped back, "Surely, you've heard of rape and pillage."

"Really, Major? I thought the war had ended some time ago. Though clearly it hasn't for you. I wouldn't have believed that the British army would sink to the levels of some of the other allied forces. I can see I was mistaken. It's my understanding that there have been quite a few cases like this one, and that none of the guilty men have been held to account. It's disgraceful. You, Major, are a disgrace."

Forsythe turned his gaze on her and narrowed his eyes.

"How dare you! I don't understand you, Mrs. Mueller, you're a half English half French girl and yet it seems that all your sympathies lie with these bloody Germans. Have you any understanding of what these people did to the millions in those camps we have liberated?"

"Yes, of course I know. I know better than you, Major, I was there, you see, first in Auschwitz and then in Dachau…."

"What? You mean you worked there?" He stepped towards her, threatening. "You're a damn Nazi, aren't you? I should have known." Frances pulled back the sleeve of her cardigan and thrust her wrist under Forsythe's nose.

"No, Major Forsythe, I was an inmate." Forsythe grabbed at her wrist and rubbed at the tattooed numbers; she pulled her hand from his grasp. "I'm sorry, Major Forsythe. I can't work with you anymore," she said.

"You don't work with me, Mrs. Mueller; you work for me. Let me remind you of that!" spat Forsythe.

"Well, not anymore, I don't. What a shame you blame all these poor people for your mistake at Dunkirk. Your mistake, Major, but they are paying for it because you are so filled with hate! You can stick your bloody job up your very British arse." She turned and left the room as Forsythe screeched after her.

"You get back here, young woman. I haven't given you permission to leave!"

She shut the door behind her and gave Phillips a grimace as she walked past him. He rewarded her with a grin.

"Someone had to put the old sod right," he said. She gave him a smile and a wink as she turned and closed the door behind her.

Chapter 30

Richard Forsythe had left his office and was glad to be out of the town. He had left the worries of running the town behind and was enjoying the drive through the countryside to the Mueller's farm. It had been going on for two weeks since he had argued with Frances Mueller, and the entire episode had caused him to re-evaluate his life.

He had never married; he had given his life to the British army and had done rather well for himself until that bloody battle at Dunkirk. He hadn't panicked, no, he hadn't done that. He had just underestimated the strength and whereabouts of the opposition and sent his men right into enemy fire, losing over half of them. There had been an enquiry into his mistake, and they cleared him of any wrongdoing. He had hoped after that it would all be forgotten, but certain people had vilified him. His excellent record as a serving officer until Dunkirk had been somewhat brushed aside, and his career had taken a bit of a turn for the worse. Which is how he had ended up in a small town in Germany, trying to sort out the court system and the headache of running the damn town for the British army.

He missed the girl, though. She was so pretty to look at. Much nicer than the faces of those miserable German lawyers who had been encouraged to take over the running of their own justice system. She had been the best interpreter they had, by far, and he had looked forward to the days when he worked with her. She had to involve herself in other matters though, and that is why he had to let her go.

Let her go. Who was he kidding? The girl had walked out on him. My God, she had stood up to him and spoken to him in a manner he had never been spoken to before. She had completely put him down, and the only woman ever to have done that in the past had been his mother. He dwelt on his mother for a while. He hoped she was doing alright in Blighty, and wondered what she would be up to, who she'd be sorting out in the village where they lived in the Cotswolds.

She was a small woman, his mother, but strong-willed and she wouldn't suffer fools. Frances Mueller reminded him of her. She hadn't suffered him; so maybe that made him a fool. Perhaps it was a foolish thing that he was doing now, going to the farm to ask her to return to work with him. Apologies were no simple thing for him to make, but he somewhat missed the girl and her interfering. Since she had gone, his days had become long and mundane.

He turned into the drive of Schonen Felder and crackled his way up the drive. Impressed by the façade of the Mueller house, he stopped the car and got out of the vehicle. There didn't appear to be anyone about, except there was the sound of a lonely violin, playing a piece he recognised but couldn't put a name to. The playing he thought was superlative; the player was clearly a real talent. He knocked hard on the door, but the playing continued. Whoever was playing must not have heard him. He stood for a moment, deciding what to do. He had come this far and so was certainly not going back to town without achieving what he had set out to do. He walked to the rear of the house and looked in at what appeared to be the kitchen window. He noticed an elderly, severe looking woman working inside, and he gave the window a rap which made her jump. Crossing the kitchen to the door, she snatched it open, giving him a frown and in very poor English asked him what he wanted.

"Is there anyone in charge here?" he asked brusquely.

"Herr Mueller, down with the horses." She pointed towards the stables. "There."

"Frau Mueller is she at home?" he asked.

"Which Frau Mueller you are looking for?"

Forsythe found the woman's manner surly and decided he had wasted enough of his time on her. He turned his back on her and took the path through the garden and bumped into Peter Mueller coming the other way, followed by the dogs who made a beeline for him and, much to his annoyance, jumped up, scraping their muddy paws down his uniform. Peter gave the command for them to stop, which they eventually did, tearing off in another direction to look for more mischief, as Forsythe brushed himself down.

"Sorry about my dogs. Can I help?" asked Peter, holding out his hand to Forsythe who felt for the first time obliged to take the hand of a German. "Peter Mueller. Please excuse my poor English."

"Ah yes, I'm Major Forsythe." Introductions over, Forsythe continued, "I'm looking for your daughter-in-law, I need to talk to her."

"She's here Major, I can hear her playing." Forsythe was taken aback.

"That's her?"

"French virtuoso before the war," explained Peter. Forsythe was wracking his brain. He knew about music and his mother was mad about the violin. They had attended many concerts in London, and all over the country together before the war came and ruined everything.

"Who?" he asked.

"As you rightly said, my daughter-in-law, Frances Mueller. You may know her as Frances Lamont." Forsythe's eyebrows shot up and disappeared under the peak of his cap.

"I had no idea; my mother is an avid fan."

"And you, Major?" asked Peter. "You're not. You don't get on, I believe."

"Oh! What on earth has the silly girl been telling you? We had a bit of a misunderstanding, that's all. I understand now, these creative people are oversensitive. I'd like to talk to her," said Forsythe as they reached the kitchen door.

"Come in then, Major,"

Peter turned to Anna and spoke in German, instructing her to make the coffee and to take it to the lounge. "You'd better make one for Frances too, just in case she agrees to speak to the Major." Anna turned to Forsythe and gave him a scowl and he wondered exactly what it was that Peter had said to her. The woman made him feel uncomfortable; he believed from the look he received that she was more than capable of killing him.

"As you say, Major Forsythe," said Peter Mueller with a smile which relaxed Forsythe, "creatives can be a little oversensitive. The coffee is Ersatz, I'm afraid. The proper stuff we can't get, but I'm sure you know that. Come."

Forsythe was relieved to leave the kitchen, the woman, and the rack of knives behind, and go to the lounge where he waited. He heard Peter Mueller's footsteps as they climbed the stairs and a few moments later the music stopped.

He looked out of the window at the front drive and as the door to the lounge swung open, he turned to find Frances Mueller framed in the doorway. She had a frown on her face and was setting Forsythe with her amber eyes, which he found disconcerting.

"What do you want, Major?" she asked, making no attempt to disguise her displeasure upon seeing him.

"Can we talk, Mrs. Mueller?"

"I'm not sure we have anything to say to one another, have we?"

Anna arrived with a tray and a pot of Ersatz, milk, sugar, and two cups. Frances could see that Forsythe was feeling uncomfortable and was rather glad of it. As Anna turned to leave, Frances lifted her eyebrows and screwed up her face at Anna, who struggled not to grin or grimace back at her. Forsythe shuffled uncomfortably and walked across the room to the table and poured coffee into the two cups.

"Would you join me, Mrs. Mueller… Frances, please?" He had used her first name and his usual unbending demeanour, had relaxed slightly. Frances took a seat opposite him and gave him a questioning look.

"Right, I'll be mother," he said in an attempt at joviality. "Do you take milk and sugar?"

"Milk, thank you."

"I heard you playing when I arrived. I know the music but can't put a name to it."

"Sonata in D Minor Saint-Saens. What is it that you want, Major?"

"Ah yes, the neglected masterpiece."

Frances gave a surprised smile. "Yes," she said.

"You play wonderfully. My mother is a great fan of yours. As am I, of course. I had no idea, no idea at all."

"Why should you. I'm sure though, that you haven't come all this way to discuss music with me. Have I done something else wrong? Is that why you're here?" Forsythe shook his head.

"No, I rather think it's me that has done something wrong. I want you to come back and work for me again. Work with me, I mean. You really are the best interpreter we have, and things have become much more difficult without you."

"I can't, Major, I'm sorry. I just can't work for someone who shows a total lack of understanding or sympathy for what these people are going through."

"How about if I try a little harder to understand them? I've given some thought to the way I've been carrying out my command. It's not really working, and…." He stumbled over his words. "Well," he said, "I think you may have a point."

What Frances wanted to say is too bloody right I've got a point, but as she opened her mouth, she suddenly recognised a way of turning Forsythe's visit to her advantage.

"I'll come back and work with you, Major, if you help me track my husband down. If you promise to contact the hospital and the French authorities and see what camp they sent him to."

"I will," said Forsythe and then with a nerve which even surprised himself he added, "if you'll join me for dinner on Saturday." Completely taken by surprise, Frances stared at him for some moments and eventually he looked at the floor with embarrassment, damning himself for the stupid invitation and acting like an absolute fool. Frances pushed her advantage.

"If you help me track down my husband and give me permission to visit Bergen Belsen Camp…"

"What?" Forsythe exploded.

"If you sort out permission for me to visit Bergen Belsen too, I'll have dinner with you on Saturday, Major Forsythe." Forsythe exhaled noisily.

"What the devil do you want to visit Belsen for? It's a hellhole I've been told."

"I may have friends there; I have to go to find out if any of them made it."

He paced the room, returning to the window, glancing out, giving her demands some thought. It was a long time since he had taken a young woman to dinner and the thought of being seated opposite Frances Mueller, or Lamont as he preferred to think of her, pleased him a great deal. He turned and found her gaze on him.

"I'll see what I can do on both counts," he said.

"Really?" He nodded and gave her the suggestion of a smile. The first she'd ever seen from him.

"I promise. So, do we have a deal then? Dinner on Saturday at the Officer's Club in Bonn. I'll pick you up here at seven." Frances gave a shrug.

"I can trust you to keep your word, can't I?"

"On my honour as a British soldier."

"Then yes, Major Forsythe, I rather think that we have a deal."

"And I'll expect you back to work tomorrow morning on the dot," he said, placing his coffee cup back on the table. "And don't be late."

And with that he turned and left, humming to himself, for the first time in an age and leaving Frances open mouthed, staring after him and wondering what the hell she had done. She had accepted a dinner date with a man she detested.

Chapter 31

Richard Forsythe kept his word, and Frances kept hers. He picked her up as he had promised, the following Saturday, though not at seven but at six o'clock, after having explained to her on the Friday that the table was booked for seven. Frances had been in a dilemma for some days over what she would wear and even asked Anna's advice.

"What would you normally wear on a date?" Anna asked her.

"It's not a date, Anna. You know why I am doing this. To get his help to find Kristian," she said.

"Ah, but does the Sergeant Major think it's a date?"

"I don't know what he thinks Anna, and he's a Major, an officer, not a Sergeant Major."

"He asked if he could take you to dinner, didn't he?" Anna asked.

"Well yes."

"Then if he's paying, he thinks he's taking you on a date, so you had better dress for a date if you want his help."

In the end, Frances settled on a pretty day dress which was pale green with cream print. She decided on tying back her hair which she thought gave her a more serious and mature look and wore little makeup.

Forsythe turned up at six on the dot. He'd arranged the use of a staff car instead of turning up in his usual military vehicle. Frances was dreading the drive to Bonn but after an initial nervousness from both parties, the conversation soon got round to music, which kept them in talking for almost the entire journey and meal, until Forsythe reached across the table and took Frances's left hand. She was shocked and tried to pull away, but Forsythe held on tight and said, "I can't bear to think of those numbers being tattooed onto your wrist, Frances. The people who did that to you are animals."

She pulled her hand free and replied, "Yes, well, I can hardly argue with you on that, Major Forsythe."

"Richard," he said, "I was rather hoping we were friends now. We are, aren't we?" She nodded.

"Yes, Richard, I rather think we are." She couldn't help herself from asking with a cheeky smile, "Am I allowed to call you Richard during the week or on just weekends?" which brought a peal of laughter from him, which surprised her as she didn't think him capable of it.

"Weekends and when there is no one else around. It wouldn't do, you know, to be on first name terms at work."

"No," she said, "of course it wouldn't."

* * *

And so, she returned to the Townhall and continued as an interpreter. Forsythe even encouraged her to bring any local problems to his attention, which, often with her advice, he did his best to sort out.

The dinner was the start of a friendship which Peter Mueller encouraged; he thought company other than that of the three elderly people at Schonen Felder would do Frances good. He knew that she saw Sara often, but Sara fed what he considered to be Frances's fantasy, that Kristian would return home. It was well over a year since he had left for Kiel and it was now highly unlikely that his son would return, although he didn't push the point with Frances or Freya. Frances wouldn't hear of it, and Freya wouldn't think of it. He grieved alone.

Forsythe became a regular visitor to the farm and rarely turned up without an offering of some sort. Real coffee, tea, sugar, chocolate, and other long forgotten delights found their way into the Mueller's' pantry, which remained well guarded by Anna.

As well as seeking Frances's company, he would also spend time at the stables with Peter, admiring the horses and learning from him about bloodlines and breeding. As time passed, Frances found herself looking forward to the visits and dinner dates. He was an intelligent man with an excellent knowledge of classical music, and they conversed for many hours and in great depth. She would often pick up the violin Mueller had given her and play for him, and for Peter and Freya, too. She knew that Forsythe was getting rather too fond of her, but let it carry on as she enjoyed the attention, she received from him.

At dinner one time he brought up the subject of her relationship with Mueller. Panicking that he may not help her in her search if he knew her true feelings, she told him what she thought he wanted to hear.

"Our marriage has only ever been a temporary thing. Kristian felt I would be better protected if I took his name," she told him and foolishly thought that would be all that Forsythe needed to know. But he questioned her about it, and she found herself tying herself up with lies.

"But then why did he even bother looking for you if he felt nothing for you? He must have gone to extraordinary lengths to find you and get you released."

"He is a man of honour, that's all," she told him. "He promised to get me out of Drancy and failed. That probably would have been it, but one of his old crew saw me on a news reel at the cinema and informed him of my whereabouts, which at the time was Auschwitz. Kristian told me it was easy from there to find out where I was."

"So, you feel nothing for the man?" Forsythe asked her and she found that she was unable to meet his eyes.

In the end, she said, "Gratitude is what I feel."

"But you must have felt more at some point. You were lovers, for goodness' sake." She flashed him a look.

"I was frightened and alone and it was Christmas and well it just happened."

"It damn well shouldn't have done; the man clearly took advantage of you and yet you tell me he is a man of honour."

"Look, Richard, I owe him, and I owe his family. You know they are good people. That's all. It is merely a payback. Nothing more and nothing less."

She knew it pleased Forsythe to hear her deny any relationship, so that is the story she clung to. But then in the secrecy of her bed, she would conjure up Mueller in her mind: the scent of him, the boyish smile, the passion of his kisses and the sound of his voice, telling her what she wanted to hear, that he loved her. She knew she would never, nor could ever stop loving him.

* * *

Mueller stayed with the Cousteaus until mid-September, and then came the journey across France and into Germany, defeated Germany. The war had ended, but he was still a wanted man. The Brits would hold him responsible for a man's death. A man from his own side, the losing side. The victors would hold him responsible for killing one of their enemies. How wonderfully ironic, he thought.

When he left, the Cousteaus packed him up with as much food as he could carry and gave him a good pair of boots and a warm coat. Marianne also gave him her precious savings, which wasn't much but meant a great deal to him. He promised that should he make it back to safety he would make certain she got her money back, and more.

"The money doesn't matter," she told him, "It's you, Kristian, you, who's important. Get home, Kristian, find Frances, and make things right." And that became his mantra: 'Find Frances, make things right.'

He knew he had to take care. He had no idea what he was going to find when he reached home. From information via the wireless and through the newspapers, he knew that his country had been split into four so-called zones, each part governed by an allied power. If reports were correct, Schonen Felder would be in the British Zone, and he thanked God that that was the case. He heard it said that the Russians had the corn, the French the wine, the Americans the scenery and the British the ruins, and that seemed quite right to him, as the British had mostly been responsible for flattening his homeland.

And so, he crept across the border into Germany like a wild animal, moving only at night enjoying the food the Cousteaus had provided while it lasted, then having to turn to scavenging. Food had become scarce, and the picking was meagre.

In his head, he celebrated crossing the border. It was a significant stage in his journey. Only then he found he was still under French jurisdiction. He had entered the French zone. He panicked, believing they would be on the lookout for him, until he realised that his worn-out clothes and filthy appearance didn't even warrant a second glance. He had become, like many of the thousands on the road, a displaced person.

He gave himself a new identity, a German who had been living and working in Belgium. He'd say he'd been kicked out of the country and was making his way back to his homeland. The countryside was crawling with filthy remnants of humanity just like him, whose only belongings were the clothes on their backs. The lucky ones had carts with bits and pieces from better times piled high, though more often not so high. Occasionally he would tag along for a while with others, and he would learn of the horrors they had experienced or heard of second hand.

With the German surrender, those horrors should have ceased, but it seemed there were many who wanted payment and retribution, and were more than happy to take it, not giving a fuck where from. He heard tales of women and young girls of only twelve or thirteen, raped not once but tens of times in the wake of the Russian advance. Of children thrown from bridges, and babies brained against walls, and men shot down like animals just for fun, and with each story, the anger in him smouldered and grew.

As he got further into Germany, many of the people he came across had fled from the Eastern sector. Many more he was told had committed suicide, women mostly, so great was their shame for the way the Russians had handled them. He also found that the treatment these people received from other Allied troops was little better. He and his countrymen and women were all dogs, and animals had no rights.

* * *

It was also September, but at the end of the month, when Forsythe turned up at Schonen Felder with information regarding Mueller. He found Frances sitting in the garden making the most of the last of the summer sunshine, sipping at a coffee and reading over a piece of music.

"Ah, there you are. What have you got there?" He greeted her, and she put down the music and rewarded him with a smile.

"Richard, what are you doing here? I'm just looking over this new piece. It's something I haven't played before."

"Ahh, I've received news for you, two lots as it happens."

"What? About Kristian?" she asked, and he couldn't help but recognise the excitement in her voice, and he felt a disappointment in his chest.

"Yes, about Kristian," he said, sitting beside her on the bench. "We tracked him down to a satellite camp just outside Paris. They discharged him from the hospital and sent him there."

"That's marvellous news. So, we can get him home?" she cut in.

"No, my dear, I'm afraid not. It seems that he and another Chappy escaped, getting on for a year ago. They found a body..."

He heard her intake of breath, and her hand flew to her mouth, horror written on her face as she gasped. "Not Kristian's!" He wanted to say yes, but he found he couldn't lie, not to her.

"No, not Kristian's, the man he escaped with. He'd been shot by the guards. Frances, it's almost a year; there's been no word since his escape. I think it's time for you to accept that Kristian Mueller is dead."

"No! No. You're wrong, he isn't dead. I know he isn't dead." She stood and left him staring after her as she fled into the kitchen, breaking into floods of tears when she saw Anna.

~ 227 ~

Forsythe followed her inside to try to make her see sense, but as soon as she saw him, she ran from the kitchen to her room, leaving him to deliver the news to Peter and Freya Mueller. He also gave them the second piece of news, which was the granting of a pass to visit Bergen Belsen, not the camp itself but the old German army camp nearby, into which many of the inmates of the camp had been moved. The British Army had destroyed Bergen Belsen not long after they liberated it.

"I'd go with her, but I don't think it's doable for me to take time at the moment," he told Peter, who was struggling to digest the news given to him regarding his son. Peter had told the women he believed Kristian to be dead but inside him the hope had always remained that he would return home.

"Do you think you could go if I sort it out?" asked Forsythe.

"What? Where?" asked Peter.

"Belsen, could you go with Frances?"

"Yes, of course I'll go," snapped Peter, wondering why the bloody man was still there and whether he was totally devoid of feeling. "I think, Richard, if you don't mind, could you leave us, to give us a little time to come to terms with the news regarding our son?"

Forsythe left feeling an ass. He'd just delivered what was clearly shocking news to Peter Mueller, and he'd outstayed his welcome. He wished he could understand emotion a little better. He knew when he liked or disliked people, or in fact when they liked or disliked him. And he understood that when people laughed, they were happy and when they cried, they were sad, but all the little nuances in between confused him somewhat. And now there was Frances, who he thought liked him and he certainly liked her, telling him there was no relationship with Mueller, and then running off in a state when he gave her the information he'd been asked to find out. He concluded that too many feelings were not a good thing to have, and he was the lucky one to have so few.

Chapter 32

"I don't know what it is about you Mueller men and this girl," Freya chided Peter, with a total lack of feeling for Frances, who was seated in the car next to him. It was tipping down with rain and Freya was holding a coat over her head to try and keep dry.

"Don't worry, Mutti, I'll look after him," Frances made light of the situation. "I know you love me anyway," she said, giving Freya a smile.

Freya Mueller gave her a stern look. "Well, just make sure you come back safely, both of you. I'll make sure Anna has some food ready for you; it's going to be a long day. Have you got your sandwiches and coffee flasks?"

"Anna made sure of that. We put them in the car an age ago," said Peter. "Now go inside or you'll get soaked. Go on!"

As Freya went back towards the house, Peter Mueller pulled away from Schonen Felder, and they headed out on the road towards Hanover, which was 250 kms away. They had filled the car up with petrol from the farm's allowance, and they had a couple of full cans in the car along with food, ID papers and the pass which Forsythe had sorted for them. Forsythe had also issued them with a coupon just in case they needed extra fuel to get them home. He estimated the journey would take them possibly up to five hours and Peter agreed.

The estimate was correct. They were stopped frequently at checkpoints and made Hanover by lunchtime. Here they ate the sandwiches, drank the coffee, and left the car. The second leg of their journey was to Celle, which was about thirty-minutes away by train if there were no holdups.

That part of their journey was incredibly slow, uncomfortable, and wet. Frances and Peter had wrapped themselves up as well as they could against the October weather in wax coats. They both sat side by side on a hard seat in an open wagon under a shared umbrella, which thankfully Freya had thrust upon them as they left home in the early hours of the morning.

"Is it far from Celle, Peter? The camp I mean," Frances asked.

"I'm not sure, Forsythe thinks about another thirty-minute car journey. Hopefully we can find someone to take us."

"Will we, do you think? It would be awful if we got to Celle and can get no further." Peter Mueller raised his eyebrows in a way that Frances found heartrendingly reminiscent of Kristian. Neither of them had mentioned him on the journey yet, and she knew if she brought up the fact that she didn't accept he was dead, then Peter would get angry with her again. He had several times already since Forsythe had broken the news. It was easy for her to forget that he was suffering, too.

"Do you really think you are going to find anyone you know at the camp who has survived?" Peter asked.

"I don't know. All I know is that I must see. Richard contacted the camp admin and gave my tattoo number to see if there was anyone who entered Auschwitz at the same time as Miriam and me, but no one got back to him. I do know, though, that if anyone could survive then Miriam will have done." Peter shook his head at her.

"A hiding to nothing, I fear."

Once at Celle, they made their way to the British headquarters and had a bit of a wait until they were seen by the town commander's secretary, who took their papers to his superior. He turned out to be an amiable man who listened to a shortened version of Frances's story and then bent over backwards to help her.

"I should think we can find someone spare to run you there. It's not too far. This side of Bergen. You know we burned the camp down, and that we have moved the inmates to a German Panzer camp not far away? The other place was so full of disease; typhus, tuberculosis, and every other stinking thing going." Frances and Peter nodded.

"Yes, thank you, Captain, we do know," said Frances.

"Well, good luck then, Frau Mueller. I hope your journey proves worthwhile."

* * *

The driver dropped them at the administration block at the displaced persons' camp, which housed the remnants of the inmates of Bergen-Belsen. He agreed to wait outside for them for as long as it took; he was in no hurry to return to Celle.

Frances and Peter waited a few minutes in a waiting room, part of a huge building which smelled of ink and paper, until a woman came their way who could help them. She introduced herself as Alice Evans. Frances told her story in as shortened a form as she could and explained that Richard Forsythe had made enquiries some weeks ago regarding the possibility of survivors she might know.

Alice had been assigned to her case and was one of the many young women who had the thankless task of trying to organise records of surviving inmates from the camp. She was apologetic that there had been no reply to Frances's search and told them that when the camp was liberated back in January, there were some 60,000 half-starved prisoners along with 13,000 unburied corpses.

"We're just about on top of everything now." She touched Frances lightly on the arm and looked at her with concern. "I think it's highly unlikely we will find anyone you know. To survive Auschwitz for so long, and then in a weakened state survive for any time here," she shook her head. "Well, you would have to be some woman," she said.

"Ah, but you see Miriam is. She is the quintessential survivor," Frances stated. Alice Evans nodded and gave her a warm smile.

"Well, let's see what we can do then, shall we? Let's start with your number and see if we can find anyone who has arrived from Auschwitz with a number from around the same time you arrived there."

"35921," said Frances. The woman noted the information, leaving them and returning to the room containing all the files of information.

"My God, Frances," said Peter, "we could be here for a week. The record keeping facility must be vast."

"I bet she will know exactly where to look," said Frances. "The Brits will have learnt a thing or two from you Germans regarding the recording of information." Peter gave a grunt. He couldn't argue with that comment. If it was one thing Germans were good at, it was organisation.

"Are you alright, Frances?" he asked, picking up on her state of nervousness.

"Strangely jittery," she said. "Suppose there is someone I know here. What will I say to them?"

After a wait of some fifteen minutes, there was the sound of heels on wood coming their way, and as the door opened, both Frances and Peter stood up to be greeted by a huge smile from Alice Evans.

"Unbelievable!" she shrieked. "We have a woman with the number 35924."

"It's Miriam," cried Frances, "It's Miriam, she's here. Peter, Miriam is alive." She turned to Alice Evans. "Where is she? Where can I find her?"

"Just hold on," said Alice. "We must make sure she wants to see you. I'll phone down to the women's camp, and someone will find your friend and bring her here. If she chooses to see you, that is. The choice is hers, Frau Mueller. These people have been through so much, we don't force them into anything." Realising what she had said, she apologised, "I'm so sorry, you know what they have been through, of course." Frances gave her a forgiving smile.

"You will tell her it's Frances, won't you? She won't know me as Frau Mueller."

The woman nodded and left them again.

Frances was like a cat on a hot tin roof. She was pacing the waiting room until Alice returned and gave her the thumbs up.

"Your friend will be here in a few minutes."

"The toilet, I need the toilet," Frances said.

"Well then, you'd better come this way," said Alice with a laugh, "and quickly, by the looks of things."

When Frances returned to the waiting room, she continued with her nervous pacing until Peter took her by the shoulders and prevented her from any further movement.

"Frances, do you want me to stay or go while you talk to your friend?" he asked.

"Perhaps you could give us a few minutes, maybe fifteen, but where will you go?" she asked. The more she thought, the more she panicked. Miriam would have expected her to take revenge. She had promised the orchestra girls she would. Maybe, she thought, Miriam would see things differently. Maybe she had learnt to forgive. Could she take that chance? Here she was with a German man in tow; she would need to break her news to Miriam gently.

"I'll just hang around outside," Peter said, "or I could sit in the car with that young soldier who brought us here, huh? I won't be far away if you want me."

"I'd love you to meet her, Peter, but I need to check with her. See how she's feeling about, well, you know?"

He nodded. "Socialising with a German. I understand, Frances. The famous Miriam. I'd love to meet her. I'll see you later then. In about fifteen minutes. I will understand if she prefers it to be just you and her."

He left her in the room alone with her thoughts. Those thoughts were dark and concerned the death of her baby and the woman who killed him. Frances wondered how she would feel when she came to face with Miriam again. It was only a very short time until she heard new approaching footsteps, which stopped outside the door. She watched, heart beating madly, as the handle turned and the door opened, framing a young woman with dark hair and eyes.

"Hello rich girl," said Miriam. "I'm surprised to see you here after what I did."

Both women stood stock still for some moments, weighing each other up, gauging each other's mood. Then a slow smile spread across each of their faces and the two of them were across the space that separated them and, in each other's arms, tears unashamedly flowing down the faces of them both.

"I knew it. I knew you'd survive, Miriam. Everyone told me I was mad, but I knew, I did, I did," gabbled Frances.

"And you have too," said Miriam, sobbing into Frances's hair. "I always hoped. I am sorry for what I did. Do you understand why? Tell me you do, Frances; I've been wracked with guilt. They'd never have allowed you to keep a baby in Auschwitz. You do know that? It would have been taken away from you. It would have destroyed you. And at the time, I hated you too."

"You hated me for falling in love?"

"I was jealous. I loved you, do love you. You must know that, and I hated you for not telling me the truth. We were family, Frances, that's what I thought." Frances pulled away from the embrace and searched Miriam's eyes.

"We are family. And I love you too. Miriam let's not talk about what happened. It was a lifetime ago, and although I didn't understand at the time, I do know they'd have taken him. And I know I wouldn't be here now if it wasn't for you."

Miriam nodded and forced a little smile. "He found you then, your Kapitan?"

"Yes, yes, he found me. At Dachau eighteen months or more ago. Come on, let's sit down we have a lot of catching up to do." They pulled two seats side by side and sat down holding each other's hands.

"Dachau, what the hell were you doing there?" Miriam asked.

Frances filled Miriam in on the details of her visit to the Russian Front and her return, after which they sent her to Dachau. She told her of the concert for Adolf Hitler, and Otto, and what he did to her. Then she told her of how Mueller had found her, and how the incarceration and the treatment she had received at the hands of the Nazis had left her in what she felt was a state of madness.

"Well, girl, you look pretty good now. Are you fully recovered?" asked Miriam.

"There are times still when something will trigger a response in me, I'd rather not have. A voice, a smell, a sound. And there are flashbacks, lots of flashbacks. I am terrified when I see someone in uniform, and it's difficult for me to get out of my comfort zone, away from the farm. Sometimes I still sleep on the floor if the bed becomes... it sounds ridiculous...."

"What? Too comfortable. Do you think I don't know?"

"Of course, you know," said Frances with a frown, and then followed up with a laugh. "Anyway, enough of me. What about you? I can't believe it. How in the hell did you end up here? What happened? Why did they move you? What did the bastards do?"

"Quite a few of us were moved here in November last year. We were supposed to be exchange prisoners. Those swine in charge knew the tide was turning and panicked. They thought they might buy their miserable lives by exchanging a few prisoners. My God, Frances, it was bad. I was amongst the lucky ones, if you could call any of us that. At least I was lucky enough to be moved by train. Some poor sods here have told me how they were made to walk. Death marches, they called them; so many people died, thousands of them.

"The conditions on the train, though, were even worse than when we were moved from Drancy. Freezing conditions, packed cattle carts, but at least they fed us: we were important to them, for a while at least."

Miriam broke into tears which, through all the horrors that they'd been through in Auschwitz, Frances had never witnessed before. She gave her friend a hug and time to recover before nodding her encouragement for Miriam to carry on.

"As we crossed into Germany, we came under fire, especially at night. They, the Nazi pigs, got off the train as the sirens sounded, and they took shelter. They left us to take our chances. It was odd. In that cart there was absolute quiet. I think we had been through so much at Auschwitz that we were all too tired to complain, even to each other. God, look at me crying like a baby." Miriam turned to Frances. "Not a pretty sight, huh?"

"You are to me. You're the best sight in the world, and your face looks different, better than it did last time I saw you. And just look at your clothes."

"Ah, you noticed my face. I've had some surgery; a British doctor who specialises in facial surgery has begun to rebuild my cheekbone."

"That's marvellous," said Frances.

"Not so bad now, eh?"

"No, not so bad, but then you were always beautiful to me."

They sat for a few moments, just holding hands, and smiling at one another. Occasionally, one of them would chuckle, overwhelmed because they were back in each other's company.

"So, finish your story. I want to know," Frances said eventually.

"Well, for the last part of the journey, they made us walk. We passed through villages and sometimes small towns, where some people were curious, but most were indifferent. Anyone falling behind was beaten, sometimes to death, but never in sight of the civilians."

There was a knock on the door.

"Ah, that will be Peter," said Frances. Miriam gave her a questioning look. "Kristian's father, he came with me. Do you mind?" Miriam shook her head and Frances opened the door admitting Peter Mueller. "Peter, this is Miriam, Miriam, Peter." Miriam took Peter's extended hand and held it for a while before shaking it warmly.

"My God, if that's the father, no wonder you fell for the son," squawked Miriam. Peter lifted his eyebrows, uncertain what they had said. They had spoken in French, and Frances laughed.

"You've just received a compliment," she told him. "You're the lucky one. This girl doesn't hand out very many." Peter gave them both a winning smile.

"So where is Kristian?" asked Miriam.

"He's been wounded and made a prisoner of war in France, but we have had help from the Brits tracking him down and he'll be home soon."

"That's wonderful," said Miriam, looking at Peter, "You'll be happy to have your son back," she said. Peter had picked up on what was being said and glanced at Frances, which, thankfully, she missed, and then shook his head at Miriam. She nodded, showing she understood.

"Sit down, Peter," said Frances, "Miriam is just about to tell me about the liberation, aren't you, Miriam?"

Miriam turned to Peter. "Are you sure you want to hear it?" she asked.

He nodded. "I have to hear it."

"I will try to explain in German. Frances can fill in the bits I don't know."

She told them how at first the British armies had come to an arrangement with the Germans that there would be a 19 km area around the camp, an exclusion zone. She continued with the story slowly, stopping from time to time to give Frances the time to interpret the parts of the story that Peter was struggling to keep up with, or understand.

"Himmler agreed that they should hand the camp over with no fighting and many SS escaped across the zone. Kramer...."

"Kramer?" Frances shrieked. "The same Kramer?" Miriam nodded.

"The same Kramer who commanded Birkenau, yes, he stayed. I think he thought he was going to get away with it all. He was arrested along with Irma Grese who had also made the move."

"Irma?" Frances shrieked a second time.

"The very same. The Brits wondered what they had come into and were at first angry and then overwhelmed by what they found. Any surviving SS and the guards were made to bury the corpses when the camp was handed over to them. Typhus was rife; quite frankly it was a miracle that any of us survived."

She told them how all the food from army rations they could find was made into a soup.

"Everything went in," said Miriam. "The British were so desperate to nourish us survivors. The trouble was that no one seemed to understand until it was too late for some, that for people who have been starving to death to suddenly start eating was a death sentence in itself, and thousands more of us died. I took care to take things slowly. I warned others, but people desperate for food will eat all they can. It's only natural, I suppose."

Frances nodded her agreement, thinking back to her first meal after her release from Dachau, at the hotel with Kristian, when she had stuffed as much food as she could, and then had thrown it all back up.

"So, we had food of sorts. If the food didn't kill us, they deloused us. Anyone standing was regarded as fit and anyone who couldn't stand was hospitalised. All in all, to shift everyone out of Belsen to the present camp was a mammoth task, but it had to be done to get a handle on all the infections."

"How long did it take to move everyone out?" asked Peter.

"Only a month. They burned the last hut in Belsen on May 21st. I haven't told you the best, Frances. A lorry arrived with what we thought was food for us women, and do you know what was in it?" Both Peter and Frances shook their heads. "Lipstick. We were all given a lipstick."

"That's wonderful, isn't it? How thoughtful they were," said Frances. Miriam smiled and nodded madly, leaving Peter confused.

"God girl, we were all so excited. Can you imagine? Better than any food. Then they took us to Harrods."

"Harrods?" questioned Peter, hearing a word he recognised.

"Well, that's what it became known as. Named after some big swanky shop in London. They gave us real clothes to wear. Freshly laundered. It was heaven. They even let us choose. What do you think?" she said, referring to the clothes she was wearing.

The talk between the two women continued for some time, and Frances found out that Alma Rose had suddenly taken ill and died. Miriam wasn't sure what had happened to the orchestra girls, but both women hoped that some of them had survived in Auschwitz until the liberation, as they were spared selections. Maria Mandel, Frances learnt, had left Auschwitz for Muhldorf.

"And has since gone into hiding, so people say," informed Miriam.

"My God, she went to Dachau. And Mengele?" asked Frances.

"Disappeared."

"Hmm. He was so clever, Miriam; he'd have had plans in place. Do you think they will find these people?"

"They will search for them. There is a man called Simon Wiesenthal. He went through five camps and survived; can you imagine? He has already started making a list of Nazi war criminals and swears he will ferret them out himself with or without help from the Allies. Simon says every bastard must be tried and their guilt proven in court. He has a small group of people to help him and I'm joining them," said Miriam. Frances touched her on the shoulder.

"That's wonderful, Miriam," she said.

Eventually, Peter felt he had to draw the conversation to a close if they were to make the journey back before nightfall. The two women embraced again and struggled to let go of one another.

"I will see you again, won't I?" sobbed Frances.

"I hope so, but where?"

Frances turned to Peter Mueller. "Miriam can come to Schonen Felder, can't she, Peter?"

He nodded his agreement. "Of course. It will be an honour for us if you visit, Miriam."

"We'll get Alice to write our address. Promise me you'll come. You'll be able to meet Kristian. He'll be back soon."

Miriam nodded. "I'll come; I promise you." Miriam lay her hands on Frances's shoulders. "Shalom ve lehitra'ot. Do you know that phrase?" she asked.

"I know that phrase," said Frances thinking back to Steven. "Shalom ve lehitra'ot, my dear friend." Then turning to Peter, she said, "It's time to go home."

* * *

The journey back to Schonen Felder started well enough. They spent the conversation in the car back to Celle, going back over some of the information that they had gathered from Miriam.

"She's wonderful, isn't she?" Frances said.

"Yes, she is, but then I knew she would be."

"How?"

"Because you told me she was. And you, Frances, you're a pretty wonderful girl, too. And it takes one to know one." They smiled at one another. "What I don't get though," continued Peter, "is how on earth you two thought being given lipstick instead of food was such a wonderful thing."

"Don't you see? They were being treated as women, for the first time for some of them like Miriam, in years. It will have done them so much better than any food."

"And the phrase you said to one another when we left?"

"Shalom ve lehitra'ot? Goodbye, I'll see you. We'll meet again…. And we will, of course."

On the train from Hanover, Frances was on a high, talking non-stop about her friend to Peter, telling him of all the things that Miriam taught her regarding the art of survival, the things that they laughed at in Drancy and Auschwitz, which they had, and often.

"It's brilliant that we've found her, isn't it, Peter?" Peter Mueller gave Frances a nod.

"Yes, my dear, it's very good indeed," he said.

"And now all we need to make things even more brilliant is to get Kristian home, isn't it?" Peter Mueller turned to her. His expression was one of extreme pain. Frances swallowed, as for the first time, she recognised the level of his grief and the realisation of her own, which until then she had kept hidden, even from herself. Her face screwed up and then collapsed.

"He's not coming back, Peter, is he?" Peter Mueller didn't reply. Instead, his eyes filled with tears and for the first time since Karin's death, he silently wept, and Frances succumbed to her own sorrow, sobbing in his arms, head lying on his chest.

"I can't live without him," she muttered.

"Yes, yes, you can. You will learn to. We all will learn to, because there is no other way."

"No, I don't want to. I won't live without him." Peter Mueller gently shook her.

"You are a young woman," he said, "who, against all odds, has been given the gift of life, Frances. You will learn to carry on because it would be disrespectful to those millions of people who had their lives taken from them not to. And I'm not talking just about the camps but soldiers and civilians, men, women, and children from across Europe who somehow got caught up in this bloody war and paid the ultimate price."

Chapter 33

December 1945

Richard Forsythe was a man in turmoil. In four days' time he would go home to Blighty, and he had thought he would be taking the woman of his dreams back, too.

He had helped fulfil her wishes to track down the man she called her husband to a POW camp in France, and he had hoped that would be enough, but despite being certain of the source of his information, the damned fellow hadn't been there. He couldn't understand why she was bothering with the chap at all after all she had been through. And then the dashed fellow forced her into some form of marriage so that his conscience felt better.

The man was dead; he had made some ridiculous attempt at escaping in the middle of the last winter with some other idiot. They had found one body, but not his, it seemed. And so there had been a lack of records recording his demise, and that had fuelled Frances and had made her even more eager to find him. He was convinced that she saw no future in the relationship, and he had guessed already that her tireless efforts were all for his parents' sake. She had said as much; it was for all that they had done for her, and he recognised how fond of her they were, and she of them. Even he with his dislike of the Germans had to admit that Peter Mueller appeared to be a decent fellow. He had learnt to tolerate him, even to like him. He had even gotten used to the old harridan in the kitchen and Freya Mueller could be charming at times. Attractive, too.

Women. He had learned to keep away from them for most of his life. He wondered why it was that things never ran smoothly as soon as women were involved. That's why he had kept away from them and never married, despite being in his mid-forties. There had been one or two likely gals along the highway of life. He'd even made the offer to Lady Jaqueline Partridge and for some reason she had turned him down. Now though he felt the time was right. It had to be if he weren't to miss out on a son and heir and someone to warm his slippers, fill his pipe, and be his companion in the autumn of his life. Mother, he had had to accept, wouldn't live forever.

Today could well be the last chance he would get to ask Frances to become his partner and the mother of his child. He knew all about her desire to carry on playing, but once they wed, he could put pay to that. In three days', time, they would both be attending the party that marked the end of the unit's stay in Germany. Barraclough the new commander of their part of the British zone would be there, along with some top-ranking officers and their wives and girls, and even a few German officials. It promised to be some affair and Frances was going to be the highlight of it all when she played, and she would be with him.

She was fond of him; he was certain of that, despite the tough beginning they had when he had been put in charge of the court system. She sought him out whenever she needed help, and once they had recovered from their initial poor start, and he'd learnt who she was, he had been more than happy to assist her. She just needed to accept that Mueller had disappeared without a trace, like millions of others. It was time for her to put her life back together and get out of the dung hole that Germany had become. There was another winter coming, and many believed it was going to be even worse than the last one, which had polished off thousands from the cold and hunger. Well, at least the British zone had staved off typhoid, unlike the Soviet zone.

England was the place for Frances. Even the Muellers hinted as much. Maybe if they all exerted a little more pressure, she would see sense. He stepped outside into the watery winter sunshine and went in search of his driver. There was no time like the present. He would call in on the Muellers and take along a few little extras if he could find some. Tea, perhaps, and some coffee, maybe some stockings for Frances and Freya.

* * *

The man turned into the long drive that led up to the house known as Schonen Felder. He looked careworn and beaten. Over the last few months, he had walked many kilometres; his shoes bore witness to the fact. They had shed their sole a long distance back; he had shed his own soul way before that, and now there was a deep, smouldering, anger in him waiting to vent.

He couldn't pinpoint exactly when that anger began; maybe it was when he heard of the deaths of his old crewmates, or perhaps it was when he saw those boys from his last mission sprawled out on the casing of the boat, as the plane gunned them down. It might have been when he saw the boat sink, or later when he turned murderer, or when he carried a friend as he died. It could have been when he saw those first pictures in the papers of the suffering of those remains of humanity that had been found in the death camps across Europe and in Germany itself. No, he couldn't pinpoint when it had happened, but it had, and he felt it tearing at him and turning him into a vengeful man, a man he didn't know, and a man he didn't like.

* * *

As his jeep drew level with the tall scarecrow figure making its way up the drive, Forsythe tapped his driver on the shoulder and ordered him to stop. The scarecrow man lifted his shaggy head and Forsythe looked into piercing blue eyes that stared at him from a filthy, gaunt, and bearded countenance. He extended his cane and prodded the man on the shoulder, noticing how his body and jaw stiffened.

"This is private property. What does the likes of you want here?" he asked. "If you're looking for work, there is none."

The man took hold of the tip of the cane, forcing it away from his body and for a moment both men stared unblinkingly at one another.

"What's happened to the family?" asked the man in passable English, and it angered Forsythe as he detected an arrogance in him and an edge to the voice.

"What's it to you?" he asked.

"I know them. You! Are you billeted here? Are they gone?"

"I don't answer questions from your sort, because I don't have to," snapped Forsythe. "Now clear off. There's nothing for you here." He pulled back on his cane, but the man still had hold of the other end.

Forsythe narrowed his eyes to inspect his antagonist. He wanted to believe the man was just another homeless person, searching the country for shelter, or something to steal. People like that were rarely interested in work. Once more he met the man's steady gaze, and in that moment, he knew that Mueller was home.

"Mueller," he breathed.

Mueller gave a harsh laugh. "So, you know who I am. And now, after me getting this far, you'll take me back, I suppose."

"To the Froggies? Actually, old chap, I've been trying to track you down to get you back here to your family."

Forsythe saw the confusion and relief in Mueller's bearded face as he asked, "My family, they're safe?"

Forsythe nodded and felt he had no alternative other than to offer Mueller a lift. With an effort he hauled himself into the back of the jeep and Forsythe was struck by the sheer exhaustion on the man's face as again he was fixed by his blue gaze. As the jeep pulled away, Mueller asked, "Tell me about my family?"

"Your father has kept us in fresh produce for the last few weeks and your wife…"

"Frances. Ah, I should have guessed, and what has Frances kept you in, Major?"

Forsythe's pale complexion heated under Mueller's steady gaze, and he answered through gritted teeth, causing Mueller's eyebrows to rise.

"Your wife, Kapitan Mueller, has proved invaluable in her help as an interpreter."

Mueller nodded, gave a sardonic smile, and said, "Careful, old chap, you're wearing your heart on your sleeve."

Forsythe snapped. He thought he was home and dry, and now the bloody fellow was back. "Yes, maybe I am, Mueller. Yes, I admit I do have feelings for your wife. In fact, I'm on my way now to try to talk her into coming back to England with me."

"Why?"

"Why the hell do you think, man?" blurted Forsythe.

"Then I'm sorry for you."

In desperation, Forsythe looked to the heavens. "Good God, is that your only comment?"

"I'm guessing you must have talked. That you know our situation. She must have told you that there is no relationship between us."

Forsythe neither denied nor agreed that Frances had told him she had no relationship with him, but Mueller could see that Forsythe was quietly elated.

The car crackled its way along the drive of the house and Forsythe's driver drew the car up in front of the entrance.

Frances viewed the approach of the army jeep from some distance away, as she exercised Majesty. She wondered what on earth it was, that Forsythe wanted to make him call at the house a day earlier than expected. Maybe the programme of music she had chosen to play at the Officer's club Christmas get together hadn't met the approval of the organisers, or the other musicians. Ah well, she would take Majesty back to the barn and give her a good rubdown, and then make her way to the house to find out. There was no rush. Forsythe would make himself at home and chat to Peter or Freya until she got back.

As she rubbed at Majesty's coat, she thought it would be strange to have a new unit of soldiers around, and she hoped they would prove as friendly as the present lot. She had mixed feelings about Forsythe; he had, in the end, helped her in her search for Kristian, but he bothered her. He had become a little too attached to her. She felt uncomfortable at times because she knew she had used him to a certain extent in her search for Kristian. Still another couple of days and he'd be gone, so it didn't hurt to be nice to him until then. The poor man she learned had suffered a great deal for the decision he'd made at Dunkirk. He had spoken of it in depth to her many times over, as it played on his mind. She could understand that.

She wondered if the new administrator, Forsythe's replacement, would still need her help. No doubt about it, the one or two extras of provisions that she had received had certainly kept Anna happy, and they would be missed. She had to admit that in a strange way she would miss Forsythe, too.

The Muellers, and herself included, had been lucky though, unlike many they had held on to almost everything. The farmers, it seemed, were the new elite in Germany, particularly since the Soviets had refused to honour their agreement to supply food from the eastern zone. Peter was held in high esteem and had been asked to sit on the Agricultural Council and yes, Peter had proved to be a clever man and a good man. Despite having had friends in high places, he had kept himself and his family clean and free of any Nazi stigma.

She had fared even better. She had taken Peter Mueller's advice and contacted her bank and solicitor to find that she was an exceedingly wealthy woman. She had a very buoyant bank account, her aunt's property in Paris, and the large house in Neuilly that she and Steven had bought together and lived in a lifetime ago. Her money, furthermore, was in Francs and not in Reich marks, which were losing value daily, as the German economy came crashing down. The new currency, it seemed, was cigarettes.

* * *

After seeing the mare settled down, Frances made her way back to the house. She was in no rush, as she knew that Peter and Forsythe would have plenty to discuss. It surprised her when she saw Sara's bicycle thrown down by the kitchen door and wondered why she had also made an unexpected visit. Going into the kitchen, total disorder met her. Forsythe's driver was sitting drinking ersatz coffee. He acknowledged her with a smile as she entered to find Freya, Anna and Sara all sobbing loudly and hugging each other over a half-finished meal of bread and cheese.

She felt a jolt of fear run through her body. "What is it? What's happened?" she asked.

The three women turned, and with relief, Frances saw they were weeping tears of joy.

"Kristian!" shrieked Freya.

"What?" asked Frances. "There's news of him?"

"He's here, He's home." Freya threw her arms around her daughter-in-law, hugging her tightly. "He's in the sitting room with Peter and Major Forsythe...."

Before Freya had finished her sentence, Frances was through the door into the hall and into the sitting room, jacket, and boots still on. She threw the door open and firstly saw Forsythe nearest the door and Peter Mueller seated in an armchair. Her eyes quickly dismissed them and moved to the figure standing at the far end of the room, gazing into the garden.

Mueller turned as the door opened, and she stood for a moment, surprised by his appearance. Stupidly, she had expected him to look the same as he had when he left over a year ago. His clothes were casual, beige jersey and brown trousers. He looked gaunt and tired, his clothes hung on him and his hair was long and untidy, and wet from just bathing.

"Kristian," she breathed almost to herself.

Then she was across the room, flinging her arms about him, her face weeping into his chest, not noticing his lack of response, his lack of warmth.

"I knew it. I knew you'd be back. I told them all." She turned as the other women entered the room. "Didn't I tell you? Thank God, Kristian, thank God."

He let her continue for a while, leaning on him, weeping. Then he took her by the shoulders, and pushed her away to arm's length, looking at her without a smile. He gave a harsh laugh.

"Behold the vanquished foe. Are you happy now, Frances?" he asked.

She shook her head, not hearing the bitterness in his voice, only hearing his frustration in defeat. "Don't be silly. You told me once that we are all losers when it comes to war. Don't you remember?"

"Well now, ask the victor over there how he feels about that," he said cuttingly, referring to Forsythe.

Forsythe shifted uncomfortably. He was a little confused; he didn't understand much of their language, but he thought he understood that there was no relationship between Frances and Mueller, and yet there she was weeping over him and embracing him.

"Richard has been good to us, Kristian. Come on, come, and sit down. Look at you, you are exhausted, that's all. You need to eat and then rest." She stood on tiptoe to kiss him on the cheek, but he retreated from her like a scolded cat. Then he recovered and turned his gaze on her and she found no warmth in his eyes.

"Nothing's changed, Frances, you should know that," he said.

"But it can, can't it, Kris? I've changed such a lot since you've been away. I've thought over and accepted things. I've come to terms with what happened to me."

Mueller threw his head back and mocked her. "Well, bully for you, my dear. What about the rest of us?"

Peter Mueller crossed the room to his son's side and laid an arm on his shoulder. "Frances is right, Kristian, you're tired, don't say anything now that you might regret. Some food and a good rest could change the way you're feeling."

"You're right, Pa, I am most dreadfully tired, but over the last few months I've had time to think too, and no amount of food or sleep will make me feel any different." He set his mouth in a hard line and turned back to Frances. "Nothing has changed. It's like I told you before, Frances, on the day I left. Whatever we had, if anything, is over." Frances felt the tears prickling her eyes and he drove the dagger in, still deeper. "Besides, there's a girl you see, in France. A French girl."

The room was silent as they all registered what he had said. They all watched as Frances took some deep breaths and then turned from Mueller and walked over to Richard Forsythe head held high.

"Please, could you take me into town, Richard? I'll just grab a few clothes and see you outside."

Mueller didn't wait to see her leave; he left the room too, with Sara close on his heels. She grabbed his arm, and he spun round to face her.

"When did you become so cruel, Kristian?" she asked. "Frances has done nothing but search for you for the last year. You are all she has thought about. She's done everything she could to take care of your parents and keep them positive, too."

"As it happens, she needn't have bothered searching, need she? I've got home without her help. Now leave it, Sara. It's nothing to do with you. You understand nothing!" he snapped.

He turned and walked away towards the staircase. She watched him go, open mouthed.

Chapter 34

Bonn December 1945

Fool! Fool to think even for one minute that things could ever be alright between them.

Frances had lost count of the number of times she had paced the floor of her suite in the Grand Apollo since she had arrived some hours before. Unable to remain at Schonen Felder following Kristian's onslaught, she had asked Richard Forsythe to find her a suite at the hotel and he had. The Apollo, still run by Germans but where Germans were forbidden to stay. Allies only. And then, as if she hadn't had enough on her mind, Forsythe had set about professing his feelings for her. Why the hell did men have such a dreadful sense of timing? she wondered.

What a mess everything had become. Angry and hurt, she agreed to leave Germany with Forsythe in three days' time. That would be the morning following the party at the Officer's club, which was to be a combined Christmas get-together and send off for those who were going back to England. She thought she had made it clear to Forsythe that she would be glad of his company on the journey, and that was all, but he had pressed her to spend just a couple of days at his home in the Cotswolds, assuring her he lived there with his mother. She had agreed to that too; it was so close to the town where she had grown up, and she wanted to revisit her childhood happy times, before moving on either to London or Paris. She still hadn't decided which.

She had spent the last year dreaming of a utopia when Mueller returned. She had done her best to clear her head of all the bad things that had happened, and now look. She was married to a man who cared nothing for her; he was just repaying a debt, a debt for services rendered. Was that the way of it then? And yet the kisses, though few, had been sweet and the caresses tender. Was it all meaningless to him? Well, he was an expert, wasn't he, hadn't Sophie Heyne said as much? "There never was anyone as good as you." And she should know, Sophie was a bloody connoisseur!

And then there were Miriam's words, too. "Did he ever tell you he loved you?" Answer? No, never. But he'd told her twice that it was over, and she had to respect his wishes. And so, she was determined not to see him again before she left Germany with Forsythe. She needed Sara's help. There were things she still had to do at Schonen Felder. She needed to call her and hoped to goodness the phone lines were up and working from Bonn to the Kohl residence.

* * *

Two days later, she thought how strange it was driving up to the place that had been her home for the past eighteen months, knowing that this would be the last time. Forsythe had got hold of a car for her to run around in for a couple of days. She didn't ask where from, and he didn't tell her. She didn't tell him that her driving skills were questionable. As she drew up in front of the entrance, Freya ran out to meet her, grasping her in a tight embrace that brought them both to tears.

"Anna and I have packed your clothes, Frances. I'll get Peter to put them in the car for you. I don't know what to say to you. I love you like my own. I want you to stay," sobbed Freya.

"You know I can't. Kristian has made it clear that there is no place here for me, Freya. He has met someone else." She forced a smile. "He's fallen in love. Finally, eh? I won't get in the way of that. He brought me here to protect me until the war ended. Nothing more."

"Oh Frances, I can't believe that. You've made up your mind to go, I can see that. You will keep in touch, won't you? I couldn't bear it...."

"Of course, I'll write often, and then perhaps you will come to Paris when things are more settled. You're my family now, aren't you? Is Anna in the kitchen?"

"Where else?"

"Of course. I'll just go and find her for a while and see you again before I leave. I want to see Peter too, of course. Is he at the stables?"

Freya forced a smile. "No, he's working in the study; you'll be in trouble if you don't see him. I hope you know," Frances nodded.

"Shall I go round the back to the kitchen?"

"Whichever. You don't need permission to do anything here."

Frances took the back route through the garden. She stood for a while, remembering the first time she had seen it, the day she had arrived with Kristian over eighteen months before. It had been early summer then and everything was in full bloom or budding, full of promise. Now there was little to see apart from a dusting of frost on the bare earth. She pulled her fur jacket closer around her to keep out the cold.

Knocking on the kitchen window, she caught Anna's attention and ran in through the back door to another tearful embrace.

"I don't know what's wrong with that boy," said Anna. "I thought I knew him, but I don't. I'd like to take my stick to him, but I suppose he's too old for that." Frances gave a weak smile through her tears and Anna took her back into her arms. "I wish you would stay, but I know you can't. You will take care of yourself, Frances, won't you? These are such difficult times for a woman to be on her own."

Frances made light of it. "Of course, I will. I've survived until now, haven't I? And I can cook now too, thanks to you, so I won't starve anyway." Then the tears took over once again. "You'd better write to me Anna, promise me."

Anna nodded. "I'm not much good at letter writing, but for you I will try." They embraced once more.

"And now I'm going to the stables to say farewell to my four-legged friends and Alf and Willie if they are around. I'll see you before I leave, won't I? We'll have a coffee." Anna nodded and followed her to the door and watched her disappear through the garden down to the stables.

As she crunched her way down the gravel path, Frances thought again how odd it was that this was the last time she would see Majesty and her foal, who was now a yearling. They were both in the adjoining paddock next to the barn. As she made her way towards the gate, Majesty gave an excited whinny and trotted over, but Frances saw her eyes were looking past her, to somewhere else. She turned to see Mueller walking across the yard towards her, dressed for riding in breeches, pullover, and wax jacket. Looking around for some sort of escape but finding none, she felt herself go hot, and the blood rushed into her face. He wasn't supposed to be here. He was supposed to be out riding with Sara. It had been arranged.

"Frances." He acknowledged her at least. He'd used her name though, and she thought that was not a good start.

"I'm sorry. I didn't come here to see you, or make things difficult," she apologised. "I thought…"

"You thought I would be out riding with Sara? So, it was all organised between the two of you, I suppose. And I would have been, but

Bismarck's thrown a shoe, you see, so I came back." He walked over to the fence and threw the saddle he was carrying down on top of it.

"I'm sorry... I wouldn't have come," she stumbled on her words. "I, I just wanted to say goodbye to Majesty." Mueller rubbed at the mare's nose and neck and received a loving snort in return. "See, you're not here for months and as soon as you're back, I get dumped," Frances complained.

He gave a quick smile. "You've done an excellent job with the foal, and Pa tells me that you are now a fine horsewoman. What did you call him in the end?"

"What?"

"The foal." Frances felt a fool. Of course, he was referring to the foal. She had so much she wanted to say to him, but all the words were stuck in her throat. "So, what did you call him?" Mueller asked again.

"Kapitan." She gave a little laugh, which to her sounded hysterical. "I called him Kapitan."

"Ah, good choice." He gave her the hint of a smile and looked down at the floor and scuffed his feet around, then looked up and met her gaze. "So," he continued, "what are you going to do with him?"

"What do you mean?"

"He's yours, isn't he? Will you take him with you do you think?" It was her turn to look at the floor.

"No, of course not. He belongs here. I wouldn't do that to him."

"No, of course you wouldn't." He gave a tired sigh and leaned forward onto the fence. "I was harsh on you the other day. It was inexcusable," he said, and then was thoughtful for a few moments. "Have you any regrets, Froggy?" he suddenly asked.

She shrugged, struggling against the tears that were threatening. It would have been easier if he'd carried on being unpleasant.

"About us?" She felt her voice catch in her throat. He nodded, and she thought for a while before carrying on. "No, no, of course not. No regrets about having a relationship with you. You helped me grow up you know. All this acrimony though, I have regrets about all this mess." She leant on the fence, turning away from him, clicking at the horses whilst trying to regain her control. "What about you? Do you have regrets?" she asked, turning back to him. He shook his head.

"No man would regret making love to you, Froggy." he said. She thought back to the times on UBA almost three years before.

"It's odd, isn't it? I think some of my happiest times were on board that bloody boat." She looked at him and forced a smile, "God, what good men they are! I'll never forget them, you know."

Mueller paled. He turned away from her and took a couple of deep breaths, then turning back, he blurted out, "You need to know. UBA was sunk, Froggy, all men lost, they're gone, all of them."

There was a strangled cry from her which tore at Mueller's guts. She ran from him into the barn, finding a free stall to hideaway in, and there she broke into uncontrollable sobbing. Following quickly behind her, he was apologetic. "You didn't need to know. I shouldn't have told you. It was foolish of me. I'm so sorry, Froggy."

"You're lying, aren't you? You must be. Tell me you're lying, Kristian," she begged through her tears, searching his eyes for the answer she wanted to hear. "It's just another way to hurt me, isn't it? It's not true, is it?"

Her grief was tearing into him. He wanted it to stop. Her to stop. Taking her by the shoulders, he pleaded, "Hush Froggy, please hush."

"Paul. Paul, he can't be gone. Tell me he's not gone, and Klaus? No, and not Dieter, not little Dieter, please God."

With each member of his old crew that she named; a dagger was driven into him. He felt himself buckling beneath the added weight of her grief on top of his own, and he couldn't bear it. Wrapping his arms around her, he pulled her close and kissed her forehead, and then he tried to kiss away the salt tears from her eyes, but still they fell and still she continued naming his men, his crew, his friends, one by one.

"Koenig, and Gotz? He'll never sing again or try out that technique. Ehrhart? His family…. No Kristian, please tell me it's a lie. It's not true, you are lying, you must be. Please say you are?"

"Hush please, Froggy, don't," he begged, kissing her eyes and her cheeks where the tears were falling, and then her mouth, preventing her from speaking more names, tasting her tears, and the depth of her sorrow.

She reached up, putting her arms around his neck, returning his kisses, until almost together they pulled apart and looked into one another's eyes. It was she who reached up once more to him, her sorrow turning to passion and anger. Taking his face in her hands, she continued to kiss him, staring up at him, determined not to bend to his will, to show him she could take charge, that he didn't matter. She threw down a gauntlet; refusing to close her eyes, refusing to mutter endearments. And he took the gauntlet up and returned like with like. Staring into the fire that was kindling in her eyes with each kiss. And so, it went on, until she felt herself falter from the onslaught of his kisses, felt her eyes begin to close, felt once more that she was falling under his spell... so she bit him.

"Shit!" He pushed her away, tasting the blood, dabbing it away from his lip with his hand. "That bloody well hurt, Froggy."

"Good," she spat.

He stared at her for a few seconds, sucking his lip, gauging her mood, watching the shallow quickness of her breaths, feeling her excitement. He nodded, staring back into her eyes again and with the hint of a smile, he asked, "Are we playing dirty, Froggy? Is that what you want to do?"

She swallowed as the passion inside her welled up into her throat so that she was unable to speak.

"Well then, no answer must mean yes," he said, pushing her backwards, lifting her slight form and slamming her into the back of the stall so that the back of her head crashed into the wood of the wall.

She cried out, "Ouch! You bastard," as he shoved his right knee between her legs and pushed her shoulder against the wall with his right hand, lifting her skirt with the other. He felt the softness of the skin of her thighs and grabbed at the lace of her knickers, pulling them down, waiting for some sort of resistance from her, which didn't come. Instead, she helped him, stepping out of them as she toyed with the buttons on his flies, finding his penis swollen and ready for her.

Exploring the dampness between her thighs, he pushed his fingers gently inside her, and she gave a low moan which caught in her throat as already she could feel the muscles of her inner core starting to spasm.

Their breathing was fast and furious, their desire for one another consuming. He bent his knees slightly to encircle her buttocks with his arms, lifting her from the floor, and she wrapped her legs around his hips and threw her arms round his neck to help him take her weight as he entered her. He thrust into her, feeling her body go rigid, knowing that she was close, pushing into her deeper, staring into her eyes until she closed them in the throes of her orgasm. Her head collapsed onto his neck, and he felt the warmth of her gentle panting breath as he reached his own ecstasy.

After, she gave him time for his breathing to calm, and then she removed her arms from him, and he cradled her as she slipped down his body to the floor. Turning her back on him, she retrieved her knickers, using them to dry herself.

"I'm late for a rehearsal. I have to go." She knew she was garbling but couldn't stop. She fought to control herself. "Goodbye, Kristian," she said, turning back round to face him. She held her head high, holding his gaze and her knickers. Holding her hand outstretched because she hadn't got a clue what else to do. He foolishly took it. "I hope you don't mind if I take my clothes. I've left the bracelet and violin with Anna in the kitchen," she said.

Keeping hold of her hand, he replied, and she felt the gentleness in his voice, "You didn't need to do that. They were gifts, Froggy."

Pulling away from his grasp, she snapped, "I don't need gifts to remember you by, Kristian. Why don't you give them to your girl in France, and oh yes, you can give her these too?" She flung her semen-soaked knickers, which hit him on the arm. Then she walked calmly from the barn straight into Sara, who was tying her horse to the fence across the other side of the yard.

"Frances?" she called, "Hold on, wait."

She called back, not wanting Sara to see the state she was in. "I can't, Sar, I'm late for a rehearsal. I... I must go... now." Taking no notice, Sara ran up the path to catch up.

"Kristian hasn't turned up. I thought I'd ride over and meet him on the way." Noticing Frances's tears, she asked, "What's wrong, Froggy? What's happened?" Knowing there could only be one explanation for the state Frances was in, she exclaimed, "Oh no, where is he?"

"He's in the barn, Sar. I'm so ashamed, I whored myself."

"What?"

"I behaved like a whore; I threw myself at him." Sara lifted her eyebrows, and despite the obvious gravity of the situation, a giggle escaped her.

"You did? Well, lucky Kristian. Is he lucky?"

"He'll hate me for the way I behaved. I know he will," sobbed Frances.

Sara looked at her with something near wonderment. "So? Spill."

"God, Sar, it shouldn't have happened. It was madness and all my fault. Look, I really do have to go. I'll see you tonight though, won't I?"

Sara wrapped her arms around her. "For God's sake, Frances, stay a while. Surely you don't need to rush off. You're too upset to go anywhere at the moment. You certainly can't drive."

"I most certainly do need to go, and I have to drive. I'm already late for the bloody rehearsal. Would you keep Kristian away from the house while I get my things together? I don't want to see him again. I couldn't face him after what's just happened."

Sara took her arms from around her. "Are you sure you're alright?" she asked.

"Yes, really, I'll be fine. I have to be, don't I?"

* * *

Watching Frances make her way back to the house, Sara then turned and made for the barn. As she entered, she was confronted by Mueller's back. He was seated on a bale of straw at the far end of the building, bent forward, head in hands. He didn't hear her approach. She laid a hand on his shoulder, and he grasped it, turning, hoping to find Frances returned, unable to hide his disappointment upon seeing Sara.

"She's gone then, Sar?" he said, the question being more of a statement.

"Isn't that what you wanted?"

He gave a slight laugh and said, "No, no, of course it's not what I wanted."

"It certainly sounded that way two days ago," she replied, "and what have you done to your lip?"

"It's not what I wanted, Sar, but it's for the best. Froggy is better off without me, you see. It's better for her if she goes. She bit me, by the way. That's what's wrong with my lip."

Sara seated herself on the bale next to him. "It looks sore."

"It is," he said. Sara gave a sigh of exasperation.

"You know two days ago; I'd have agreed with you that it was in Froggy's best interest to go. That was some outburst from you, Kristian. But now I find you head in hands with a bitten lip and more upset than I've seen you since you were eight. What the hell is going on with you? Frances thinks you hate her because in her words she just whored herself. What's that all about?"

He gave Sara a weak smile. "Is that what she said? I'd say I took advantage of her. And I don't want a bloody sermon, so don't even start."

"I'm not going to give you one. I know you, Kristian Mueller, probably better than anyone. Why won't you just admit that you're in love at last? It's always been obvious to me. You wouldn't have brought Froggy home if you weren't. Oh, you'd have got her out of the camp, but that would have been the end."

~ 255 ~

Mueller bit his damaged lip without thinking and winced. "Well, she's gone, Sar, so that is the end of it."

"And you're going to just sit back and let her go."

"Yes, that's exactly what I'm going to do."

In her frustration, Sara gave him a shove. "Why Kristian, for Christ's sake?"

He turned on her, raising his voice. "Because! Because Sar."

"Because what?" she shouted back, giving him a second shove.

"Because I am filled with shame. Shame for myself and shame for my country. Shame for the way I treated her. She told me things. She cried out to me, and I told her she was a madwoman. I turned my back on her when she needed me most, preferring to believe that it was she who was at fault, she who was mad, rather than all those mad bastards in Berlin. There you have it. Now leave me alone, Sara. Please go, and just leave me alone, eh?"

Seeing his grief, she threw her arms around him, and he collapsed into them, laying his head against hers as she said, "Don't you think we have all felt that shame? She told us the night before you left for Kiel that she forgave us all, because the things she had told us were so unbelievable."

"Unbelievable but true," he said, then he gave a sniff. "She's better off without me, like I've said. How can I ask her to stay here, Sar? We're an occupied country now. We've been carved up. Do you think they are going to make things easy for us, huh? It's going to be hard for years. Froggy will be better off out of it. Don't you think I've thought it all through? My God, it's all I've thought of for months. Now leave it, please."

"Tell me you don't love her and then I'll leave it, I promise."

He unwound himself from her embrace and looked her in the face. "Of course, I bloody well love her. I felt something the first time I set eyes on her. They laid her on my bunk and there was a stray curl in her mouth, and I pushed it back. All I wanted was to keep her safe, Sar. That's all I've ever wanted, and I've failed. I love her more than my own life. I swear I do, and that's why I can let her go, you see. For her."

"Do you not think Frances should have some say in her life? You shouldn't underestimate her strength, you know. Look what she's been through. What she's survived."

"Oh, I would never underestimate Froggy. I know what she's been through. Now more than ever. That's why she deserves more than I can give her. She deserves better than a life here. Better than me."

"You're wrong, Kristian. What Froggy needs is to know she's loved. You really injured her with your talk of another woman. How could you do that on top of everything else?"

Mueller stood up and paced the floor. "I wanted her to hate me. I thought it would make things easier."

Sara snapped, "Who for? Who were you making things easier for? Is there a girl, huh? Is there another girl, Kristian?"

"No, no, of course not. Well, not the way you are implying."

"What am I implying, do you think? Is there another girl in France?"

"Marianne, she looked after me..." began Mueller.

"I bet she did!"

"She saved my life, Sar. She's just a kid, only nineteen."

"And you bedded her!" He turned away.

"I'm not proud of it. But you have to understand the way things were. I thought there was a good chance I wouldn't make it back. She'd lost her man, and we were both lonely, and then the war ended and...." He shrugged.

"God, Kristian, I hope you haven't left her with a little German in her belly."

"I was careful, always." He puffed out his cheeks and exhaled, sitting deep in thought for a few moments before he spoke. "What the hell do I do, Sar? I've really cocked up, haven't I?"

Sara shrugged. "Yes, you have. And I don't know. How did you leave things? I assume not great, as you are both in pieces."

Mueller forced a laugh. "We shook hands," he said.

"You shook hands." She shook her head. "Is this the same boy every girl in town either wept over or wanted to lay? Unbelievable!" Sara paced the floor of the barn, thinking. "You must tell Frances how you feel, Kristian. She deserves to know."

"How? It's all too late. Tomorrow morning she'll be gone, and tonight it's that sodding party. It's too late to change things. Maybe that's a sign huh? It's just the way it's meant to be."

"I'm going to that damn party by the way," announced Sara.

"The devil you are! How come?" asked Mueller with some surprise.

"It might just be that my fiancée is taking me."

Mueller looked at Sara wide eyed, then despite everything, he burst into laughter. "Fiancée? Why the hell didn't you tell me? Why the hell has no one told me?"

"I think my news got swept under the carpet because of your dramatic appearance, that's why."

"So, come on then, who's fool enough to take you on?" asked Mueller.

"Lieutenant Jack Burton, American 12th army."

"Hah! A bloody Yank. What ever happened to all the good German boys?"

"What ever happened to all the good German girls? You don't choose who you fall in love with Kristian, haven't your learnt that at least?"

He scowled at her. "Whatever happened to non-fraternising?"

"Ah, well, your wife helped us with that. We met here in March, in fact. He has now been given special permission to fraternise with me. Come tonight and you'll meet him. He's a musician too, plays in a swing band that the Brits have nabbed for the night."

"Another bloody musician! Tempting as your offer is, no thanks. I'll meet him some other time."

"What's happened to your balls, Kris? Perhaps I need to check them out?" Mueller retreated a little. Sara had taken him by the balls on several occasions when they were youngsters, as a way of persuading him she was right, when he had known very well that she was wrong. He recalled the pain of it.

"You can sod off, Sara," he said, retreating a little further still. Sara watched him for a few moments, then with a smile, she resorted to other childhood methods.

"I dare you. I dare you to come tonight and meet Jack and tell Froggy that you love her."

Mueller shook his head at her. "That's not fair is it, using a dare?" He thought for a moment, his interest sparked. "How would I get in anyway? If I came that is. Invitation only surely. I can't just walk in?"

"True," said Sara, "but I know how you can get in. It's at the Grande in Bonn. The Brits now use it as their officers' club. You're right though, there will be guards at the entrance, but there's a fire escape around the back. Maybe I could open the door for you from the inside. What do you say?"

Mueller gave a sniff. "I'll think about it. What time is Froggy playing?"

"Get there by eight. Dinner suit if not in uniform and I think it is best that you're not. You might stand out a bit. If you do come, behave, please. We could give you a lift if you like."

"I said I'll think about it, Sar. If I come, I'll make my own way there."

Chapter 35

There was a knock at the door of Frances's hotel room. She was deep in thought. Since returning from the rehearsal for the evening's performance, the only thing that had been on her mind, as usual, had been Mueller. She was thinking about their meeting, and lovemaking, if you could call it that. What the hell had she been trying to prove? And to whom? Him? Herself? She'd behaved like a complete idiot. A whore.

The knock drew her from her reverie, and she looked at her watch, the one Freya had given to her. It was 6:30 pm, and she was nowhere near ready. That would be Richard, she thought, come early to batter her senses with further unwanted protestations. She took a deep breath and opened the door to find Sara on the other side.

"Frances, what are you doing? Why aren't you ready? Aren't you due at the Officer's club at 7:00?"

"Yes, yes. Come in, Sara. What on earth are you doing here?"

"I have this for you." Sara produced the violin Mueller had given her, the one she had left at Schonen Felder. "I told Kristian that you were having to borrow a violin. He said to tell you to use this tonight, and then to take it with you when you leave tomorrow. Or you can leave it with me if you're set on returning it."

Frances took the case with a sigh. "That's kind of him, Sar, thank him for me, will you? I confess I will feel better playing an instrument that I know."

"Of course, I'll thank him, but come on, look at you. You're not even dressed. I'll give you a hand." Sara crossed to the wardrobe and removed a bottle green satin gown.

"I wasn't going to wear that, Sar. I had that made specially. You know I did. There's a black one hanging up. I'll wear that instead."

"Rubbish! Come on, chop, chop, this one is the one for tonight."

Sara undid the satin covered buttons on the back of the gown and held it open for Frances to step into. It fit her like a second skin. The bodice was boned, leaving her shoulders naked except for thin straps. It was tight across the hips, then gently flared in folds to her feet.

Sara's eyes lit up. "Wow, that's some gown. Now what about your hair, loose?"

"No, I will have to tie up the sides or it will get in the way when I play. I have your combs here somewhere. I think they're in the bathroom. I found some jet earrings, too. Now I can finish myself, Sar. You get back to Jack and enjoy yourself. I'll see you soon."

Sara gave her a kiss on the cheek. "Good luck, Froggy. I'll see you later."

As she left, she bumped into Forsythe walking up the hall and called back, "Frances, Richards's here."

Frances called out from the bathroom, "Sorry Richard, I lost track of time. Give me five minutes. Help yourself to a drink."

"Don't rush. You've had a lot on your mind. Are you sure you are up to playing?" he shouted through to the bathroom.

"Yes, yes, of course I am," she called again. "I'm looking forward to it."

He was a decent man, Richard Forsythe, she thought. They had got on well once they had both got over their poor start. She knew he was more than a little impressed by her musical ability and that coloured his judgement of her, but that wasn't unusual. She thought about Otto and his comments about her talent, and even Steven had initially only shown interest in her because of the music. The music, she thought, I am nothing without music, just a shell. And yet Mueller had seen something more, he must have. He had no interest in music. It meant nothing to him.

What a dreadful mess everything had become. The intensity of her feelings for Mueller had ruined her for any other relationship. Love or hate him, Mueller filled her mind night and day. Sometimes, like now, she experienced a feeling of such guilt that she thought of Steven so rarely.

She glanced at her reflection in the mirror before she went back into the lounge to greet Forsythe. She looked good and she knew it. The thought of playing again for a live audience had given her the spark she needed. It was there in her eyes, and that gave her confidence. She had clipped up the sides of her wayward hair in one of the latest fashions. Her gown pleased her, as it should, it cost a great deal on the black market. It was special and had been for Mueller, and she wished he could see her in it.

Mueller walked the perimeter of the hotel that was now the British Officer's Club, searching for a way in. The entrances and exits were well guarded, as he knew they would be. He thought he was certainly going to have to resort to the fire escape if he was to get in. He had spoken to his parents about his feelings for Frances that afternoon, and it overjoyed them with the prospect of him and Frances finally sorting things out and settling down as a married couple. His father had even found him petrol to get him to Bonn and back.

He noticed a guard eyeing him up. He had been hanging around for too long, and the man was becoming suspicious. The time for thinking had passed, and he was going to have to act. He walked back round to the rear of the building, finding there was a guard posted at that door too, but further along and set in the shadows was the fire escape. He took his shoes off and slipped them into the pockets of his dinner jacket, praying they wouldn't fall out and alert the guard as he climbed stealthily up the steps of the metal framework. He thanked God there was a thick blanket of clouds making the winter night still darker.

With great care, he made his way and got to the top with scarcely a sound. He paused and listened for voices on the other side of the door and, hearing nothing, pushed his weight against it, only to find it locked. He cursed inwardly, wondering what the hell to do when the sound from a window being opened to the right of where he stood drew his attention and probably that of the guard. He jumped back from the door and into the shadows. There was whispering from the open window. Sara was calling to him softly.

"Kristian, Kris. Are you there?"

"Of course, I'm bloody well here. What's happened to the door?" he whispered back.

"I knew you'd come. I couldn't open the door, neither could Jack. We tried. The bloody thing's stuck," continued Sara.

"Look, Sar, this isn't the place for a conversation. I can't get in, so clearly, I'm not meant to be here."

"Bollocks!" came the whispered expletive from the window. "You can climb onto the outside of the fire escape," she continued, "and it looks like from there you can reach across to the window here."

"Oh, great, and what if I can't?" Mueller spoke in hushed tones. "There's a guard down there with a bloody big rifle. That's if I don't kill myself in the fall, of course."

"You can do it, I'm sure of it. Come on, come, and look."

Mueller came out from the shadows of the framework once more and threw Sara a withering glance as he assessed the distance from the fire escape to the window. He was tall enough and thought he might just be able to stretch his right arm across and get a hold on the inside of the windowsill whilst hanging on to the fire escape frame with his left hand. The crunch was going to be when he let go of the frame with his left hand. He was just going to hope that his right arm would take his weight momentarily, until he could swing his other arm across to share the load.

"I don't know, Sar, it's quite a stretch," he whispered up to her.

"Come on, I'll help you," she replied, then she gave a little shriek, and hearing a man's voice, Kristian jumped back into the shadows. Seconds later, she was back at the window again. "Kristian, it's Jack. He's here. Come on, we can both pull you in."

Mueller felt the start of an adrenaline rush. He was rising to the challenge of outwitting the enemy once more. He replaced his shoes. Any sound now, he thought, and he was a dead man, anyway. He swung his body onto the outside of the frame and stretched across to the windowsill with his right arm. Feeling the safety of another man hanging on to him, he let go of the fire escape and swung his other hand into the window space, dangling for a couple of seconds until he was hauled through the window and onto the floor of a linen cupboard by a young GI.

Jack Burton held out his hand to help Mueller to his feet and introduced himself with a broad grin.

"I knew you'd come; I knew you could do it," said Sara with a laugh as she used her hands to brush Mueller's dress suit down. "Of course, that was the straightforward part of the evening, wasn't it? The hard part involves Froggy."

Mueller slapped Sara's hands away and turned to Burton. "Kristian Mueller and I'm very pleased to meet you," he said in his best English offering Burton his hand, and then referring to Sara, "Have you any idea at all what you're taking on here, Jack? She's been trying to get me killed since we were kids." Jack smiled as Sara took control.

"Shush, Kristian. Right, it's quarter to eight. You stay here and Jack will bring you a drink," she ordered. "Best to keep out of Forsythe's sight. We'll let you know when Frances is about to play." She opened the door of the cupboard and pulled Burton through the door after her, making sure the door was properly closed behind her. Once out, she couldn't resist rapping on it. "You stay there and don't move until we say," she ordered.

Mueller settled down on the floor in the corner, listening to the sounds of partying and wondering if by being here, he had made one of the most stupid decisions ever. Life in Germany for the foreseeable future would not be a ball. Most likely it was going to be hell, and yet that was what he was going to offer Frances.

About ten minutes later, there was a knock on the cupboard door and Jack Burton appeared, beers in hand, one of which he passed to Mueller.

"Come on Kristian, time to put in an appearance," he said. "Just mingle. There are quite a few blokes here not in uniform, so you won't stand out. Frances has just arrived at the far end of the ballroom and the orchestra is tuning up. I'll stick with you. Let's find a good place to watch. Sara will find us. What have you done to your lip, by the way?"

"Frances," said Mueller with a grimace.

Jack Burton gave Mueller a knowing smile as he made his way through the ballroom, keeping to the left side, which, like the other, had rectangular pillars running along it. A large wooden dance floor took up the centre of the room, with staging at one end already occupied by members of the military orchestra. There were tables and chairs set out for those wishing to eat and seating for Frances's performance. Dotted around on the carpeted area were more comfortable chairs and lower tables for those who wished for a more relaxed evening.

As the two men walked the length of the room towards the staging, Mueller recognized Konrad Adenauer and pointed him out to Jack.

"Good God, I'm surprised that Adenauer has graced the Brits with his presence, after the way they treated him in October. They removed the old guy from office, didn't they?" Jack remarked.

"Oh, the Brits will fete him. They will have realised by now what a mistake they've made," said Mueller wryly. "Adenauer is one of the few who can bring some sort of order back to Germany, you see. Let's not go any closer to the front, Jack. I'd rather watch from here. I don't want Froggy to see me; it might put her off."

There was some clapping of hands and a ripple of anticipation as Frances made her way to the raised stage, looking impeccable. The dress clung to the contours of her body and her amber eyes were alight with excitement at the thought of playing for an audience again. Her professionalism shone from her and was obvious to everyone.

Once on stage, she turned to the small military orchestra and quickly gave a final tuning to her violin. She gave the members of the orchestra a nod and a smile to signify that she was ready to begin. There was silence in the hall, broken only by a low, almost inaudible whistle from Jack Burton. "My God, that's some girl. Mueller, you're a lucky fella," he whispered.

Mueller gave him a quick smile, struggling to tear his eyes away from Frances for one second as he replied, "Yes, I know I am."

A hush had fallen on the audience as Frances raised her bow and for fifteen minutes delighted her audience and the orchestra who accompanied her by playing 'The Lark Ascending' by Vaughan Williams. She stepped forward after taking a bow and held up her hands to quieten down the applause.

"Well now," she began, "I thought I'd better get you all on side by playing a piece by a British composer, and what a fine piece." The audience cheered, and she had to wait again for them to settle down. "That, of course, was by Ralph Vaughan Williams, The Lark Ascending. I'd like to change the mood now with a short piece by Paganini, Caprice number 24."

This was a piece of music she had set herself the task of perfecting. Known for being one of the most difficult pieces written for solo violin, if she could master it, she would know that she had found her form again. She held her audience enthralled for the 5 minutes it took to play it and received a standing ovation at the end.

As the applause continued, Sara joined Mueller and Jack, who were standing in the shadows of the pillars.

"Wow, that girl is good," she said to Mueller, who nodded, still unable to look away from Frances and madly clapped with the rest of the audience. Frances was enjoying the appreciation and was in no rush to continue, waiting until the applause abated before stepping forward once again.

"Thank you, thank you so much," she began. "You know, I was always taught to leave an audience wanting more, so I would like to play just one more piece for you this evening. As some of you know, the war for me has been quite a journey, and has taken me to some unusual and difficult places where I met some wonderful people. French, English, Jewish, Polish, and German. Many of those people have since lost their lives." She paused to gain control of her emotions, struggling to finish what she wanted to say as her voice broke. "I would like to dedicate this piece of music to all of them." She felt the tears well up and fought to control them. "Especially, I would like to dedicate this piece to my late husband, Steven Meyer, my teacher, and my friend. This is Massenet's Meditation."

* * *

As Frances took her final bow, Richard Forsythe rushed forward to take her hand, helping her step down from the stage. He pecked her on the cheek and congratulated her on a magnificent performance. They were making their way back to a large group of top brass officers when Mueller walked out from behind a pillar, stopping them dead in their tracks.

Frances felt her pulse rate quicken. "Kristian, what on earth are you doing here?" she asked, fighting against the lump she felt in her throat.

As Forsythe, in unison, also asked, "How the bloody hell did you get in here?"

Mueller raised his eyebrows at them both. "Ladies first, I think," he said. "I came to see you, Froggy. And to answer your question, Forsythe, I broke in, past your guards I'm afraid."

"Well, you can bloody well break out again and under your own steam, or I can get some chaps to help you if you like."

Mueller felt his hackles rise and was about to give a curt reply but was prevented from doing so by the arrival of Konrad Adenauer

"Ah young Mueller, isn't it?" said Adenauer, laying a hand on his shoulder and extinguishing the heat from the situation with Forsythe.

Mueller turned to him. "Yes, Sir, it is."

"I heard you were missing. When did you get back?"

"Just a couple of days ago."

"It's good to see you, my boy, you look remarkably well for what you have been through. How are your parents?"

"Coping, Sir, thankfully."

Somewhat deflated, Forsythe led Frances away and over to a group of British officers, who also congratulated her on her performance. Forsythe introduced her to Brigadier Barraclough, Military Governor of North Rhine, and was until he left the next day, Forsythe's commanding officer. Frances took the hand of a neat man with thinning hair who sported a moustache. He was covered with medals, she noted.

~ 266 ~

"Ah, Miss Lamont. I very much enjoyed your performance. Perhaps you and Major Forsythe would like to join me at my table?"

Frances glanced quickly at Forsythe, who nodded gratefully at Barraclough, and accepted the invitation. Once seated, Frances set herself the task of trying to listen in on Kristian's conversation with Adenauer. She was disappointed. There was too much conversation around the table at which she was sitting. She found, along with the general hubbub, Mueller's conversation with Adenauer was drowned out. He had come to see her. Why? she wondered. Maybe it wasn't her he had come to see. Maybe he had come along to meet Sara and Burton. He had taken a risk surely by turning up whatever the reason. She glanced towards him and met his eyes. He quickly looked away. He was watching her. Was he watching her? He had caught her watching him. Her mind was in a spin.

"I seem to remember you were reading law at Bonn, am I right?" Adenauer asked Mueller.

"Yes, I completed the course and then joined the Kriegsmarine."

"And you left Bonn with a first, I think."

Mueller nodded, "It all seems a long time ago now, Sir. Another lifetime ago." Adenauer returned the nod and smiled as Mueller cast a glance in Frances's direction, not for the first time he noticed.

"It's young men like you we are going to rely upon to rebuild Germany. I could do with a young lawyer. I am working on forming a Rhineland branch of the Christian Democratic Union Party. How would you like to work for me, Kristian?"

Kristian puffed out his cheeks and exhaled. The offer was a brilliant opportunity for him to rebuild his life, but there was still an enormous shadow across it. "I'd like that very much, Sir, but you may not want me," he said. "I'm a wanted man, you see."

Mueller told Adenauer the story of his internment in the camp in France, and his meeting with Otto, and the unfortunate accident which ended his life. He told him how he and Fackler had escaped the camp and how Fackler had been shot and later died. How he had been lucky enough to have been nursed back to health by the Cousteaus and had then made his way home.

"So, you see, Sir, I have no discharge papers, no ID, and I probably have a price on my head. Not the ideal employee for you and your party, I'm afraid."

Adenauer took Mueller by the arm. "Come on," he said, leading him over to the group of British officers surrounding Frances. Catching

Barraclough's eye, he said, "Barraclough? You owe me, I think. This is Kristian Mueller, one of our Grey Wolves. A good lad from an excellent family. He's got himself into a bit of bother with the French. I'd like you to help him. Let's say it's payback for you removing me from my office as mayor, eh?"

Mueller thought Barraclough looked discomforted by the reminder that he had removed one of the best German administrators from office, and from an important post in the Rhine. He knew Barraclough was no fool, and would know full well, that Adenauer was a decent man. He would probably be regretting he had acted hastily as far as his removal from office was concerned. Mueller held out his hand to Barraclough who rewarded him with a welcoming smile.

"One of the Grey Wolves, eh? You gave us the run-around for a good while. I think you could have beaten us in the Atlantic, Mueller."

"I agree with you, Sir, and Donitz knew that. Those in Berlin couldn't see it though. They were fools, I'm afraid."

"Well, lucky for us then, eh? So, you've been upsetting the Frenchie's, have you? Good show. What have you been up to then?"

Mueller related his tale, once again keeping his voice low, not wanting to broadcast the fact that he had no papers to his name.

Barraclough rubbed his chin thoughtfully. "So, Mueller, what you haven't told me is why you took a swipe at the man in the first place."

"No, Sir, I haven't."

"Well?"

Mueller swallowed before saying, "He raped my wife, you see."

"The devil he did!" spat Barraclough. He knitted his brows together in thought. "Just a minute, isn't the lovely Frances your wife?"

"Yes, she is," said Mueller.

"Then, I'd say the bugger deserved to die. My God, the French will love this. A crime of passion, eh?"

"But I didn't kill him, Sir, it was the fall that did that," Mueller reminded him.

"Yes, of course it was, but surely no one would blame you, even if you had killed him. What's wrong with your lip, by the way?"

Mueller looked towards Frances, caught her eye, and raised his voice enough for her to hear.

"My wife bit me, Sir."

Barraclough looked from one to the other, taking in the grin of satisfaction that Mueller was giving Frances, and her answering look of absolute horror. He gave a slow smile. "Jolly good, Mueller, eh? Leave it with me. I'd grab that girl of yours for a dance if I were you, before she's spirited away by Forsythe. The man's got a thing about her you know, though can't say as I blame him."

Right on cue, Forsythe whispered in Frances's ear and the two of them made for the dance floor, leaving Mueller to stare after them as Konrad Adenauer re-joined him.

"All well?" he asked.

"Yes, all good, Herr Adenauer. Thank you."

"Then I will expect a visit from you at my office in Bonn on Monday. I hope you don't think I'm interfering, my boy, but I heard your wife is leaving for England tomorrow. I've been watching you. Watching you both." Adenauer laid a fatherly hand on Mueller's shoulder. "Fight for that girl, Kristian, that's my advice."

"I intend to, Sir," he replied.

Chapter 36

May 1946

Frances yawned as she slipped out of her clothes and prepared for bed. She had just one more concert, then she was going to take time out for a few months. She had to. Things had worked out really well for her since she had come home to Paris, and she had found that she was more than capable of running her own career. She didn't need anyone to do it for her. Steven's face shot through her head as if to remind her that he had managed her affairs for all those years. But she had been a child then and she had needed help. He had organised everything so perfectly. Had it really been four years since his death? It seemed more in some ways. She had certainly had a bundle of life experiences thrown at her since losing him and of course dear Jaques had lost his life that day, too.

Richard Forsythe had suggested he could take care of her affairs for her when she had got back to England. She had stayed with him and his mother for a few days running up to Christmas, but both he and his mother had got a little pushy and she feared that she had gotten a little rude. And so, she had said her farewells and made the journey to the home of her childhood.

The town hadn't changed. It was still the lovely little market town that she remembered. She booked into the Lord Leycester Hotel for a few days. If she looked out the window of her room to the other side of the road, she could see the towers of the castle stretching towards the skyline. And if she looked to the left, she could see part of the old town wall and the girl's school she had attended.

While there, she had taken a walk to her old home. Just a ten-minute walk across the river bridge was all it was. The view of the castle from that bridge was one of the town's gems. The view from her old home was even better. The garden ran down to the river and from the end of it you could see the weir which ran up to the castle walls.

That town held many memories for her, but she cut short her stay, deciding her real home was Paris. Once there she had made straight for the Conservatoire, where she was welcomed with open arms. The girl who had survived the Nazi death camps had made her way home again. Many concerts were organised. The conservatoire was cashing in on her story, but it had been to her advantage too and her career was relaunched in Europe.

She wondered how they all were at Schonen Felder and immediately regretted that thought. Schonen Felder had pushed its way into her head as it always did. She had tried to fill her mind with other things, as she did every night, to try and blank out that place. Schonen Felder, where she most wanted to be. He wouldn't be there though. A laugh caught in her throat as she considered that bizarrely Kristian was somewhere in France. With her. His French girl. Padding across the bedroom of her house in Neuilly, she poured herself a glass of red wine. When Mueller encroached on her thoughts and entered her head space, that's what she did, she poured herself a glass of red. As she sipped it, she felt better. Better, until the glass was empty, and then she poured herself another to make her feel even better still. Never more than two if she had a concert the next evening. She would need a clear head for rehearsals. If there was no concert, and no rehearsals, then the number of glasses didn't matter.

Had he come to see her that night that she performed at the Officer's Club? She shook her head and took a gulp of wine. Over and over and over. That bloody night! It was etched into her brain and wouldn't budge. Thank heaven then for the music, it drowned those thoughts out. And thank goodness for the wine because that helped, too.

Maybe, she thought, he had an arranged meeting with Adenauer. Or perhaps Sara took him there to meet Jack. No, that didn't make any more sense than it had on all the previous nights she had had those same thoughts.

He had asked her for a last dance. Richard had stood by her side, and she had felt his anger at Kristian's intrusion. But she didn't care, and anyway she had wanted to feel Kristian's arms around her for one last time.

"It's alright, Richard," she said. "It's just one dance."

She had stood proudly straight and formal, not letting him see how eager she was for his embrace. He had taken her right hand and she had felt a shot of longing rip through her body at his touch. She controlled herself and let her left-hand rest lightly on his shoulder and kept her eyes averted from his. But then as they moved with the music, he had pulled her close and she hadn't the strength or inclination to fight the feelings that coursed through her body. She had sighed and laid her head on his shoulder. She wanted him to kiss her. She wanted to kiss him and shout out to the rest of the room, "See. This man is mine. It's me he loves. He belongs to me and no one else."

He had asked for a last dance for old times' sake. A last dance before she left his life forever, and he left hers, to be with another French girl.

She gave a guttural scream and tears fell from her eyes as they had that night when she had said, "I'm sorry Kristian. I can't do this," and she had pushed her way out of his arms and ran into the night.

* * *

Mueller had accepted Conrad Adenauer's offer of a job on the Monday following the bash at the British Officer's Club. He had been told quite a few times lately that he was a lucky man, and he accepted that he was. He had survived the war, one of the few U-boat Kapitans to do so, plus he had dropped into a job working for one of the most influential German politicians of the day. A man who was held in high esteem by the occupying forces. He would give the job up now, and his life too, to hold Frances in his arms and smell the scent of her skin. To bury his face into the unruly mass of chestnut hair and lose himself in her amber eyes.

No matter how many times he went back over that bloody evening, he couldn't work out what the hell had gone wrong. Sara had planned it all. He had made it safely into the venue, and that was quite an achievement in itself. He watched Frances play from behind a pillar and been so bloody proud of her. Her performance had been superlative not to mention how wonderful she looked in that bottle green gown. He always knew that was the colour for her.

Had it been a mistake to go there? Sara and Jack had said no. Sara had accused him of messing things up. Had he? "Ask her for a dance and tell her how you feel." That's what Sara had suggested. Frances was leaving that night with Forsythe for England; it was his final chance to put things right between them. His feeble attempt at putting things right had gone horribly bloody wrong though.

Following the chat with Barraclough, he had watched and waited for the right moment to ask her for a dance. Forsythe had stuck to her side like glue but then he wandered off to get a drink and he saw his chance. Forsythe came back pretty damn quickly when he saw that he was weaving his way across the dance floor to Frances's side. Once there he did as Sara suggested and asked Frances for a dance, as Forsythe stood bristling by her side.

"A last dance for old times' sake, Froggy," he said, just as the orchestra struck up with Moonlight Serenade.

She turned to Forsythe and said, "Just one dance. It will be alright."

She held her hand out to him. He took it and pulled her onto the dance floor. She pulled back against him and formally took his right hand, laying her left on his shoulder, standing stiffly erect, keeping a proper distance between them. Then as they moved to the music, he felt her relax, and he pulled her in closer to his body. She laid her head on his shoulder with a sigh, and they melted into one another.

Then suddenly she had stopped moving, and for a moment he thought the music had stopped playing, and she said, "I can't do this, Kristian." And with that she was gone. Sara had rushed after her, thinking she had made for the ladies' room, but she wasn't there. She had disappeared into the night along with Forsythe.

Mueller sighed and put the pen he had been toying with onto his desk. He picked up the telegram he had received the night before and read it through once again. It was from France, from Marianne. In it, she informed him she had seen reported in a recent Parisian newspaper, that Frances Lamont was due to perform with the Orchestre de la Société des concerts du Conservatoire, Orchestre National de Lyon, Concerts Colonne and Orchestre National de France. There had been an article written about her. How she had gone home to France where she belonged, after suffering at the hands of the Nazis during the war. When he had received the telegram, he had been elated. No more searching the newspapers for a mention of Frances; he knew exactly where she would be the next day.

He rubbed his forehead thoughtfully. It was good of Marianne to have taken the time to contact him, and she certainly deserved the happiness that she'd spoken of in her last letter. He'd returned the money he owed her plus a good bit extra and told her how Frances had disappeared off the face of the earth. She'd replied and thanked him and told him of her engagement to the man who owned a neighbouring farm. She'd known him for years and liked him. His wife had passed away sometime before and left him with three children to fend for. He smiled inwardly. She'd enjoy that, he thought, taking care of them all, and still she'd found time to contact him, but that was the sort of girl she was.

His eyes scanned the telegram again; three concerts already missed. That just left the one with the Orchestre National de France and that was tomorrow evening, in Paris. Time was running out. He looked at his watch. It was almost 9 a.m. Adenauer would be in his office within the next few minutes. Right on cue, Mueller heard his voice greeting his secretary as he arrived, and he decided to catch the man early before he had time to immerse himself into his work. It was then that he wouldn't look too kindly at being interrupted. He made his way along the corridor and entered the secretary's office. The woman gave him a hearty smile as he went in.

"Good morning, Kristian," she said. "Did you actually go home yesterday, or have you been here all night?"

The hours he spent in his office had been noticed, and she enjoyed teasing him about the fact that he never appeared to find time to socialise or relax. It was true; since Frances had run out on him, he had turned all his energies into working for Adenauer and in searching for her. On weekends, he would go to Schonen Felder and either help with the farm work or exercise the horses. He was in no mood to be sociable, preferring his own sad company where he could revisit all the mistakes he had made over and over again.

He spent the evenings in Bonn trawling through foreign newspapers where he would, if he were lucky, find mention of Frances, but always the places she had played and never where she was going to play. This was why the telegram was so important to him. He knew where she was going to be the next day, where he could find her.

"I came in early, Maggie. I could do with a chat with the old man if he isn't too busy," he said, giving her one of his gap-toothed smiles which seemed to do the trick.

"Well, I'll see if he has time to see you then," she said, smiling back at him. "Hold on." She crossed the room to the door of Adenauer's office and gave it a brisk knock. "Herr Adenauer, Kristian would like a word with you if you can spare him the time."

There was a slight pause until the door opened, revealing Konrad Adenauer. "Come in, my boy. Have we got a problem?" he asked.

Mueller entered the office and took the chair offered to him by Adenauer, who seated himself behind his desk.

"No, no, we're all fine here. I've found Frances, Herr Adenauer," he said. "I received a telegram last night from a friend. Frances is performing tomorrow night in Paris. I was wondering…"

"That's wonderful news, isn't it?" interrupted Adenauer. "How long will it take you to pack up your things and leave? Is there anything outstanding that needs to be seen to, Kristian?"

"I think I could have all the important stuff sorted by midmorning, Sir."

"Then don't let me keep you. Sort it and call in at my office before you leave. Which theatre is Frances playing at and how do you intend to travel?"

"The theatre Des Champs-Élysées. Car, I think, Sir. If I get a good run, I could do it in ten hours or so, if I don't have problems at the borders."

* * *

By 11:30, that morning, Mueller was back with Adenauer's secretary.

"Your lucky day." She smiled. "I've been kept very busy sorting things for you."

Mueller raised his eyebrows at her. "What things?"

"You have a hotel reservation for as long as you need it at Hotel Grande Power. It's about a six-minute walk to the theatre from there and hardly much more to Quai d'Orsay. I've made things easy for you."

"Maggie, I haven't a clue what's going on. Quai d'Orsay?"

"The old man will explain," she whispered, as Adenauer's office door opened.

"Ah, there you are, Kristian. Come in. I've got a minor job for you to do while you're in Paris. I have a letter here that I want you to hand deliver to Georges Bidault at the French Foreign Office. You must make certain that you only give it to him in person. Is that clear?"

"Of course, Sir."

"Good. Maggie has been busy. She has sorted out an excellent hotel, and papers which state that you are on diplomatic business. They will give you safe conduct over the borders. They should help you get fuel too, should you need it." Adenauer waved his hand. "Off you go, and I don't want to see you back in your office until next Tuesday at the earliest. Is that clear?"

Mueller's head was spinning. He was being sent to Paris on a diplomatic errand which would coincide with finding Frances, and he was being given a week to do it. "I can't thank you enough, Sir," he said.

Adenauer gave him a fatherly look. "You can thank me by not messing up, Kristian, on either count."

* * *

On his way back to his apartment, Mueller had time to chew over the errand given him by Adenauer, who lately had become chairman of the Christian Democratic Union party. He was to deliver by hand a letter from Adenauer to Georges Bidault who was head of the Quai d'Orsay, the French Foreign Office. That was hardly surprising, he thought. He knew from his work that Adenauer and Bidault had been communicating for some time in an attempt at a reconciliation between France and Germany. He also knew that much of the communication had been secretive, as Bidault wanted to appear to be steering France toward coercive measures to keep Germany weak, like his predecessor de Gaulle. He knew, too, that there had been close contact between politicians from the French Moral Re-Armament Party with other Christian Democrats in Europe with the hope that European unity could be facilitated through a Franco-German reconciliation. He was all in favour of that, though he reckoned there was little immediate hope. He couldn't see unity in Europe happening for a good while.

Once back at his apartment, he grabbed a suitcase and packed a few clothes, taking care to remember a dinner suit for his night at the theatre, and more importantly his ID, and then he was off.

The journey was uneventful, apart from the length of it. He crossed into the French zone and into Belgium and then made his way into France itself, passing all border checks without question. He eventually arrived at Hotel Grande Power and checked in just before midnight, too tired to take in his surroundings other than the grand frontage of the hotel with its wrought iron and glass canopy. The door attendant parked his car for him, and he followed the night manager up the fine twisting oak staircase to his apartment, ordering a snack and a large brandy as a nightcap, though doubting he would need any help that night to lull him into a deep sleep.

Maggie, he thought, had done a grand job in getting him rooms which looked out onto the busy Rue Francious. The hotel was on one corner of a crossroad and the other three corners comprised similar stone built six-storey buildings. He couldn't help comparing the view from his window to views of Cologne and most of the other German cities which the Brits, with some help later from the Yanks, had flattened. He was in no doubt after learning of the atrocities committed by the Nazi party that Hitler and his henchmen had to be stopped, but to bomb cities to the extreme, with no conscience for the harm done to civilians, and laying waste to the hundreds of years of history, seemed somewhat barbaric to him.

His apartment he found had a small balcony, which delighted him, as it gave a wonderful view of the illuminated Eifel Tower, and it was here that he stood for a good half hour sipping at his brandy and mulling a few things over before turning in. He awoke pleasantly refreshed to the sounds of a busy city and checked his watch: 8.30 a.m. By now he would have started work, and here he was stretched out in a luxurious bedroom in a very comfortable bed. He reckoned he just had time for a quick bath before breakfast, then it was off to Quai d'Orsay, hopefully to find Georges Bidault and to deliver Konrad Adenauer's letter. If all went to plan, he thought he would have a few hours for a little sightseeing before his evening trip to the Theatre de Champs-Élysées.

He had to admit that he was nervous. The last time he and Frances were together hadn't gone well. He had thought he had a plan in place then, but somehow things hadn't worked out as he had expected them to. He laughed to himself as the thought crossed his mind that things rarely did work out as he expected them to, as far as Frances was concerned. How would tonight go? he wondered. Was he about to make a complete arse of himself? She might have moved on. There could be a new man in her life. There had been no mention of one in the press, but that meant nothing.

Chapter 37

The day so far had been a success, thought Mueller. He had delivered Adenauer's letter into the hands of Georges Bidault, who turned out to be a pleasant man. He had then spent a few hours sightseeing and then had returned to the hotel to get changed and down a couple of drinks in the oak panelled bar.

On the way to the theatre, he stopped for an early dinner in one of the many restaurants which, despite the economic climate in France, as in the rest of Europe, seemed to be doing a pretty good trade. Paris, he thought, was a law unto itself. He had read that there had been an influx of people to the city following the end of the war, and that there was a huge shortage of housing and of food. Walking the streets that evening, he thought you would never believe it.

His plans took a turn for the worse on arrival at the theatre. He found that there were no tickets available for the concert; it was a complete sell-out. He pleaded with the girl in the ticket office and in the end, she suggested he should wait in the bar, and she would see if, by any chance, there were tickets that had not been collected. He was still waiting after the concert had started and the first piece of music had been playing for a good fifteen minutes, before the girl found him. With a lingering smile she passed him a ticket, which he gratefully accepted and paid for. The programme he bought informed him that Frances was not involved in the first half of the concert, and so he decided to stay in the bar until after the interval with a couple more brandies to soothe his nerves.

And now here he was waiting in her dressing room, concert over, bow tie untied and collar of his shirt undone, looking more relaxed than he felt. He knew her well enough to know that she would lap up the compliments, and why not? She had been superb. He had rushed to the stage door of the theatre and talked the door attendant into letting him in by explaining that he was Mademoiselle Lamont's husband, and that he had turned up to give her a surprise. He smiled to himself. At least he hadn't had to lie, and she certainly was going to have one hell of a surprise when she saw him. He heard women's voices outside the dressing room and recognised one of them as belonging to Frances.

"I am so tired, Emily," he heard her say. "I think I could sleep for a week."

"At least tomorrow you have a day off. I don't know how you manage to stand for all that time in your condition," came the reply. And then the door opened and there she was, fiddle in hand, looking glorious in the loose-fitting black evening gown which fell from her shoulders to her feet in folds. He heard her intake of breath before she recovered herself and forced a smile.

"Kristian? What on earth are you doing in Paris?" she asked.

"Business.... I had some business for Konrad and found that you were playing here tonight. You were brilliant, by the way. I thought I should call in to see how you are... you see." I'm garbling, he thought.

"Well, as you can see, I'm fine, thank you," she said, placing her violin back into its case.

"Are you sure? You're not ill, are you?" he asked, thinking back to the conversation he had just heard and wondering if his understanding of it was quite right.

"No, of course not." She forced a laugh. "Whatever made you think that?"

"The conversation you just had outside. I heard you say you were tired, and someone mentioned a condition?" He paused. "Are you pregnant, Frances?" he asked.

She looked down at the floor, refusing to meet his eyes, and shrugged. "My condition has nothing to do with you, Kristian, if that's what you're thinking," she muttered.

There was a knock on the door and one of the theatre staff shouted, "Your taxi is waiting, Mademoiselle Lamont."

"Yes, thank you," she shouted back. "Look, I have to go, Kristian," she said, trying to keep her voice level. "It was really kind of you to come. Give my love to everyone back home, won't you? Tell them I'll write soon, as I promised I would."

He grasped her arm and shook his head. "We need to talk, don't we?"

"Do we?" She turned her eyes on him, and he felt the heat from the fire in them. "It was you, I think, that said there was nothing more to say, wasn't it?"

"Things have changed since then, it seems. Why did you run out on me without a word?"

"It doesn't matter why, does it? Under the circumstances—" She turned away from him, with the pretence of sorting out her belongings.

"Sod the circumstances, Froggy," Mueller snapped, "If I have nothing to do with your condition, as you put it, then who, huh? Who is your condition to do with? The jolly old major?"

She turned to him, a look of disbelief on her face. "What? Don't be so ridiculous. Do you really think?"

"It's not that ridiculous, is it? You have a penchant for older men, don't you?"

She turned her amber eyes on him. He saw the hurt reflected there for a moment, and the tears that filled them, before he felt her hand deliver the blow to his face. He understood too late the cruelty of his comment.

"God, Froggy, I'm so sorry. I deserved that."

"Yes, you did," she said, fighting the tears back. "Go, Kristian. Please, just go, will you?"

He nodded and walked to the door, leaving it open as he left. Frances took several deep breaths to control herself. He'd done it again; he'd just shown up, and now her life was in turmoil all over again. How did he do it? She'd worked so hard to carry on after leaving Germany. She found on returning to Paris that she still had many useful contacts in the field of music. Those contacts had bent over backwards to put her in touch with the right people, and she had bookings galore for the next couple of years. And she'd done it on her own. She didn't need anyone; she didn't need him! Angrily throwing her belongings into a small green suitcase and grabbing her wrap and violin case, she made her way to the stage door, just in time to see Mueller paying off the taxi driver.

"What the hell, Kristian?" she shrieked and flew at him, lashing out with her suitcase. "What the hell are you doing? You've no bloody right to interfere," she said, swinging the case in his direction a second time.

Mueller grabbed it, prising it from her fingers before she could wield it at him once more.

"I told you, didn't I, that we need to talk? I'll walk you back home." He grabbed her by the wrist and walked away from the theatre, dragging her behind him.

"Let me go, Kristian," she fumed. "I'm too bloody tired to walk home, and I've bloody well nothing at all to say to you."

He carried on walking, still holding her wrist, still pulling her along. Not even knowing if they were going in the right direction towards Neuilly, and only assuming that's where she would be staying.

"I think you should curb your tongue," he said, "What would your adoring public think of you if they heard you cursing the way you're doing? It's hardly fitting, is it? An hour's walk, Froggy, that will calm you down and give us time to talk. First, though, we'll go for a meal."

"I'm not going for a meal with you. I don't want a bloody meal," she spat, now swinging her violin case towards him. He stopped walking and dropped her suitcase to the floor, keeping hold of her wrist and swinging her round to face him. Giving her the chance to swing the violin case at him for a second time, he made a grab for her other wrist and set his jaw in the look she knew meant he'd had enough. He fixed her with his eyes.

"Frances, if you swing that case at me again, I swear I will take it from you, and it will end up in the Seine. Do you understand me?" She met his gaze, eyes wide, and blinked at him.

"You wouldn't," she said uncertainly.

He lifted his eyebrows quizzically. "I think you know I would. And then you'd be famous for being the virtuoso who lost two of these…" He shook the case, "Stradi things. Just calm down, eh? You're behaving like a spoilt brat. I thought you had grown up." He scanned the street. "Ah, a restaurant."

She sighed. "I told you I don't want a meal."

"That's fine, I do," he said, crossing the road and pulling her towards the door of the restaurant, which had a worn out and tired look about it, so unlike the ones he remembered in Brest or when touring Paris whilst on leave. The front of the house was approaching them.

"Kristian, if you must have a bloody meal, then speak in French, will you? Or you could find yourself strung up. We French have long memories," she whispered.

"Ah Mademoiselle Lamont," said the front of the house with a smile, "Your usual table is taken, I'm afraid." She made to answer.

"That's fine," cut in Mueller, following her suggestion, and speaking in French. "A table for two. Can you take the lady's coat and these cases please?" he asked.

The front of house nodded, taking the cases and coat offered up by Frances.

"Well, at least your French has improved," she said.

Mueller nodded, a half-smile on his lips. "Marianne," he said, gleefully noting the scowl he received from her as they walked to their table.

There was a ripple of applause as they crossed the restaurant floor from several diners, who had clearly been at that evening's concert. Frances immediately rose to the occasion, smiling and thanking them, shaking hands, followed by Mueller shaking his head.

Once both were seated, their waiter approached the table, menus in hand. He passed one to Frances.

"The lady isn't eating," said Mueller. "I'll order now. Just a main course. I'll have a steak, medium, potato dauphinoise, and vegetables, oh, and a bottle of champagne."

"Your best champagne," said Frances with a smile.

"And just one glass," parried Mueller. "The lady would like a jug of water and a glass, please. Thank you." He noted the look he was receiving from the lady with a raise of his eyebrows. "Better behave, Froggy, in front of your adoring public," he warned.

She leant across the table towards him. "Pig," she muttered, and he rewarded her with a broad boyish smile which tore right into her chest wall.

"So why did you run away from me?" he asked.

She shrugged, "It doesn't matter."

"It matters to me. One minute we were dancing and from what I remember you were quite enjoying being in my arms and then kaput! The girl's gone. Why?"

She shook her head, looking down at the table, refusing to meet his gaze, which he had set upon her. Refusing to even look up when the champagne arrived but finding it too much when the waiter served the meal. She watched Mueller cut into the steak, chewing it, enjoying it.

"It's a good steak," he said, washing it down with the champagne. "Potatoes are good too, nice rich sauce."

Frances felt her mouth water. It had been hours since she had eaten and then it had been just a snack. "Can I try, just a little?" she asked.

He put down his knife and fork, sat back in his chair, and briefly studied her, chin in hand. "Are you hungry, Froggy?"

"Kristian don't keep calling me Froggy, not here, not where people can hear, French people. Remember the revolution, what they did to people they didn't like," she whispered. "And yes, I'm starving."

He pushed his plate towards her. "Go on. Have it."

"What about you?"

"I ate earlier. I got it for you. I knew you'd be hungry; you see." She glanced at him, giving him a half smile. Then she pulled the plate towards her, attacking the meal with gusto. "You told me once that you never ate before playing and that you were always starving afterwards," continued Mueller, "and I see what you mean. Slow down, you're having a feeding frenzy."

"You remembered that?" she mumbled through a mouthful of food.

"Of course, I remembered that. I haven't forgotten anything that you've told me."

She cocked her head at him. "Can I have some champagne?"

"If you tell me why you left me."

She swallowed. "I don't like goodbyes, that's all," she said, and then carried on eating until the plate was clean. Afterwards she sat back, refusing to meet his eyes, satiated, thoughtful. And then she sighed. "You told Richard Forsythe that you wanted a last dance with me. I knew at the end of it we'd say goodbye. It was… so final…. I didn't like it. That's all."

"You knew that we would say goodbye, did you?" questioned Mueller. She nodded. "You stole my thunder by running out that night, you know," he continued.

"What do you mean?" she asked.

"We'll talk as I walk you home. Come on."

She knew him well enough to know he was going to walk her home, and that there was very little she could do about it. She was finding out how much she'd missed him. Nothing had changed. Her heart was lurching, and she knew she was still in love with him. He would walk her back home and tell her why he was in Paris and twist her arm to tell him who had fathered her child. Then at the end of it he would tell her how happy he and Marianne were, and that would be that. At least she could try to drag things out longer. Be with him for a while more.

"Can I have a pudding first and some more champagne?" She lifted her head and looked at him through molten eyes. He was smiling back at her, meeting her gaze.

"I knew you'd be more pleasant after you'd eaten," he said and called the waiter over for her to order.

As they walked, they talked.

"It's quite extraordinary, isn't it? You coming to Paris while I am playing? Quite a coincidence," she mused.

Mueller wanted to get things off to a good start by being honest. "It was Marianne who told me you were playing. I came to find you, and it tied in with some work for Konrad."

She gave him a scowl. "I suppose this Marianne told you over the breakfast table, did she? How wonderfully domestic."

He decided not to reply to her caustic remark and changed the subject. "It's a beautiful city, Paris, especially this time of the year, and it's a beautiful night for a walk. Let's try not to fight, shall we?"

She was quiet for a while, wondering whether to pursue the topic of Marianne, and decided for the time being to let it drop.

"There are lots of cracks in the old place if you look carefully," she said. "It needs tens of thousands of francs spent on it and we can't even blame you lot and the occupation. Paris has been a neglected city for a long time."

"Not as many cracks here as there are in Cologne, Froggy," Mueller said wryly.

She smiled briefly at his comment before changing the subject. "You didn't have to come here, you know. If you'd sent the paperwork to the Neuilly house, I would have found it at some point. I would have sent it back," she said.

"I have no idea what you are talking about. What paperwork?"

"The paperwork for the divorce. That's why you're here, isn't it?"

"Is it?"

She looked up at him as they walked. "I won't stand in your way, Kristian. I've thought things through over and over. I know that our marriage was only meant to be just a temporary thing to keep me safe. And please know that I really appreciate what you did and what your parents did, of course, taking me in and all." He'd stopped walking, and she turned back to him. "What?" she asked.

"I said you stole my thunder the night you ran out on me, Froggy. Haven't you wondered what I was going to say, huh?"

She shrugged. "I think you said it all, Kristian, didn't you, the day you came home." She clutched at her stomach, suddenly crying out.

Mueller grabbed her shoulders, concern written on his face. "What's the matter? Frances, are you alright?"

"Hmm, yes, I think so." She giggled. Too much champagne, thought Mueller.

"There's a great deal of movement going on here," she said, rubbing her belly. "I think I am being thanked for the meal." And the champagne, thought Mueller with a sigh of relief.

They had walked past the Arc de Triomphe and were a good way along the Avenue du Roule.

"You scared me, Froggy. Look is there somewhere we can sit for a while?"

"I'm fine... really. I just want to get home and get some sleep," she replied.

"I think we should sit. I'd like to sit." He puffed out his cheeks as she'd seen him do so many times before when he was thinking. "I really do need to talk to you, you see."

"The church then, Saint Pierre," she said, giving him a questioning glance. "There are benches outside. It's just a little further."

They carried on walking to the Eglise Saint Pierre and found a bench in the garden which surrounded the church. "Impressive," said Mueller, sweeping the building with an appreciative glance. "How old?"

"Not very. I think it opened in 1914."

Mueller sniffed, "Not even as old as me then." They both sat in silence for a while, each lost in their own thoughts.

"Is the bump behaving now?" Mueller asked after a couple of minutes.

"A bit of wriggling going on," she said. "It's the strangest sensation, having something growing inside you."

He nodded thoughtfully, considering, trying to imagine that sensation and failing. "Can I feel it, do you think?" he asked.

"Them. You can feel them, Kristian," she said, taking his hand and laying it on her belly. "You know they are yours, of course."

He turned to her, looking into her amber gaze, giving her another of his boyish smiles which made her heart jump into her throat yet again.

"Of course, I know," he said, shaking his head, blue eyes wide with wonder, as he felt the babies pushing against his hand.

"Them you said. My God is there a litter of little Muellers in there?" he asked, eyes even wider.

"No, just two, and that's quite enough," she informed him.

He stood and moved to the front of her, squatting down, and leaning forward, he deposited two kisses on her stomach, and afterwards laid his head against it. She sighed, combing her fingers through his hair, caressing his cheek, and cradling his jaw, running her finger over the sculpted cheekbones. He turned his face into her hand and kissed the palm.

"I'm so sorry," he muttered softly. Then he stood and returned to seat himself beside her and, with a sigh, she turned to him.

"Don't be sorry. You deserve to be happy; you've been through so much. I'm happy for you, really, I am. I'd never stop you from seeing your children, you know. If you want to, that is."

"Shush, Frances. Just for a minute say nothing, eh? Let me unburden myself while I feel I can. Now. Here."

"But you don't need to. You don't need to explain anything."

"But I do, you see, so just listen. Just let me talk, eh?" He took her hand, toying with the fingers, and noisily exhaled. "That night, the night you ran out on me, I was going to tell you something, something I should have said three years ago."

"What?"

"Froggy, please. I've never said this before. It's difficult for me, so just listen, huh?" He paused for a few moments and then took a deep breath and after exhaling again, he continued. "I was going to tell you that I love you, have loved you since...." He shook his head. "I don't know when it happened, but I knew I was in love with you that Christmas day on UBA and even before then. And that's when I should have told you, and I'm so sorry that I didn't."

"But the day you came home, you told me you didn't want me. God, Kristian, you told me that there was someone else. Do you know what that did to me? I had been waiting and praying for you to come home for more than a year. You can't say this now. Not now, just because I'm pregnant. You think you can say all of this, and I'll play happy bloody families, don't you?"

"No. No. I've been looking for you since you left. I want to explain." He reached out and laid his hand on her cheek. "Let me explain. When I found out, when I heard and read about what you'd been through in those bloody camps, I was so ashamed. I even considered not coming home at all. I thought it would be easier for you to think I was dead. It was Marianne that made me see I had to come back. She said I was only half a man—"

"Oh! And we all know which bloody half of you it was that she enjoyed, don't we!" mocked Frances as tears sprang into her eyes. She stood and moved away from him. Away from the bench, towards the church building. And when she reached it, she laid her head against the cool stone, trying to quench the fire in her brain. He'd said he loved her. Those were the words she dreamt of him saying. But now he'd said them, they filled her with anger, and she wondered if he'd told them a year ago to another French girl.

He followed her over to the porch of the church and put a hand on her shoulder. "This isn't going so well, Froggy, is it? You stopped me before I'd finished, by the way. What Marianne said was that I'm only half a man without you, and she's right, I am, you see."

"Marianne said that?" She turned to face him, tears running down her cheeks. He nodded and wiped the tears gently away with his hand. "Well then, perhaps she's not so bad after all." And then she shook her head. "I don't understand. Marianne said you should come home..." He took her hands.

"She did, and she was right. But then I saw some dreadful things on my journey back home. I saw some dreadful things on patrol too, of course, but that was war. This was much worse. People beating each other, killing for a morsel. Women selling their bodies to buy food for their children. Women and young girls raped, not just once, Froggy, and God knows that's bad enough, but over and over, and then committing suicide because they couldn't bear the shame. I saw and heard things that disgusted me. The state of Germany, the German people, the way we were treating each other, the way the occupying forces were treating good people. It all disgusted me. I didn't want it for you. I thought you'd be better off somewhere else, anywhere else. Then when Forsythe told me he was going to ask you to go to England, I figured it was the best thing for you, and if you hated me, then it would be all the easier for you to leave."

"How about what I wanted for me, Kristian? Shouldn't I have had a say in that?" she gasped through her tears.

"That's what Sara made me see. She talked me into breaking into the Officer's club. I was supposed to tell you all this that night, and I would have done. You weren't supposed to run out on me and leave early, that wasn't on the cards at all. You really did wreck the entire plan."

"You broke into the Officer's club? They could have shot you, for goodness' sake."

"Well, luckily!"

He held her gaze for a moment until she asked, "What about when you left for Kiel?" He gave her a tired smile.

"I would have told you the fateful day of the picnic; the way I felt, I mean, I intended to. I behaved like a spoilt child, didn't I? I wanted you so badly and you said no."

"No, I didn't. I said I just needed time."

"Which I didn't give you, did I? I thought you were playing a game with me, you see, so I went off and got pissed out of my brain and became thoroughly maudlin. I was convinced I wasn't going to get through the bloody war, and truthfully, I was scared shitless of what I was going back to. If I'd held you that morning before I left, I wouldn't have let you go. I'd have refused to leave. They would have had to prise you from my arms and then shoot me. It was easier for me to walk away and easier for you to not know the truth about how I was feeling."

"You think you made it easy for me, do you?" she snapped. "I wrote, and you didn't reply." Her body had become taught, and she clenched her hands fist-like. She exhaled, allowing some of the tension to leave her body. "Can you even guess how I felt not hearing a bloody word from you? Asking your mother every time one of your letters arrived if you'd even mentioned me." He took her by the shoulders, shaking her gently, trying to explain.

"The mission they gave me was a bloody suicide mission, Froggy. I didn't want to raise your hopes. I didn't want my folks to know, either. I'm here against all odds you see. I reckon we've been given another chance, haven't we?" She twisted, freeing herself from his grasp.

"A chance at what, for God's sake? I don't know what you're even asking me." He blew out his cheeks in exasperation and exhaled.

"I'm asking you to come home. I'm offering you a meagre existence in a broken country with broken people. There," he nodded at her, "and you'd be a damn fool if you said yes." She looked away from him and sniffed.

"What time is it?" she asked, turning to him, and totally changing the subject. He looked at his watch, annoyed that she'd ignored his outpouring.

"It's 1:15, alright? Damn well 1:15,"

"I'm tired. I need to get home, Kristian."

Mueller chewed his lip. "I'm sorry, you're tired," he said, picking up the suitcase and passing her the violin. He walked back towards the road, irritated that things had gone so badly. "Well, come on, let's get you home."

They carried on walking towards her home in silence. He was beginning to feel foolish, beginning to wish that he'd kept his feelings to himself. Locked away is where they should have stayed. He'd opened himself up to her, torn himself wide open, and she hadn't said a thing to staunch his wound; she was letting him bleed. Then, without a word from her, he felt her fingers touch his palm and then lightly grasp his hand. He looked down at her and she was smiling to herself.

"Do you think you can make that offer any more attractive?" she asked, looking up at him. He thought for a moment.

"Yes, I do. On top of that marvellous offer, I've already made you, you get half a man."

"Which half?" she asked, and he saw the smile tugging at the corners of her mouth.

"Well now, which half do you want?" he replied, looking into her eyes.

"Well, that's the thing, isn't it? I want all of you, every bit, Kristian. I want your soul, too."

"Oh, you took that from me a long time ago, Froggy."

They carried on walking a while more, both in thought, and then he felt her thread her arm through his and snuggle in closer to his body.

"Is that a yes, then?" he asked, not daring to look at her. She muttered, almost but not quite to herself.

"For wherever you go, I will go; wherever you lodge, I will lodge; your people shall be my people, and your God my God. Where you die, I will die, and there they will bury me. Thus, and more may the Lord do to me if anything but death parts me from you."

He stopped walking, she looked up and their eyes locked for a few moments until he shook his head and raised his eyebrows.

"Jesus Froggy, I didn't have you down as a bible scholar."

"We studied the book of Ruth at school. Girls' school," she explained. "I suppose they were trying to teach us obedience to men, or some such foolish thing. I remember thinking at the time what an idiot Ruth was."

"And do you still?" he asked as they carried on walking again. She looked up at him.

"I think I've changed my mind."

"Ah. And what made you change it?" he asked.

It was her who stopped walking. She pulled him back and raised her eyes to his and he lost himself in the depth of them.

"I fell in love. Completely. For the first time," she said.

Mueller gave a sniff and looked away from her to hide his embarrassment, as his eyes filled up with unaccustomed tears. He wiped his hand across his face, noisily exhaled, and turned back to her.

"Christ, Froggy, you know how to cripple a man. That drew more tears than a kick in the balls."

She laughed at his discomfort and then pointed to a large three-storey stone house with full-length windows on the corner of a wide street, planted with cherry and almond trees, and full of similar properties.

"That's some townhouse," said Mueller as they crossed the street and reached the door.

"Yes, it is, although only half of it is ours. It's still quite grand, though. Otto grabbed it when I moved out and went to Edie's. I thought I'd hate it when I came back, but I don't." Mueller smiled at her and kissed her gently on the forehead.

"Good. So, Frau Mueller, I will see you in the morning for breakfast, and you can take me sight-seeing." He looked at his watch. "That's in just a few hours. Get some sleep, you must be exhausted."

He took the key from her hand, opened the door, pushing her towards it, turning her around and kissing her forehead gently once again before turning back towards the city. As he walked away, she called him softly.

"Kristian." He stopped walking and turned back. "You bragged once that if there was a proper bed, you'd make love to me all night and all day." She watched as he straightened.

"That wasn't bragging, that was fact," he called back.

"Well, is it still fact, now that you're a pen pusher and no longer a man of action?"

He saw the wanton look on her face and crossed the road back to the house. She was smiling at him, amber eyes kindling, and he took her outstretched hand.

"I can't answer your question, Froggy. I don't know the answer, you see." He gave a suggestive smile, meeting the fire in her eyes with his own blue gaze. "But I think we are going to find out."

A review is so important to an author, so if you feel you can, and would like to, please leave one on Amazon. There are other platforms too where you can leave reviews, such as Goodreads and Book Bub.
Look out for War Torn 3